...ves:
Love or Money

BRONWYN JAMESON
KATHERINE GARBERA
MAUREEN CHILD

MILLS & BOON

First published in Great Britain 2011
by Mills & Boon, an imprint of Harlequin (UK) Limited,
Eton House, 18-24 Paradise Road, Richmond, Surrey TW9 1SR

SOCIETY WIVES: SECRET LIVES
© by Harlequin Enterprises II B.V./S.à.r.l 2011

The Bought-and-Paid-for Wife, The Once-A-Mistress Wife and *The Part-Time Wife* were first published in Great Britain by Harlequin Mills & Boon Limited.

The Bought-and-Paid-for Wife © Harlequin Books S.A. 2006
The Once-A-Mistress Wife © Harlequin Books S.A. 2006
The Part-Time Wife © Harlequin Books S.A. 2006

ISBN: 978 0 263 88355 8

05-1011

Printed and bound in Spain
by Blackprint CPI, Barcelona

THE BOUGHT-AND-PAID-FOR WIFE

BY
BRONWYN JAMESON

Dear Reader,

When I was asked if I would like to participate in SECRET LIVES OF SOCIETY WIVES, I jumped in with an enthusiastic, "Yes, please." Just hearing the series name conjured up all kinds of juicy, scandalous premises...not to mention the "it" TV show at the time. The invitation came, you see, midway through the first season of *Desperate Housewives*, and I'm a big fan.

Now, I live a long way—ten thousand miles, give or take—from Connecticut and a similar distance from the glamorous, high-society lifestyle this series embodies. But it was no hardship researching and inventing my little piece of Eastwick, Connecticut. From Vanessa's home to the polo charity benefit to the country club wedding, it was a Bentley-load of fun!

As for my hero... I have a New York friend to thank for Tristan. Jen's offhand comment about sexy Australian footballers in their short shorts and great legs inspired me to create this background for my rugged, difficult, take-no-prisoners alpha. I hope you enjoy him as much as Vanessa does!

Cheers,

Bronwyn Jameson

Bronwyn Jameson spent much of her childhood with her head buried in a book. As a teenager, she discovered romance novels, and it was only a matter of time before she turned her love of reading them into a love of writing them. Bronwyn shares an idyllic piece of the Australian farming heartland with her husband and three sons, a thousand sheep, a dozen horses, assorted wildlife and one kelpie dog. She still chooses to spend her limited downtime with a good book. Bronwyn loves to hear from readers. Write to her at bronwyn@bronwynjameson. com.

For all my readers, with a special mention
to those who've written to me. I treasure
every note and letter and card.
And to Mrs White, the number one
advocate for my own little "Lew."
Thank you, K.

One

He'd seen pictures. He'd expected beautiful. After all, when a man chooses a trophy wife, he wants one other men will covet. But Tristan Thorpe hadn't appreciated the extent of that beauty—or its powerful clout—until ~~g impact.~~ ~~five-and-a-bit feet of breathtak-~~ ~~colonial opened in a~~

Vanessa Thorpe. His father's widow. The enemy.

In every one of those society diary pictures she looked as glossy and polished as a trophy prize should… which had left Tristan speculating over how much was real—the platinum hair? the full lips? the petite but perfectly curved body?—and how much came courtesy of his father's wealth.

He hadn't wondered about the sparklers at her throat

and in her ears. Those, he knew, were real. Unlike her other multi-faceted assets, the diamonds appeared on the listed valuations of Stuart Thorpe's estate.

But here, now, seeing her in the flesh for the first time, Tristan didn't notice anything fake. All he saw was the very real sparkle in her silvery-green eyes and the smile. Warmer than the August sun at his back now that the rain had cleared, it lit her whole face with pleasure and licked his body with instant male appreciation.

That hot shot of hormones lasted all of a second, which was as long as it took for shock to freeze the smile on her perfect pink lips.

"It's…*you*."

Her whispered gasp came coated with dismay and, although she didn't move, Tristan saw the recoil in her expression. She wanted to back away. Hell, she probably wanted to slam the door in his face, and a perverse part of him wished she would give it a go. The long flight from Australia and the snarled afternoon traffic following a heavy rainstorm had him edgy enough to enjoy that kind of confrontation.

Logic, however, wind of confrontation.
cautioned him to remain cool.
duchess." And because he wasn't the least bit
smiled, as slow and mocking as his drawled greeting.
"Obviously, you were expecting someone else."

"Obviously."

Tristan arched an eyebrow. "Didn't you say I was welcome here any time?"

"I don't recall—"

"Two years ago," he reminded her. After her hus-

band's death. Seeing as she had to call his estranged family on the other side of the world to inform them of his passing, why not extend her largesse? An ex-waitress with expectations of a cool hundred million in inheritance could afford to appear generous.

Right now she didn't look so generous. In fact she looked downright inhospitable. "Why are you here, Tristan? The court date isn't until next month."

"If it's even necessary."

Surprise and suspicion narrowed her eyes. "Have you changed your mind? Are you dropping your contest of the will?"

"Not a chance."

"Then what do you want?"

"There's been a new development." Tristan paused, savoring the moment. He'd flown nearly ten thousand miles for this. He wanted to drag it out, to see her flail, before he brought her down. "I think you'll change your mind about keeping that court date."

For a second she stared at him, her expression reveal-ing nothing but annoyance. Behind her, somewhere vast interior, a phone started to tightening her lips, before she spo her momentary distraction glance, a

"If this is another of your attempts to obstruct execution of Stuart's will—" the hostility in her eyes and her voice confirmed that's exactly what she thought "—please take it to my lawyer, the same as you've done with every other new development the past two years. Nothing has changed in that regard. Now, if you'll excuse me…"

Oh, no. No way would he be dismissed. Not with that snooty voice, not with that imperious lift of her perfect little chin.

Tristan didn't stop to consider propriety or good manners. To prevent her closing the door on him, he stepped forward. To halt her leaving, he reached out and caught her by the arm.

The *bare* arm, he realized as the shock of her warm and female softness shot through his system.

Vaguely, beneath that purr of awareness, he felt her stillness and heard the hitch of her breath. Shock, no doubt, that he'd dare lay a hand on her.

"You don't want to close that door on me." His voice sounded rough, a deep growl in the tense silence. And he realized that the shrill ringing of the telephone had stopped, whether because someone had picked up or the caller had quit, he didn't know and couldn't care. "You don't want me taking this public."

"No?"

"If you're smart—" And she was. They might have dealt with each other largely through lawyers, but he never underestimated the smarts behind that cool blond look. "—you'll keep this between you and me."

Their eyes flashed with raw antagonism and something else. The same something that still buzzed through his system and tightened his gut. The same something that made him release his grip on her arm without breaking eye contact, even when he heard the rubbery squelch of rapidly approaching sneakers on the foyer's marble floor.

"Take the call if you need," he said. "I can wait."

Their eyes met, clashed, held, and he saw a flash of something in her face, quicksilver fast. Then it and she were gone, from the room but not from his blood.

Damn it to blazes, he could not be attracted to her. He would not allow it.

With a growl of aggravation, he shut his eyes and rubbed the back of his neck. Twenty-six hours he'd been traveling. Longer from when he left his Northern Beaches' home for the airport in Sydney's south end.

He was tired and he was wired, running on adrenaline and fixation on his goal.

How could he believe anything he felt right now? How could he trust anything in the turmoil of emotions elicited by his return to Eastwick, Connecticut? To this, the home where he'd grown up, where he'd felt cherished and secure, only to have that comfort blanket yanked from under his adolescent feet without any warning.

Guess what, darling? We're going to live in Australia. You and your sisters and your mother. Won't that be exciting?

Twenty years later he was back and his heightened responses—the heat, the bitterness—weren't all about Vanessa Thorpe.

He expelled a long breath and forced himself to move farther inside.

She'd changed things, of course. The colors, the furnishings, the mood. His footsteps echoed in the cavernous foyer, soaring to the two-story ceiling and bouncing off walls painted in a medley of pale blues. Where he remembered the warmth of a childhood home, now he felt nothing but an outsider's detachment.

Ignoring the tight sensation in his gut, he executed a slow three-sixty and took in the matched mahogany hall stand and side table, the pair of watercolor seascapes, the vase of long-stemmed blooms. The place was as perfectly put together as Vanessa Thorpe, as carefully executed as had been her plan to snare a multimillionaire three times her age.

For two years Tristan had fought the will that gave her everything bar a token bequest to him, Stuart Thorpe's only child, a deliberate act to show he'd chosen wife over son as his beneficiary. Tristan had filed motion after motion while he searched for a loophole, an angle, a reason.

He'd never doubted that he would win. He always did.

Finally, from out of the blue, he'd caught his lucky break. An anonymous allegation contradicting what his legal team had learned about the young widow. Initially, all they'd heard was good—Saint Vanessa with all her charity committees and voluntary work and her unstinting devotion to an ailing husband.

But a second round of discreet inquiries had revealed another slant on Vanessa Thorpe. No solid evidence, but enough rumors from enough different sources to point toward the smoke of a secretly guarded fire. Evidence would not be easily attained two years after the fact but it might not prove necessary.

He was banking on an admission of guilt to close this thing off, granting his mother all that was rightfully hers. Winning would not make up for her life's disappointments and unhappiness, but it would serve to reverse the gross injustice of her divorce settlement.

Twenty years late but it would redress the balance. It was just and fair. And at long last, it would set things right in Tristan's mind.

Vanessa put down the receiver and slumped over the library desk, weak with relief. Plans had changed. Andy would not be arriving at the door any minute, making her meeting with Tristan Thorpe even more difficult than it promised to be.

And she knew, from experience, that anything involving Tristan would prove more difficult than it needed to be.

Time after time he'd proven that, obstructing the execution of probate at every turn, refusing each effort to compromise, threatening to never give up until he had his due. All because he'd cast one look at her age, another at her background and thought *Hello, gold digger*.

Vanessa knew plenty about narrow-minded bigots, but still she'd given this one time to reassess. She'd called, she'd extended that invitation to visit, she'd given him every opportunity to take a fair settlement from the estate. She'd thought he deserved it, even though Stuart had decided otherwise.

But Tristan remained inflexible. A greedy, heartless brute and bully. Too bad she refused to be intimidated.

Reflexively she lifted a hand to rub at her arm. She hated that his touch had left a remnant warmth, that she'd felt the same heat from eyes the changeable blue of summer on the Sound. From the depth of his dark drawl and the scent of rain on his clothes and the contrast between civilized suit and uncivilized—

An abrupt knock at the library door brought her head up with a guilty start. But it was only Gloria, her brow puckered with concern. "Is everything all right, hon? Do you need to go out? Because if you do, I can deal with *himself*."

The last was issued with a sniff of disdain that made Vanessa smile. For a brief second she considered taking that option, mostly because it would tick him off. But she needed to find out what he wanted and why he'd felt a need to deliver his latest pain-in-the-butt objection in person.

Not that she believed he'd discovered anything new. At least, nothing that could influence the estate distribution.

"Everything's fine, thanks. Andy's had to cancel our trip to the city but that's turned out to be a blessing. As for *himself*—" she said it with a mocking smile as she rose to her feet "—I can handle him."

"I know you're plenty tough, but he's a big one."

"The bigger they are…"

Gloria harrumphed. "You better make sure he doesn't break anything valuable when he falls. And if he does fix on making trouble, I'm here."

"No," Vanessa said, getting serious. "You will not be here because your working day finished thirty minutes ago. Now, go home and fuss over your Bennie. As soon as I'm done with our guest, I'm heading up to Lexford anyway."

"Is everything all right up there? Is L—"

"Everything's fine," she repeated. And because she didn't want to extend the conversation by fielding further queries, she put a firm hand on Gloria's shoulder and propelled her toward the door. "I'll see you tomorrow. Now, shoo."

Wanting a glass of water before facing the dreaded enemy, Vanessa headed to the kitchen…and stumbled upon him en route—not in the formal sitting room as instructed, but in the keeping room.

No, no, no. Her heart beat fast with agitation. This was *her* place. The only room decorated with *her* things. The only room small enough and cozy enough and informal enough to relax in with a good book or to visit with friends.

Tristan Thorpe did not fit anywhere in that picture. Not the friends bit, and definitely not the small and cozy part. He'd made his mark as a pro football player in Australia, and she could see why he'd been such a forceful presence on the field. It wasn't only his height, broad-shouldered build and wide male stance. He also exuded an aura of purpose and determination, a hard edge that his tailored suit and expensive grooming could not disguise.

Even standing with his back to the door, without the full-on impact of his intense blue gaze and the decisive set of his strong-boned face, he created an uneasy awareness in Vanessa's flesh. She wasn't used to seeing a man in her house, especially one this blatantly male.

But he's here, she told herself. *He is what he is. Deal with it.*

That pragmatic mantra had pulled her through a lot in twenty-nine years—more difficulties of more importance than Tristan. Most of them had been solved by her godsend marriage to Stuart and she could not afford to lose that resolution. Not now; not ever.

She started into the room and at the sound of her first footfall, his head came up. A thousand nerves jumped to life as he swung around to face her. She lifted her chin an inch higher. Straightened her shoulders and fixed her face with the cool, polite expression that had gotten her through the most terrifying of social events.

Let him call her *duchess*. She didn't care.

And then she noticed what had held his attention— what he now held delicately balanced in his big hands— and her heart lurched with *I-do-care* anxiety. It was the *Girl with Flowers*, the most treasured in her collection of Lladro figurines.

That fretfulness must have registered in her expression because he regarded her narrowly. "Bad news?"

Vanessa knew he referred to the phone call, but she nodded toward the figurine. "Only if you drop that."

Heart in mouth she watched him turn it over in his hands, first one way and then the other. As a football player he'd been magic with his hands, according to Stuart. But magic or not, she didn't want Tristan's hands on her things. She didn't want to look at them a week or a month or a year from now, and remember this man in her home.

As much as she wanted to keep her distance, she couldn't help herself. She had to cross the room and take the statuette from his hands.

"When I mentioned bad news, I meant the phone call."

The brush of their fingers unsettled Vanessa more than she'd anticipated. She felt the fine tremor in her hand and prayed he didn't hear the telltale rattle as she put the figurine down.

"There's no bad news," she said, recovering her poise. She indicated a wingback chair with one hand. "Would you like to sit?"

"I'm comfortable standing."

Leaning against a cabinet with the heels of his hands resting on its edge, he looked at ease. Except the tightness around the corners of his mouth and the tick of a muscle in his jaw gave him away. Not to mention the intentness of the sharp blue gaze fixed on her face.

Like a lion, she decided, lolling in the grass of the veldt, but with every muscle coiled as he waited for the chance to pounce. Paint her pelt black and white and call her zebra, because she was the prey.

The vividness of that mental image created a shiver up her spine, but she snapped straight in automatic reflex. *Do not let the enemy see your fear.* It was a lesson she'd learned as a child, one she'd tried to instill into her younger brother, Lew.

One she'd used often in her new life, adapting to the scrutiny of Eastwick society.

As much as she wanted to put distance between herself and the enemy, she stood her ground and met his unsettling gaze. "Would you care to tell me about this new development? Because I can't think of a thing that would make any difference to your claim on Stuart's estate."

"You're aware of every letter in that will, Vanessa. Surely you've worked this out."

"You've tried to obstruct every letter of that will. I can't believe there's one you missed!"

"We didn't miss this one, duchess. You were just clever enough to beat us…then."

Vanessa huffed out a breath. "I have no idea what you're talking about. Stop playing games, Tristan. I don't have the time or the patience."

For a long moment he didn't respond, although she realized—belatedly—that he no longer lounged against the cabinet. He'd straightened, closing down the gap between them. But she refused to ask for space. She refused to acknowledge that his proximity bothered her.

"Is he the same one?"

She blinked, baffled by his question. "Who?"

"The man you were expecting this afternoon. The one who put that smile on your face when you answered the door. The one who called."

Was he crazy? "The same what? What are you talking about?"

"I'm asking if this man—Andy, isn't it?—is the one who's going to cost you a hundred million dollars."

Vanessa's heart seized with shock and a terrible realization.

"Well?" he asked, not giving her a chance to recover, to respond. "Is he the man you were sleeping with while you were married to my father?"

Two

Oh. My. Lord. He was talking about the adultery clause. The one left over from Stuart's first marriage, to Tristan's mother.

When Tristan had signaled his intention to challenge the will, her lawyer, Jack Cartwright, had gone over every clause with painstaking care, making sure Vanessa understood and that he wouldn't receive any nasty surprises from the opposing attorney.

She'd given that clause no more thought. She had no reason to. But now Tristan thought she'd had a lover...that she *still* had a lover.

That comprehension took a moment to sink in, and then she couldn't prevent her shock from bubbling into laughter.

"You think this is funny?"

"I think," she said, recovering, "this is ludicrous. Where would you get such an idea?"

"My lawyer's asked around. There are rumors."

She stared at him in disbelief. "After almost two years of this dispute, you've decided to invent rumors?"

"I didn't invent anything."

"No? Then where did these rumors suddenly sprout from?"

He took a second to answer, just long enough for Vanessa to note that the muscle still ticked in his jaw. "I received a letter."

"From?"

"Does it matter?"

"Yes, it does," she fired back at him, her earlier disbelief growing indignant. "It matters that someone is slandering me."

He regarded her in silence, a long taut moment that fanned Vanessa's gathering fury.

"I'm giving you the chance to deal with me privately, here and now," he said finally, his voice low and even. "Or would you prefer to take this to court? Would you like to answer all the questions about who and where and how often under oath? Would you like all your society friends to hear—"

"You bastard. Don't you dare even think about spreading your lies."

"Not lies." Something glinted, brief and dangerous in his eyes. "I intend to dig deep, Vanessa, if that's what it takes to discover all your dirty little secrets. I will find every truth about you. Every last detail."

Vanessa's head whirled with the implications of his

threat. She had to get away from him, to cool down, to think, but when she tried to escape he blocked her exit. And when she attempted to stare him down, he shifted closer, hemming her into the corner where she couldn't move without touching him.

Her resentment rose in a thick, choking wave. She wanted to sound icy, imperious, but instead her voice quivered with rage. "You start by turning up at my home uninvited. You manhandle me. You threaten me with your nasty lies. And now you're resorting to physical intimidation. I can hardly wait to see what you try next."

Their eyes clashed in a lightning bolt that was eight parts antagonism, two parts challenge. She knew, a split second before he moved, before his hands came up to trap her against the wall, that the two parts challenge was two parts too much. And still she couldn't back down, even when his gaze dropped to her lips and caused a slow sweet ripple in her blood. Even when he muttered something low and unintelligible—perhaps an oath, perhaps a warning—beneath his breath.

Then his mouth descended to hers, catching her gasp of indignation.

For a second she was too stunned by the sensation of his lips pressed against hers to react. Everything was new, untried, unfamiliar. The bold presence of his mouth, the rough texture of his skin, the elemental taste of rain and sun and man.

Everything was unexpected except the electric charge that flushed through her skin and tightened her breasts. That was the same as when he'd touched her, the same as when he'd watched her walk away, the same as when she'd turned at the library door and caught him staring.

She heard the accelerated thud of her heartbeat and scrambled to compose herself, to reject that unwanted response. But then he shifted his weight slightly and she felt the brush of his jacket against her bare arm. For some reason that slide of body-warmed fabric seemed more intimate than the kiss itself, and the effect shimmered through her skin like liquid silk.

The hands she'd raised to shove him away flattened against his chest and the slow beat of his heart resonated into her palms. With a shock she realized that she wasn't only touching him but kissing him back, just now, for one split second. *Oh, no. A thousand times no.* Her eyes jolted open, wide and appalled, as she pushed with renewed purpose.

His mouth stilled for one measured second before he let her go. The message was clear. He'd instigated this. He was ending it. Damn him. And damn her traitorous body for reacting to whatever weird male-female chemistry was going on between them.

Red-hot anger hazed her vision and she lashed out without conscious thought. He dodged her easily, catching her arm before she came close to landing a blow. And that only infuriated her more. She wrenched at her captured arm and the jerky action caught the Lladro *Girl with Flowers* she'd set down on the cabinet.

In slow motion she saw the delicate figurine start to topple but she couldn't move fast enough. The sound of its shattering impact on the marble floor filled the silence for several long brittle seconds. Vanessa pressed the back of one trembling hand to her mouth, as if that might silence the anguished cry deep inside her.

But when she started to duck down, he intercepted her, his hand on her arm holding her steady. "Leave it. It's only an ornament."

An ornament, yes, but this one was a gift from her childhood—a symbol of where she'd come from and all she'd dreamed of leaving behind.

But only a symbol, her pragmatic side reminded her. She'd had to grow up too practical for dreams and symbolism. This incident signified only one thing: she'd allowed Tristan Thorpe to cut through her cool, to upset her enough that she'd lashed out in temper.

And she would eat dirt before she gave him the satisfaction of knowing how deeply he'd affected her.

"Are you all right?"

The softened edge to his voice caught her off guard, but she shrugged that aside along with his touch. He was probably worried that she'd start weeping and wailing. Or that she'd turn and throw some more of her *ornaments* at his infuriating head.

No doubt it was as hard and as cold as the marble tiles underfoot.

Gathering the shards of her poise, she turned and met his eyes. "I will be fine once you get out of my house."

The concern she'd detected in his voice turned steel-hard. The muscle she'd noted earlier jumped in his jaw again. "You enjoy your house while you can, duchess."

"Meaning?"

"It won't be yours once I prove your adultery. Not the house, not any of these pretty things you're so concerned about breaking. All bought and paid for with Thorpe money."

"Good luck with that," she said coldly, while the anger resurged with new fervor. She had to get out of here before she did start hurling things at him, if only to show how little they mattered. "If you'll excuse me, I have another appointment. If you have anything else to say, please say it through my lawyer."

"That's it?"

"Except for one last thing… Please close the door on your way out."

Tristan hadn't planned on following her. After closing the front door, he'd been intent on getting to one place only—his attorney's office in Stamford. He had a letter to deliver. He had instructions to employ the best investigator—a team of them, if necessary—to follow up every rumor about her secret assignations, to find this mystery man whatever the cost.

Even though he'd prodded her about seeing *the same man* today, he didn't believe she would be foolish enough to flaunt her lover so openly. Not when she stood to lose everything she'd set her cap at when she had married the old man.

With all his focus trained on what she'd said and not said, on what he'd done and wished he hadn't, Tristan drove straight through the intersection of White Birch Lane and Beauford when he should have turned right. Half a mile farther on he realized his error and pulled over. Waiting for a gap in the traffic, he beat himself up about missing the turn. And while he was at it, he beat himself up some more for making such a hash of his first meeting with Vanessa Thorpe.

Sure she provoked him. Everything about her had needled him long before he came face-to-face with her kick-gut beauty. But did he have to react to every goading statement, every challenging eye-meet, every disdainful lift of her chin?

Did he have to kiss her?

The hell of it was he didn't remember making a choice. One second they were going at it, biting verbal chunks out of each other's hides, the next he had her backed against the wall tasting the provocation of her lush lips. And the hell of *that* was how swiftly her taste had aroused his hunger.

He'd wanted so much more than one quick bite. His hands had itched to touch that distracting dip in her chin, to feel the creamy softness of her skin, to pull her tight against his body.

He could blame the long day, his lack of sleep, the edgy turmoil of returning to Eastwick, but in the end he could only hold himself responsible. He'd let her get to him.

He wouldn't make that mistake again.

The flow of traffic eased and he checked his mirror just as a champagne colored convertible whizzed by. He didn't have to see the vanity plates to know it was her. Everything on the list of possessions they'd sparred over this past year was indelibly printed on his brain.

He hadn't planned on following her any more than he'd planned on kissing her, but as he steered into a gap in traffic Tristan had a hunch that this would turn out a whole lot more fulfilling and less frustrating than that ill-conceived meeting of mouths.

"I'm so glad you suggested this," Vanessa said.

This was to meet by the water at Old Poynton, where the breeze drifting off Long Island Sound tempered the warmth of the late afternoon sun; where breathing the fresh marine air cooled the edgy heat of Vanessa's temper…a little.

And *you* was Andy Silverman, who'd suggested the outdoor walk-and-talk when he'd called earlier to change plans.

Andy had grown up in the same Yonkers neighborhood as Vanessa's family, and she'd recognized him as soon as he commenced working at Twelve Oaks, the special-needs facility that had been home to her younger brother for the past seven years. They met regularly to discuss Lew's program and his progress, and Andy had become more than her brother's counselor.

Now she counted him as a friend…the only friend who knew and understood Lew and the difficulties posed by his autism.

"Tough day at the country club?" Despite the light-hearted comment, she felt a serious edge to Andy's sidelong look. "You want to talk about it?"

"Haven't we just done that?"

They'd talked about Lew, as they always did, and about why Andy had cancelled their trip to the city. Storms, like today's, were one of several triggers that upset Lew's need for calm and routine order.

"Your brother has bad days all the time," Andy said now. "You're used to that."

No. She didn't think she would ever call herself *used to* Andy's autism or his most difficult, sometimes violently damaging, days. But she conceded Andy's perceptive point. He knew there was more worrying her today than Lew.

"I'm not sure you want to hear this," she said.

"Hey, I'm a professional listener."

That made her smile. "Do you charge extra for out-of-hours consultations, Dr. Silverman?"

They'd reached the end of the promenade. Andy paused and leaned against the stone wall that separated the walkway from the beach. He folded his arms across his chest. His open face and calm expression were part of what made him so good at his job. "Go ahead and spit it out. You know you want to."

Not so much *want to* as *need to*, Vanessa silently amended. Her gaze shifted beyond her companion, tracking two windsurfers as they rode a gust of air across the clean blue surface of the Sound. Then one of the surfers slowed, faltered, and toppled into the water, his charmed ride on the wind over.

"Wouldn't it be nice if we all had such soft landings," she mused out loud.

"You've lost me."

With a small sigh, she turned her attention back to Andy and his invitation to *spit it out*. "It's Tristan Thorpe."

Andy tsked in sympathy. "Isn't it always?"

"He's here. In Eastwick."

"For the trial? I thought that wasn't till next month."

"He's here because he thinks he's found a way to beat me without going to court." All semblance of relaxation destroyed, Vanessa paced away a couple of steps, then swung back. "Which he hasn't, but that won't stop him making trouble."

"Only if you let him."

She laughed, a short, sharp, humorless sound. "How can I stop him? He has it in his head that I'm a nasty sly adulterer and he's here to prove it!"

To his credit, Andy barely blinked at that disclosure. She supposed, in his line of work, he heard all manner of shockers. "That's not a problem if there's nothing to substantiate."

"Of course there's nothing to substantiate!"

"But you're upset because people might believe that of you, despite your innocence?"

"I'm upset because…because…"

Because he believes it. Because he kissed me. Because I can't stop thinking about that.

"My point exactly," Andy said, misinterpreting her stumble into silence. "Your friends know you well enough to not believe whatever he might put about."

"My friends know. You know. I know," she countered hotly, "but he's always thought the worst of me. Now he believes I'm not only an Anna Nicole Smith clone who took advantage of a susceptible older man, but I kept a lover on the side to share my ill-gotten spoils." She exhaled on a note of disgust. "I don't even know why I'm surprised."

Andy regarded her closely for a long moment. "He's really got you stewing, hasn't he?"

Oh, yes. In ways she didn't want to think about, let alone talk about. She'd let him kiss her, she'd breathed the scent of him into her lungs, and then she'd raised her hand, for pity's sake, when she despised violence born of temper and heated words and uncontrolled emotions.

"He got me so riled," she said with quiet intensity, her stomach twisting with the pain of those long-ago memories. "I wanted to hit him, Andy."

"But you didn't."

Only because he stopped me.

She could still feel the steely grip of his hand, the pressure of his fingers wrapped around her wrist, and the need to lash out raging in her blood. And the worst of it? Not the loss of her treasured gift but the ac-knowledgment, on the hour-plus drive up here, that she hadn't been lashing out at him but at her fickle body's unexpected and unwanted response.

"I told myself not to let him get under my skin. I invited him into my home when I wanted to slam the door in his face. I tried to be polite and calm. But the man is just so…so…" Unable to find a suitable descrip-tor, she spread her hands in a silent gesture of appeal. Except she doubted the dictionary contained a single word strong enough, hot enough, complex enough to cover all that Tristan had evoked in her that afternoon. "And it's not only him that has me stewing."

Suddenly she couldn't stand still any longer. Hook-ing an arm through one of Andy's folded ones, she forced him into motion, walking back toward the strip of tourist boutiques and sidewalk eateries opposite the small beach and marina.

"Someone sent him a letter. An accusation. That's how this latest crusade of his started." She tugged at his arm in agitation. "Who would do such a thing?"

"Did he show you this letter?"

Vanessa shook her head and in Andy's raised brows she read another question. "Are you thinking that this letter might not exist?"

"If I were you," he said carefully, "I'd want to see it."

At the time she'd been too astounded and too het up by his allegations. She hadn't thought of asking to see the evidence. Frowning, she walked and she chewed the whole exchange and its implications over in her mind. "Why would he invent this letter and come all the way over here to prove its claims? That only makes sense if he believes he *can* prove it. And that only makes sense if someone—such as his correspondent—has convinced him they have something on me."

And that made no sense because she had never slept around.

Not once. Not ever.

"It's not as if I have a pool boy," she continued, "or a tennis pro or a personal trainer. The only male staff I employ regularly is Gloria's Bennie, and that's only for odd jobs to keep her happy. I see Jack, my attorney, regularly but everyone knows he's a besotted new husband and soon-to-be father."

"And you see me."

Andy's evenly spoken comment hung in the air a second before she grasped its significance. Then she stopped in her tracks, shaking her head with a slowly dawning realization. Usually they met behind the walls of Twelve Oaks' sprawling estate, in one of the formal meeting rooms or the less formal library, or they walked around the estate's spacious grounds.

But on occasions they did meet in the nearby town of Lexford, for lunch or a coffee. And they'd also met once or twice here at the shore where Andy lived.

"Do you think some busybody could have seen—" she waggled her hand between them, unable to voice the *us* that might link their friendship in a nonplatonic way "—and misconstrued?"

"It's possible."

Vanessa stared at him wide-eyed. Then, pity help her, she couldn't suppress an involuntary giggle.

"Pretty funny, huh?"

"I'm sorry." Sobering instantly, she reached out and put her hand on his arm. And that was the thing with Andy—she could touch him and feel no spark, no jolt, no prickling of heat. Nothing but a comfortable warmth similar to what she'd established with her husband and still missed so very much. "I didn't mean to offend you. You know I love you like a brother."

"*I* know that, but what about someone watching us?"

Shock immobilized her for a split second. Then she drew back her hand and her body, suddenly aware of how close they stood. As they'd done on countless other innocent occasions.

With an audience?

They continued walking, but Vanessa couldn't stop herself from glancing at each car and passing pedestrian. Scores of people were out enjoying the gorgeous summer twilight, yet she felt exposed.

Despite the warmth of the air she felt a chill run over her skin. "I hate the thought that someone might have been following me."

"That's something I've never quite understood."

She cut him a narrow look. "The fact that I don't like being spied on?"

"The fact you've kept Lew and your visits to Twelve Oaks secret."

"That has nothing to do with being spied on."

"Maybe not," he said in his usual mild manner. "But if the good folk of Eastwick knew about your brother, then they'd also understand why you need to drive up here so often and why you meet with me. That would take care of one possible misinterpretation."

As usual, Andy was right. Except up until now she hadn't seen any need to share this most personal part of her life. Only Stuart—plus a handful of trusted professionals and some old friends from her pre-Eastwick days—knew about Lew. Together they had decided to keep his long-term tenancy at Twelve Oaks private.

"Are you ashamed of—"

"Of course not!" Vanessa swung around to face Andy, all thoughts of being spied upon lost in the fierceness of her answer. "Don't you dare suggest that Lew is some sort of embarrassment. I would take out a paid page in the *New York Times* if I thought it would help, but what would be the point? All that would accomplish is a whole lot of talk and finger-pointing from small-minded people who don't understand."

"And this is the society you want to live in?"

"No. This is the society I *chose* to live in when I married Stuart."

Because that choice included Twelve Oaks, the exclusive facility that provided Lew with the best environment, the right therapy, everything he needed to grow and flourish as an individual. She hadn't even dreamed of accessing such an expensive option before she met her future husband. In fact she'd been at the end of her tether, out of options for caring for Lew and dealing with his increasingly violent tendencies as he grew from a boy into a man.

"Besides," she continued, "not everyone in Eastwick is narrow-minded. If they knew, my friends would want to visit, to help, and you know how Lew is with new people and changes to his routine. He is happy and I'm happy visiting and doing my voluntary work without it being talked about all over town. I've had enough *poor Vanessa*s to last a lifetime, thank you very much!"

They resumed walking, Andy silent in a way that suggested he didn't agree. Was she being selfish, making it easier on herself, protecting her cushy life? After Stuart's death she had wanted to confide in her friends, because Lord knows she'd felt so incredibly alone and lonely. But then she had Gloria, who'd come from the same background, who knew Lew. Plus Andy. Two of the best friends she could have because, unlike her Eastwick friends, they'd known her when she was plain Vanessa Kotzur.

It had been easier to keep the status quo, for so many reasons.

What about now? her pragmatic side wanted to know.

"I need to see the letter," she said with quiet resolve.

Before she made any decision on what else to do, she had to see the evidence.

Andy nodded grimly. "And you need to set him straight about me."

Vanessa's whole system bucked in protest. She could actually feel her feet dragging on the pavement as they neared the street where she'd parked her car.

"Perhaps I can do this without even mentioning Lew. I'll say I do voluntary work at Twelve Oaks." Which she did. "And we're working together on a program…a new music therapy program which I'm looking at funding. And that I'm interested in extending the equestrian therapy facility."

This wasn't even bending the truth. She intended making a very significant donation from Stuart's estate, once it was finalized, to help with both of those programs as well as funding positions for adolescents from low-income families.

Andy's frown looked unconvinced. "He's looking for proof of adultery, Vanessa. He'll have you investigated."

"And find out what? That I drive up to Lexford two or three times a week, to a special-needs home where I'm listed as a volunteer?"

"A home with a resident who shares your surname. Any investigator worth his salt is going to make the connection."

Didn't he ever tire of being so calm and logical and right? Blast him. Because he *was* right, and already her mind had leaped ahead to the next correlation a professional investigator—or his eagle-eyed employer—may make.

Lew Kotzur had moved into Twelve Oaks the same month that his sister Vanessa quit her two waitressing jobs to marry Stuart Thorpe. The man who pulled strings to get young Lew into the place. The man behind the trust fund that paid all his bills.

A sick feeling of fatalism settled over her as they stopped beside her car. Even before Andy spoke. "The way I see it, you have two options, Vanessa."

"I get to choose my poison?"

He didn't smile at her attempt at levity. His calm, level gaze held hers as he laid those choices on the line. "Either you let Thorpe investigate and risk him spreading nasty stuff about why you keep your brother hidden away from your new society friends. Or you tell him yourself and explain your motivation. There're your choices, Vanessa. It's up to you."

Three

There wasn't any choice. Sitting in her car, watching Andy's loping stride carry him off toward the marina, Vanessa knew exactly what she had to do. Swallow her poison quickly, before she had time to think about how bitter it would taste going down.

She dug her cell phone from her purse. Stared at the keypad so long that the numbers swam before her eyes. Closed her eyes until the crashing wave of dread passed.

This isn't about you, Ms. Pragmatist lectured. *Think about Lew. Think about how disruptive and upsetting this could end up for everyone at Twelve Oaks if an investigator started hanging around, grilling staff and residents.*

She didn't have Tristan's cell number, but she did have several Eastwick hotels in her phone's directory. How hard could he be to find?

Not very, as it turned out.

On her second attempt, the receptionist at the Hotel Marabella put her straight through to his suite. She didn't have a chance to second think, or to do any more than draw a deep breath and silently wail, *why the Marabella?* She preferred to think he'd have chosen one of the big chains instead of the tasteful Mediterranean-style boutique hotel whose restaurant was among her favorites.

Perhaps his secretary chose it. Or a travel agent. Business executives did not make their own—

"Hello."

Vanessa started so violently she almost dropped her phone.

By the time she'd recovered and compelled her heart to stop racing and pressed the tiny handset to her ear, he was repeating his greeting and asking if anyone was there. His voice was unmistakable, a deep, thick drawl colored by his years down under. That color matched the sun-tinged ends of his rich brown hair, the deep tan of his skin, but not the alert intensity of his eyes.

She felt a ripple of hot-cold response, as if those eyes were on her again. Those eyes and his mouth—

"It's Vanessa," she said quickly, staunching that memory. "Vanessa Thorpe."

Silence.

"I wasn't expecting to find you in."

"You weren't expecting…" he murmured, slightly puzzled, slightly mocking. "And yet you called?"

"I thought you might be out for dinner. I intended leaving a message."

"A different message to the one you left me with earlier?"

Vanessa counted to five slowly. He knew she'd been spitting mad when she ordered him out of her house. And he knew why, blast him. She was not going to let that cynical taunt get to her. She had to do this. For Lew. For Andy. For her own guilty conscience. "I need to talk to you."

"I'm listening."

"I meant, in person."

In the next beat of silence she could almost feel his stillness, that hard-edged intensity fixed on her from fifty-odd miles away. Ridiculous, she knew, but that didn't stop a tight feeling of apprehension from gripping her stomach.

"Tomorrow?" he asked.

With a full schedule of committee meetings plus a trip to Lexford to see how Lew was doing after today's dramas, her only free hour was first thing in the morning. And the idea of inviting him to her home, or arranging to meet for breakfast somewhere else, caused every cell in her body to scream in protest. Breakfast meant straight out of bed. Breakfast also meant a long night of worry and endless opportunity to change her mind.

"Tonight would suit me better." Vanessa closed her eyes and tried to block out how bad an idea this might turn out to be. "Do you have plans?"

"I have a dinner reservation downstairs."

"I'm sure they will hold your table."

"I'm sure they would," he countered. "If I asked them to."

She sucked in a breath, but she couldn't suck back her sharp retort. "Are you deliberately trying to antagonize me?"

"I don't think either one of us has to try. Do you?"

Okay. So he wasn't going to make this easy, but that didn't mean she would give up. "Are you dining alone?"

"Why do you ask? Would you like to break bread with me?"

"I would like," she enunciated, after ungritting her teeth, "to speak to you. If you're dining alone, I thought that may provide an opportunity without intruding on your plans."

Another pause in which she could almost hear him sizing up the implications of her request. Then, he said, "I'll have the restaurant add another setting."

"Just a chair," she said quickly. "I won't be eating so please don't wait for me. I'll be there in an hour."

"I look forward to it, duchess."

Tristan had drawled that closing line with a liberal dose of mockery, but he *did* look forward to Vanessa's arrival. Very much. He couldn't wait to see how she explained her rapid turnaround from *get out of my house* to *I need to talk*. He could have made it easy on her by changing his dinner booking and meeting her downstairs in the lounge bar or the more private library. He could have offered to drive out to her house, to save her the trip into town.

But after witnessing her rendezvous at Old Poynton, knowing she'd rushed helter-skelter to her lover right after scoffing at the letter's allegations, he was in no mood for making anything easy for Vanessa.

So. She wanted to talk. Most likely to spin a story concocted during that intense seaside heart-to-heart. He couldn't imagine her confessing but she might attempt to explain away her secret meetings with lover boy. Whichever way she played it, he was ready.

This time she wouldn't catch him unawares.

This time he would keep his hormones on ice.

Resisting the urge to check his watch, he poured a second glass of wine and pushed his dinner plate aside. He'd requested a table at the end of the terrace, where, in secluded peace, he could pretend to enjoy the food and the shimmer of reflected moonlight off the darkened waters of the Sound. Where he wouldn't be scanning the door for the distinctive shimmer of moonlight-blond hair.

Still, he sensed her arrival several minutes later. Without turning he knew her footsteps and felt the quickening of anticipation in his blood. When he started to rise from his chair, she waved him back down. Her warm smile was all for the waiter who fussed over seating her—not opposite but catercorner to him.

"So madam, too, can enjoy the view."

She thanked Josef and while he took her order for some ridiculous froufrou coffee, Tristan kicked back in his chair and tried not to notice that she still wore the same pink sundress.

Because she hadn't yet gone home? Because she'd spent all this time at Old Poynton...doing what?

Only walking? Only talking?

The questions—and the possibility in the answers—snarled through him, sharp and mean. For a long moment he continued to stare at her, waiting for Josef to leave. Waiting for her to acknowledge his presence. Waiting for the impulse to ask those questions to pass so he could speak with some civility.

He took a sip from his very civilized *sauvignon blanc*. "Traffic bad?"

She'd been fussing with her purse, setting it just so on the table, but she looked up sharply.

"You said an hour."

"Have I held you up?" Her expression was polite, her voice as cool and dry as his wine. "If you have another appointment, you should have said when I called. I didn't mean—"

"My only appointment is upstairs, with my bed. It's been a long day."

Across the table, their gazes met and held. Comprehension flickered in her eyes, like an unspoken wince of sympathy. "I'm sorry. You must have started the day yesterday, on the other side of the world."

And didn't that seem a long time ago? He should have been wiped out but instead he felt energized. By her presence, by her proximity, by the subtle drift of her perfume in the still night air. But mostly by the promise of another skirmish in their ongoing battle.

"I'm sure you didn't come here to talk about my long day." And there was something in her eyes or in his primed-for-combat blood, that pushed him to add, "Or my current need to get horizontal."

"No." She answered without pause, without dropping

eye contact, without responding to his deliberate provocation. "I didn't."

"So. What do you want?"

"I want to see the letter."

Tristan arched an eyebrow. "You don't believe it exists?"

"Is there any reason I should?"

"I've flown ten thousand miles today on the strength of it."

"So you say."

Rocking back in his chair, he met the steady challenge of her gaze. "If the lover doesn't exist and the letter doesn't exist, why are you worried?"

"Do I look worried?"

"You're here."

Irritation flared in her eyes but before she could respond, Josef arrived with her coffee. She smiled up at the young waiter, her annoyance instantly concealed by an expression as warm and friendly as when she'd opened the door that afternoon. Then Tristan cleared his throat and the subtle reminder of his presence wiped all the warmth from her face. Exactly the same as when she'd found him on her doorstep.

"I am here," she said tightly, "to see this letter. If it exists."

"Oh, it exists, duchess. Same as your lover." Turning the wineglass with his fingers, he waited a second before continuing. "A little young, isn't he?"

A frown marred the smooth perfection of her face. "Josef?"

"Lover boy. At Old Poynton."

"How do you…" Her voice trailed off and her eyes widened as the inference took hold. "You followed me this afternoon?"

"Inadvertently."

"You *accidentally* followed me? *For fifty miles?*"

One shoulder lifted in a negligent shrug. "I took a wrong turn. You sped by. I thought it might be interesting to find out who you needed to see in such a godfire hurry."

Vanessa stared across at him with a growing sense of horror and violation. Not the chill shivers of earlier, when she'd thought about being spied on, but a hot wave of outrage. Because *he'd* done this. Not some anonymous stranger, but this man. Sitting beside her and passing this off as if it were a big fat nothing.

For a long second she had to fight the urge to hurl something at him. The closest something was her cinnamon mocha macchiato, untouched and still hot enough to do serious damage. The need steamed through her, curling her fingers so tightly around the coffee cup's handle, she was afraid it might crack under the pressure.

Not good, Vanessa. Not cool. Not restrained. Not gracious.

Not any of the things she loved about this lifestyle she'd adopted.

Through sheer force of willpower she loosened her grip, but she couldn't risk speaking for fear of the words she might hurl in lieu of the physical. She couldn't even look at him, in case that fired her rage anew. To remind herself of the very public venue and her very elegant surroundings and the very real need to gather some restraint, she looked past his shoulder at the restaurant and the other diners.

Even on a Tuesday night the Marabella's celebrated restaurant was close to capacity, the crowd an even mix of well-heeled tourists and business suits and elegantly dressed locals. Many she recognized; several she knew well enough to call friends. Frank Forrester, one of Stuart's old golfing buddies, tipped his silver head and winked broadly when he caught her eye.

Smiling back, she breathed a silent sigh of relief that Frank's company didn't include his wife. The last thing she needed was Delia Forrester sauntering over to flutter eyelashes and flaunt her latest chest augmentation at the new man in town. And if Delia were present, she *would* notice Tristan. She *would* saunter and flutter and flaunt because that's what Delia did in the presence of men, despite the husband she gave every appearance of doting on.

"What's the matter, duchess? Afraid you'll be seen with me?"

Tristan's soft drawl cut through her reflection, drawing her attention back to him. When her gaze collided with his—sharp, steady, the rich ocean blue darkened like night on the water—she experienced a brief pulse of disorientation, almost like vertigo.

"Not at all," she replied crisply, shaking off that weird sensation. What was the matter with her? Why did she let him get to her so easily, in so many ways? "We are here to discuss business, the same as these gentlemen—" she spread her hands, indicating the sprinkling of suits around them "—and the real estate reps over by the door."

When his gaze followed hers, taking in the company, Vanessa's heart gave a tiny bump of discovery.

She'd hit upon the ideal segue back to Andy and this afternoon's meeting and the ridiculous misconception about an affair. "I don't mind being seen with you, Tristan," she said in a smooth, even voice, while her insides tightened and twisted over where this conversation might lead. "It's no different from two people meeting, say, at the shore, to talk business."

"Your meeting this afternoon was business?"

Lifting her chin, she met his sardonic gaze. "I do voluntary work at a facility for the developmentally disabled up near Lexford. Andy works there as a counselor."

"And you meet him, about your volunteering, at the shore? After hours?"

"Not usually." She moistened her lips. Chose the next words with careful precision. "Andy isn't only a work associate, you see. We grew up in the same neighborhood, went to the same school. He's a good friend and we do meet after hours, sometimes, and not always to talk about my volunteering. Given his profession, Andy is a good listener."

"And today—this afternoon—you needed to talk."

"To vent," she corrected.

"About me."

"Who else?"

He didn't counter for a tick, and there was something in his expression that started a drumbeat of tension in her blood, a beat that slowed and thickened when his gaze dropped to her lips. "Did you tell him about our kiss?"

The intimacy of his words washed through her, at first warm and strong with remembered sensations and then all wrong. *Our kiss* denoted sharing. A lovers' kiss, hushed with reverence and sweet with romance, not imbued with bitter disdain and the bite of angry words.

She shook her head. "That wasn't a kiss."

"No?"

"It was a power play, and you know it."

A note of surprise flickered in the darkened depths of his eyes. "Was it really so bad?"

"As far as kisses go, it fell a long way short of good."

He rocked back in his chair, his expression trickily hard to gauge. Then he shocked the devil out of her by laughing—a low, lazy chuckle that stayed on his lips and tingled through her body like the sparks of a slow-burning fuse.

"Here's where I should say, I can do better."

"To which I would reply, you won't ever get that second chance."

Treacherous territory, Ms. Pragmatist warned her. She'd challenged him before. In the keeping room today, for example, and even before today's first face-to-face confrontation they'd employed words to cut and thrust, in terse e-mails and messages delivered via their respective attorneys.

But this verbal sparring held a different edge.

This came in the shadow of laughter, with a lazy smile and a dangerous shot of pleasure because Vanessa sensed that, finally, she had managed to surprise him in a positive way. That shouldn't have pleased her quite so much. She should have felt repelled by the prospect of another kiss, a real kiss, with no agenda other than exploring—

No. She jolted upright, appalled that she'd been staring at his lips. That she'd allowed the marine-scented air and the witchery of a full moon to lure her from her evening's task.

No more, Ms. Pragmatist admonished. *Get to the point and get out of here.*

"Andy is not my lover. He never was. He never will be." She laid it on the line in a resolute rush. "If he is named in that letter, I think it's only fair that he should know."

"There are no names."

"Can I see?"

"Now?" He showed his hands, palms up, empty. "Not possible. It's in my lawyer's hands."

"You didn't waste any time."

"You had your chance this afternoon, when I came to your house. It was you who suggested we deal through our lawyers."

Yes, she remembered. She also remembered what had made her so spitting mad that she'd kicked him out without seeing the letter. Blast him and her own sorry self for not asking over the phone. She could have saved herself the drive and the aggravation and the gossip she'd no doubt started by meeting him in this public place.

Tight frustration prickled at the back of her throat, but she lifted her chin and ruthlessly shoved that emotion aside. "Could you please arrange for a copy to be sent to my lawyer's office tomorrow?"

"First thing," he replied with surprising compliance.

Prepared for their usual slanging match, Vanessa stared at him through narrowed eyes. What was the hitch? What angle was he playing? He held her gaze for a long moment, steady, blue, guileless, and there was nothing left to say.

Nothing left to do, except get out of there before she started trusting his word.

"Fine." With a brief, decisive nod, she reached for her purse. A shadow fell across their table. And Frank Forrester's distinctive longtime smoker's voice rasped through the silence.

"Sorry for the intrusion, but I couldn't leave without saying hello to my second favorite blonde. Given my rusty old ticker—" he tapped a thin hand against his chest and winked "—I don't put off till tomorrow."

Although Frank often quipped about his age and his heart condition, Vanessa couldn't voice her usual light-hearted reproach. Not only because he'd interrupted her getaway, either. Up close he looked a decade older than his years, frail and slight and stooped.

Smiling up at him, she only hoped her shock at his appearance didn't show on her face.

"Your company is never an intrusion," she assured him. And because it was the gracious thing to do, she added, "Would you care to join us? For coffee or a nightcap?"

"No, no. I'm on my way home. Can't dally." But he made no move to leave and his gaze glinted with genuine interest—or curiosity—as it edged toward her companion and back.

As much as she'd have liked to, Vanessa couldn't ignore the hint. "Tristan, meet Frank Forrester. Frank, this is Stuart's son. From Australia."

"You don't say?" Frank shook his head slowly, his gaze beetling in on the younger man's face. "You've grown some since I last saw you, lad. You were a weedy young beanpole then. It must be at least fifteen years."

"Twenty," Tristan said. And he was on his feet, shaking hands. Being clapped on the back in the male version of an embrace.

"Welcome back to Eastwick, lad. Welcome home!"

Vanessa blinked with surprise. She hadn't considered they might know one another, despite the former bank president's longtime friendship with Stuart. And as for the *welcome home*—the concept of Tristan belonging here in Eastwick was almost as unsettling as seeing him in her home that afternoon.

"Suppose you're here on business," Frank mused. "You started up a telecom, didn't you? Heard you'd turned it into one of the Pacific's major players."

"I'm surprised you've heard of us."

Frank made a gruff sound. "Your father was a proud man. He wasn't above crowing your successes."

If this came as a surprise to Tristan, he didn't show it. No shift in his expression, no acknowledgment, no mention of his father. Just a smoothly offered, "I recently sold out of the company, as it happens."

"You don't say."

"It was an attractive offer."

"Made a killing, eh?"

Tristan's smile came quick and unexpected, its impact a devil of awareness that settled low in her belly. She had to force herself to concentrate on his words. Not the sharp line of his jaw or the curve of his lips. Not the sudden recall of those lips against hers, but his words.

He's sold his business. Does that mean this trip is open-ended? That nothing will prevent him staying in Eastwick for as long as it took?

"Are you asking as a friend or a banker?" he asked.

Frank chuckled. "I'm an old man. Retired, didn't you know?"

"Once a banker, always a banker."

Suppressing a smile, Vanessa looked away. Apparently she needed her own mantra: *once a brute, always a brute*. Just to remind herself what lurked behind that slow, charismatic grin.

"You'll have to come for dinner one night," Frank suggested. "If you're in town for more than a day or two."

"That depends—" she felt the glancing touch of a sharp blue gaze "—on my business."

"Are you staying with Vanessa? Even better. Why don't you both come?"

Staying with her? In her home? Her heart did a little stumbling hitch as their eyes met. *No way*.

They both spoke at once.

"He's not staying with me, actually."

"I'm staying here. At the Marabella."

Oblivious to the sudden tension in the air, Frank dug around in his jacket until he unearthed a card. He pressed it into Tristan's hand. "Even more reason to join us for a meal, lad. Call me when you know your plans."

They said their goodbyes and Frank started to leave. Then he stopped, one hand raised, as if struck by a sudden notion. He turned back. "Is that polo do this weekend, Vanessa?"

"It's on Sunday, yes. But I don't—"

"Perfect!" Frank spoke over the top of her objection. "Why don't you join us?"

"Polo?"

Tristan sounded dubious and Frank nodded sympathetically. "Damn sissy sport if you ask me, but my wife seems to like it."

Champagne, celebrities, studly Argentinean players. Of course Delia liked the polo.

Vanessa did not, particularly, but Sunday's match was a fund-raiser for *Eastwick Cares,* one of her favored charities since it dealt with at-risk youth. The kind of place she and Lew might have needed, had their lives taken a slightly different turn. So, no, she couldn't *not* go to the polo match, although the idea of sharing the same luncheon tent as Tristan and Delia made her stomach pitch.

"Everybody will be there," Frank continued. "Great chance to catch up. Ain't that right, Vanessa?"

Something sharpened in Tristan's gaze as it fastened on her face. A sense of purpose that she instantly recognized for what it was: he would go to the polo match, all right. And he would use the opportunity to quiz people about her.

"That's right, Frank. Anybody who's anybody will be there." She smiled, but the effort felt as forced as her jovial tone. "Unfortunately that means all the invitations were snapped up months ago."

Frank waved that away with a tremulous hand. "Delia will rake up a ticket if need be. Let me know, lad."

With a sinking heart, Vanessa watched his unsteady meandering departure. Delia could wangle an extra invitation if she set her mind and her saccharine-sweet charm and Frank's checkbook to it. There was nothing Vanessa could do without appearing petty or vindictive, and right now all she wanted was escape.

But as she gathered up her purse she felt Tristan's focus switch to her.

The instant she turned into the sharp cast of those blue, blue eyes, she knew what was coming next. Like a freight train barreling through the night, she saw the oncoming light and couldn't do a thing to divert the wreck.

"Who is Delia?" he asked, right on cue.

Twenty years ago, when Tristan left Eastwick, Frank had been married to his first wife. Now Vanessa would have to explain the new, younger, recently acquired model and he would draw the inevitable comparison. Vanessa had heard it all before. She and Delia were not kindred spirits—as Delia had wanted to believe when she first sailed into the choppy waters of Eastwick society—but they had both improved their financial and social status immeasurably when they married significantly older men.

She could not speak for Delia's motives, but she had married Stuart for his money. It was the one fact Tristan had got absolutely right.

Four

"Delia is Frank's current wife."

"His current wife?" Tristan asked. "How many Mrs. Forresters have there been, exactly?"

"Delia is the third."

Not unusual in a place as affluent as Fairfield County, with men as wealthy as Frank Forrester. Or Stuart Thorpe. "Has she been the current Mrs. Forrester for long?"

"Delia and Frank met at this same charity polo event last summer. She was working as a freelance journalist, I believe, and she chose to feature Frank in an article on business leaders who'd retired here on the gold coast. They married soon after."

Alerted by the measured choice to her words and the defensive tilt of her chin, Tristan narrowed his eyes. "Love at first sight?"

"Is that so hard to believe?"

"I haven't met Delia. You tell me."

"You know, that's never come up in conversation," she countered coolly. "I'm not that close to Delia and, frankly, I'm not comfortable discussing her."

Tristan studied her for a moment, his interest piqued by the words and the attitude. Obviously she got along fine with Frank…but not his wife? He had to wonder about that.

And since she was tucking her dinky little purse under her arm with a note of I'm-about-to-leave finality, he might as well wonder out loud.

"Is there something I should know about her before I start making social engagements?" He gestured toward the door, indicating she should precede him. Wariness clouded her green eyes and her mouth tightened slightly because, naturally, she'd have liked to walk away. Alone.

Too bad because he intended seeing her to her car.

And getting a response to his question about Delia.

"Is there a reason you're not close?" he persisted after they'd cleared the tables and were crossing the restaurant foyer. She wasn't exactly dawdling but he kept up easily, a hand low on her back steering her toward the elevators. "Because I'd have thought you would have plenty in common."

Halting abruptly, she turned to him. Green sparks flared in her eyes. "Don't presume too much, Tristan. You've never met Delia. And you only think you know me."

For a moment the inherent challenge in her words was secondary to the impact of her nearness. She'd turned into his ushering arm, so swiftly that the swing of her hair brushed his arm and shoulder. Several strands had caught against his dark jacket, and when he inhaled—a quick flare of his nostrils, a sharp suck of air— he breathed her delicate floral scent and the combination rocked his brain and libido with dizzying temptation.

He knew better than to touch but he did it anyway.

With his free hand he lifted those rogue strands from his jacket and coiled them around his fingers. Her hair was as fine and silky soft as he'd imagined but surprisingly cool, unlike the flush of heat in her throat and the softening of her full lips.

Completely unlike the bolt of energy that crackled in the air as their eyes met and held.

"Is that a challenge?" he asked.

She blinked slowly, as if lost in the moment and the dangerous vibration pulsing between them. "What do you mean?"

"To get to know you better."

Behind them the elevator announced its arrival. The subtle electronic distraction brought her head up and back, breaking eye contact and forcing him to release her hair. A couple exited the elevator, hand in hand and so absorbed in each other they'd have walked right through him and Vanessa—or a herd of stampeding buffalo—if he hadn't backed out of the way.

"Not at all," she responded once they were alone again. "It was a statement of fact. You haven't met Delia Forrester and yet you presumed a similarity between us."

"You're unalike?"

"We are different." She held his gaze. "Very different."

He thought she would say more—it was there in

her eyes, a darkening of purpose, a fleeting moment of gravity—but then she made a little gesture he interpreted as forget-about-it and started walking.

He caught up with her in two strides.

"I'm going to take the stairs," she said crisply. Then, when he continued at her side, she cut him a sharp look. "There's no need for you to accompany me."

"I'll see you to your car."

"I am valet parked. There's no need."

He didn't argue, he just kept walking, not to be difficult or perverse but to see her safely to her car. It was the right thing to do. So was letting go the subject of Delia Forrester—he would find out the differences soon enough.

He would make up his own mind.

While waiting for her car, they made stilted small talk about the hotel and its first-rate service and, when her Mercedes Cabriolet appeared, about the car itself. Then, before she slid into the driver's seat, came a moment of awkwardness, as she said goodbye in a stiffly formal way.

"Not goodbye." Tristan dismissed the valet with a look and met her eyes over the sports car's low door. "I will see you at the polo match. Frank said everyone will be there—I assume that includes you?"

"Please don't do this," she said in a rush of entreaty. "Please don't use this as a venue to ask questions about me."

"This afternoon you didn't have any qualms. I recall you wishing me luck."

"This afternoon you caught me by surprise."

The surprise of that kiss, of each touch, of their unwanted attraction, arced between them in the tense stillness of the night. Nothing needed to be said; it was all there, in the unspoken moment. As was the root of their conflict, the part that was no surprise. "And now you're suggesting I shouldn't ask questions about you?"

"I'm asking that you respect the privacy of others." She moistened her lips, and the sweet warmth of her kiss licked through his veins again. "You said this was between you and me, but it's not. You will hurt others, if you go around asking questions and starting rumors and drawing attention to our feud. Think about it, please. Think about doing the right thing."

Standing so close, Tristan felt the candor of her appeal reach out and take a grip. She'd never asked anything of him before, not so directly, not with a *please* that chased the memory of her taste and the scent of her hair on a wild scrambling scurry beyond his blood and his male hormones to a closely guarded place beyond.

"I am doing the right thing," he assured her...and reminded himself. "I've never doubted that."

For a brief instant he thought there was more, a response or another appeal, and deep in his gut he hoped for the latter. A *please, Tristan* that was only about them and had nothing to do with their conflict. But then she pressed her lips together and just before she slid into the driver's seat, he glimpsed something else deep in her eyes, something that shifted like a darkening shadow.

Whatever was going on with her, he would find out.

Steel coated his resolve and his voice as he watched the glossy vehicle glide from beneath the hotel portico onto the street. "If you have nothing to hide, duchess, then why that appeal? What do you have to fear? And who the hell are you protecting?"

A block away from the Marabella, Vanessa expelled a soft gust of held back breath. Finally she was able to breathe and think again—two basics she had difficulty with in Tristan's company. And now she was functioning at something like normality, the tight, sick feeling she'd experienced earlier returned with a vengeance.

Tonight had been a complete waste of time. Had she really thought she could sit at the same table and pretend he hadn't turned her world on its head with his arrival and his condemnation and his hot-blooded kiss?

"Not a kiss," she reminded herself vehemently, and a fat lot of good that did! Rolling her shoulders and gripping the steering wheel tightly did not halt the rush of heat, either. Even now, all these hours later, she could still feel the sizzle.

What was that about?

The sad part was, Vanessa didn't know. She'd never experienced anything like this before. Ever. No boyfriends, no stolen kisses, no illicit make out sessions. Nothing but work and caring for Lew and then a whole new world of opportunity through her friendship with Stuart Thorpe.

"Why him?" She thumped the steering wheel with one fisted hand. "Why did it have to be him?"

Tonight, unfortunately, she'd witnessed an unexpected side to her nemesis. Smiling in the moonlight, challenging her over his kissing technique, charming and at ease with Frank Forrester, showing her to her car like a gentleman.

She growled low in her throat and thumped the wheel again.

And what are you going to do about it, duchess?

Hearing the silent question in *his* dark chocolate drawl did not help her mood of frustrated disquiet.

"Nothing," she muttered, but that response hung over her like a dark-shadowed indictment of her failure tonight. She shifted in her seat and reconsidered. Okay. About this unwanted attraction, she would do nothing.

But that wasn't her real problem…

She still had no proof of the letter's validity, and he believed he had grounds to steal her security and Lew's future away from her.

Paused at an intersection, she checked for traffic. Down the street to her left stood the offices of Cartwright and Associates, a place she'd come to know oh so well in the past two years. The place where she should have taken the news of Tristan's arrival and allegations this afternoon.

As Stuart's lawyer and now hers, Jack Cartwright was one of the handful of people who knew about Lew, and right now she could do with his clear head and logical approach. She checked the dashboard clock and winced. Although Jack and his wife Lily were close friends, they were expecting their first baby in a month's time and calling this late felt like an imposition.

Not that she wasn't tempted…but, no. First thing in the morning she would call and arrange a meeting. The earlier the better.

* * *

After sleeping poorly Vanessa was up and dressed before dawn, but she managed to hold off calling the Cartwright home until seven o'clock. Then she kicked herself because Jack had gone into the office already. She exchanged small talk with Lily for all of six seconds before the other woman picked up on the strain in her voice. "Is everything all right, Vanessa?"

"No, not really. Tristan Thorpe's in town." Which, really, was the sum total of her problems. "I need to talk to Jack. I'll call him at the office."

"I have a better idea. Why don't you come over here and have breakfast with us?" Lily suggested. "Jack will be home in an hour or so. He went in early to brief an associate on a court appearance because he's taking the morning off. Doctor's appointment."

"Is everything all right?"

Lily chuckled. "As far as I know, but Mr. Protective insists on taking me, every time."

Vanessa didn't want to intrude on their morning plans but Lily insisted. And right on eight o'clock she was following her heavily pregnant friend into the kitchen of the Cartwrights' two-story colonial home. And it was a home, as bright and cheerful and welcoming as the glowing Lily.

Lily was a recent addition to the circle of friends known as the Debs Club and Vanessa had felt an immediate kinship. Possibly because she, too, had grown up in a tough environment unlike the rest of the group who truly were debs. Lily, too, had struggled to fit into this privileged society in the early months of her marriage, but she and Jack had worked things out and now the happiness she deserved showed on her face.

"Jack's not home yet." Lily rolled her eyes but with a cheerfulness that said she didn't mind. Her man would be home soon and that suited her fine. "I called to let him know you were coming over so he shouldn't be long. Can I get you coffee? Tea? Juice?"

"Oh, please, you don't have to wait on me. Sit down."

"And take a weight off?"

"Yes. Exactly." For the first time she let her eyes rest on the other woman's belly and she felt an unfamiliar twinge of longing, a reaction she hid behind a smile. "Are you sure that's not twins in there?"

"Sometimes I swear there are three." Lily paused in the middle of making a pot of tea. Her expressive blue eyes grew dreamy. "Not that I would mind."

Of course she wouldn't. Her down-to-earth honesty combined with her caring nature and a street-smart wisdom had made her a wonderful social worker and would make her an equally wonderful mother.

Lucky kids, Vanessa thought, and the pang in her middle intensified.

"So." Teapot in hand, Lily waddled across to the table and lowered herself carefully into a chair. "Tell me about Tristan Thorpe."

For once Vanessa was relieved to bring him into the conversation—anything to stifle this bizarre attack of motherhood envy. She had no idea where that had sprung from, all of a sudden. "He arrived yesterday. He's staying at the Marabella. He's even more aggra-vating face-to-face."

"You've seen him already?" Lily propped her chin in a hand, all eager-eyed curiosity. "Do tell."

Where should she start? What could she say without giving away the depth of her confusion and conflict? Just saying *face-to-face* had brought a guilty warmth to her cheeks, mostly because it put her in mind of mouth-to-mouth.

And hadn't *that* wild sensual memory kept her company all through the night!

"There's probably no need for me to tell you anything," she said, recalling one of the other things that had kept her awake. "You will hear it all on the grapevine soon enough."

"All?"

"I met with him at the Marabella restaurant last night."

"You went to dinner with him?" Surprise rounded Lily's eyes. "Did anyone survive?"

Vanessa pulled a face. "Barely. As luck would have it, Frank Forrester happened along."

"With Delia?"

"No, but he'll tell her that he ran into us. You know Delia. She needs to know everything that's going on."

"Unfortunately, yes."

Delia had really stuck her claws into Lily, for no apparent reason other than her friendship with the Debs. That ugliness had exposed a whole new side of Delia Forrester—a side that turned Vanessa ice-cold with anxiety when she thought about—

"Hey, what's the matter?"

Vanessa blinked, and realized that her worried frown had drawn Lily's question. She started to wave her friend's concern aside, then changed her mind. Of all the Debs, Lily would most likely understand.

"I was thinking about how these people—the Delias of this world—can tear a person apart for no reason. A whisper here, a catty comment there, and before you know it everyone is talking and wondering." She took a breath. "Have you heard any rumors about me?"

"What kind of rumors?"

"Oh, that I'm meeting a man in secret. That I have been for years."

"Where on earth did this come from?" Lily's eyes narrowed. "Tristan?"

"He says he got a letter, from someone over here—" she spread her hands to indicate Eastwick, their home "—claiming there is proof."

Something flickered in Lily's eyes and she sat up straighter. She opened her mouth, about to speak, but then her focus shifted, distracted by the sound of footsteps. As her husband came into view her expression transformed, growing bright and soft and incandescent with love.

Although Jack greeted Vanessa with an apology for his tardiness, it was a fleeting acknowledgment of her presence. Because then he was smiling at his wife as he leaned over and pressed a chaste kiss to her forehead and touched a gently protective hand to her stomach.

It was nothing and it was everything, a symbol of the intimacy of their small family circle and a reminder of what she, Vanessa, had never experienced and could never contemplate for herself.

Suddenly her throat felt thick with a desperate sense

of yearning. It was ridiculous, hopeless, frustrating. She didn't even want this love, this coupledom, this family deal. She had everything she wanted, everything necessary and important, and there was no room or time or emotional energy left for anything else.

"So, I hear that Tristan Thorpe is in town." Jack straightened, his expression smoothing into business professional. It seemed that the news had traveled even faster than she'd anticipated. "Is he here to make trouble?"

"He got a letter," Lily supplied, and her husband went very still. His eyes narrowed on Vanessa. "The same as the others?"

"The…others?" Vanessa repeated stupidly, and in the same instant it struck her what they meant.

Two anonymous extortion letters had been sent several months back, one to Jack and one to Caroline Keating-Spence. She shook her head slowly, kicking herself for not considering this connection.

"I don't know. I haven't seen the letter yet." Her heart beat hard in her chest, a thick pulse of dismay, as she looked from Jack's still countenance to Lily's worried frown and back again. As the full ramifications took hold. "Do you really think this could be the same person? That it might be the same man…the one Abby thinks killed Bunny?"

Five

Tristan had a breakfast meeting, too. Not with his lawyer but with the private investigator engaged by his lawyer to look into Vanessa's alleged adultery. The P.I. turned out to be a retired cop who was punctual, professional and personable.

Tristan dismissed him anyway.

His decision was split-second, gut instinct. Sitting in a Stamford coffee house watching the guy demolish a towering stack of pancakes while he delivered the lowdown on his snooping techniques, he pictured Vanessa's face when she'd appealed to his sense of fair play. Same as last night, he felt the grip of her emotion as she looked him in the eye and hit him with the reminder that this was between the two of them.

That didn't mean he'd changed his mind, only his tactics.

Instead of employing a third party to dig into her affairs, he'd take up the shovel himself.

Instead of arranging for the letter to be sent to her lawyer, he collected it and brought it back to Eastwick. His aim: to deliver it personally.

Turning into White Birch Lane, he pulled over to make way for a horse float and the need to brake and control his deceleration alerted him that he'd been driving too fast. Worse, he realized that his haste was geared by a different anticipation from his first visit to her home. Edgy, yes, but colored by memories of her smile and her taste and the spark of a fiery inner passion when she faced up to his hard-line tactics.

Vanessa might look the picture of Nordic cool but he'd seen her gather that poise around herself like a protective cloak. Measured, learned, practiced—whatever, he knew it was fake and he couldn't help wondering why she felt the need to adopt a facade. He couldn't help wondering what she was hiding, and a frown pulled hard at his brow.

He'd spent a good portion of the night wondering about her, uncomfortable with how much he wanted to know. It was an alarm and a warning.

Get to know her, yes, but don't forget why.

After the lumbering trailer disappeared, Tristan continued at a more sedate pace. He allowed himself to glance around, to take in the big homes set back from the road on finely manicured acreages. His frown deepened as he contemplated Frank Forrester's reference to coming home.

He didn't feel any more sense of homecoming today

than yesterday, not even when he turned into the drive where he'd learned to ride a bicycle, not passing the first tree he'd climbed, not even looking out over the grass where he'd first kicked a football.

All he felt was the same gut-kick of bitterness and the keener edge of anticipation. He had to remind himself, again, of his purpose.

He wasn't here to see her, to visit with her, to spar with her—he was here to deliver the letter.

That didn't prevent the crunch of disappointment when the housekeeper—Gloria—opened the door and informed him, with great glee, that Mrs. Thorpe was out and not expected home until late in the afternoon.

Okay. This could still work. In fact, if Gloria didn't mind talking, this could work out even better.

"I didn't ever get that tea yesterday." He smiled and was rewarded with the suspicious narrowing of the woman's eyes. "Is the invitation still open?"

"I guess I could manage a pot of tea."

She stepped back and let him precede her into the foyer.

"So," he said, picking up his shovel and turning the first sod. "Have you worked for Mrs. Thorpe a long time?"

After visiting with Gloria, Tristan returned to his hotel to catch up on some business. He'd sold his share in Telfour very recently and was still fielding calls and e-mails daily. Then there was his position on two company boards plus an enticing offer to join a business start-up, which had influenced his decision to sell.

He was still considering that direction and monitoring a couple of other options.

The busyness suited him fine. He didn't know how to do nothing and immersing himself in his normal business world served as the perfect touchstone with reality. He'd needed that after the last twenty-four hours.

Thus immersed, he picked up the buzzing phone expecting to hear his assistant's voice, only to be disappointed.

Delia Forrester hadn't waited for him to call. He didn't much care for the woman's overly familiar manner but he accepted her invitation to join their party at Sunday's polo match, regardless.

After the call, his concentration was shot so he headed to the hotel's pool. His natural inclination was to swim hard, to burn off the excess energy in his limbs and his blood and his hormones. But after a couple of hard laps he forced himself to ease off to a lazy crawl. He refused to cede control to a situation and a woman and an untenable attraction.

Up and down the pool he loped, distracting himself by thinking about last night's encounter with Frank Forrester, conjuring up vague memories of him and his first wife—Lyn? Linda? Lydia?—spending weekends out of the city at the Thorpe home.

And now, for all the brightness of his conversation, Frank looked worn out. Had his father aged as badly? Had he grown frail and stooped?

Worn out from keeping up with a young, fast, social-climbing wife when he should have been taking it easy with his life's companion, enjoying the rewards he'd earned through decades of hard work?

Without realizing it, Tristan had upped his tempo to a solid churning pace, driven by those thoughts and by the effort of *not* thinking about his father with Vanessa.

Too young, too alive, too passionate.

All wrong.

He forced himself to stop churning—physically and mentally—at the end of the lap. Rolling onto his back, he kicked away from the edge and there she was, standing at the end of the pool, as if conjured straight out of his reflections.

Or possibly not, he decided on a longer second glance.

Dressed in a pale blue suit, with her hair pulled back and pinned up out of view, her eyes and half her face hidden behind a pair of large sunglasses, she looked older, stiffer, all polish and composure and money.

She didn't look happy, either, but then he'd expected as much when he decided not to leave the letter with Gloria.

He knew he'd hear about it—and that she'd possibly come gunning for him—but he hadn't expected her this early in the day. Not when he'd been told she had a full day of important charity committee meetings.

Despite all that, he felt the same adrenaline spike as last night in the restaurant and this morning walking up to her door. The same, only with an added rush of heat, which didn't thrill him. To compose himself, he swam another lap and back, forcing himself to turn his arms over—slow and unconcerned.

Then he climbed from the pool in a long, lazy motion and collected his towel from a nearby lounger. All the while, he felt her watching him and his body's unwelcome response undid all the good work of those relaxing last laps.

Thank God for jumbo-size hotel towels.

Walking back to where she stood, Tristan subjected her to the same thorough once-over. Payback, he justified. She didn't move a muscle, even when he came to a halt much too close, and he wondered if her shoes—very proper, with heels and all to match the suit—had melted into the poolside tile.

"A little overdressed for a dip, aren't you?"

A small furrow between her brows deepened. She moistened her lips, as if perhaps her mouth had all dried out. "I didn't come here to swim."

"Pity. It's the weather for it."

"Yes, it's hot but—"

"You want to get out of the sun?" Tristan inclined his head toward the nearest setting with a big shady umbrella. What a difference a day makes. Twenty-four hours ago he'd been in the business suit, knocking at her door. Now she was on his turf and he aimed to milk the reversal in power for all it was worth.

"No." She shook her head. "I only came for the letter. Gloria rang to tell me you'd called around but you wouldn't leave it."

"I didn't know if I should."

She made an annoyed sound with her tongue and teeth.

"Last night you specifically asked that we keep this between you and me," he reasoned.

"Which is why you insinuated yourself into my house and interrogated my housekeeper?"

Ah. He'd thought she mightn't approve of that. "Gloria kindly made me tea."

"Did she kindly tell you what you needed to know?"

"She told me you were tied up with meetings all day." He allowed his gaze to drift over her charity-meeting outfit. "Yet here you are."

He sensed her gathering frustration, but she took a minute to glance around the surroundings and the little clusters of tourists and the discreetly hovering staff. If she'd been about to stomp on his bare foot with one of her weapon-shaped heels or to launch herself fully clothed into the pool, she resisted. Her elegantly dimpled chin came up a fraction. "I am here to fetch the letter. Do you have it or don't you?"

"I have it, although—" he patted his hips and chest where he might have found pockets, had he been wearing clothes "—not on me."

Despite the dark Jackie O.-size shades, he tracked the shift of her gaze as she followed his hands down his torso. Then, as if suddenly aware of what she was doing and where she was looking, her head snapped up. "I didn't mean *on you*. Is it in your room?"

"It is. You want to come up and get it?"

"No," she replied primly. "I would like you to go up and get it. I will wait in the lounge."

Vanessa didn't give him a chance to bait her further. She turned smartly on her heel and walked away. Yes, he tracked her departure all the way across the long terrace. Yes, that filled her sensory memory with images of his bare tanned length wet and glistening from the pool. Of those muscles flexing and shifting as he toweled himself off. Of the blatant male beauty of a strong toned abdomen, of dark hair sprinkled across his chest and trailing down his midline and disappearing into his brief swimming trunks.

Heat flared in her skin then shivered through her flesh as she crossed from the wicked midafternoon sunshine into the cool shade of the hotel interior. She chose a secluded seat away from the terrace windows and surreptitiously fanned her face while she waited.

And waited.

She ordered an iced water and checked her watch. And realized the waiting and waiting had actually been for little more than five minutes. Time, it seemed, had taken on a strange elongated dimension since she opened the door exactly twenty-four hours ago.

In that time so little had happened and yet so much had changed. None of it made sense…except, possibly, the buff body. He'd been an elite athlete, after all, and any woman with functional eyesight would have found herself admiring those tight muscles.

It wasn't personal.

Vanessa exhaled through her nose, exasperated with herself. She didn't check her watch again.

Assuming he showered and dressed, he could be five or ten minutes or more. And although she hoped he did shower and dress, she didn't want to think about him showering and dressing.

To pass the time she scoped the room, wincing when she noticed Vern and Liz Kramer at a table not too far away. Vern and Stuart went way back. While she liked

the Kramers, she didn't want to deal with another intro-
duction and everything-is-fine conversation like last
night's episode with Frank. She just wanted to get the
letter and get out of here.

The letter.

Another shiver feathered over her skin with the realization of a purpose and an anxiety forgotten from the
second she saw Tristan's strong, tan body slicing effort-
lessly through the azure water. Finally she would get to
see this piece of evidence. She could make her decision
on how to proceed: whether to take Andy's advice and
tell all, or follow Jack's counsel in revealing as little as
necessary.

Since this morning's breakfast discussion, she'd had
little time to weigh the options. Jack's version tempted
her because doing nothing, saying nothing, was always
easier. But was it best for Lew? She just didn't know.
But seeing the letter—her heart raced as a tall, familiar,
fully-dressed figure entered the room—she hoped,
would make up her mind.

Although she'd watched him arrive, Vanessa looked
away to take a long sip from her water. Then he was
there, standing beside her chair, an envelope in his hand.
Her whole stomach went into free fall and she had to
close her eyes against a dizzying attack of anxiety.

"Are you all right?" he asked.

She nodded. From the corner of her eye she saw Liz
Kramer peering their way and she sucked in a quick
breath. "Can we go somewhere more private? I'm afraid
some more old friends are about to come over here."

To his credit, he didn't turn and look. "There's the

guest library downstairs. Or I could arrange a private meeting room—"

"The library will do fine. Thank you."

Tristan stood back, hands in pockets, while she turned the envelope over in her hands. He tried not to notice the pale trepidation on her face. Or the tremor of her fingers as she drew the single sheet of folded paper from inside.

But he couldn't ignore the tightening in his chest and gut, the desire to reach out and...hell...do what? Take the bloody letter back? Ignore his reason for holding onto it this morning, so he could hand it to her and judge her reaction?

Logic said she wouldn't look so uncharacteristically nervous—she of the cool poise and composure—unless she were guilty.

Damn it all to blazes, he needed that guilt. He should be turning up the heat, pushing and prodding her into a hot-tempered admission. Except she looked too fearful and vulnerable and he couldn't. Not yet.

"It's white," she murmured, so low he wouldn't have made out the words if he weren't so intensely focused on her face. Her lips. The wide bemused eyes she suddenly raised up to his. "This is the original? Not a copy?"

"That's the original." Then, when she continued to sit there studying the paper and the envelope, he asked, "Aren't you going to read it?"

Perhaps she'd been building up her nerve or delaying the inevitable, because now she unfolded the letter and scanned it quickly. When she got to the end, she stared at the page for a full minute. He couldn't tell *what* she was thinking only that she *was* thinking. In the silence of the large library room, deserted but for them, he could almost hear the wheels turning and the gears engaging.

But when she finally spoke it wasn't to point out the lack of concrete proof in the letter's content, as he'd expected. It was to ask, "Why would somebody do this?"

Hands deep in his pockets, Tristan shrugged. "To create trouble for you."

"Well, they've succeeded there," she said dryly, surprising him again...and reminding him of her first baffling reaction.

He nodded toward the letter. "You commented on the white paper." She'd also asked if it was a copy. "What's going on, Vanessa? What aren't you telling me?"

"I..."

Vanessa paused, her chest tight with indecision. Despite Jack's instructions to divulge as little as possible, she wanted to share. Yesterday, no. Out by the poolside, no way. But this man had shown a new consideration, in fetching the letter so promptly, in whisking her away to a private room without question, in standing aside and letting her read in peace.

Besides, telling him about the letters would take the focus off her and the secret she didn't want to share. This one he would probably hear anyway, if he hadn't already, on the town grapevine.

"A couple of months back," she commenced slowly, decision made, "two people I know here in Eastwick each received an anonymous letter. I thought...I had thought...this one might be connected."

"Now you think not, because the paper's different?"

"And there's no demand of any kind."

He went still. "Are you saying these other letters contained extortion demands?"

"Yes."

"Demanding what? What's the link?"

"Did you know Bunny Baldwin?" she asked. "Lucinda was her real name but everybody called her Bunny. She was married to Nathan Baldwin, a friend of Stuart's. I thought you might have known them when you lived here."

"It's been twenty years."

"You remembered Frank Forrester."

"He and his first wife spent a lot of time at our house."

Oh. She looked away, unaccountably stung by the sudden hard cast to his eyes. *Our house.* Did he still feel that attachment? Was that why he was so bound and determined to win the estate back?

She wanted to ask, to know his true motivation, but he cut through her thoughts and reminded her of the subject at hand.

"I take it this Bunny Baldwin is the link between the letters?"

"Yes." A sick, tight feeling twisted her stomach as she thought about poor Bunny. Although the woman had been fearsomely intimidating—and had cast some speculation about Vanessa marrying so spectacularly well— she'd also been mother to one of Vanessa's closest friends. "She passed away a few months ago. They thought it was a heart attack but Abby, her daughter, discovered her journals missing. Long story short, the police are now reinvestigating her death."

"Because of some missing journals?"

"Have you heard of the *Eastwick Social Diary*?"

His answer was a noncommittal, "Refresh my memory."

"It's a gossipy newsletter and Web site column about who's who and doing what—" or *whom* "—in Eastwick. Bunny was the writer and editor, and the journals contain her notes and sources plus all the material she chose not to print."

"Chose not to?"

Too agitated to sit, Vanessa rose to her feet and slowly circled the seating arrangement. This connection to his letter and its allegations had to be broached, as much as she dreaded how the conversation would go down. "I gather she thought some stories were too scandalous or damaging or potentially libelous to print."

That's all she had to say. The sharp speculation in his eyes indicated he'd joined the dots without needing further clues. "These journals were stolen and the thief has attempted to blackmail persons named in the journal?"

"That seems the likely explanation."

"And you think it's possible the same person sent the letter to me?"

"I thought so." She lifted her hands and let them drop. "But then it's not the same stationery."

"You think a blackmailer uses the same paper every time?"

"I don't know. I don't know what to think. Do you?"

"There's no hint of extortion," he said after a moment's pause. "And if this person did have blackmail in mind, he'd have sent the letter to you. To entice *you* to pay hush money."

She exhaled on a long note of resignation. Yes, he was right. Although… "Do you believe there's no connection to Bunny and the journals? Because this is rather a big coincidence, a third anonymous letter whose source could have been the same as the first two."

He regarded her silently for a long second. "What are you trying to sell me here? What's your angle?"

"I don't have an angle. I'm just trying to work out the motivation behind this letter."

"And?"

Surprised he'd detected the nebulous hint of more in her words, she looked back at him warily. Then, she decided to tell him. "What if the thief read something in the journals and misinterpreted? What if the person referred to as having an affair wasn't me at all? A lot of the diary pieces are *guess who, don't sue*. Names are not named. What if he has the wrong person?"

"That doesn't explain why he sent the letter to me."

Vanessa narrowed her eyes. "You aren't prepared to listen to my side at all, are you?"

"I listened."

"And now what? You'll have me investigated?"

"Yes," he said, that blue gaze unflinchingly direct. "I will continue to investigate. I also think we should speak to the police."

"The police?"

"You said they were investigating Bunny's death and, I imagine, the extortion demands. Whether it's connected or not, they should see this letter."

Six

"I heard a whisper that Tristan Thorpe's in town."

Felicity Farnsworth's casual comment dropped like a brick into the calm pool of after-lunch conversation, bringing all eyes straight to Vanessa.

Blast.

She'd rather hoped the drama surrounding Emma's upcoming wedding—she wanted small, while her parents had invited half of Eastwick—would keep the focus off her. That's the way she preferred things anyway, including at the regular Debs Club luncheons. These women—Felicity, Lily, Abby Talbot, Emma Dearborn and Mary Duvall—were her friends. Smart, warm, kind, inclusive, they'd invited her into their group, onto their charity committees and into their confidence.

Now, more than ever, she felt the weight of guilt

because she hadn't been so forthcoming. In six years of regular get-togethers she'd tiptoed around her past and her reason for marrying Stuart and becoming part of Eastwick society.

Although she had shared much of her angst in battling Tristan over the will, hence the girlfriends' questions now.

"Is he here about the will contest?" Abby asked.

"Where is he staying?" Caroline wanted to know. "Have you met him, Vanessa?"

"Yes, have you seen the beast?" Felicity continued.

Carefully Vanessa put down her coffee. "Yes, I've met with him." *I've also fought with him, kissed him, ogled him in swimmers, and accompanied him to the police station.* "He's staying at the Marabella and, yes, he is here about the will. In a way."

"You sound remarkably calm," Emma decided. "Is that a good sign? Or are you sedated?"

"Is he dropping the contest?" Felicity asked. "He must know he's beating a dead horse."

"Tristan doesn't think so," Vanessa replied. "In fact, he's here because he believes he's found a way to beat me."

They all responded pretty much at once, a mixture of scoffing remarks and how-so questions. And so she filled them in on the letter's allegations, the no-adultery clause in Stuart's will, and finally this morning's meeting with the detectives handling Bunny's case.

Silence followed, an unusual happenstance when this group met. Abby recovered first, although she looked pale and strained. Not only had she lost her mother in sudden and suspicious circumstances, but she'd had to fight tooth and nail to have her suspicions recognized. "What did the police say?"

A lot, Vanessa answered silently, most of it uncomfortable questions about her relationship with Tristan and the—nonexistent—man referred to in the letter. To her friends she said, "They took us seriously enough when we showed them the letter. They asked a lot of questions, but in the end I'm not sure they think it's the same person."

"Why not?" Abby leaned forward, intent and focused. "It sounds exactly like the others."

Felicity nodded. "The lowlife who took the journals is selecting blackmail opportunities straight from the pages. It's only a matter of time before he hits pay dirt."

They all fell silent a moment, considering, before Emma asked, "Wouldn't he have tried to blackmail Vanessa though?"

"Would you have paid?" Felicity turned to Vanessa. "If the letter had come to you?"

"Why would I pay when the allegation is false?"

A couple of them exchanged looks, no one met her eye, and in the ensuing silence the bottom fell out of Vanessa's stomach. "You think I had a lover? While I was married to Stuart?"

"No, sweetie." Emma put a hand on hers. "Not us."

"Then...who?"

"There's been some talk," Caroline said.

And they hadn't told her? Hadn't mentioned these suspicions once? In all this time?

"You have to admit, you do keep parts of your life off-limits."

Felicity had spoken no less than the truth. Vanessa

had been secretive and this was the perfect opportunity to confide in her friends and garner their advice. That's what friends were for, after all. Not that she had much experience, especially with her peers, and that made this hard task even tougher.

Her intentions were good, but the words lodged in her throat. Before she could coax them free, Lily returned from the bathroom and there was much fussing over how long she'd been gone.

"I ran into Delia Forrester," she explained. "I couldn't get away."

"Poor you," Caroline murmured.

"Whatever did she want?" Emma asked.

"A favor." Lily pulled a wry face. "She needs an extra invitation to the polo benefit. Vanessa, it seems she's invited your good friend Tristan Thorpe."

Polo turned out to be a hard, fast and physical game—not for sissies as Frank Forrester had maintained. After several chukkers and with the help of some sideline experts, Tristan was catching on to the skilful intricacies of play and enjoying the breakneck end-to-end pace. As Frank's binoculars rarely strayed from the field, he wondered if the old bloke had been referring to the off-field action rather than the polo itself.

Tristan had a healthy cynicism for the games played by the beautiful people, and this charity benefit had brought out the best—and worst—players. Which brought his thoughts winging straight to Delia.

Frank had introduced his wife as "My favorite blonde," instantly tying her to the woman he'd referred to as his second-favorite at the Marabella restaurant. In those first few seconds Tristan rejected the connection out of hand. The two women were as different as Vanessa had claimed.

With her glossy facade and saccharine-sweet affectations, Delia was the kind of woman he'd expected—and wanted—to find living in his father's house. Vanessa Thorpe was not. The truth didn't slam into him. It had been creeping up on him for days, with every meeting, every new discovery, every disarming touch of warmth or vulnerability.

Acknowledging his error of judgment did unsettle him, however.

If he'd misjudged her character by the width of the Nullabor, could he also be wrong about other things?

Since seeing her response to the letter he'd been thinking a lot about the sender's motivation. He'd assumed someone had a vendetta against her. Back in Australia he'd believed it—a pushy young social climber could make plenty of enemies without even trying. But since arriving in Eastwick, the worst he'd heard about her was, "She holds her cards close to her chest."

A loud cheer rolled through the spectators' gallery, rousing Tristan from his introspection. The local team's number three had goaled, leveling the score. He'd learned early on that the Argentinean import was a great favorite with the partisan polo crowd.

Vanessa, too, had her fans. This Tristan measured from the locals' responses to him.

Too polite for blatant rudeness, many met him with a cool look or shook his hand with stiff formality. Others were more direct. Vern Kramer, for example, stated outright that he sympathized with his plight—"You're his son, after all"—but didn't approve his tactics. Vern was another of his father's oldest friends and one of the more vocal sideline polo experts.

Right now he was protesting an umpiring decision with much gusto. His wife took a large step back, disowning him with a wry shake of her head. "He's not mine. I don't know him."

Tristan waited a moment, watching the umpire award a penalty against the local team and smiling at the roasting that ensued. Then he acknowledged Liz Kramer whose large backward step had brought her—unwittingly—to his side. "How are you, Mrs. Kramer?"

"Well, thank you." Her greeting was polite, her tone frosty. Par for the course, although from Liz it stung. She'd been a close friend of his mother's, a frequent visitor at their home, and he remembered her fondly. "And you, Tristan? Are you enjoying being back home?"

Not the first time he'd been asked a variation of that question and he didn't understand the assumption any better with each repetition. "My home is in Sydney," he said, sick of making the polite answer. "This is a business trip."

"And are you enjoying that?"

There was a bite to her voice that suggested she knew his business. "Not particularly."

"Which makes me wonder why you're persisting."

"I have my reasons."

Eyes front, watching a melee of horses and mallets, he felt rather than saw Liz's gaze fix on his face. "How is your mother?"

"Recovering."

"She's been ill?"

He cut her a look and saw genuine concern in her eyes. It suddenly struck him that of all the conversations he'd had since arriving in Eastwick, Liz was the first to ask after his mother. He decided to tell her straight. "Breast cancer. She's had a tough few years."

"I'm sorry to hear that."

They watched the game in silence for several minutes. Then Liz said, "I hope she found the happiness she was chasing."

Tristan frowned. "Chasing?"

"When she left your father."

"I'd hardly define being tossed out with nothing as leaving."

He tried to keep the bitterness from his voice but wasn't sure he succeeded. Not when Liz made a soft clucking noise with her tongue, part sympathy, part reprimand. "She took *you*, Tristan, the most valuable thing from her marriage. Stuart was a long time getting over that."

But he *had* got over it. With the help of a beautiful new wife, and that stuck in Tristan's craw in a dozen disturbing ways now that he'd met Vanessa.

His gaze shifted beyond Liz, and—as he'd had done countless times in the past hours—he unerringly found Vanessa in the crowd. Despite the number and size of the hats blocking his view, despite the subtlety of her dress, despite the way she'd pinned her distinctive hair beneath a pretty little lace and net construction.

The awareness was there, like a visual magnetism. He didn't seek her out. He looked up and like sunshine, she was there. Since acknowledging how much his attitude to her had changed, since recognizing the dangerous pull of this attraction, he'd kept his distance. Not exactly avoiding her, just proving to himself that he could resist the urge.

"He was so lucky to find Vanessa. She is a treasure."

He looked back at Liz, found she'd followed the direction of his gaze. "I've heard that more than once today," he said dryly. "A treasure. A good gal. An angel."

"Feeling like you've been cast with horns and a trident?"

"Somewhat."

With a soft chuckle, Liz lifted her empty champagne flute and looked him in the eye. For the first time he saw the familiar sparkle of her humor. "If you'd like to take the first step toward redemption, you can fetch me a refill."

Vanessa thought she felt him watching her. Again. But when she turned in that direction—and all day she'd known exactly where he stood, sat, lounged—she found her imagination was playing tricks. Again.

This time he was intent in conversation with Liz Kramer. With his head dipped toward the shorter woman so a lock of sun-tinged hair fell across his forehead, he looked younger and warmer and more at ease than Vanessa had seen him. Then someone moved and blocked her view and she turned away, heart racing and her mouth gone dry.

Anxiety, she decided. And trepidation because of what he might be discussing with Liz and with countless others before her.

And who are you kidding?

Not her pragmatic self, obviously. She knew these re
sponses had nothing to do with their conflict and everything to do with the man.

Was he ignoring her on purpose?

No, Ms. Pragmatist answered. *He is doing what he
set out to do.* Mixing, meeting, talking. And learning absolutely nothing because there was nothing for him to
discover—at least nothing that wasn't rumor and
whispers about her secretive side.

Thinking of the *talk* her friends had told her about
took her mind off Tristan, at least. Not that being talked
about was a biggie for Vanessa—she'd grown up with
fingers pointed her way. *That's the girl with the
freakoid brother. Did you hear her daddy got arrested
again last night? They're such a loser family.* She
didn't care what others said about her; she did mind
that her friends might have believed her capable of infidelity.

And she hated that she'd frozen when she should
have told them the reason for her mysterious behavior.

The sea of summer frocks and lightweight suits, of
hats and champagne flutes and imported longneck beers
shifted again, parting as if by a divine hand to reveal him
again. Walking toward her, a bottle of vintage Veuve
Clicquot in one hand, a pair of flutes in the other. Dressed
simply in a pale gray suit and open-necked white shirt—
no more, no less than a hundred other men in the crowd—
he commanded attention with his size, his presence, the
way he moved with an athlete's grace and purpose.

She felt a burst of sensation, as though the pop of a

champagne cork had sent all the bubbles fizzing through her veins.

Not good, Vanessa. Not good at all.

In a bid to appear involved, she turned back to Felicity and Reed, Emma and Garrett, Jack and Lily...and discovered that while she'd been lost in introspection they'd moved on. Vaguely she recalled Lily wanting to sit down. Or Jack insisting she sit. Possibly she'd waved them on.

Now she was alone. And feigning surprise when she heard the rich drawl of Tristan's voice at her back. His actual words were swallowed by the thumping of her heart as she swung around.

He stood close enough for her to feel the impact of his electric blue gaze. A thousand watts all plugged in to her. He probably bought the whole wow-where-did-you-spring-from act because her mouth had gone slack and her throat tight and breathless while she just stood there staring up at him.

Help, her pragmatic self whimpered weakly. She feared that side of her was about to go down for the count.

"I noticed your lack of champagne." The corner of his mouth quirked in a kind of crooked half smile. "I gather that's a transgression here."

The only transgression she could think of was her weak-kneed, weak-willed desire for a man she'd declared her enemy five days ago. How could this be happening?

That deadly attractive half smile had turned quizzical and Vanessa gave herself a mental shake. "Thank you," she said, a trifle huskily. "But no."

"This bottle is straight from Liz Kramer's stash, just opened, unspiked. Scout's honor."

"So you say, but you don't look like a Boy Scout. Can I trust your word?"

Something flickered in his eyes and in her blood. Perhaps that was the last gurgle of Ms. Pragmatist going under, because she appeared to be flirting with him. She, Vanessa Kotzur Thorpe, who had never flirted in her life.

He filled one of the slender glasses, then handed her the bottle. She regarded it suspiciously. "Take it," he said. "So I can defend my Boy Scout honor."

Their fingers brushed as she took the bottle, a thrilling little contact of skin on skin. She had barely recovered when he lifted the glass to his mouth. Their eyes met over the rim as he took a long, slow sip and the connection somehow seemed steeped in intimacy.

Without breaking eye contact, without saying a word, he held out the glass and temptation whispered through her blood. She wanted to take it from his hand, to place her lips on the same spot, to taste his heat on the icy cool glass.

More, she wanted to stretch on her toes and lick the golden chill from his lips. To kiss him the way she'd wanted to the first time.

"You still don't trust me?"

Vanessa wet her lips. "It's not that. I'm not drinking."

"Driving?"

"I don't drink." She volunteered the information without thought…and then kicked herself sharply. *Pay attention*. She didn't want to explain why she never touched alcohol, nor did she want to see in his eyes that he'd worked out the reason by snooping into her background.

She switched her gaze to the game, pretending to watch without seeing anything but a blur of activity. A team of monkeys mounted on camels could have taken to the field and she wouldn't have noticed...although she supposed they'd have needed extra-long-handled mallets.

After a moment the thick ache in her chest reminded her to relax and breathe. Today Tristan appeared relaxed, as if he were enjoying this as a social occasion rather than as an investigative opportunity. Perhaps he'd taken her appeal outside the Marabella to heart.

Perhaps he was biding his time.

Play thundered by close to the sideline and the air thickened with the scent of sweat and earth and the clash of contact between players. Vanessa blinked and focused. The umpire blew a foul eliciting a heated debate on who'd crossed whose line on the ball.

"How are you enjoying the polo?" she asked, genuinely curious.

"I like the game."

"But not the rest?"

He considered that a long moment, appearing to give it more weight than the casual inquiry commanded. "I'm enjoying today more than I'd thought. I hadn't realized so many people would remember me or want to know me. Given your popularity, I thought I might be the pariah."

"You're not?"

His small smile caused a large clamor in her system. "Can't say I haven't felt some coolness."

"Which hasn't dulled the curiosity."

"No."

Vanessa cast a glance over the crowd and found a degree of that curiousity trained on them. Many of the locals—her friends included—would be conjecturing over her chumminess with the enemy. A frown pulled at her brow so she considered the changed dynamic between them. She couldn't work out what had changed. The heat, the awareness, the attraction, she'd felt before, but today there was another element she couldn't pin down.

They weren't exactly comfortable and relaxed together but the tension had altered.

It reminded her of the one time she'd sat on a horse. The riding lessons were a birthday present from Stuart, but when the instructor hoisted her into the saddle she hadn't enjoyed the sensation one little bit. She'd hated losing touch with earth, of not knowing if the exhilaration would last or bring her crashing onto her backside.

She cast a cautious sideways glance at Tristan and caught him watching her. A weird sense of yearning fluttered to life in her chest, and her frown deepened as she quickly looked away. *Oh yes,* Ms. Pragmatist nodded. *You are so going to land on your backside.*

"Worried about what they're thinking?" he asked.

"Well, I am fraternizing with the enemy."

"I'm not the enemy, Vanessa." He eyes on hers were darkly serious. "Your real enemy is the person who wrote that letter."

Vanessa lost Tristan to Delia during the halftime divot-stomp and didn't see him again—no, that wasn't true, she couldn't help *seeing* him, but she didn't *talk to* him again—until she was walking toward her car at the end of the day. This time her wow-where-did-you-spring-from reaction wasn't contrived. One second she was picking her way carefully across a soggy patch of ground, trying not to identify the heavy weight pressing down on her chest as going-home-alone gloom, the next he was there at her side.

The weight lifted leaving her feeling ridiculously pleased...until she felt his gaze fix on her smile for an unnervingly long moment. Then she thought, *must stop grinning like a loon. Must think of something to say that doesn't sound like I'm ridiculously, pleased.*

"Did you enjoy the second half?" she asked, getting the smile under control. "I lost you during the break."

"I didn't know they really did that."

"Walk the divots? It's a time-honored tradition and the perfect chance to mix. Don't they do that at your Aussie football games?"

"Our mixer tradition is aimed at the kids. They all flock onto the ground for a kick at halftime."

Picturing the mayhem of hundreds of kids let lose on a football field, Vanessa allowed herself a half smile. "Slightly wilder and noisier than a divot-stomp, I imagine."

"Slightly."

"You looked as if you were enjoying yourself." Straight away she wished she'd kept that observation to herself. She also wished that the sight of Delia hanging off his arm, laughing, reaching up to brush something—or nothing—from his collar wasn't stuck in her visual memory. She had no hold on him and no right to the sharp stab of possessiveness.

"I enjoyed today," he said noncommittally.

"You seemed to fit right in."

He cut her a sideways look, as though trying to work out if she was having him on. Then something shifted in his expression, his gaze grew keen with perception. "And you, Vanessa. You fit in as if you were born to this life."

The warm glow of enjoyment brought on by his seeking her out and fanned by their banter, faded and died. But she might as well confirm what he'd probably already gleaned from Gloria or who knows where else. "My parents both worked for people like these, in the city. I spent some time observing the life."

"And you dreamed of living it?"

She shrugged. "What girl doesn't dream? It's the Cinderella fantasy."

They stopped beside her car, the last left in this row of the parking field, and she was searching her purse for her keys when he asked, "Why my father?"

Vanessa looked up sharply, not quite sure she'd heard him correctly. If she had, then she didn't understand the question. Intense blue eyes collided with hers for a heart-jolting moment before he looked away.

Before he waved a hand at the field still littered with Bentleys and Porsches and Mercedes. "You wanted this life, you could have had it with any man you wanted. Why my father?"

For a second she stared back at him, stunned by the question and then by its subtext. She'd set out to trap a rich man because of a childhood Cinderella fantasy. Then she kicked herself hard for her stupidity.

She'd known he held that opinion right from the first

time she spoke to him, so why should the question shock her now?

"I hope to God I'm reading you wrong," she said tightly, "and that you're not suggesting I could have done better than Stuart."

"Not better. Younger."

"Because a *younger* man could have given me what?" She huffed out a contemptuous breath. "For the life of me I cannot think of any man—younger, older, whatever—as kind and generous and concerned for others as Stuart Thorpe."

"What about your other needs, Vanessa?"

His meaning was clear in the dark burning light in his eyes, in the way he closed down the distance between them, in the sexual energy that seemed to pulse in the air as his gaze trailed slowly over her face and lingered on her mouth.

She shook her head slowly. This part of her marriage she discussed with no one. Not Gloria, not Andy, not Emma or Lily or any of her girlfriends. She'd promised to keep the platonic nature of their relationship a secret, to protect Stuart's pride as a man and to prevent the scuttlebutt of gossip.

"You're young," he persisted. "Didn't you want a family?"

"No."

It wasn't a lie, despite her recent pangs of baby envy. She'd already brought up her brother, taking over his care when she was little more than a child herself. She'd used up all her nurturing spirit. She had no emotional energy left for babies of her own. None whatsoever.

"No," she repeated, more adamantly. "I didn't want a family and I didn't need a lover. Your father gave me everything I wanted, everything I ever dreamed of wanting, and more. And he chose to leave his estate to me. Why can't you accept those truths? Why can't you go back to Australia and let me be?"

Seven

Go home to Australia and let her be?

No, Tristan couldn't do that. He could never quit a task half-done.

He still needed to know everything about Vanessa, but before he even approached her in the parking lot after the polo match he'd accepted that his motivation had shifted focus.

That's what drove him to ask why she'd chosen his father.

Frustration. Self-defense. Finding that full-bodied smile trained on him for the very first time, he'd felt a primal rush of possessiveness, a *she-should-be-mine* kick that transcended desire. He'd needed a reminder, damn fast, of why he couldn't get in that car and drive her back to his hotel and claim her as his own.

Her fervent response had done the trick. It had also convinced him of one of two things: either Vanessa had genuinely cared for her husband or she was one bloody fine actress.

And if he was out-of-the-ballpark wrong about her relationship with his father, was he wrong about other things?

Questions and conflicting answers chased through his mind all night long. At dawn he plunged his restless body into the hotel pool and slugged out a hundred laps. Afterward he'd intended returning to his suite and to his regular, controllable Monday morning of work, where questions had answers, where decisions triggered action, where results ensued.

Where he never backed down from the tough issues…or from digging too deeply because of a woman's heartfelt appeal. *I'm asking that you respect the privacy of others. Think about it, please. Think about doing the right thing.*

That plea still had his conscience tied in knots a week later.

Instead of working, he found himself driving out of town and into the sprawling midcountry estates, heading for White Birch Lane and a score of knotted intangibles. He needed facts. He needed truths.

Not only about Vanessa, but about the father he'd not spoken to since he left Eastwick as a twelve-year-old.

Focused on that result, he didn't consider the early hour until he was driving up to the closed and silent mansion. It was too early for her to be gone for the day but not too early, he discovered, to find her in the garden.

The morning sun was less than an hour old, its light as pale as her hair. As diaphanous as the shell-pink sweep of nothing that shaped her body. The image was soft and ethereal, an artist's rendition of *Girl with Flowers*, and Tristan stood transfixed by her beauty for a minute too long. Twenty yards of lawn and several bays of massed rose bushes away, he sensed her sudden stillness and the shock in her eyes when his presence registered.

The polite thing to do was acknowledge her, maybe with a teasing remark about wandering the grounds in her negligée, then retreat so she could dress in something more…substantial. The sensible thing was to turn on his heel and get the hell out of there without taking any more notice about what she was wearing or not wearing.

But he had noticed. His body ached with its impolite and not-sensible response to noticing.

The best he could do was keep a bed of rose bushes between them as he approached, an extra thorny-branched barrier to the one he was busy erecting in his mind.

She's out of bounds. She loved your father. She was his wife for five years.

No matter what resulted from their legal wrangle, from the letter's allegations, from his investigations, she could never be his.

The massed shrubs shielded much of her body from view, but it didn't help. He could still see her face, her throat, the skin framed by lace at her shoulders and breasts. And he could see what had brought her out of doors so early.

One of her gloved hands held a bunch of long-stemmed blooms; the other wielded a pair of lethal-looking shears. The part of his body that had noticed the diaphanous nightdress and the shape of her body beneath took due note.

"I hope I didn't startle you too much. Those things—" he inclined his head to indicate the shears "—look like they could do serious damage."

"I heard you drive up, so no."

"Yet you looked surprised."

"I thought you were Gloria, arriving early."

Her accompanying shrug caused her negligee's deep neckline to dip, and Tristan's hand itched to reach out and slide it back into place. With a silent curse he shoved both hands in his pockets, out of temptation's way. "I'm not Gloria."

"No," she said, as soft as the morning. "You're not."

Their gazes meshed for what felt like a long time. He could feel the pulse of attraction between them, a silent energy that hummed in the summer's morning. She felt it too— he could see it in her eyes and in the slight flush of her cheeks.

Hell. She felt it too.

He buried his hands deeper in his shorts. "I should have called first."

"It's fine, really."

"Really?"

"You saved me a phone call." A frown of concentration formed between her brows and turned her eyes serious. "I wanted to talk to you about what I said yesterday…or what I didn't say."

"About?"

"Your father. The will. I'm not backing down on anything I said, but on my way home yesterday and last night and this morning I was thinking—" She paused and although her eyes were clear, the dark smudges beneath flagged her lack of sleep. "I may have given the impression that Stuart didn't want you to have anything. That is not true."

"He left me a thousand bucks. To show he hadn't forgotten me."

"That was the lawyers' doing and not what I meant. He would have made you a beneficiary, Tristan, if you'd come to see him when he asked."

"Guess I must have missed that."

"I guess so," she said with a damn-you note to her voice. With great care she snipped off another pink bud and added it to her collection. The petals quavered—because her hands were shaking?—and when she looked up again, her eyes glistened with moisture. "Ignoring his letter, not even bothering to reply—that was just plain cruel, Tristan. He was your father and he was dying. Would it have hurt to swallow your pride and pick up the phone?"

Hit hard by the husky edge to her voice and the sheen of emotion in her eyes, it took a moment for the words and the message to register. Then everything inside him went still. "What letter?"

"He wanted to see you or at least to speak to you, to explain his side of the story. I suggested he write—that he might find that easier than trying to explain over the phone."

"And he sent it?"

"I posted it myself." She stared back at him, at first with that same hard edge as earlier and then with slowly dawning comprehension. "You really didn't receive it, did you? And when I tried to call…"

He'd deliberately stonewalled her, not taking the calls and then not returning her increasingly insistent messages until it was too late. His father had passed away an hour before.

What-might-have-been frustration swelled inside him, tightening his chest, his throat, his expression. "If he wanted to talk to me so badly, why the hell did he leave it so late?"

"Because he was as proud and as stubborn as you! He poured his heart and his soul into that letter and when you didn't reply, when he got nothing but stony silence, he gave up."

"But you didn't."

In her eyes, he saw that truth. She'd pushed Stuart to write the letter. And she'd made those calls when his father was hospitalized, a last ditch effort to reconcile them: the husband she'd loved and his only child.

"That's when he made up his mind about the will." Carefully she closed the shears and clicked the safety lock into place. The metallic snick punctuated the finality of his father's decision. Closed, done, ended. "He said you'd made your own life in Australia. You were a success. You didn't need his money and you didn't need him."

She was right. At thirty his time of needing a father had long passed into a faded, bitter memory of the years when he'd silently yearned for that support. Even if he had read the letter or if he'd taken her calls, he doubted it would have led to anything but cold, hard words. "Too little, too late."

For a moment he thought she might dispute that, but then she changed tack—he saw the switch in her expression and the set of her mouth as she gathered up her bunch of cut roses and started to move off. "You might not believe this," she said, "but he never forgot you were his son. He told me once how glad he was that your football career took off, because that made it so easy to keep up the connection. The more your star rose, the more stories he found in the press."

"His son, the famous footballer."

A vehement spark lit her eyes. "It wasn't like that, Tristan! Of course he was proud of your success—what parent wouldn't be? But this was about knowing some part of you, about having that connection. He learned all about your Aussie Rules game and he read all the match reports and stats. He watched the games on cable.

"One night I found him sitting in the dark, in the theater room where he watched the games. And the television was showing, I don't know, ice-skating or rhythmic gymnastics or something I knew he wouldn't watch. I thought he'd gone to sleep so I turned on the light to rouse him and send him back to bed."

She paused in a gap between two heavily-laden bushes, her expression as soft as the mass of creamy-pink roses that framed her slender curves. And, damn it her eyes had gone all dewy again. He braced himself, against the punch-to-the-heart sensation the sight of her caused and against whatever she was about to tell him.

"He didn't turn around because he didn't want me to see his tears, but I heard them in his voice. I knew he was sitting there in the dark crying. He told me later that you'd been playing your two hundredth game and they'd run a special on you during the halftime break. He was so proud and I was so damn mad at you both for not doing something about your rift."

Rift? The gap between him and his father had been more in the scope of a canyon. If there'd ever been any chance of bridging it… "That was up to him."

"Would you have listened?"

For several seconds they stood, gazes locked, the atmosphere taut with that one telling question. And when he didn't answer, she shook her head sadly. "I didn't think so."

"It makes no difference."

"You're that callous?"

"I am what I am."

She nodded slowly. And the disappointment in her eyes hit him like a full-throttle shoulder charge. "You are also more like your father than you know."

"Kind. Generous. Concerned," he quoted back at her.

"Proud. Stubborn. Unprepared to step back from your line in the sand." Her eyes narrowed with a mixture of challenge and speculation. "Why is the inheritance so important to you? Your success at football carried on into business. You just sold your company, advantageously, I gather. You can't need the money."

"Money isn't everything, duchess."

"Is it the house you want?" she persisted, ignoring his gibe. "Does it have special meaning?"

"Not any more. Does it to you?"

"It meant a lot to Stuart, so, yes."

"I'm asking about you." And even as he asked the question, he felt its significance tighten in his chest. "Is this your idea of home, Vanessa?"

"It's the only place I've ever felt happy to call home."

"You're happy here, living this life?"

She looked him square in the eye. "Yes, I am. I work hard on fund-raising committees. I love the volunteering work I do."

"A regular philanthropist, are you?"

It was a cheap shot but she took it on the chin without flinching. He sensed, in the briefest of pauses before she responded, that she'd taken a lot of hits in her life. That she was a lot less delicate than she looked. "I do what I can. And just so there are no misconceptions—I like most everything about my life. I like the security of money, of knowing all my needs are taken care of."

"Not to mention the things that money can buy."

"I don't care about the things."

Really? "You told me you love your car. Your clothes aren't from Wal-Mart. And what about the trinkets?" Forgetting the self-defensive caution that had driven him to keep a garden's width between them, he rounded the end of the bay and closed down that separation. "If *things* don't matter, then why were you so upset when the figurine smashed?"

"It was a gift."

"From Stuart?"

A shadow flitted across her expression but her gaze remained clear and unwavering and disarmingly honest.

"A New York socialite my mother worked for gave me that figurine for my twelfth birthday."

"Generous of her."

"Yes and no. It was nothing to her but a kind gesture to the housemaid's poor daughter. But to me...that little statue became my talisman. I kept it as a reminder of where it came from and where I came from. But, you know, it doesn't matter that it broke." She gave a little shrug. "I don't need it anymore."

Maybe not, but there was something about her explanation's matter-of-fact tone that belied the lingering shadows in her eyes. She could shrug it off all she wanted now, but he'd been there. He'd witnessed the extent of her distress.

Damn it all to blazes, he'd caused it by backing her into the corner and shocking her with his kiss.

And here he was, forgetting himself again. Standing too close, infiltrating her personal space, breathing the sweet scent of roses and aching with the need to take her in his arms, to touch her petal-soft skin, to kiss every shadowed memory from her eyes and every other man from her rose-pink lips.

The physical desire he understood and could handle. It had been there from the outset, crackling in the air whenever they got too close. But this was more—dangerously, insidiously more—when he needed less.

"You mightn't need it," he said gruffly, "but it matters."

"No. What matters is how Stuart wanted his wealth distributed. We talked about this—about which charities and the best way to help—but everything is tied up because of your legal challenge. Why are you doing this?" Her eyes darkened with determination. "Why, Tristan? Is it only about winning? Is it only about defeating me?"

"This isn't about you."

"Then what is it about?"

The first time she'd asked about his motivation, Tristan had turned it into a cross-examination. And she'd answered every one of his questions with honesty. The least he could do was offer equal candor. "It's about justice, Vanessa."

"Justice for whom?"

"My mother." He met her puzzled eyes. "Did you know she got nothing from my parents' divorce?"

"You can't be serious."

"Deadly. After fifteen years of marriage…nothing."

"Is that how you count yourself, Tristan? As nothing?" Her voice rose with abject disbelief. "Is that how your mother counted what she took from Stuart?"

He'd heard the same message from Liz Kramer. *She took you, Tristan, the most valuable thing.*

But the other side to that equation set his jaw and his voice with hard-edged conviction. "She counted herself lucky to gain full custody." Except to do so, to prevent an ugly court battle and a possible injunction preventing her move to Australia, she'd ceded her claim on a property settlement. "I guess that kind of payoff made me worth a hell of a lot."

For a long moment his words hung between them, a cynically-edged statement that conveyed more of his past hurt than he'd intended. He could see that by her reaction, by the softening in her expression and the husky note in her voice. "He thought Andrea would reject that offer. He thought they would negotiate and reach an agreement of shared property and shared custody. He didn't want to lose you, Tristan."

"Then why didn't he fight to keep me?"

She shook her head sadly. "He didn't want to take you from your mother. It broke his heart to lose his whole family like that."

"*He* kicked us out. *He* divorced my mother. *His* choices, Vanessa."

"I was under the impression that Andrea was at fault," she said after a moment's hesitation. "That she had an affair…which Stuart found out about and forgave. The first time."

Tristan went still. "What do you mean, the first time?"

"I mean…" She paused, her face wreathed in uneasiness. "How much of this do you know? I'm not sure it's my place—"

"You don't think I need to hear this?"

She nodded once, a brief concession to his point, and moistened her lips. "He took her back because he still loved her and because she promised it was a once-only thing, because she was lonely, he was working too hard. He took her back and when she announced she was pregnant, he was ecstatic."

"I know the twins aren't Stuart's," he reassured her grimly. "I know they're only my half sisters."

"And that's what broke his heart, don't you see? She never told him. She let him believe they were his and she kept seeing the father before they were born and afterward. When he caught her out again, when he did the paternity test and discovered the truth…that's why the marriage ended, Tristan. And that's why Stuart felt so strongly about adultery."

He didn't have to believe her but he did. It made too much sense not to. It tied everything together in a neat bow…and brought them looping back to his reason for being here in Eastwick. His reason for wanting, so vehemently, to defeat her.

"That's why he added that clause to his will," he said slowly. Not a question, but a statement.

Not because he suspected Vanessa of cheating, as Tristan had believed, but because of his own mother's infidelity. Not one mistake, as she'd led Tristan to believe, but repeated betrayals. Which put her subsequent choices into perspective, too.

Her acceptance of the divorce settlement.

Her flight to Australia, in pursuit of the twins' father.

Her objection to his challenge of Stuart's will.

"Does Andrea know why you're doing this? Is it what she wants?"

Vanessa's soft voice cut straight into his thought process, as if she'd read his mind.

And when he didn't answer, she added, "I thought as much."

That jolted him hard. The initial questions, the way she'd read him so accurately, the knowledge that she'd turned his beliefs inside out.

Yet this had been his pursuit for two years, his conviction for longer. He would not toss it without hearing the truth from his mother. Not without considering all he'd learned this morning, away from the influence of steady green eyes and rose scented skin.

Resolve tightened his features as he nodded to her bundle of flowers. "Shouldn't you be putting those in water?"

She blinked with surprise, as if she'd been so intent on their discussion that she'd forgotten her morning's purpose. "I...yes."

"I need to go. I have some decisions to make."

Hope fluttered like a bird's wing in her eyes. "You'll let me know...once you've decided."

"You'll be the first."

He nodded goodbye and had gone maybe ten strides before she called his name. He paused. Turned to look over his shoulder and was floored again by the picture she made with the sunlight silhouetting her body and legs through that filmy pink robe.

Like the roses, he figured she'd forgotten her state of dress. Or undress. For both their sakes, he wasn't about to point out what was clearly defined by the unforgiving light.

"The letter I told you about, from your father—I kept a copy. It's yours, Tristan. If you like, I can go and get it for you."

Eight

After Vanessa offered him the letter, Tristan had stood staring at her down the paved path, face and body both set hard and still as a Grecian statue. There'd been a dizzy moment when her imagination played memory tricks, stripping away his clothes to reveal sun-gilded skin and rippling pool-wet muscles. When he pointed out—his voice dark and quietly dangerous—that if she were going to fetch anything, it should be more clothes, she'd shaken her head with confusion.

How did he know she was picturing him near-naked? Was she that transparent?

One slow sweep of his shuttered gaze and she realized that, yes, courtesy of the sun's backlighting, she *was* pretty darn transparent.

Oh, she'd played down her discomfiture. Ignoring

any reference to clothing, she'd lifted her chin and invited him to wait in the foyer while she located the letter and a file box of photos and clippings and other memorabilia Stuart had kept.

At first she'd thought he wouldn't bother taking them. Later she'd decided that his lack of response as she pushed them into his hands was all a crock. Vanessa understood the pretense. She, too, was a master at hiding her heart.

With an offhand shrug and a polite thanks he took them, presumably back to his hotel.

Vanessa should have been overjoyed to see the back of him and that morning's intense emotional drama. She should have been thrilled that they'd finally talked through some of the misunderstandings and misinformation, and that he might now reconsider his stance on the will. But, no, his departure had left her feeling hollow and restless and anxious, her mind buzzing with more questions.

Twice she picked up the phone, once her car keys and purse, with a view to pressing him for answers. Did he have any ideas on who had written the letter that brought him to Eastwick? Would he continue to investigate its allegations? Or was his challenge of the will now over?

But she forced herself to wait. He needed time to digest Stuart's heartfelt words, to come to grips with the truth of his split from Andrea and their subsequent custody settlement.

The hollowness in her middle grew into a raw ache when she thought about what he'd believed and what his mother had let him believe. From experience, Vanessa knew that twelve was a vulnerable age to have a parent cut from your life. To go through that in a new country, in a new school, without your friends, believing you'd been traded like a chattel in your parents' divorce…

She hadn't looked at this from Tristan's side before. So much about the man now made sense. Those hard edges, his drive to succeed, this pursuit of an inheritance he didn't need. It wasn't all about doing the right thing by his mother; it was also about himself and the father he'd believed didn't want him.

She could almost forgive him his resentment. If only he'd returned her calls or given her a chance to explain earlier, they could have avoided all this. And that thought added to her turmoil while she waited to discover what would happen next.

Tuesday morning she forced herself to push aside another restless night and her frustrating angst as she set about her usual routine…although she did take care to dress this time, before venturing out into the garden. Tuesday was one of her regular days at Twelve Oaks, and she cut enough blooms for several arrangements at the grand house and put them in water.

Next, she headed to the kitchen and mixed a double batch of chocolate cherry muffins. The precise processes involved in baking always calmed her. Picturing her brother's blissed-out grin when he opened the container and discovered his favorite treat always brought a smile to her face. It still hovered—a happy curve of affection—when the timer chimed and she pulled the baking trays from the oven.

They'd turned out perfectly. Her smile broadened

with satisfaction. Then she turned and looked up, and everything—her smile, her brain, her legs—froze.

But only for a split second. The instant their gazes connected she felt an ungoverned rush of heat all the way from her quick fix ponytail to her freshly painted toes.

"Where did you spring from?" she asked, her voice husky with astonishment. And, yes, a note of pleasure because of the way Tristan was looking at her and because, well, simply because he was here.

"Gloria let me in. I followed her up the drive."

Vanessa had been so absorbed in her task she hadn't heard the housekeeper's arrival. After depositing the trays on cooling racks, she put a hand to her rapidly beating heart. "This is two mornings in a row you've sneaked up on me. You have to stop doing that."

"Just evening up the score. You surprise me all the time." He paused, taking in the sunshine yellow dress she'd chosen to empower her mood, before his gaze returned to her face. "Although at least today you're dressed."

Which did nothing to hide her reaction to the appreciation in his eyes or the satisfaction of knowing she surprised him. She felt the flush rolling through her skin and the tightening of her nipples against the lace of her bra. Today she might be dressed, but she had no bouquet of roses to hide behind.

"Where's Gloria?" she asked, shifting the conversation to neutral ground.

"Putting away the…things…you loaned me."

The letter and photos? Her eyes widened. "Oh, no. You didn't have to return them. They are yours to keep."

"I don't need them."

"Maybe, but I want you to have them. Stuart would have wanted that."

Something quickened in his eyes, a flash of emotion, of sorrow or regret, but he lifted a shoulder and it was gone. Shed like a stray leaf.

He strolled farther into the room and inclined his head toward the marble island. "You bake?"

So. He didn't want to talk about the letter or his father. Vanessa's stomach dipped with disappointment. But what could she do? Perhaps if he stayed a while, perhaps if she went along with the teasing note to his question and kept it light, she could steer the conversation back.

"Yes, I bake." She arched her eyebrows at the racks of cooling muffins. "Behold the evidence."

Palms flattened on the countertop, he leaned over to breathe the rich aroma. His eyes rose up to hers, and the look of sybaritic pleasure on his face turned her knees to jelly. "Chocolate chip?"

"Chocolate cherry. With coconut."

"Are they as good as they smell?"

Showing off a bit, she deftly loosened the first batch of muffins and turned them onto the cooling rack. A dozen, each one perfectly formed. She looked up and smiled. "Better."

"Do you cook anything else?"

"I know my way around a kitchen."

He chuckled, and that unexpected appreciation did nothing to help strengthen Vanessa's jelly-knees. "Maybe I should have taken Frank's prompt and angled to come stay here instead of the Marabella."

"Oh, I don't think that would have been a good idea," she countered. "The two of us trying to share a house."

It was only banter, deliberately lighthearted as they danced around the reason for his visit and the topic she desperately wanted to address. But in the short hesitation before he answered, Vanessa caught the glimmer of heat in his eyes and the mood changed. An unspoken acknowledgment of their attraction stretched between them, as palpable as the rich scent of oven-warm chocolate.

"No," he said, much too seriously. "Not a good idea."

To break the tension, she offered him coffee. Perhaps, then, she could broach the question of what next.

"Do I get anything with the coffee?"

Muffins, Ms. Pragmatist muttered in her ear. *He's talking about muffins*. "I guess I can spare you one."

"The rest being for…?"

Fussing with the coffee making, she answered automatically. "The guys at Twelve Oaks."

"This is the place where you volunteer? Where your friend Andy works?"

"Yes."

"Interesting name. Twelve Oaks."

Vanessa looked up sharply. Nothing showed in his expression beyond curiosity but, still, she was so used to *not* talking about Twelve Oaks, to protecting this part of her life from scrutiny. "That's the name of the estate," she explained carefully. "A grand old Georgian home with separate servants' quarters and stables and a small farm. The owner willed it to a foundation that worked with the developmentally disabled and they developed it into a residential facility."

"What do you do there?"

"I help the therapists. Tuesdays it's with arts and crafts. On Thursdays we cook." She rolled her eyes. "Chick stuff."

He didn't counter with a teasing quip as she'd imagined, and she felt him looking at her differently, with a new respect or admiration that she did not deserve. If not for Lew, she would never have known about Twelve Oaks. She would never have gotten involved.

"I don't do very much, as it happens, and what I do is not exactly selfless."

"How long is your session this morning?"

Frowning at his question—where had that come from?—she looked up and got tangled in the intentness of his blue, blue eyes. "Does it matter?"

"I had this idea of going with you." He let go a huff of breath. "Bad idea."

"Why?"

"I have a plane to catch this afternoon."

Although this only half answered Vanessa's *why*, it snagged her attention in a whole new way. Her pulse started to beat faster. "Where are you going?"

"To see my mother."

"You're going back to Australia?" she asked in a rising rush of alarm.

"Florida. My mother moved to the States last year."

"I did not know that," she murmured, barely audible above the *thump thump thump* of her heartbeat.

"That's what I came to tell you. In case I don't come back."

Only a few days ago she'd begged him to go home, to leave her alone, but now.... Vanessa drew a breath and blew it out in a rush. "Does this mean you're finished here?"

"Not quite."

She barely had time to absorb that enigmatic reply before he circled the island and offered his hand. Vanessa's mouth turned dry as she stared at the long, lean fingers, the strong knuckles, the thick male wrist. Moistening her lips, she asked, "Is this a peace offering? An apology? Or just goodbye?"

"Maybe it's all three." He took her hand, engulfing it in heat, in rough-textured sensation, and in the notion that a truce might send their relationship veering into new, uncharted territory. "And maybe I'm doing what I have to do. To set things right."

"That's important to you, isn't it? Setting things right?"

"Yes."

"And doing things right?"

"Always."

Butterfly nerves beat a tattoo in her stomach as she met his steadfast gaze. "So now you know your father's thoughts and feelings and wishes, you will do the right thing? You will set matters right?"

"That has always been my intention, Vanessa." His grip on her hand altered, a minute easing of pressure, a realignment of palms. And just as smoothly he redirected the conversation. "You remember the night you came to see me, at the Marabella?"

"Which part, exactly?"

"The part where you maligned my...expertise."

He was talking about his kissing expertise. The certainty skimmed through her in a quicksilver flash and, wow, she had not seen it coming. Not even when he suggested he wanted to set things right; and that he always did things right.

"If my memory serves me—" which it did, word for word, beat for beat "—I said you wouldn't ever get a second chance."

"And I thought I'd give you a chance to reconsider."

Intense curiosity tingled in a dozen places, in her accelerated pulse. He was saying goodbye, leaving and possibly not coming back. Would it hurt to succumb to temptation, to feel his mouth on hers without the blaze of antagonism that fired their first kiss?

Not if she approached it with eyes wide open, as an experiment, a new experience…

"Five seconds." She straightened her shoulders and met his eyes. "You have five seconds to prove your expertise."

He stared at her a moment.

Vanessa shrugged. "Take it or leave it."

Something shifted in his expression, a slight flare of his nostrils, a subtle tightening of the lines at the corners of his eyes. *Challenge accepted. Game on.* Vanessa had half a second to think *I am so out of my league* before he tugged on her hand, bringing her infinitesimally closer.

Eyes holding hers, he lifted that hand to his mouth.

He kissed her fingertips first, one after the other, and then he pressed his mouth to the center of her palm. It was unexpectedly subtle, dangerously seductive, and when he gently nipped the flesh at the base of her thumb, intensely erotic. Heat bloomed in her skin, in her blood, in her breasts and her thighs.

She wanted more, a real kiss, the touch of his hands, but he let her go. Just like that.

He left without a word, but she got the message. His goodbye kiss was an apology for the other and a sign that he could do things right. So very, very right.

He'd reached the front door before she remembered the other reason for this visit. "Wait," she called after him. "Stuart's letter. I want you to have it."

She didn't know if he heard her or not. He kept on walking and didn't turn back.

Emma Dearborn had wanted an intimate fuss-free wedding with just family and closest friends, partly because of the short time frame she had in which to finalize her vows with fiancé, Garratt Keating, but mostly because that's the way Emma liked things. But then she let her parents get involved and, well, the lavish event took over the Eastwick Country Club ballroom and gardens and anyone who was anyone in Eastwick society made the guest list for the evening affair.

In the end it didn't matter. Emma only had eyes for her new husband.

After the ceremony, the Debs gravitated together to share their relief that it had gone so beautifully and their praise of Felicity's wedding planning magic. Somehow she'd pulled it all off while also taking her place as Emma's maid of honor.

"I don't know how you did it, Felicity." Abby Talbot shook her head. "You are a genius."

Felicity smiled and said, "I know."

But then ever since falling for Reed Kelly her smile had been a constant, as big and bright and sparkly as the monster pink diamond on her engagement finger.

"Look at her." Lily directed their attention to the dance floor. "Could she be any happier?"

Emma and Garrett waltzed by, lost in each other, and Vanessa felt her heart squeeze with a mixture of joy for her friend and good old-fashioned bride-envy. But she kept on smiling. Between weddings, babies and engagements, she needed to get used to this feeling.

The smile faded when she saw Delia making a beeline for their group, a look of predatory purpose painted on her face. Vanessa didn't have time to issue a warning before the woman swept up in a cloud of Valentino chiffon and her signature perfume, made exclusively for her in France.

Caroline Keating-Spence once suggested that Poison would have worked just as well as her signature scent. Delia had not been amused.

"Are we all having fun?" she asked with an inclusive smile. Her wide-eyed gaze came to rest on Lily's pregnant belly. "Oh, dear, you are getting huge. Should you be standing?"

Lily assured her she was fine.

Delia, being Delia, ignored her. "Where is that darling husband of yours? Surely he isn't neglecting you.... Is that him over there? Talking to *your* beau." She placed a solicitous hand on Felicity's arm and lowered her voice. "I do hope today hasn't been too awkward for you both."

Felicity's fiancé, Reed, had been engaged to Emma but she'd broken it off when Garrett resurfaced in her life. Then Reed and Felicity got together and, well, it had been awkward for a little while, but that was history.

"How sweet of you to be concerned, Delia." Felicity batted her lashes. "But why should there be any awkwardness?"

Delia gave her a poor-dear look. Then her attention shifted to her next victim. Abby. "And where is your gorgeous man, Abigail? I haven't seen him once tonight."

"Luke couldn't be here, unfortunately."

"Really? He's missing the wedding of one of your dearest friends? And so soon after your poor mother's passing."

"He's away on business," Abby supplied tightly.

"He spends a lot of time away, doesn't he? Are you sure it's business? You know how these men can be...."

Reacting to her pointed barbs only incited Delia and they'd decided long ago not to play her game. But after the stress of recent months Abby was a vulnerable target. Vanessa could see the gleam of moisture in her eyes. She needed rescuing, fast.

"We probably don't know as much about men as you, Delia," she said with a gracious smile. "I doubt many women do."

Delia laughed it off but her eyes glittered with malice. However she was fixing to respond, it would not be pretty. Vanessa braced herself.

But it was Mary Duvall's voice that broached the sudden tension. "Oh, look. I believe Emma is preparing to throw the bouquet. We mustn't miss this!"

Of course, Mary was mistaken but they all kept moving, intent on getting as far away as possible from the razor-sharp slice of Delia's tongue. With talk of rustling up a dance, Felicity went in search of Reed. Lily hooked her arm through Abby's and suggested they quench their thirst with cold drinks, which left Vanessa and Mary.

"Is this how it feels to escape the firing squad?" Vanessa's smile echoed the wry tone of her voice. "Nice diversion, by the way."

"I needed to do something. I was next in line."

"I think you were pretty safe. You haven't been back in Eastwick long enough for Delia to select the most damaging weapon."

Mary didn't reply. In fact she looked pale and uneasy—enough that Vanessa felt badly about her blithe comment. But before she could apologize, Mary excused herself and hurried off to the bathroom.

Vanessa frowned after her. She didn't know Mary Duvall well. An old schoolfriend of Emma and Abby and Felicity, she'd lived in Europe ever since graduating from college but had recently returned to Eastwick at the behest of her dying grandfather. There was definitely something going on with her, and Vanessa couldn't help wondering if it was connected to Bunny and the diaries.

Perhaps Mary, too, was the victim of an extortion attempt.

They knew of two thwarted attempts but what if other letters had been sent and not reported? Other victims could have agreed to buy the blackmailer's silence. As for the letter to Tristan—its lack of an extortion demand didn't make sense. Unless it was just a random, unconnected piece of mischief-making…

Her gaze shifted back to where they'd left Delia. Could she be responsible? One part of Vanessa screamed, *Hell, yes*, because Delia thrived on making strife. On the other hand, she seemed to get her kicks from delivering pointed barbs face-to-face, watching for a reaction, and then driving another dart into the wound.

Letter writing was not Delia's weapon of choice.

And the note alleging Vanessa's adultery wasn't written in Delia's bitchy style.

Off to her right Vanessa detected the rapid swish of apricot Valentino and she turned to track the woman's progress. It seemed Delia had her sights on someone over by the entrance. As much as Vanessa—and all the Debs—would have loved to peg Delia as the villain, the current Mrs. Forrester had no need to blackmail. Not with a doting husband to keep her in designer dresses and plastic surgery.

Vanessa turned away and saw Lily beckoning, Jack at her side. Perfect. Vanessa wanted to get them alone, to quiz Jack on any recent developments with the extortion letters and to ask if he'd heard anything from Tristan's lawyers.

Three days had passed since he'd walked out of her kitchen. There'd been a note of finality to his parting words that suggested he wouldn't be back, and Vanessa discerned that any news would be relayed via their legal counsels.

The three days had crawled by, not in edgy anticipation of an end to her legal struggle, but under a heavy pall of disappointment. For two years she'd wanted nothing more fervently than to end her feud with Tristan Thorpe. Now she had her wish and it felt like a giant anticlimax.

All because of that damn kiss.

You are a sad case. Ms. Pragmatist shook her head in disgust. *What does a twenty-nine-year-old virgin know about kissing anyway? We both know he was only proving a point, settling a score, taking the points from one challenge because he was on the brink of losing another.*

She started toward Lily and Jack's table but had only taken half a dozen steps when she sensed a disturbance back by the door…where she'd last seen Delia. She paused, swung her head to look across her shoulder, and her gaze collided with the cause of every disturbance in her recent life.

Tristan Thorpe. Here. His expression filled with purpose as he shouldered aside whoever held him back.

He looked dark and forbidding and gorgeous.

And he was heading her way.

Nine

What was Tristan doing here? What had happened to bring him back so soon? What could be so important that he would crash Emma's wedding?

Vanessa's mind raced with questions while her heart raced with an insane desire to fly across the ballroom and fling herself into his arms. She'd taken half a dozen—sedate, controlled, nonflying—steps in that direction when Jack Cartwright cut into her path.

"You aren't leaving?" he asked, when she frowned at her blocked view of the door.

"No. I was just going to…see someone."

"Is this someone a better dancer than me?" Jack shifted, turning to look in the direction she'd been headed and revealing that *this someone* had also been intercepted.

By Delia.

Her arm was hooked through his. Her voluptuous body angled in close. Her perfectly coiffed head tilted back as she made some kind of appeal. And when she led him onto the dance floor, jealousy sliced through Vanessa, swift and sharp.

Appalled by her response, she looked away…but not quickly enough. Jack's eagle-eyed gaze trained on the couple. "What is Thorpe doing here?"

"Dancing with Delia, it would appear."

Jack made a scoffing noise. "Let's hope it's only dancing."

His meaning sat all kinds of uncomfortable in Vanessa's stomach, but as she watched the couple circling the floor she couldn't impugn his comment. They danced close enough that Delia's filmy skirt swirled around Tristan's legs. Her head was tilted, allowing her to look intently into his face. Her fingers lifted to touch the back of his hair and Vanessa swallowed hard to stem the rising pall of red-hot anger and disgust.

How dare she paw him like that, here at Emma's wedding, in view of half of Eastwick and her own husband. How dare he let her. When Frank had been the one local gracious enough to welcome him home and invite him into their social circle.

"About the dancing…" Jack drew her attention back to him. "My wife suggested you might like to do me the honor. She being somewhat incapacitated in the waltzing department."

Vanessa glanced across at Lily, who patted her middle and grimaced. She supposed her friend had caught her looking alone and forlorn. That was Lily, always looking out for others. She made a shooing gesture with her hand and mouthed, "Go on."

Vanessa sighed. As much as didn't want to be anywhere near the Delia-Tristan floor show, she knew she wouldn't be able to stop watching from the sidelines. Like a horror movie, she'd be drawn and repelled and disgusted and completely unable to look away.

At least dancing with Jack she could pretend to be unaffected.

"I'd love to dance." She offered him a smile and her hand. "Thank you."

Dancing with Delia gave Tristan a new appreciation of the term *grin and bear it*. She'd rescued him from the pair of doormen who'd followed him inside, so he owed her. Not that he couldn't have dealt with them, but that would have gotten him kicked out on his backside. He'd already drawn attention when he plowed right past the lightweight security, all because he'd caught sight of Vanessa and suffered a momentary brain snap.

But Delia had stepped in and forestalled a large-scale disturbance. "He's my guest, darlings. There's no need to check the list. Unless you want to trouble the Dearborns in the middle of their only daughter's wedding…"

How could he refuse her invitation to dance? He figured that one more turn of the floor should be enough gratitude, although if she touched his neck again or made another heavily-suggestive sexual remark, he was walking away. If they threw him out, so be it. He'd grow some patience and wait outside—as he should have done all along—to confront Vanessa with the new hard evidence.

No smoke screens this time. No turning him inside out with her tear-filled eyes and husky-voiced stories of his father's last wishes and years of regret. No more playing him for a fool with her protestations of innocence.

Either this bloke from Twelve Oaks was her lover or he wasn't. In which case, Tristan needed to know who the hell the guy was and why she insisted on hiding him away like a guilty secret.

He'd noticed the second she joined the dancing. Hell, how could he not notice? Even in a ballroom dripping with diamonds and designer one-offs, Vanessa's classic beauty shone. It wasn't her dress—an understated glimmer of silvery-blue—or the cool sparkle of her jewelry when it caught the light of the ballroom's massed chandeliers.

It was her; and it was him. The awareness he'd felt from the moment they met had strengthened into a living, breathing devil with teeth. He couldn't stop himself wanting her; he couldn't stop himself watching her.

And before tonight was out, he would make good his promise to know her every secret.

"Ah. So that's what brings you here."

Tristan concentrated his focus on Delia, and found hers zeroed in on Vanessa. There was something in her tone and in the set of her face that raised his protective hackles. But he kept his own expression impassive as he used the waltz's natural moves to turn her away from the object of her scrutiny. "I have no idea what you're talking about."

Delia laughed, a crystalline tinkle that grated over every raised hackle. "It's all right, darling." She leaned even closer and employed a stage whisper. "Your secret's safe with me."

"There is no secret, Delia."

"No?" She widened her eyes, all fake credulousness. "Have I read those long, lingering looks all wrong then?"

Damn. Was he so obvious?

"Married all those years to an old, ailing man," Delia continued, low and confiding. "No offense to your father, darling, but I can understand why she's mooning after you. I know I miss sex with a young, fit man."

Whoa. Tristan went still inside. Vanessa was watching him? That's what Delia was referencing?

"We're very alike, she and I. Not that Ms. High-and-Mighty would ever admit it. She belongs to the Debs Club." Delia sniffed. "As if she was ever a debutante!"

"Were you, Delia?"

She blinked. Then, as if realizing she'd gone a step too far, she laughed it off. "Of course I wasn't a deb. I never went in for all that snooty WASP stuff back then. I was too busy having a good time."

"But you like it well enough now?"

"Of course I do, darling. I love this lifestyle and everything it offers, just like our Vanessa. Pretty clothes, pretty jewels, pretty men." She caressed his shoulder and the ends of his hair with an overly-familiar hand and her voice dropped an octave. "I especially love the men."

Delia wasn't as easy to shed as the doormen. Fortified by French champagne and his acquiescence during their dance, her advances grew even bolder. When she suggested they adjourn to his hotel room, Tristan drew the line. He delivered her back to her husband—poor sod—and suggested he take her home.

Then he went hunting for Vanessa.

She was still dancing, but with an older man he didn't recognize or care to meet. Although he approached with an aim of taking her somewhere private to talk, keeping Delia's busy hands above the belt had stretched his patience to a thin twanging cord. Suddenly he didn't want more friction—unless it was the kind created by this woman against his body.

The only way that was going to happen was under the guise of dancing.

But after he sent her partner packing, she ignored his proffered hand. "I've had enough dancing."

"I haven't," he said shortly, taking her into his arms.

"I need a break."

Tristan stood firm. "You looked like you were enjoying yourself with your other partners."

"Not half as much as you."

Ah. So this was about Delia. She *had* been watching. Primal satisfaction roared through his veins and pooled low in his body. He pulled her closer and despite the resistance resonating through her stiffly-held body, she felt right.

The perfect warm-blooded, sweet-scented antidote to Delia's venom.

And, what the hell, Vanessa felt so right that he drew their joined hands to his lips and kissed her knuckles.

She recoiled as if he'd bitten her. Which he might

have done, with the same lazy eroticism as in her kitchen, if she'd let him. Judging by the wariness in her eyes, that wasn't happening any time soon. "What was that for?" she asked.

"Just trying to relax you." He tugged her nearer again. "At the moment you're dancing with all the suppleness of a tackle-dummy."

"Did you consider that might be because I'd rather be dancing with the tackle-dummy?"

Smiling at the image, he swept her into an exaggerated turn. She had to relax to keep up and once she was dancing again, he asked, "Because of Delia?"

She didn't have to answer. He felt the response in her grip and the falter of her step. He stopped teasing and took pity. If Jack Cartwright had pulled Delia-like moves on Vanessa, Tristan would have laid the bastard out cold in the middle of the dance floor.

Tristan didn't bother debating the wisdom of such fierce possessiveness. He tucked her under his chin and bent to speak near her ear. "For your information, I wasn't enjoying myself."

"Then why did you dance with her?"

"She saved me getting kicked out of here."

Finally she relaxed a little, although Tristan fancied he could hear her brain ticking. He figured she'd want to know why he'd crashed the wedding reception and he'd have to tell her. End of warm, relaxed perfect woman in his arms. Resurgence of hostilities. Damn.

When she tipped her head back to look up into his face, he contemplated kissing her. To silence the inevitable question, to buy some more time, and because he'd spent the last three days regretting the lost opportunity in her kitchen. When she hit him with the five-second challenge, he'd wanted to shock her in return and knew he'd done so by ignoring her lips.

Talk about outsmarting himself.

But she didn't ask the expected; she surprised him again. "I hope you don't take anything Delia says too seriously."

Tristan didn't carry tales or repeat rumors. He had to consider what he said carefully. "I gather you two aren't buddies."

"No. I think…" Her brow puckered, thoughtful, worried, and his whole body tightened with the urge to kiss it smooth. To take that anxiety from her and make it better. "I think she imagined we were kindred spirits because of…superficial similarities." She cut him a fierce look. "We're not alike. At all. She likes to play games."

"And make mischief?"

Their eyes met, no clash, no surprise.

But she shook her head.

"You don't think she could have sent the letters to me?" Because as far as Tristan could tell, Delia was the only person in Eastwick society with a gripe against Vanessa.

"The thought did cross my mind, but she likes hand-delivering those verbal gems. She lives for reaction. The letters don't seem li—" She stopped midword. Sucked in a breath, her eyes wide. "You said letters, plural. *Letters* to you."

Intent on each other and the conversation they'd

danced to a halt on the edge of the floor. Another couple bumped Tristan's back and he turned Vanessa in his arms, shielding her from their curious gazes. "We should take this somewhere private."

"You did say letters?" she persisted.

"There's a second. Delivered Tuesday."

He ushered her out into the gardens, much too far and too slowly for Vanessa's impatient imagination. By the time they'd cleared the perimeter of the pool area and the clusters of wedding guests spilled from the ballroom into gardens festooned with lights, scores of questions clamored for answers.

Barely knowing where to begin, she spun around to face him. "You went to Florida. How did this person know where to find you?"

"It was delivered to the Marabella before I left. I thought it was Stuart's letter—the one you loaned me and said I should have. I thought you'd sent it in. You seemed so insistent."

"I am."

A corner of his mouth kicked up, acknowledging that.

"And when did you discover it wasn't from me?"

"After talking to my mother last night." He gave a tight shrug. "I couldn't sleep. I'd put the envelope in my pocket and I decided to read it again."

The letter he'd returned because he thought he'd never read it again. *Right.*

But that was another story, for another time. Right now she needed to know about this second letter of Tristan's. "This letter…is it from the same person?"

His eyes met hers, dark and unreadable. "It appears so."

"The same allegations?"

"Dates. Times. Places."

That she'd met an imaginary lover? Vanessa shook her head. Apparently this last week had proved nothing. Instead of anger she felt a choking wave of disappointment. "And you believe this piece of fiction?"

"There's more." He reached into the inside pocket of his suit jacket, and in that second's pause her heart stalled with a prescient sense of doom. "A photo."

She stared at the enlarged print but she didn't take it from his hand. Even upside down, in the shadows of a dimly lit garden, she could see enough.

"Who is he, Vanessa? If he's not your lover, then who?" He asked quietly, without accusation or antagonism, and her heart started to beat with a strong, thick pulse of hope. This week *had* meant something. He was prepared to listen.

She lifted her chin and met his eyes and the words came easily.

"His name is Lew Kotzur. He's my brother."

"Why didn't you tell me about your brother before?"

They'd left the wedding after her revelation, seeking privacy from the chance of interruption. He drove and Vanessa talked, at first in fractured snippets and then with growing fluency. She discovered a cathartic release in finally sharing about Lew and his autism and the wonders Twelve Oaks had wrought on his behavior and esteem.

Except for an occasional prompt, Tristan didn't interrupt. He let her talk until she was done and she realized they'd arrived at the shore. The beach would be packed with sightseers during the day, but at night they were alone with the moonlight and his opening question.

"I wanted to," she answered candidly, aware of all the times she'd prevaricated and danced around the full truth. "That night I came to the restaurant, after I talked to Andy down at Poynton, I intended telling you."

"But you didn't."

"There was too much anger and resentment still hovering from our first meeting. And then Frank came over to visit." And she was making excuses when there wasn't any excuse. She'd chickened out or frozen up or let her temper get the better of her logic. "It seems that every time we get together, there is some emotional drama or other and I get sidetracked."

"The other morning in your kitchen you told me about Twelve Oaks. That was the perfect opportunity."

"It was. I know. A missed opportunity."

When he didn't respond, she turned and found him angled in the driver's seat, his fingers drumming against the steering wheel, a slight frown drawing his brows together as he watched her with silent intensity.

Was he watching her mouth? And thinking of another missed opportunity?

She shook that thought aside and stared ahead, through the windshield. *Concentrate*, Ms. Pragmatist scolded. *This is your chance to clear away the final misunderstandings. Do not get sidetracked.*

"Does anyone know about Lew?"

"Gloria. Andy. Jack and some other professionals. But no one else in Eastwick. None of my friends."

"Why not?"

Expecting the question, she'd already grown tense and wary. She didn't expect her way of thinking would make sense to a man like Tristan, who charged after his goals and damn the consequences. She didn't want to open herself and her background up to his judgment. "That's not an easy question," she prevaricated. "I'm not sure you will understand."

"Try me."

She exhaled a shaky breath. "Lew has been my responsibility since I was a teenager."

"What happened to your parents?"

"A long story, another time." *Hopefully, never.* "But even when they were around, they weren't around much. They were working or—" she shrugged "—whatever. I'm eight years older, so it fell on me to look after my little brother from when he was in diapers."

"You were just a kid yourself."

His voice was tight with anger and, pity help her, this was exactly what she'd feared. "Please, do not give me that poor-Vanessa look because I never minded. Not for one second. I wanted to look out for him," she said fiercely. "He needed someone to."

"Because of the autism."

Vanessa nodded. "He was always…different. And you know how kids can be with that."

"Not in the same league, but yes."

She cut him a look. "When you moved at Australia?"

"A long story, another time."

For a second their connection held the warm strength of understanding, and that sensation helped her shuck some of her tense reservations. *It might be okay to share. He may understand more than I'd imagined.*

"Anyway," she continued with more confidence, "I grew up protecting Lew from ugly insults and neighborhood bullies, and I had to fight tooth and nail to get anyone to acknowledge he had a serious problem. His well-being was my responsibility years before my mother passed away and I became his guardian."

"How old were you?"

"Twenty-one."

In the brief pause that followed, he must have done the math. Two years a widow. Five years married. Not much left over. "And along came Stuart Thorpe."

"The answer to my prayers," she said.

"How did you meet?"

"Oh, I'm pretty sure you know I was a waitress."

"That's not what I asked."

Vanessa lifted a shoulder and let it drop, shifting uneasily under his watchful gaze. *Tell him*, Ms. P. whispered. *Tell him everything and the slate will be clean.*

"One of my jobs was in the city, in a restaurant near Stuart's office. He was a regular, a lovely man who was always friendly and who remembered what we'd talked about a week before." When she paused to moisten her dry mouth, she tensed, anticipating his dig about Stuart's tips or about her scheming to snag a millionaire. But he remained silent, watchful, waiting for the rest. "One day he came in when I'd just had a call from Lew's school. He was on a last warning for his violent behavior and I was at wit's end. I told Stuart and he offered to come to the school with me."

On the wheel, his long fingers clenched and straight-ened. A reflexive action? In response to Stuart's visit to the school?

"I didn't accept his offer."

"Why not?"

"Lew was my responsibility and to be honest—" she looked up at him through her lashes "—I wondered what he would want in return."

Even in the tricky moonlight, she could see the harsh lines of cynicism etched in his expression. She hated that look and its cause, but he'd requested the true story not a rose-colored adaptation.

"The next week," she continued, "he brought all the information about Twelve Oaks."

"The answer to your prayers."

His murmured aside made a mockery of her earlier comment and that stung deeply. Damn him and all this rotten history. She felt as if she'd started a swift slide back to the start, to that day when he'd appeared at her door with his scorn and derision riding shotgun alongside.

"I didn't have the money for a place like Twelve Oaks," she told him. "And the very thought of entrust-ing Lew into the care of strangers made me sick. I threw the brochures in the trash, but Stuart persisted. He sent a car the next weekend, to take me and Lew up there for a look around. I saw these young men, so content and confident, and I saw all the possibilities for Lew."

"So he offered you marriage, and everything that goes with it, in return for Twelve Oaks."

He could have used more brutal language. He could have come right out and accused her of selling herself into marriage. It was no less than the truth. A deal, a trade, and a regular bargain from her side.

Except she hadn't accepted everything.

She lifted her chin and met his eyes. "Stuart and I had a contract, a private handshake deal. I wanted Lew taken care of, for his entire life. In return I became Stuart's friend, companion, hostess. A trophy wife, yes, and he loved to play on that, buying me all the pretty things you mock. Taking me places I'd be photographed on his arm.

"But we kept separate bedrooms. I was his wife in name only. I was never his lover."

Ten

"That's why I laughed so hard at your adultery allegation. Not because it was funny but because it shocked me with its utter implausibility. And there you were standing in my keeping room vowing to prove my guilt—" she released a breath of laughter, soft and self-effacing "—when it would have been easier to prove I couldn't have had a lover!"

Tristan almost choked on his next breath. His head whipped around to stare at her. "Are you implying you've never had a lover?"

For a moment she studied her hands, and he wondered if she was reconsidering her provocative claim. *It would have been easier to prove I couldn't have had a lover.* By sleeping with her? By discovering that she was untouched?

That notion turned visual, sensual, carnal, a sweet thick rush of desire that settled between his thighs.

"You're a virgin?"

"Is that so hard to believe?"

"You're thirty years—"

"Not quite," she interrupted.

"About to turn thirty and a widow. You're so damn beautiful you could have any man you wanted. Yes, it's hard to swallow."

Slowly she raised her eyes to his. "You think I'm beautiful?"

She didn't know? He shook his head in disbelief. Women. "I knew you were beautiful before I hit your doorstep and then you opened the door…" He lifted a hand and let it fall, lost for words to describe that impact.

"How did you know?"

I knew when I found myself lifting my jaw off the mat. But he didn't think that's what she meant.

"You said you knew, before…" she prompted.

"I'd seen your photo. On that society Web site."

Her eyes narrowed a fraction, but that didn't conceal the glimmer of surprise. Or pleasure. "You were checking me out?"

"I like to know what I'm up against."

"Did that help?"

"No."

They sat a minute in silence. The car and the night created a cocoon of intimacy, but the mood was not exactly comfortable, not really relaxed. Not a big surprise given her disclosure. He felt he needed to say something—something other than "This changes everything" and "Come back to my hotel room." Both seemed premature but the longer the silence stretched, the harder that notion hammered through his body.

She had never slept with his father.

She had never slept with any man.

He shifted in his seat, turning to look at her. "Thank you for telling me. I appreciate your honesty."

"It's a weight off." When she gave her trademark little shrug, her silvery dress glistened in the moonlight. She waited for his eyes to drift back up to her face. "Can I ask something of you in return?"

"As long as it's not another five-second challenge."

A hint of a smile teased her lips, drawing his attention and reminding him how he'd outsmarted himself in her kitchen.

"I'd like to know how you got on in Florida," she said. "When you went to visit your mother."

Tristan found it easier to talk about than he'd imagined. Perhaps because of her honesty, perhaps because of the soothing backdrop of beach and water and velvet-dark night, perhaps because they'd already shared so much that he felt Vanessa knew him better than anyone outside his immediate family.

She suggested they walk and he agreed. As they strolled along the boulevard, he told her how his mother had eventually confirmed what he'd learned from Vanessa and from Stuart's letter about the adulterous affair with the twins' father and the subsequent fallout. He didn't tell Vanessa how his mother had attempted to justify her deception or how she'd wept buckets as she begged his forgiveness.

Not wanting to think about that emotional mael-strom, he kept on talking about the twins—his half-sisters—and his hometown of Perth where he'd lived until his career took off. Prompted by Vanessa's percep-tive comments and questions, he divulged the culture shock of landing in a new country in the middle of a school year. The Yankee kid with a strange accent, who didn't know a thing about any of the local sports.

"Is that why you took up Australian football?" she asked. "To fit in?"

"It was easier than cricket. At least I knew how to kick a football."

"And so the Yankee kid mastered the Aussie game and showed those locals."

"It sure didn't do me any harm." In fact, the market-ers had used that unique spin to turn him into a house-hold name and that high profile hadn't hurt him in the world of business. "It put me where I am today. I'm not sorry about that."

He felt her gaze on him, sharp with contemplation. Already he'd revealed more than he'd intended, more than he was comfortable sharing with anyone. He sure as hell didn't want to defend that last statement.

He didn't have to because she suddenly tripped and might have fallen if he hadn't caught her. "All right?" he asked.

"My heel is stuck." Steadying herself on his arm, she tried to pull her shoe free and failed.

Tristan hunkered down to take a look and found the stiletto wedged tightly in the gap between two paving stones. If not for a delicate lacing of straps around her ankle, her foot would have come free and left the shoe behind.

But there were the straps. And a delicate foot and ankle and toes with their nails painted a pearly pink. And something about that sight turned his fingers into thumbs and hazed his vision.

"Put your hands on my shoulders," he instructed, his voice deep and gruff with that sudden rush of desire. "This might take a while."

"There's a buckle at the side, Can't you see it?"

Yeah, he could see it. Just. But he was enjoying this unique perspective, with her weight resting on him and his hand cradling her foot. He felt no way inclined to give it up too soon.

The strap came loose and he traced his thumb over the imprint left in her skin. Through her sheer stockings he could feel the warmth of her skin and the scent of roses twined through him, enticing him, when he palmed the backs of her calves, he thought he heard her draw a shudder of breath and her hands flexed and tightened on his shoulders.

He came to his feet in a long, slow slide of body against body and she tilted her face to meet his kiss with a soft sigh of relief. This was the kiss he'd wanted that morning in the kitchen; it felt like a kiss he'd been wanting all his life. A sensuous giving and taking as they learned each other's lips and mouths and tongues with a heat that threatened to engulf them both.

Eventually they came apart, their breathing an elevated rasp in the stillness.

"What now?" she asked.

Everything inside Tristan was still and hard. "That's up to you."

"What are my choices?"

"I can take you home," he said. "Or I can take you back to my hotel. Your choice, Vanessa."

Vanessa chose his hotel because she wanted this between them. No third parties. No history, just them and this night and the latent promise of that kiss.

But after he'd parked his car and turned off the engine, her insides jumped with misgivings. "What are we doing?" she asked. "What is this about?"

"That's up to you," he repeated. And the way he looked at her with all that contained male intensity did nothing to calm her nerves. "Do you want to go upstairs? Yes or no?"

For the entire ten-minute drive from the shore, her pragmatic side had screeched an increasingly strident *no.* But there was a *yes,* as well, a whispered temptation of a voice that beat in her accelerated pulse and in a dozen places she'd barely known existed before this man strode into her life.

Perhaps knowing he would stride back out again influenced her choice. She could have this night, she could savor the experience, she could say goodbye and get on with real life. All before she turned thirty at midnight.

She sucked in a quick breath and nodded. "Yes."

He took her by the hand and led her to the elevators. Keeping her knees from shaking took all her concentration. She'd made her decision. She was pretty sure she would go through with this…experience.

Upstairs in his top-floor suite, she wasn't so sure. When the door clicked shut behind them, her nerves shot through the roof. She bought some time pretending interest in her surroundings, ambling a slow investigative circle of the living room and keeping her eyes averted from the turned-back bed she glimpsed through the half-open door to his bedroom.

Eventually she'd seen the entire suite, balcony and bathroom included. She strolled back into the living room and pulled up short. Bare from the waist up, Tristan was hunkered down at the silent stereo. Soft light spilled from a standing lamp and played over the long muscles of his back. Perhaps she made a sound, because he looked up sharply and came to his feet. And in that instant his face looked so tense and hard and untouchable, she felt an urgent need to bolt.

Her mouth went dry. Her heart raced. But her feet remained glued to the spot.

A muscle jumped in his cheek and she realized, with a startled sense of discovery, that he looked nervous, too. She found that oddly reassuring.

"Would you like a drink?" he asked.

"If I were ever to start, tonight would be the night. But…no."

He stood, silently watching her for another second. Butterflies flapped in her stomach. She couldn't stand the tension any longer. "What now?"

"Take off your jewelry," he said in a low controlled voice.

She lifted a hand to touch the delicate diamond and sapphire necklace. "You don't like it?"

"No."

"And the dress?"

Slowly he started to cross the room toward her. She saw the flare of his nostrils, the unwavering intensity of his eyes, the clench and flex of his hand, and all her senses sharpened with anticipation. He stopped in front of her, his gaze a long, slow slide of approval. "I like the dress."

"I'm glad," she said simply.

An unexpected tenderness lurked deep in his eyes as he took one of her hands and tugged her closer. His kiss started gentle, a brush of lips, a teasing shift of pressure from top lip to bottom and back again. A kiss that was everything his look had promised. Vanessa spread her hands over his chest, exploring the heady contrast of coarse hair and hot, smooth skin. He nipped at her bottom lip and dragged it between his teeth, a move so unexpected and incredibly sensual, it curled her toes.

Warm and dizzy with desire, she swayed nearer and closed her eyes.

Her hands slid over his shoulders, her fingers laced in his hair, and she made a muted sound of discovery at its softness. He took the invitation to deepen the kiss, opening her mouth with the pressure of his and sliding his tongue inside. The kiss exploded with heat in the beat of a second, and she surrendered to the unrestrained pleasure.

When he retreated, she followed, sliding tongue against tongue and learning his dark male flavor. Desire sang in her veins as she sank into his mouth and discovered a new angle to the kiss.

She could have lapped this up forever but he slowly eased her back to earth with a luscious series of kisses that trailed from her lips to her chin and along the edge of her jaw. He pulled back far enough to look into her eyes and murmur, "Better?"

She smiled and something primal beat in his eyes.

"Turn around."

Dipping one shoulder, she turned within his arms. Her heart raced like a bird in flight while she waited in anticipation of what came next. His hands skimmed up her arms and cupped her shoulders in rough-textured heat. When he leaned forward and spoke at her ear, the deep resonance of his voice pulsed through her body.

Her breasts grew tight and heavy. Heat bloomed all through her skin. And she had to ask him to repeat his request because no words registered, only sensation.

"Hold your hair up out of the way."

With both hands she lifted the long tresses high. She felt his hands at her nape and then the necklace fell free. He caught it in one hand and added the matching earrings. When he nuzzled the side of her exposed throat, Vanessa's knees all but gave way.

But his hands curled around her hips and held her steady, captive to the hot kisses he peppered along one shoulder and then the other.

She couldn't contain the low needy sound that escaped her throat. The same need shuddered through her, an aching desire to press herself against him, soft to hard. As if he'd heard her silent plea, he pulled her back into his body. She felt the hard jut of his arousal, heard the rough growl rumble in his chest.

Arching her back she pressed closer and his hands slid up to span her rib cage. The tips of his thumbs brushed the underside of her breasts and she shivered with expectancy. She'd never experienced anything like this intensity of sensations. And she was still fully clothed.

The thought of doing this naked brought a flush of heat to her throat and face, and when he turned her in his arms she found the same raw need reflected in his eyes.

"Okay?" he asked.

"Oh, yeah."

He kissed that satisfied sound from her mouth, a long, deep extended kiss that left her breathless and panting. Then he took her hand and led her into the bedroom. He kissed her again and looked down into her eyes. "Shall we lose the dress?"

Her nerves skittered and her breath caught on her whispered, "Yes."

"Nervous?"

"A little."

"Yeah," he said, but his fingers seemed sure and steady on her dress fastening. "I know."

The loosened bodice fell forward and she caught it in her hands. "What do you have to be nervous about?"

He paused, eyes serious on hers. "Doing it right."

Well, sure, but at least he had experience on his side. She, on the other hand, was acting on impulse. And the sensations he aroused with the sure touch of his hands and the heat of his mouth and the erotic wet slide of his tongue.

Before she could think, *I'm not quite ready to be seen in my underwear*, her dress lay in a silken pool at her feet and she was being seen in her underwear. With high heeled sandals. She felt gauche and exposed, but when she saw the primitive desire on his face she lifted her chin and forced her hands to rest at her sides.

He stepped in and cupped her breasts, his thumbs stroking over her aroused nipples until pleasure pierced her body and stretched straight to her core. When he removed her bra, an arrow of fear immobilized her for the first exposed moment but the touch of his bare hands brought her zinging back to life. The pad of his thumb circled her areola and grazed her nipple.

"Easy," he murmured when her knees dipped and wobbled. "I've got you."

He eased her to the bed and followed her down.

His mouth found her breast. Sliding her fingers through his hair, she sifted the strands in a fretful echo of the pull of his mouth. *Oh, yes,* Ms. P. whispered, *he definitely has you.* Then his hot tongue swirled over her nipple and her back arched from the bed. She cried out, a ragged appeal for release.

He left her breasts to slide lower, hooking his fingers into her underwear and peeling them away. A restless fire licked through her body. His hands were on her legs, his mouth on her thighs, his fingers finding her wet and ready.

Then he left her alone and she felt the abandonment in every turned-on cell. Her eyes fluttered open to find him beside the bed. Shoes already gone, he stood to unzip his trousers and her mouth went dry. She'd known he was a big man, hard and uncompromising, and that had never been more apparent than when he straightened, naked and very, very aroused.

Apprehension flickered through her and she swallowed.

Perhaps this wasn't such a good idea after all.

Perhaps she could have remained a virgin for life.

But then he finished donning protection and returned to her side, kissing the worry from her lips, reassuring her that he'd look after her, touching her supersensitive flesh with a delicious pressure that spiraled low in her belly.

"Please," she whispered, catching at his body and pulling him close. She wanted this now, while she felt like this, ready to go up in flames. "Please, can we do it?"

Heat blazed in his eyes as he moved over her, spreading her thighs and pressing a slow, deep kiss to her open mouth as he eased into her body. Restraint tightened his face. "Are you sure?"

In answer, she lifted her hips into the insistent press of his sex.

Eyes fixed on hers, he eased his way with the measured rock of his hips. Sweat broke out on his forehead when he stopped, and she felt a momentary panic.

"Don't stop." Her hands slid down his back and her nails found purchase in the taut muscles of his buttocks. "Please. Don't stop."

"I'm just," he said tightly, "going slow."

He pressed a little deeper and a tremor quivered through the long sweat-dampened muscles of his back. In that moment she recognized the effort in his restraint and knew it was for her, in deference to her first time, and she felt an overwhelming wave of tenderness.

She lifted a trembling hand to touch his mouth, and he muttered something low and fierce, an oath or a promise, and then he was inside her all the way, filling her to the brink with his heat and with the enormity of the moment.

She rocked her hips, adjusting to the unfamiliar, surprised by the lack of pain, and wanting it to never end. But he'd started to move with a slow, smooth cadence, rising over her with a look of burning intensity that caused her heart to stall out. She picked up the rhythm and held his gaze through each rolling thrust, moving with him as he drove toward his completion.

He didn't leave her behind. He reached between them, finding her and stroking her until her world narrowed and converged on one wildly spinning pleasure point. She heard him call her name as he followed, a hoarse shout of release that hung in the cooling air and wound its way around her heart.

Tristan watched Vanessa sleep, at last seeing her with her guard completely down. No clothes, no makeup, no facade of sophistication. Just Vanessa, her delicate beauty incandescent in the soft lamplight. So beautiful and proud and complex and fierce, she made him ache in a dozen ways and a dozen places.

Propped on an elbow he watched her and he willed her to wake, impatient to start over. He wasn't proud of how he'd judged and treated her so harshly and he intended making it up to her every way he could. Thinking about what she'd revealed in the car, about her childhood and her care and protection of her brother when she'd been too young for such responsibility, fuelled his resolve.

He'd got it so wrong. This time he intended getting it right and he couldn't wait to start.

Leaning close he kissed the soft sleepiness of her mouth and the sexy dent in her chin and traced a fine blue vein across the near-translucent skin of her breast.

The nipple peaked and she came awake instantly. It took another second for her memory to catch up and the flush to rise from her throat. She met his eyes but a note of shyness kept her expression wary.

He couldn't halt the surge of possessive male pride that gripped him. He wasn't sure he wanted to. He smiled and shook his head. "A virgin."

"You didn't believe me?"

Trick question. Something in her tone warned him to take care with his answer. "I didn't understand how that could be possible."

"I think lack of opportunity sums it up."

"You didn't have boyfriends?"

"No. I was either working or looking after Lew. And the boys I knew weren't interested in having him tag along." She rolled a shoulder dismissively. He sensed she didn't care that she'd missed the teen-dating scene. "And then I was married at twenty-two."

For a moment he said nothing, his need to know warring with his need to leave the past behind.

But he did need to know. That was his problem—he was greedy to know everything about her, even the bits better left buried. "This contract you made when you married. Didn't you ever want to break it?"

"No. I never looked at Stuart that way. He was more like a…"

In her hesitation he sensed what she was reluctant to admit. "A father?"

"Like the father I wished I'd had. I'm sorry, but that's the truth. And, you know, I think that was why Stuart suggested this arrangement in the first place. He never got over losing his family. He was desperately lonely, especially when he got older and his health problems caused him to cut right back on his work."

"He was semiretired?"

"Yes. That's when he started coming into the restaurant more often. He was a bit lost." She smiled, a wistful little curve of her lips that fisted around his heart. "At first he just wanted to help. Then he got invested in me and Lew. I think he saw us as a substitute family."

It hurt, but not as much as before he'd read the apology in Stuart's letter. And she'd needed the support of a father figure, it seemed. Desperately.

"Your parents—you said they weren't around much."

"No. And when they were…I often wished they weren't." Sadness, dark and profound, shadowed her expression. "They didn't handle Lew's difficulties. They didn't know how to handle him. My father had a violent temper."

"Against you and your brother?"

"Only my mom. And she drank to counter it. We were the classic dysfunctional family."

"And no one saw this?" he demanded, angry at the injustice of everything she'd told him and his impotence to change it. "Nobody helped?"

"My parents were working, too, providing in their own modest way. And if the authorities had gotten involved, Lew and I might have been fostered out and split up. We coped, okay? Much better than if a kid like

Lew had landed in the foster system. And I ended up here, living in Fastwick, with everything I ever wanted."

"Except a family."

She looked up sharply. "Lew is my family. I don't want it any other way, Tristan. I have no regrets over marrying Stuart. He knew it was for the money and we were both happy with that choice."

"And me," he asked. "Do you have any regrets about me?"

She studied him a long while and a myriad of emotions darkened her silvery gaze. "That would depend."

"On?"

"On how this ends up."

"At the moment I was wondering about so far." He lifted a hand and touched a mark on her throat. *His* mark on her throat. His body tightened in response. "Do you regret this?"

"Not yet."

It was a start. And she was still here, in his bed, which had to count for something.

"Will you stay?" He tugged at the sheet she'd pulled up to cover her nakedness until she relented and let it go. Then he turned her into his arms and looked deep into her eyes. "I want to make it up to you, Vanessa. Will you let me?"

Eleven

Vanessa stayed. A fitful sleeper even in her own bed, she hadn't counted on sleeping soundly and waking to the sound of running water. Jackknifing upright, she discovered Tristan lounging in the doorway to the bathroom. He was naked, which she noticed straight away, and looking cat-got-the-cream satisfied and very much at ease.

She frowned at the thought. How long had he been standing there, watching her sleep?

Disconcerted, she pulled the sheet up beneath her chin.

He arched his eyebrow in a way that reminded her he'd seen it all already, from much closer. "I'm glad you're awake."

"Oh?" she asked, immediately suspicious.

"I'm running a bath for you. If you hadn't roused soon, I was going to have to take drastic action."

"Such as?"

He straightened off the doorjamb and sauntered to the bed. With each approaching stride her heart kicked up another beat. He didn't say a word. Eyes locked on hers, he bent down and swung her into his arms as if she weighed nothing.

She gasped in shock and because, well, she wasn't used to being manhandled. But as he carted her back to the bathroom, she discovered she liked the manhandling too much to fight it. She made a token protest as he held her over the brimming three-cornered spa tub, but instead of dropping her into the bubbles he stepped over the rim and sank down with her in his arms.

Then he kissed her and murmured, "I'm glad you stayed," and she decided to stay a little longer.

Breakfast arrived on the heels of the bath and Vanessa felt extremely spoiled.

When she finished dressing and walked into the living room, she discovered a pancake stack lit with candles and sparklers in the center of the dining table. Her eyes widened with disbelief and her heart did a crazy painful lurch.

"Happy birthday, darling."

Not duchess. Darling.

Hot tears ached at the back of her throat and she took an age to compose herself enough to say, "Thank you." She cleared her throat. "How did you know?"

"I just took a wild stab in the dark."

Of course he knows your birth date, Ms. Pragmatist mocked. *And probably a whole lot more that he's not letting on. He was investigating you. Digging up your secrets. Remember?*

The mood nose-dived after that. Oh, she sat at the table and blew out the candles and pretended to make a wish. She was hungry enough to appreciate the fabulous breakfast spread and he'd even remembered her specialty coffee—or he'd known enough to check with the restaurant staff.

But she couldn't get past the sinking feeling that however wonderful the night, however enjoyable his company, however seductive his intent, the specter of their past conflict would rise between them.

"So." He leaned back in his chair and studied her across the table. "What have you got planned for your special day?"

"I have a date with Lew."

"Lunch?"

She nodded. "A picnic at the shore."

"You might want to rethink that." He tilted his head toward the balcony and outdoors. "Storms are forecast."

Bother. She put down her cutlery, frowning.

"We could do something else. Go somewhere else. Maybe the rain will fizzle out and we can still picnic—" He stopped. Frowned back at her. "What's the problem?"

The initial problem was the storms, which Lew loathed and feared. But the second problem superseded the first, and was now jittering around in her stomach. "You said *we*. I'm not sure that's a good idea."

"Which part? Me spending the day with you? Or me spending the day with Lew?"

Vanessa's stomach twisted into a pretzel knot. There were so many concerns, so many not-a-good-ideas she did not know where to start. "It's difficult," she said carefully. "He can be difficult."

"He's autistic. You mentioned that."

She shook her head. "I don't think you understand. He needs routine. Anything out of the ordinary— changed plans, new people, storms—makes him fret. Difficult with Lew can be sudden and violent."

"I would like to meet your brother," he said with quiet insistence.

"I'm afraid that's out of the question."

"For today? Or forever?"

She should not have to explain her decision—it was hers alone to make. But his obdurate expression demanded an answer and she knew he would push and push until she ended up losing her temper. It was better to explain while her head was cool and clear. "This isn't personal, Tristan. I don't take anyone to see Lew because his reaction to people is so extreme. He either ignores you altogether or he takes an instant shine."

"And which do you think I can't handle?"

Damn him, she had one difficult male in her life. She did not need another.

And wasn't that the crux of this whole issue? Tristan did not have a future in her life. So why introduce him into Lew's? Why set up the potential for disappointment?

Instinctively she knew that Lew would adore Tristan. They would talk sports and throw a football and swap the kind of guy-talk she couldn't even fake. And tomorrow or next week or whenever, Tristan would return to his own life and she'd be left with the constant hammering of, *Where's Tristan? Can we go visit? He said we'd go to the Yankees. Can we go today?*

Even worse, there'd come a day when Lew would finally accept that Tristan wasn't taking him to a ballgame. And she was the lucky one who would have to deal with his why-doesn't-he-want-to-be-my-friend moping.

She shook her head firmly. "My answer is still no."

"What about Stuart? Did you take him to visit Lew?"

"They met. But he didn't have an active role in Lew's life."

His gaze narrowed. "I thought you two were his surrogate family."

Damn him, did he ever let up? "I said he *thought* we might be, but it turned out to be too painful. He tried, but he didn't want a constant reminder of the son he didn't get to see and toss a ball with. That substitute didn't work."

Finally, he had no comeback. His silence was not satisfying, however. It banded tight around Vanessa's chest, an aching reminder that this father-son conflict would always come between them, driving one of them to speak out of turn and hurt the other.

An aching reminder that she needed to protect her own heart as well as Lew's.

She lifted her chin with a new determination. "I'm not debating this anymore. I am spending the day with Lew. Alone." She pushed to her feet. "I'll just get my purse and shoes."

"All right," he said with great reluctance. "But I am taking you to dinner tonight."

"No, Tristan."

Something darkened in his narrowed eyes. "Are you suggesting that this is it?"

"You told me last night, that *this* was whatever I wanted it to be."

"That was before you came upstairs and took off your clothes." He, too, came to his feet. They faced off across the discarded birthday breakfast. "This is not over, Vanessa."

"Because you say so? We can't have a relationship, Tristan. Even if I wanted to, even if we didn't have all this angst and conflict and history between us, I couldn't. I have priorities and they're all about Lew. I can't do a relationship!"

"Then why did you sleep with me? What was last night about?"

"You tell me," she fired back, instantly defensive. "Maybe I just wanted to prove my innocence!"

"You didn't think I believed you?" A muscle jumped in his jaw. His voice went very low, gruff with intensity. "I hope you are kidding."

Vanessa walked away from the table. Her heart was thundering, anxiety chased through her veins. At the French doors leading onto the balcony she whirled back around. "Look at us! We can't go a day without one of these confrontations. This is what I grew up with, Tristan. This is why I love my life with all its calm and order. That's why my marriage was so perfect."

Her impassioned little speech crackled between them a long time before he spoke. "You're pushing me away because you're scared."

"I'm pushing you away because you are so damn stubborn you won't take no for an answer!"

"I'm trying to work out what's going on with you. Last night was…" He let out a frustrated huff and shook his head. "Maybe you don't realize it, but that was amazing. I want that again, Vanessa, but I'm not going to beg. I won't go down on one knee. I won't promise you a perfect life of calm and order, because I'd rather have you with the heat and the passion and, yeah, even the fights."

Heart knocking hard against her ribs, she stared back at him. "I didn't ask for any promises. And I hate the fights."

"Yeah, I figured."

She didn't know what else to say. She'd made up her mind and she needed to get out of there. At the door she turned and found him standing in the same place, motionless but for that muscle jumping in his jaw.

She swallowed a large ache in her throat and met his shuttered gaze. There was one last thing to broach. "I can't go without asking about that letter. The second one."

"I'll hand it over to the police."

"And the will challenge?"

"You proved your point," he said flatly after a long beat of pause. "I'll talk to my lawyers tomorrow. It's all yours. Just as Stuart wanted."

Tears welled in her eyes before the door shut behind her. She dashed them away with her wrist as she strode to the elevators, eager to be somewhere private before the emotional storm erupted. She pressed the button and fixated on the floor indicator. More tears threatened and she swallowed against the harsh throb in her throat.

At least she could be thankful for one thing. He hadn't insisted on driving her to collect her car from the country club where she'd left it last night. She would take a taxi. And if the tears came, it wouldn't matter.

The elevator arrived and she stepped forward as the door opened.

"Wait." Tristan's voice called after her, from back at his suite.

Heart racing, Vanessa pressed the ground floor button. She couldn't take any more of this emotion and she was afraid that one kind word, one softening of his hard-set expression, would send her sobbing into his arms.

Counterproductive, Ms. P. decided.

The doors started to close. Vanessa breathed again.

But at the last possible moment, a large, familiar hand blocked their slide. She remembered it on her breasts, between her legs, drawing her to an exquisite climax. And the ache in her throat grew unbearable.

She straightened her shoulders and sucked in a fortifying breath. *Please don't cry. Please don't cry.*

"You forgot this."

She forced herself to focus on what he held in that extended hand.

The jewelry he'd asked her to take off before they made love. She stared at the glittering pieces in his hand, a symbol of the bought-and-paid-for wife. A symbol of the conflicted history that would always come between them.

She took them and put them in her purse and gamely met his guarded eyes. "Thank you, Tristan. For everything." The doors started to slide, and she hurried to finish. "I will never forget last night. You're right—it was amazing."

When he returned to his suite, Tristan packed his bags. There wasn't a lot to do; he'd packed for Florida never meaning to return. And now, he didn't know if he was glad or sorry that he'd come back.

He didn't dwell on working out an answer. Vanessa had made her mind up and he'd come closer to swallowing his pride and begging than he'd ever wanted to try. And for what? To buy another week in her bed? To instigate a long-distance relationship with no future, because she didn't want anything that might threaten her secure world.

She might have her priorities all screwed. She might be living at delusion-central when it came to her happiness. But she'd been right about one thing: they could never go one day without a fiery confrontation.

That's what he loved most about her: that fierce commitment that made her stand to her convictions and made a mockery of her desire for a calm, orderly existence.

He understood her reasons. After that hellish childhood, who wouldn't want security? But courtesy of Stuart's estate she had truckloads of prime greenback security.

She needed more. He hoped someday she would come to that realization, even though he'd be long gone. But before he left, he had three loose ends to tie.

First, he phoned his lawyer with orders to drop his challenge of the will. Then he called the detectives on the Bunny Baldwin case and made arrangements for an officer to collect the second nuisance letter.

The third task was all about setting things right and he didn't expect it to be easy. He figured it might take several days to track down the exact model and he was going to do everything in his power to make sure he did.

If he found it, well, it would serve as an apology and a thank-you and a goodbye.

To set his search in motion, he lifted the phone and called the number he knew by heart.

Vanessa's thirtieth birthday was hardly an unqualified success. The squally storms missed Lexford, but it only took the threat of dark clouds and thunder to put Lew on edge. She transferred the picnic to the recreation room at Twelve Oaks and spent the afternoon watching DVDs with Lew and several of his friends.

Which wouldn't have been all bad if their taste in movies didn't run to gross-out humor.

Still, the time spent with her brother reassured her that she'd made the right choice. Watching him nudge his buddies and guffaw over the lame jokes brought a poignant ache to her heart. He couldn't be happier or in a better place. And his laughter was her happiness.

"Watch this bit, Ness," he called over his shoulder. "It's a crack-up."

The boys all thought so but Vanessa rolled her eyes. She'd set her cell phone to vibrate, and when it started to hum she fought the temptation to answer.

What if it's important?

What if it's Tristan?

That made no sense after they'd ended on such a blaring note of finality. There was no reason for him to call and nothing left to say. That didn't stop her heart plummeting with disappointment when she picked up and heard Jack Cartwright's deep voice.

"I don't know what you got up to with Thorpe last night and, frankly, I don't want to know. But you pulled it off. His lawyer just called to let me know. He's dropped the contest."

There was a huge moment's hollowness. Then Jack saying, "Hello? Are you there? Vanessa?"

"No, no. I'm here."

"I don't hear you screaming with jubilation. I must say I'm disappointed in you."

"I think I'm just numb," she said honestly. "Maybe the joy beans will kick in later."

Although she doubted it. She could hardly confess that she'd known his decision earlier that morning. Not without admitting she'd possibly influenced the result between the Egyptian cotton sheets of the Marabella's Columbus suite.

Her cheeks grew hot, her body restive with remembering. Driving home from Twelve Oaks she talked herself into calling Tristan. To thank him for following through on his promise so promptly.

But the receptionist informed her that Mr. Thorpe had checked out that morning.

He was gone and it was over. Two years of torment and trouble at his hands were finally finished, and all Vanessa felt was a gaping chasm of aloneness.

Twelve

"Did you hear that David Duvall passed away last night?"

Abby shared the news of Mary's grandfather's death as soon as Vanessa and Felicity joined her on the country club terrace the following Wednesday. They had all just attended a social committee meeting, finalizing details for the Eastwick Ball. Abby had asked them to stay and have a drink with her as she had some news.

Vanessa had expected an update on the investigation into Bunny's death so this came as something of a shock. "How is Mary?" she asked. "She seemed very strained at the wedding. Maybe it was because of her grandfather…"

"He's been sick a long time, but a family death is never

easy." As soon as she finished speaking, Felicity winced and put her hand over Abby's on the table. "Me and my mouth. I'm sorry."

"Please, you don't have to cosset me." Abby smiled gamely. "I actually asked you to stay because I have some news about Mother. I wanted to tell you before you read it in tomorrow's newspaper."

"Has there been an arrest?"

"No." The corners of Abby's mouth tightened. "But the police have finally acknowledged that they're treating this as a murder investigation."

"Oh, Abby." Felicity squeezed her friend's hand. "Are you okay with this?"

"I'm pleased they appear to be doing something about my suspicions."

"Has there been new evidence?" Vanessa asked.

Abby nodded. "The police recovered a single pill near Mom. The tests show it's a placebo made to look like digitalis. I couldn't work out why no medication showed up in Mom when I'd *seen* her taking her pills!"

"Someone had swapped them for these placebos?"

"That would also explain the disappearance of her pill case."

"If the murderer took it."

Felicity and Vanessa swapped shocked looks. Up until now they'd known of Abby's suspicions, but this sounded like hard evidence. And whoever did this had to have access to Bunny's pill case and Bunny's home. They'd also known where to find the journals.

"It has to be someone we know," Vanessa mused. "Someone close to Bunny."

"The police are still trying to locate the woman Edith heard arguing with Mom that day."

"It is odd that no one saw this mystery woman."

They all agreed. Vanessa cleared her throat. "There's something odd about the letters, too."

She felt the other women's eyes on her, waiting for her to explain.

"You know the letter I mentioned, addressed to Tristan but not demanding any money....well, he received a second one."

"When did this happen?" Felicity asked.

"Last week. That's why he crashed the wedding."

"I wondered what was going on between you two. When Lily said you left with him, I thought we should report your abduction."

Vanessa felt heat in her throat and her face. "It wasn't an abduction." *It was more of a seduction, really.* "We worked out a few misunderstandings, and he's dropped the will contest."

"Are you for real?"

"That's wonderful, Vanessa. You must be thrilled!"

"I'm relieved, mainly."

Felicity was studying her with curiosity. "Those must have been some misunderstandings. Were they connected with the letters?"

"Yes, actually. The second letter was supposed to prove my adultery. There was a photo and a list of dates and places where I met this man."

"Someone followed you? And wrote all that down? How sick."

Vanessa nodded. She felt sick thinking about that

level of surveillance, all unnoticed. "Anyway, Tristan has given both letters to the police," she assured Abby. "In case they're connected to the missing diaries."

"But you don't think they are?"

Vanessa shrugged. "I don't know. There's no demand for money. They're just...odd."

The other women considered this for a long moment before Felicity spoke. "And the photo? Who did this creep think you were seeing on the sly?"

Felicity's phrasing was particularly apt and made it easier than Vanessa had anticipated to swallow her resistance to sharing this part of her life. "My brother."

"You have a brother?" Abby asked. "I don't think you've ever mentioned him."

"I haven't. That's the thing."

That hadn't been so hard, Vanessa decided afterward. Felicity and Abby had been supportive and understanding and nonjudgmental. Driving home from the country club she felt her whole body sigh with relief.

Finally.

Maybe now she could muster some enthusiasm for the rest of her life. With the lifting of conservation orders on Stuart's estate, she could start executing his wishes for distributing his wealth. She had her friends, her committee work, Lew and Twelve Oaks. Everything would soon fall back into a routine and life would resume its calm, orderly pattern.

By the time she walked in her front door, Vanessa was feeling a renewed serenity. She paused in the foyer and called for Gloria. The sound of her voice echoed through the downstairs rooms, unanswered.

She crossed to the library and opened the door to peer inside. No Gloria and she almost missed the parcel sitting in the center of her desk.

A belated birthday present?

She had no idea who it could be from.

Intrigued, she crossed the room and picked up the unmarked gift box. She was still turning it over in her hands, a frown between her brows, when Gloria appeared.

"Ah, you found it," she said.

"Yes, but what is it?" Vanessa asked. "And where did it come from?"

"A delivery man brought it. Just an hour or so ago."

"Who's it from?"

"I don't have X-ray vision. Why don't you open it and see?"

Of course she should open it. Ms. Pragmatist would have had the sucker unstuck and unwrapped and the thank-you card written by now.

She drew a quick breath and started on the box. She had a strange sensation in her belly, a feeling of momentousness that made Ms. P. shake her head in despair.

Inside the box was a tissue-wrapped…something. She peeled away the layers with shaky fingers to reveal a Lladro figurine.

"It's your *Girl with Flowers*," Gloria said unnecessarily. "Who could have sent that?"

She almost missed the card tucked inside the box. Three lines in a bold hand.

Setting things right.

A peace offering, an apology,

A goodbye.

The words he'd offered in the kitchen, the day he turned a simple kiss on the hand into sensual bliss. Gently her thumb stroked over the illegible scrawl of a signature that swam before her eyes.

"Are you all right, Nessa?"

She turned the delicate little girl over in her hands and the memory of him doing the same, that first day in the keeping room, washed through her in a debilitating wave. No, she was not all right. She was trembling with emotion, inside and out, so much so that she had to sit down.

"How on earth did he find her?" she murmured. It couldn't have been easy to locate a piece cast seventeen years ago, especially in less than a week. How had he even known which figurine to look for? Someone must have helped. Her gaze settled on Gloria. "Did you have anything to do with it?"

"All I did was point him in the right direction. It'd be just like him to hare off on a wild goose chase."

"I didn't want him chasing after anything!"

"After all he put you through?" Gloria retorted. "It was the least he could do."

Vanessa tried to summon up the same righteous indignation as her loyal housekeeper. Then she might be able to repack the gift and send it back. Hadn't she told him that the figurine itself meant nothing? Its symbolism was indelibly imprinted on her life. She didn't need a place-keeper anymore and certainly not this…substitute.

Except her heart—poor, foolish, smitten creature—
recognized this gesture as much more than replacing a
broken ornament. The figurine itself didn't matter; his
act in sending the gift did. It represented an apology for
the discord of the last two years and for the way he'd
confronted her in her home and for every misconception and accusation and altercation.

Setting things right mattered to him—he'd told her so.

She should accept that, send a prettily worded—and
sincere—thank-you note, and get on with her life.

That is what she wanted, right? That's what she'd
told him that morning in his hotel suite. In the days
since, she'd even reconciled her wretched romantic side
with that reality. She'd put Tristan Thorpe behind her,
she'd moved on with her own life, concentrating on her
true priorities.

But her gaze kept returning to the little note.

Goodbye.

Was that what she really wanted? Now, like this,
when she'd been less than truthful? Or was it her turn
to set one last thing straight...?

Tristan was in a cab en route to the airport when his
phone buzzed. He knew it was her by the telltale little
sound of her inhalation when he answered. His body did
the complete *it's-Vanessa* rattle and hum before she got
anywhere near saying those words.

"It's Vanessa. I'm glad I caught you. The hotel told
me you'd checked out and I was afraid—" She paused,
sucked in an audible breath, slowed the headlong rush
of her voice "I thought I might have missed you."

"I'm still in the city. Stuck in traffic."

"I suppose the rain isn't helping. Not at this time of morning."

"Wet up there, too?"

"It's just started to close in."

Tristan shut his eyes and shook his head. Had it come down to this? Stilted small talk about the weather interspersed by awkward seconds of silence?

Yes, he answered himself in the next cumbersome pause. *It had.*

"What do you want, Vanessa?" he asked on a sigh.

"I want to thank you for the figurine. I can't imagine how you found the *Girl with Flowers.* You must have gone to a lot of trouble and that wasn't necessary but… thank you. It's lovely and I…" He pictured the hitch of her shoulders she'd give as her voice trailed off, and in those last husky words he also heard the threat of tears. The image—of that distinctive Vanessa gesture, of her beautiful eyes misty green with moisture, of her dimpled chin lifting as she struggled for control—squeezed all the air from his lungs.

For a long beat of time he couldn't speak. Couldn't do anything but sit there, fighting the urge to offer up sentiments she didn't want to hear and which his battered pride wouldn't allow him to utter. He felt like one big, harsh, frustrated bundle of regret.

Finally, he managed to shrug and say, "It's the least I could do."

She gave an odd little laugh. "Funnily enough, Gloria said the exact same thing."

Funnily enough, that didn't surprise him. "And what about you, Vanessa?"

"Oh, I think it's a start."

"Didn't you read the note? I thought it was more of an end."

"And your way of setting things right."

Yeah, except nothing felt right. Not about leaving, not about the way things were between them. Not about this whole agonizing goodbye conversation from the back of a cab. That was all kinds of wrong.

"Before you go—" her voice, soft and resolute, cut through the rough storm of his thoughts "—there is something I need to set right."

"I'm listening."

"That morning in your hotel suite, you suggested I was running scared but I wasn't so much scared as full-out terrified." She proffered that with another rueful laugh. "I hadn't had the time—or perhaps the courage—to work out what I was doing there with you or what should happen next. It was too much, too intense, and then you hit me with wanting to meet Lew. I'm not used to sharing that part of my life. I'm not used to sharing anything quite like I did with you that night."

"Yet you did. To prove a point."

"No. I didn't sleep with you to prove anything."

That admission hit Tristan with sledgehammer force, somewhere in the region of his heart. He rolled his head back and pinched the bridge of his nose, as if that might contain the giant ball of ache inside him. "Are you sure about that?"

"Yes," she said with a quiet conviction that resonated right through the phone.

"Why did you sleep with me? Because I've been thinking about it and your explanation is the only one that makes any sense."

"Does it have to make sense? When it seems like there was no choice."

What the hell? "I gave you the chance to back out. There was no force."

"I'm not talking about force, Tristan, I'm talking about desire. At the beach…the way you touched me, the way you kissed me, the way you looked at me. You didn't have to take me back to your hotel room. You could have done anything you wanted, any way you wanted, right there."

"Beach sex is overrated."

"While making love," she countered, "isn't. At least not in my limited experience."

"Why are you telling me this?" he asked roughly, because, hell, in two hours he'd be in the air, heading back to Australia. He didn't want to think about the passion of that night, the sweet taste of her mouth, the hot silk of her body. He couldn't afford to ponder her choice of words. Not sex but *making love*. "Why now, when I'm about to leave?"

"Do you have to go?"

He couldn't have heard her right. Probably because of the rush of blood in his ears, the roar of hope racing to fill every raw aching hollow in his body. "Why would I want to stay?"

"I'm going to Twelve Oaks this afternoon. If you are still interested, I would like you to come with me." She paused, as if to gather breath or courage or both. And when she spoke again, her voice was strong and steady and blessedly sure. "I would like you to meet my brother."

He wasn't coming.

Vanessa waited an hour longer than the usual travel time from the city before resigning herself to that fact. She should have expected as much by his silence after her invitation, a silence she'd filled by blabbering about the rain and the traffic and how long the drive may take and how much Lew would enjoy meeting him and how much she looked forward to seeing him. Then she realized that his cell had dropped out.

He'd heard her invitation, though, she was sure of that. He hadn't come because he was going home. He had meant the goodbye on the note and there would be no other.

Still she waited another half hour after the extra hour, and then she sucked back the useless tears and drove up to Lexford alone. Sure, the bottom had fallen out of her world but she'd promised Lew. She would keep on doing what she had always done—looking out for him, building her days around his care, using Stuart's estate to help others in the same situation she'd found herself in before his timely intervention.

Except with every passing mile the ache of wanting what she'd witnessed between Lily and Jack, Emma and Garrett, Felicity and Reed—that devoted connection which she'd thought she could live without in her own life—grew thicker in her chest. She attempted to summon up the voice of pragmatism, to remind herself that this yearning was for a chimera of a relationship. They barely knew each other. A couple of weeks, a series of clashes, a belated understanding and one long, hot night of passion.

"This is not a relationship," she said out loud. "Will you please back me up here?"

But Ms. P. remained ominously silent while the rain continued to fall, enclosing Vanessa in a bleak gray curtain to match her mood.

Lost in her desolate musing, she didn't notice the car tailing her until its headlights flicked on and off, on and off, catching her attention in the rearview mirror. Thinking *police,* she instantly slowed and started to pull over. She hadn't been speeding, but did she miss a yield sign or…

Her heart gave a huge stutter as she glanced into her mirror again. Not a police car. No siren or flashing lights, just the warm yellow-tinged beam of headlights from a silvery gray sedan following her onto the shoulder, and a matching bright glow in the center of her chest as a tall, broad, familiar figure stepped from the driver's seat.

Fingers quaking with a nervous blend of hope and relief, Vanessa fumbled to release her seatbelt. Her door opened and somehow she spilled from the seat and straight into the hard wall of Tristan's body. For a moment that was enough: the familiar breadth of his chest, the shelter of his large frame, the sweet scent of rain on his skin. Then his arms folded around her, holding her close against the drumming beat of his heart, and she knew that nothing would be enough again, not without the comforting strength of those arms.

Despite the cool drizzle of rain neither moved for a long time, except to burrow closer, to stroke the wet strands of hair from her face, to wrap her closer into the hard heat of his body. This might not be a relationship, Vanessa thought, but it felt so perfectly right and so full of promise.

She closed her eyes and for several seconds imagined that it could be this simple; that walking into his arms might magically fix everything she'd feared would come between them. It wouldn't. After those precious few seconds, she raised her face from his chest. "When you hadn't arrived after all those hours, I thought you'd gone home."

"I thought I was home," he said with heart-stopping simplicity. A frown creased his brow. "Are you crying?"

"No."

It wasn't quite a lie, since the tears were part of the smile that formed on her lips and arrowed to her heart…or perhaps it was the other way around. When he thumbed the betraying moisture from her cheek, the smile swelled to fill her chest. "It must be the rain."

He turned his intense-eyed focus from her face to survey the sky. "I need to get you out of this."

"We're already wet," she countered, not ready to relinquish her position. "Besides, this isn't cold rain."

At least it didn't feel that way to her, not with his body heat seeping into her flesh.

When he looked set to argue the point, Vanessa held a hand up to his lips. Her expression turned serious. "You said you were home—do you mean to stay?"

"If you want me to."

Her heart started to pound. Of course she wanted him…but could it be that simple?

After another second she felt a change in his posture and his gaze narrowed on her face. "That is why you called me? Or did I read that message wrong, too."

"No, oh, no. I called because I wanted you to stay." She drew a quick breath, suddenly more nervous than she had ever been in her life. "I want you to stay, Tristan. I want to take this chance at…at whatever it is we might have together."

"What do you think that might be?"

Vanessa frowned, not understanding what he was getting at. "I don't know."

"I didn't walk away from that airport today for nothing."

"The morning in your hotel room, you said no promises."

"That morning in my hotel room, you said you had everything you wanted," he countered. "Do you want what you've got…or do you want that and more?"

A week ago the notion of *more* had terrified her. She hadn't wanted the intensity and emotional roller coaster. She hadn't wanted to open herself up to the possibility of a love this powerful and breathtaking.

Now, looking up into the intense blue of Tristan's eyes, she saw every vestige of her quiet, restful, ordered life slide away. A frisson of fear chased in its wake but she lifted her chin and moistened her lips. "I would very much like the more," she said. "If it's with you."

He kissed her, possibly because he'd been waiting too long to do so, and possibly because the magnitude of this step had tightened her expression. He kissed the rain from her lips and then from her lashes, her cheeks, the point of her chin. Then he kissed her mouth with a tenderness that sang through her blood. Everything else, every worry and every anxiety, melted in the restrained promise of that kiss.

"There will be a lot more, Vanessa. And there will be promises."

"You said no p—"

"I lied."

She swallowed. "In what way?"

"I promise to be here for you and your brother, in whatever capacity you want. I promise to support you and protect you." He stroked a thumb across her lips and the look on his face almost caused her knees to buckle. "I'd also promise to love you, but I'm afraid that might terrify you."

Strangely, it didn't…and that worried her just a little. "We don't know each other well enough for promises. What if this doesn't work out? What if we keep on clashing the way we have always done? What if this is just—"

He kissed her again, this time for a very long while. It silenced Vanessa's worries once more and she could have gone on kissing him for days, weeks, months, but the rain started to fall more heavily and he lifted his head to glare at the sky again.

"I need to get you out of this rain before you drown." He drew her back to her car, but before opening the door he paused. "We mightn't have known each other long, but I know you well enough."

Well enough that he'd stayed, to support her, to protect her, to be her rock. To love her.

The notion wasn't half as terrifying as she'd imagined. It rolled through her and settled somewhere deep and vital. *So this is love*, she thought on a note of wonder.

It felt like something she would like to get used to.

She went up on her toes to press a kiss to his mouth.

"What was that for?"

"Just something I'd like to get used to," she said with a smile. She had a feeling it wouldn't take too long to work up to more. "Would you like to meet my brother now?"

"I thought you'd never ask."

It was the perfect answer and the perfect start to a new happiness she didn't bother trying to hide. She had earned this happiness—it was hers, bought and paid for, and delivered from Australia, with love.

* * * * *

THE ONCE-A-
MISTRESS WIFE

BY
KATHERINE GARBERA

Dear Reader,

Scandals, secrets and a very sexy man from her past are all a part of this new life that Mary Duvall is carving out for herself. Since I married my sweetheart when I was twenty-one, there's not much scandal lingering in my past, but I loved the fact that Mary's life abounds with it. Her hero, Kane Brentwood, is a British gentleman who has never doubted that the one thing he wants in his life is Mary, whether as his mistress or as his wife. In my mind Kane is a mix between the devastatingly handsome Hugh Grant and the supersexy Clive Owen. Kane has all of Hugh's urban suavity and Clive's arrogant determination to win the woman he loves at all costs—like he did in the movie *Closer*—especially since Kane mirrors the same determination when it comes to Mary.

Enjoy!

Katherine

Katherine Garbera is the award-winning, bestselling author of more than twenty books and has been nominated for *Romantic Times* BOOKclub's Career Achievement Awards in Series Fantasy and Series Adventure. Katherine recently moved to the Dallas area, where she lives with her husband and their two children. Visit Katherine on the web at www.katherinegarbera.com.

This book is dedicated to the ladies of Nation Drive—
Kim, Michele and Kathy—who've made me feel
welcome and at home in Texas.

Acknowledgments:

Thanks to the other Society Wives ladies who made
working on this book such a pleasure...Maureen,
Metsy, Pat, Alison and Bronwyn.

Also a special thanks to Wanda Ottewell and Melissa
Jeglinski, for asking me to participate in this fun series!

One

Mary Duvall stood over the open casket of her grandfather, David Duvall. Tears burned the back of her eyes, but she kept them in check, very conscious that Grandfather David had always wanted her to be composed in public. That's why she'd closed the doors to the viewing room and entered it alone.

The old Mary would have wept loudly and cried her grief with sobs and moans, doing everything in her power to get those emotions out. But now she buttoned them down. Ignored everything but the need to touch his face one last time.

She touched his cold, makeup-covered skin and shivered inside. She felt so alone. She *was* all alone

now. Her parents had died years ago in a car accident—not that they'd ever been close. And her
younger brother, their perfect child, had been in the
car with them—also gone.

She liked the new life she was carving for herself
in Eastwick, Connecticut, at her grandfather's behest.
She'd returned from Paris when she'd learned his
health was failing. He'd offered to make her his heir
if she proved she was no longer the rebellious wild
child he remembered.

"I'm going to make you proud, Grandfather. No
more embarrassment over my behavior."

She leaned down, brushing her lips over his dry
forehead and wishing for just one second that he
could embrace her. Her childhood had been difficult
to say the least and Grandfather David had been as
disapproving as everyone else in the Duvall clan, but
he'd always hugged her as she left.

He was the only one to ever do anything like that.
She would miss him more than she'd realized.

A knock on the door interrupted her farewell.

She glanced at her watch. Damn, it was almost
time for the public viewing. No doubt her cousins
would be outside demanding some private time with
a man they cared about only for his money.

Mary wanted to use the Duvall estate to benefit
others. She intended to establish a trust that would
be used to create neonatal units at hospitals in lower-income areas. She also hoped to sponsor an art-

focused summer camp for underprivileged children. She had never been encouraged to paint as a child, even though her earliest memories were of having a paintbrush in her hand. She loved to create new worlds on canvas.

Her work was garnering attention in Europe and she enjoyed the money she'd made selling the serial rights to several of her pieces for a print series.

But for now, she had the viewing to get through. Before opening the door, she tucked the short note she'd written last night into the breast pocket of his suit, under his handkerchief, right over his heart.

Then she wiped the moisture from beneath her eyes and confronted her second cousins. Channing and Lorette Moorehead were the children of her grandfather's sister.

"How touching. I almost believe you cared for the old man," Channing said, escorting his sister Lorette to the casket.

"I did care for him," Mary said.

"Then why did you spend so many years breaking his heart?" Lorette asked.

Mary swallowed hard, biting back a retort that wouldn't be ladylike. Wouldn't fit the image that Grandfather wanted her to portray.

"We made our peace, Grandfather and I."

"You may have fooled Uncle David, but we aren't convinced you've changed. I will be keeping an eye on you," Channing said.

He was almost ten years older than she was, and from her earliest memories he'd always been a pompous ass. She had no fondness for Channing, but Lorette, who was only two years older than Mary, had been a close friend when they were younger. They'd roamed all over Grandfather's mansion playing games and getting into trouble. It had all ended when Lorette had turned ten and declared herself too old for childish pursuits.

"I'll leave you two to your private grieving."

The anteroom was almost empty except for a few of her friends. Their long history and regular luncheons had garnered them the name the Debs Club.

Everyone in their group seemed to be getting engaged or married; something Mary had no desire to do herself. She'd been deeply in love with a man once, and when he'd left her to marry the "right" kind of woman, she'd promised herself she'd never live with that kind of pain again.

Yet another example of how her wild lifestyle— which wasn't really that wild—had resulted in her being alone. The problem was that for most of her life Mary had never wanted to follow the rules. Almost in contradiction to the plain name—and possibly plain aspirations—her parents had given her at birth, Mary had come out of the womb a rebel.

But not any longer. She'd paid a high price for her rebelliousness, and her deathbed promise to Grandfather David meant she'd toe the line from now on.

Mary started toward her friends. They all wore black for mourning, and Mary appreciated having them here. Maybe she wasn't completely alone. She did have her friends, and they'd proven to be a solid support to her in a way that she'd never experienced before.

The outer door opened before she reached her friends, and she turned to greet the newcomer. The blood rushed to her head and she heard the pounding of her own heartbeat in her ears as she recognized the one man she'd never thought to see again.

Kane Brentwood—English lord and her ex-lover.

"Kane?"

"Mary," he said. Just her name in that deep voice of his never failed to send shivers coursing through her body.

She couldn't face him now. Not today, when she was struggling to keep her composure carefully in place. Not when she was so close to losing it.

At the sight of him, she was overwhelmed with the weight of the secrets between them. Secrets that, if revealed, would cost her everything— Grandfather's inheritance, Kane's respect and her own hard-won peace.

She tried to regain her composure, but she saw stars dancing in front of her eyes as he approached her. And then everything went black.

Kane Brentwood caught Mary just before she hit the floor. He was aware of the murmuring of voices behind him, but he didn't pay attention to anyone save the woman in his arms. His woman. She hadn't been taking very good care of herself. She'd lost weight and her skin was pale. He wondered if she'd mended bridges with her grandfather and what that had cost her.

He cupped her face. "Mary."

Her eyes blinked open, and he stared into that familiar Caribbean-blue color, reminding him of the month they'd spent at his vacation home in the British Virgin Islands. "Mary-Belle, are you okay?"

"Kane?"

"Yes, darling."

As she looked up at him, confusion knitted her brow. "I'm not your darling anymore."

A spear of anger went through him and he had to tamp down on his instinctive response, which was to take her in his arms and prove that she was still his. To prove that Mary would react to him the way she had from the first moment they met. But she was a married woman now, and he knew the way she felt about married people and affairs.

"We can discuss that later," he said.

A spark lit her eyes, the kind that in the past had always led to a spirited argument and then eventually to the bedroom. "Will your wife take part in the discussion?"

"I'm divorced. And your husband?"

She flushed and shook her head. "No husband."

No husband. She was free. He felt a surge of possessive determination. Now that he had her back in his arms, he wasn't going to let her go again. He'd done his bit for family and lineage, and that had cost him—more than he ever wanted this woman to know. They were both available again, and he was suddenly determined not to screw up the way he had before. He would not lose her again.

"Mary? Are you okay?"

He glanced over his shoulder to see four women walking toward him with a group of men a few steps behind. He tightened his hold on Mary.

"I'm fine, Emma. I didn't sleep well last night."

He wondered how much of that was due to her child. He didn't know much about the little blighters, but every book he'd read had said that they were time-consuming.

There were dark circles under her eyes, and he wished for a moment he still had the right to carry her out of this room, to find a private place. But he didn't. He lowered her to the ground, deliberately torturing himself by allowing her body to rub against his.

There were too many people around to have the discussion they needed to have. And he wanted—no, needed—to simply hold this woman who looked too fragile.

She took a step away from him, but he held onto her wrist.

"What are you doing?" she asked.

"Claiming what is mine," he said, stating the truth of why he was in Eastwick, especially now that he knew there was no husband. When he'd first read the announcement of David Duvall's death in the *Wall Street Journal,* he'd barely taken note of the fact—until he'd seen Mary's name listed as next of kin.

He'd been quietly searching for her for over a year now. His men hadn't been able to find any trace of her at the Paris apartment building where he'd last known her to live.

"I'm not yours anymore," she said again, tugging hard and pulling her hand away from him.

"Come with me," he said.

"Why?"

"I want to speak to you," he said, ignoring her friends.

"We are speaking, Mr. Brentwood."

"Alone," he said, using his hold on her waist to draw her closer to him. She had always had the ability to make him forget all rules of good breeding and react like a man. He felt the urge to do something horribly crass, such as toss her over his shoulder and carry her out of this room.

"I don't think that's a good idea."

He should never have put her on her feet. He should have kept her in his arms…where she belonged. "Don't push me, Mary-Belle. I'm not in the mood for it."

She stiffened at the nickname and gave him a hard

glare. He lowered his head, brushing his lips against hers. A surge of arousal shot through his body as her mouth opened under his—the same way it always had. He slipped his tongue between her lips, hungry for her taste. It had been too damned long since he'd sated himself on Mary.

Someone cleared their throat, and Mary pulled away from him. Kane kept his hand on her waist and gave the man who was glaring at them a withering stare.

"Who is this?" the man asked. He had thinning hair and a pinched expression on his face. He looked at Mary with ill-disguised loathing, and Kane pulled her more fully against his side, under his shoulder. Offering her his protection.

She elbowed him in the ribs, and he frowned at her but did not release her. Mary had always been so ethereal, dancing in and out of his life in a way that made him suspect he'd never be able to hold her for long. He would not waste this opportunity.

"Channing, I'd like you to meet Kane Brentwood. We met when I was living in London. Kane, this is my cousin Channing Moorehead, and his sister Lorette."

He shook hands with both of them. "I'm sorry for your loss."

"We were very close to Uncle David," Lorette said. "We've always lived our lives in an exemplary manner…to show our respect for him."

"We're all impressed, Lorette," Emma said with a touch of sarcasm.

Mary smiled gratefully at her friend, and Kane realized, with his usual sense of great timing where Mary was concerned, he'd bungled into a moment where he shouldn't have. There was a real tension between Mary and her cousins—something not unlike the tension between him and his family.

Lorette turned toward Emma to say something and Mary quietly withdrew, stepping away from the others in the anteroom. The behavior was so unlike the Mary he'd known, but grief did make people vulnerable.

He cupped her elbow and drew her farther away from the others. "What's their problem?"

"Don't worry about it, Kane. It has nothing to do with you."

"I'm not so sure you're right, Mary-Belle. I'm not going to simply walk now that I know we're both free."

"I'm a different woman now, Kane. I have an image to uphold," she said, glancing over her shoulder to make sure that no one was near. "One that makes it impossible to be your mistress."

"What image? I saw your work in a London gallery last spring. Your canvases were always remarkable, but there is something…breathtaking about these new ones."

"Thank you, Kane. But it's not my image as an artist that I'm concerned with. No one here knows anything about that part of my life."

Kane couldn't believe that she'd keep something that was such an integral part of who she was a secret. Mary had lived and breathed painting the entire time they'd been together—almost ten years. He'd had to resort to being her model a time or two to get her attention.

"What image are you concerned with, darling? That of being a mother?"

"No. My child was stillborn," she said softly, and he felt the pain in her words. He wanted to comfort her, but she shook her head.

"I was speaking of the Duvall family image. I came home to claim my heritage, Kane. A heritage that isn't as old as yours but is every bit as stringent. I have to go now. Thanks for coming."

He nodded and let her walk away. He wasn't sure what to make of the new Mary or her words. But one thing was very certain—now that he'd found her, he wasn't leaving Eastwick without laying a claim on her. The kind of claim he should have made when they'd first met, instead of letting his own arrogance force them into roles from which there was no escape.

The funeral wasn't long but went by very slowly for Mary. Afterward, everyone came to the Duvall mansion for the wake. In the midst of the crowd and condolences, Mary retreated to Grandfather David's study for a few moments of solitude. She sat in his big leather chair that smelled faintly of the tobacco he'd always smoked. She inhaled deeply, wrapping her senses in her grandfather's memory.

There was a knock on the door, and Mary knew the interruption signaled she'd been gone from the wake long enough. She answered the summons to find Emma, Caroline and Lily standing there.

"We thought we'd find you hiding out," Emma said, closing the door firmly once they were all inside.

"I'm not hiding," Mary said. Though she suspected her friends knew that she was lying, they'd never call her on it. And she needed time away from the pressure of making nice to all those people. After she was forced to be her society self for too long, she felt an itching deep inside to do something bold and crazy. To shake things up. She had no idea how her friends could survive the daily grind that was society life.

"Not even from Channing? God, that man is an ass," Caroline said.

"Maybe. Is he looking for me? Is that why you came to find me?" Mary asked.

"No Felicity and Vanessa are running interference with Channing, and Abby cornered Lorette. We're here to find out more about that dreamy man with the British accent."

The last thing she wanted to talk about was Kane. She didn't even know where to begin or what to say to her good friends. "That couldn't wait until the next Debs lunch?"

"Who knows when we'll have time for the next one with everyone getting engaged and planning

weddings," Caroline said, her eyes glittering with
that effervescent joy she brought to everything.

"There's really not much to tell. I met him when
I was in London."

"When?" Emma asked.

"My second week there. I was working in Harrods," Mary said. She remembered the way he'd
stopped at the display of women's scarves and lingered
for almost thirty minutes, never once pretending he
was going to buy one but just flirting with her.

"And that's it?" Caroline's voice held a disbeliev-
ing tone. "That was ten years ago. The man today
looked like he was more to you than a customer."

"He was. We had an…affair," Mary said because
she thought her friends would understand that better
than knowing that she'd lived in an apartment he'd
paid for and that she'd made herself available to him
whenever he'd wanted her. She'd been a kept woman.

"I knew there was more between you," Lily said.
"There was something about he way he looked at
you. And that kiss…"

Mary's lips still tingled, but she was trying very
hard to forget that. To forget everything about Kane
except the fact that he was no longer a part of her life.

"I haven't seen him in almost three years." To be
honest, she didn't want to remember the last time
she'd seen Kane.

She'd been so hurt and angry that she'd said something she never should have. When she'd returned to

Eastwick, Grandfather had said that her behavior had caused pain to others and herself, and she'd immediately thought of Kane. If she'd had the comportment then that she had now, maybe things would have turned out differently and she would still have her son…alive today.

"He definitely looked like a man who wanted to rekindle the relationship with you," Caroline stated.

"I can't. Not now. I have too much going on."

"Sure you can," Lily said. "You could at least explore the possibility."

Mary shook her head. Kane wasn't going to be a part of her life again. He was her weakness, and she knew if she allowed him back into her life, she'd have to face her past and the lies she once told. Lies that still haunted her.

Two

Kane was up early the next morning, jogging along the beach of Long Island Sound. He'd spent a restless night trying to come up with something he could use to force Mary back into his life. He knew that it was going to be hard to convince her, but he wasn't a man who was used to failure.

He'd left the family import business when he'd had his marriage to Victoria annulled. His relatives had been appalled that he hadn't done his duty and stayed married to the woman, even though their marriage had been strained from the beginning. At his family's response, Kane had realized that he meant nothing more to them than his role as heir.

He'd taken that opportunity to make a complete break with them.

He'd been living in Manhattan for the last year and a half, where he'd taken a small investment firm and turned it into one of the up-and-comers in the financial world.

He glanced at the horizon, gauging how much farther he'd run before turning back, when he spotted a familiar figure—Mary. She was sitting on the sand and staring out at the ocean. He slowed his pace to a walk to get his breathing under control before he got to her.

"Good morning, darling."

"Morning, Kane," she said, tipping her head back to look up at him. The sun left her face in shadows but brought out the warm highlights in her dark hair. Her locks whipped around her face in the breeze, and in that moment she strongly resembled the woman he'd once known. No longer buttoned-up and perfectly coiffed.

"What are you doing here?"

He put his hands on his hips, standing over her. "Jogging. I'm afraid I'm a bit sweaty. Do you mind if I join you?"

"Would it matter if I said yes?"

"It would." He was a man used to having his way. Things happened for him because he refused to take no for an answer. But with Mary, this time he wanted to be more accommodating. If she didn't want his company, he'd leave.

She rested her chin on her drawn–up knees, staring once again at the ocean and its endlessly cycling waves. "It's a public beach, I can't stop you from sitting."

He dropped to his haunches in front her, his eyes meeting hers. "I'm not interested in the beach, Mary-Belle. I'm interested in your company."

"Why? I thought we hashed this all out years ago," she said, her hands going to her hair and trying to pull it out of her face.

"We didn't," he said, shifting to sink to the sand next to her.

She sighed and the wind carried the sound away from them. He wished that the breeze could as easily clear away their past, yet at the same time he wouldn't give up those years they'd spent together for anything. Just the ending. If he could change the way things had ended he'd be a happier man.

"I can't go back to what we once had," she said.

"I'm not asking you to." He couldn't return either. He was no longer the man he'd been when he'd kept her as his mistress. Now he wanted…hell, he wasn't sure what he wanted aside from Mary back in his bed.

"Oh, well, that's— Why are you here, Kane?"

"Because you are."

"Don't say things like that."

"Even if they are true?"

"Especially if they are true. My life is complicated now. I have family obligations."

"To whom?"

"Grandfather's estate."

He rubbed the back of his neck. It was ironic that now that he was free of family responsibility, she wasn't. "What kind of obligations?"

"It's complicated. I want to use my inheritance to establish a foundation that will help lower-income families. I definitely want to create neonatal units for areas that can't otherwise afford them. And I'd also like to sponsor art programs in schools. I was also thinking to use some property that Grandfather has near the Finger Lakes in New York for a summer camp."

"That sounds ambitious. Where are you going to start?"

"I have no idea. I mean, I'm an artist, not a businessperson. Channing sits on the board of two foundations, so he knows how they operate, but I can't bring myself to ask him to help."

"Why not?"

"Because he and I don't get along. He's hoping I do something outrageous so the money will go to him and Lorette."

"Your inheritance has stipulations?"

"More than you could imagine."

"What kind?"

She made a face at him. "Let's just say that I have to be a model of social behavior."

"Not exactly the Mary I remember."

She tipped her head to the side and gave him a

genuine smile that affected his ability to breathe. He'd never forgotten how beautiful Mary was, but his attraction to her had been more than her physical appearance. It had been the zest she'd had for life. The way her laughter and smiles had filled the empty spaces in *his* life.

"Why are you staring at me, Kane?"

"Because I love your smile."

"My smile?"

He traced his finger down the side of her face, cupping her jaw and rubbing his thumb over her lips. "It's the first thing I noticed about you that day in Harrods."

"My mouth?" she asked, licking her lips, and he almost groaned out loud.

"Yes. Your lips are perfect for kissing."

She flushed a little, nibbling on her lower lip. "Yours are, too."

"Men don't have kissable lips." No one had ever said the things to him that Mary did. She didn't fear his reputation and wasn't intimidated by his wealth and family connections. She'd always treated him as though he were just another guy. And part of him liked the fact that with Mary he could simply be himself.

"Well, you do. Or maybe it's that you really know what you're about when you kiss me."

Her lips parted and her warm breath brushed over his fingers. He leaned down to capture her lips with his. At the contact, she sighed his name, opening her mouth for him. He moved to cradle her head between both of his hands.

He took his time with the kiss, relearning the taste of her and reacquainting her with his taste. He swept his tongue languidly into her mouth, pulling her more firmly into his arms and into his embrace. This was where she belonged.

Kane had always had the ability to transport her from the real world into one where only the two of them existed. In that world she'd do whatever he asked of her and never count the cost. But she couldn't afford to be that cavalier. Not now.

She pulled away from him, easily reading the signs of arousal in the man who'd been her first and only lover.

"Why did you pull away from me?"

"I can't be seen engaging in public displays of affection."

"That suits me. Let's go back to my hotel and engage in private displays of affection."

She shook her head. "Not today. I'm meeting with Grandfather's lawyer at ten. Then I'm interviewing financial planners to find someone to help me establish my trust."

"Who are you meeting with?"

"Someone from Merrill Lynch and someone from A.G. Edwards. I got their names from the phone book," she said. Truth was, she wasn't good with money and she didn't have any idea how to make her dream into reality.

"Would you consider letting me help you?"

Kane was brilliant with investments. He'd carefully invested the money he'd given her during their years together and turned it into a small fortune. She had used that money to support herself before returning to Eastwick. "Do you want to?"

"I wouldn't have offered otherwise," he said with a hint of a grin.

Her question had been inane. "You make it hard for me to think clearly."

"That's good to know."

He stood, offering her his hand and tugging her to her feet. He linked their hands together and started leading her away from the shore, toward her home.

"Will you have breakfast with me?" he asked.

His thumb rubbed over the back of her knuckles, and tingles spread up her arm. Her nipples tightened in response to his touch and his mere proximity. She always reacted this way in his presence. If she had breakfast with him, she'd probably end up making love with him. "No."

"Why not?" he asked, lifting her hand to his mouth and kissing the back of it.

She pulled her hand from his grasp. "I'm not getting involved with you again, Kane. Maybe you shouldn't help me with my inheritance."

"Why not? I'm probably more qualified than some stranger you rang up on the telephone."

"I think working with you will complicate things."

"Things? I'm not sure I understand."

She wanted to punch him in the arm. He frustrated her sometimes and she knew he was doing it deliberately right now. She took a deep breath, remembered that she always had to appear composed.

"I really don't want to give Channing or Lorette a reason to take me to court."

He took her shoulder, pulling her toward his body, wrapping one arm around her waist. He tipped her head back with his other hand, forcing her to look up at him. "I'm not taking no for an answer. I'm back in your life, and we'll take it slowly if that's what you want, but there is no way I'm leaving you again."

"Kane…don't say things like that to me."

"I mean them."

She couldn't reconcile what he was saying to what he'd said when they'd parted. His words still lingered in her mind, the emotional wounds he'd inflicted only half-healed.

"No, you don't. You told me that I was never anything more to you than a mistress, and I believed you. We don't have a great love affair to rekindle. Ours was a business-minded relationship. You paid for my living expenses and I took care of your sexual needs. That was it."

He cursed under his breath but didn't let go of her.

"It was never a business arrangement. Passion like ours can't be contained in something so tame."

Passion…one of her downfalls, if her grandfather was to be believed. Passion had a place only at her easel, where she channeled all of her rebelliousness into her art.

"Passion isn't part of my life now, Kane. You'd do well to remember that. I'm not the woman you knew. I've changed and I can't go back."

"How many times am I going to have to pay for making you my mistress?" he asked, his accent more clipped than normal. He sounded every inch the aristocrat when he talked that way.

"It's not about making you pay. Please, Kane, you have to leave. Go back home and forget about me."

"You may have changed, but I haven't. I'm still a very determined man. And you know I always get what I want."

"Do you have any idea how arrogant you sound?"

"Yes."

That startled a laugh out of her. Kane was still a mix of contradictions. A perfect gentleman in public and a total hedonist in private. She was so tempted to wrap herself around him and let him take her back to those carefree days in London. But she knew that she couldn't.

Something her grandfather had said when she'd returned to Eastwick forbade that. He'd said it was time to grow up and stop running from her responsibilities.

He'd reminded her she was the last Duvall. The only one to carry the mantle of her family's legacy.

"Arrogance isn't going to help you this time," she said, walking away from Kane.

"Yes, it is. You need me to set up this foundation of yours. It's the least I can do for an old friend."

Friend. She didn't know that they'd ever been friends. Friends shared things that she and Kane never had. They'd both played roles and lived in a world of their own making.

"Are you going to deny we were friends?" She heard the challenge in his voice.

"I'm not sure. But I will accept your offer of help. I know you're good with investments and I need someone I can trust."

Mary had a pounding headache after spending three hours in a conference room with her grandfather's attorney, Max Previn, and Channing. Max was a kind, older gentleman who had tried to smooth over the animosity that Channing had brought into the room, but it had been next to impossible.

She'd explained her plans for her inheritance to the lawyer and he'd approved, with the caveat that she remember the stipulations of the will. If at any time she did anything scandalous, the money would be forfeit and she'd have to repay any amount she'd already spent. She'd put the stipulations from her mind long enough to finish the meeting and leave the office.

Mary's car—a late-model Mercedes sedan—was parked at the curb, and she looked at that car feeling a new loathing for this life she'd been forced into. A part of her—the wild, crazy part—wanted to say the hell with it and walk away. She resented the restrictions and the instructions on how to behave that were being dictated from the grave.

But another bigger part of her mourned the baby she'd lost in childbirth, and she wanted to do what she could to ensure that no other woman ever had to live with that crushing feeling.

With her thoughts in such turmoil she couldn't get in the car and go home yet. Instead, she walked along the sidewalk in front of a row of shops until she reached her friend Emma's art gallery. Through the front window Mary could see Emma was with a customer, so she stayed outside. Featured in the display window was her latest print series—Paris. The series was composed of four different pieces that she'd simply titled for each of the seasons.

"Your work has really matured."

She glanced up at Kane, surprised to see him here. He wore a black pullover and a pair of faded jeans. His hair hung rakishly over one eye and he looked way too good. The realization stung because she didn't want to be attracted to him anymore.

"You think so? I still see room for improvement."

"The artist is never satisfied," he said, quoting back her own words.

Why did he remember so much of their time together? She certainly recalled those years in vivid detail, but that wasn't surprising since she'd lived for him for so long. She'd almost refused when he'd offered to set her up as his mistress, uncomfortable with putting herself in that situation. In the end, however, the chance to be with Kane under any circumstances had stayed her.

"What are you doing here?" she asked.

"Waiting for you. I'm going to design a financial plan for your foundation, remember?"

"Of course I remember. I meant, how did you find me here?"

"I was eating lunch across the way and spotted you."

"Oh. For a minute I thought you'd been stalking me."

The droll look on his face made her feel just a little bit foolish. But her response to him underscored something for her. She realized, for her own sanity, she couldn't allow Kane to get close enough to set up her foundation.

"I've changed my mind about accepting your help."

"Why?"

"Channing is going to be watching me like a hawk, trying to find some kind of chink in my new behavior so that he and his family can inherit instead of me."

"Darling, I'm the soul of discretion."

That was true, he always had been. It was her

reaction to Kane that worried her more than anything he would do. That and the secrets of their shared past—both the nature of their relationship and the truth she'd kept from him.

"You don't understand. If they found out I was your mistress, I'd lose everything."

"No one knows the truth except you and I," he said quietly.

She turned away from the window as Emma finished up with her customer. She didn't want her friend to see her with Kane in tow. She took a few steps away from the shop and he followed.

He put his arm around her shoulder, drawing her close to him as he directed them across the street to a small park with a gazebo in the center. Underneath the shade of a large maple tree he stopped, leaning back against the trunk.

"I'm sorry, Mary."

She was taken aback by his words. "For what?"

"For not doing things properly when we first met."

She shook her head. She'd been over their relationship so many times and she knew that a big part of her had liked being Kane's mistress. Had liked that her parents were outraged by it. She closed her eyes at how immature she'd been regardless of how sophisticated she'd felt.

"I think there's plenty of blame to share," she admitted.

He pulled her off balance and into his arms. Mary

was very aware that this was her third public embrace with him and that Channing had actually witnessed the other two.

She pushed against his chest. "Let me go."

"Not this time."

A part of her wanted a relationship with Kane. What had started as a way to outrage her parents and to rebel had turned into love on her part. And she'd never forgotten Kane. But she wasn't ready for the roller coaster of emotions being with him would entail. Especially now with so much at stake.

"I mean it. Let me go. If I'm seen like this, it will give them ammunition to use against me."

"I'll let you go on one condition."

"And that is?"

"You let me work with you to establish the trust."

"It would have to be strictly business. No more touching or kissing. I can't risk it."

"I can't make any promises to not touch you. But I can assure you that I will do my utmost to make sure no one else witnesses it."

"Then my answer will have to be no. Thanks, Kane." She paused. "I know that this sounds weird, but it's been really nice seeing you again."

She turned to walk away, but his low voice stopped her in her tracks. "That's not the answer I was looking for, Mary-Belle."

She glanced over her shoulder at him. He hadn't moved from his relaxed pose against the tree. He

looked every bit the brooding English lord she
knew him to be.

"Sorry to disappoint you."

"You won't for long. Since you're so concerned
about keeping me a secret…I'm going to blackmail
you into accepting my help."

Three

Kane watched the blood drain from Mary's face, saw her eyes narrow and her temper flare. He crossed his arms over his chest and waited for her to blast him.

She took two steps toward him and then stopped abruptly, taking several deep breaths, glancing up at the leaves of the maple until she had herself under control. The mask of her composure slipped over her features and the small glimpse he'd had of the real Mary disappeared.

"Who would you tell?"

"I think I'd start with your cousins."

"I don't believe you," she stated boldly.

Kane didn't believe it himself, but he knew he

couldn't let her walk away so easily again. Desperate times called for desperate measures, and all that. "It wouldn't be a decision I made lightly. But I'm not going to allow you to dismiss me from your life."

"Kane, please."

He'd heard those words from her so many different times. In the bedroom when she was begging him to touch her breasts. In that run-down flat in Paris that she'd fled to when he'd gotten engaged. And now when he was blackmailing her. He fought to keep focused on the end result: helping Mary and winning back a place in her life.

"I'm a different person now."

"I can see that," he said, catching a strand of her dark hair between his fingers. Her hair was still softer than silk, but now it was cut to her shoulders and straight, with none of the wild curls she used to have. It was one more thing about Mary that was so foreign to him, that he had to figure out what had caused the change.

"I want to get to know the new Mary. I'm a different man, too."

"You still seem arrogant to me."

"I am."

He wanted her. He'd been in a constant state of semiarousal since he'd read her name in the newspaper. Seeing her had brought all the lust to life in him.

"So what's it to be?" he asked.

She wrapped her arms around her waist and

glanced down at the ground. After a few moments she looked up at him. "I guess you can help me."

He felt a surge of triumph and absolutely no guilt. He wasn't about to let anything harm Mary again. As it was, she looked a little pale and her face was drawn. He knew that the process of grieving was a hard one, and Mary didn't seem to be taking care of herself. She was thinner than he'd ever seen her.

"Have you had lunch?"

"Um…what?" she asked, narrowing her eyes at him.

"Have you eaten?" He carefully enunciated each word.

He was rewarded for his silliness with a tiny smile.

"No, I haven't."

"Then we'll discuss the details of how to get started on your trust over lunch."

"Didn't you already eat?"

"Yes."

"I'll be fine. We can go back to Grandfather's—I mean, my house—and I'll grab a salad there."

"You're the boss."

"I wish. You aren't the type to let a woman tell you what to do," she said, walking across the park toward the parking lot.

"You're right," he said, falling into step beside her. "But I do always consider your desires."

She flushed. He knew her well enough to know the look on her face meant she was thinking of sex. His personality was dominant in the bedroom and out. He remembered building her to the edge of climax time and again, then waiting for her sweet cries of frustration before he finally plunged deep into her body and brought them both the relief they desperately needed.

He wrapped his arm around her waist, causing her to stop. She tipped her head back to look at him, and he noted that her pupils were dilated and her breathing was a little heavier than it had been earlier. "Do you want me, Mary-Belle?"

She opened her mouth, her small pink tongue darting out to wet her lips. "Yes."

That one little word washed over him like a satin glove on his naked skin. His blood pumped harder, his erection stirred, and his entire body longed for her. It had been too long since he'd last sated himself in her curvy body, and he wanted—no, needed—to do so again.

He lowered his head to taste her, to make up for the hurt he'd caused earlier when he'd threatened her. He'd never have the words she wanted to hear, but he would always show her with his actions what he really felt.

Their lips barely brushed. He rubbed his over hers, building the moment between them, knowing that they couldn't go much further than this one little kiss. But later, after she'd eaten and they'd discussed business…then he'd deliver on the promise of this one small kiss. Vaguely he registered the sound of footsteps behind them.

"Third time, Mary."

Kane pulled back from her ready to deck her cousin. She turned in Kane's arms—not pulling away from him—to face her cousin.

"I thought you had a company to run, Channing. I know that your inheritance is tied to the profit of Duvall-Moorehead Manufacturing. Aren't you afraid that skulking around after me is going to distract you?"

"I can handle my job *and* keep an eye on you."

"That's not your job, Moorehead," Kane said.

"Is it yours?"

"That's irrelevant. Anyone who threatens Mary will have to go through me first."

Mary led the way into the kitchen, very aware of Kane's heavy footsteps behind her. She felt so out of control, and for the first time since she'd come back to Eastwick she was glad of Grandfather's lessons in composure. The old Mary would have skipped lunch, grabbed Kane's hand and led him to her bedroom.

But now she thought about the consequences of her rash actions, what would be lost and what would be gained. So instead she was heading toward her sunny kitchen, intent on the mundane task of eating a salad.

She'd simmered all the way home thinking of the way that Channing and Kane had reacted to each other. She really was sick of the men in her life thinking she needed them to fight her battles.

Carmen, the Duvall family housekeeper, was in

the kitchen when Mary entered. "Good afternoon, Carmen."

"Good afternoon, Miss Mary. Can I help you with something?"

"I'd like a salad and some tea brought into the study. Kane, do you want anything?"

"Perrier, please."

"I'll bring it in."

Mary waited until they were in the study with the door closed before she addressed Kane again.

"I don't want you fighting my battles."

"Too bad."

"Kane, I'm serious about this. Channing is going to be around the rest of my life and, when you're gone, that kind of macho display is going to come back to haunt me."

"What makes you think I'll be gone?"

She didn't let herself dwell on those words. She ignored him, turning away and seating herself behind the desk. Her life was in flux right now. She'd experienced this type of soul-changing, life-altering event twice before. Each time it had involved a complete upheaval of everything she knew about herself and the world around her.

And each time Kane had somehow come into her life. But he never stayed. No matter how content or happy they were together, he always had one foot out the door. She'd come to accept that she was meant to spend her life alone. Not like the women in the

Debs Club, who were pairing up like animals on Noah's ark. Mary had always been a little different, and her life's path was, too.

"Ignoring me won't make me go away."

"I'm not ignoring you," she said, tossing her head and gathering her thoughts. She could never completely ignore Kane. His blatant masculinity dominated whatever space he occupied. He tempted her to forget about trusts and cousins and family and…to act like a fool again?

"You're here to work, right?" she asked, angry at herself for being so weak where he was concerned. Sometimes it really ticked her off that the only man she'd allowed herself to fall in love with was someone who could never live with her in a normal way. She wondered what that said about her.

"That's one reason."

"The only one that counts."

"If you say so."

"I do."

He took a seat across from her, pulling out a notepad from the briefcase he carried. She hadn't noticed the case earlier but did so now. She'd helped him pick it out.

"I made a few phone calls earlier and have set up a meeting for us with an attorney friend of mine. He'll talk us through the legalities of what you want to do."

Kane was a thorough man, so she wasn't surprised that he'd already started working on setting up her trust. And she knew this wasn't just business to him. For a minute she wanted to bask in the feeling of being cherished and taken care of. That was one of the reasons she'd stayed with him so long. He'd been the first person in her life to actually take care of her.

True, she'd taken care of all his sexual needs in exchange, rendering their relationship in terms of an agreement. Had she reneged on her agreement with her parents? Had they never approved of her because she'd never even tried to be the daughter they'd wanted her to be? That was a path to pursue another time.

"Thanks. We need to have a contingency built into the investment plan in case I have to pay back my inheritance."

"Why would you have to do that?"

"The will has some stipulations, remember?"

"When will the money be available to you?"

"Mr. Previn has okayed a release of the funds in three months' time. But I'll have a probationary period that will last for the following two years."

"Probationary period? What exactly are they watching you for?"

"Behavior. I'm supposed to follow the rules of comportment that were written by my great-grandmother. The rules were revised by both my grandmother and my own mother."

Kane didn't say anything and she was glad for it. She hated that stupid comportment book. She hated how every detail of her childhood had been used as an example of what not to do in her mother's version of the book.

"Sounds like a long line of rules."

He had no idea. They were stringent, too. No room for mistakes in the Duvall family. Her mother had once told Mary that she'd felt the mantle of expectation on her own shoulders once she'd married Mary's father. But to Mary that mantle had always felt like a choke hold.

"You know how family is. Your own has rules, as well."

"They don't apply to me anymore."

"Why not?" she asked. The past three years she'd deliberately cut herself off from anything that would carry information about Kane. She hadn't read the *Globe* or talked to any of the friends she had in London. It had been too painful to think of him in a new relationship with another woman, the two of them living a life together.

"When I divorced Victoria I was told to never come back again."

"Why did you divorce her?"

"That has nothing to do with your investments."

"You're right. I'm sorry, Kane. I had no right to pry."

He set down his notepad and came to where she sat, leaning one hip against the huge walnut desk. "I wouldn't deny you anything you ask for. But you were very adamant about keeping this afternoon all about business."

"I guess I was."

"Changed your mind?" he asked, stroking one finger down her face.

"I'm not sure."

Kane lifted Mary from the chair and set her on the edge of the desk. He pushed her thighs apart and stepped between her legs. Sliding his hands down her back, he grabbed her butt and pulled her forward until he could nestle his erection against the center of her body.

She gripped his upper arms and tipped her head back.

"What do you think you're doing?" she asked, leaning toward him.

"Convincing you to change your mind," he said, letting his gaze drift down her body, lingering on her breasts and her taut nipples pushing against her blouse. He remembered the way she looked—the curves of her breasts, the dark pink color of her nipples. He remembered how sensitive she was to all kinds of stimulation.

"Looks like my plan is working," he said, his eyes reconnecting with hers.

"You have a plan for sex."

"Darling, this is so much more than sex."

She closed her eyes. "I hope so."

He didn't know what to say to that. So he lowered his head and took her mouth with his. He slipped one hand into her silky hair, holding her head at the angle that gave him full access to her mouth.

He ran his tongue over her lips, teasing the both of them. Her breath brushed over his tongue as she opened her mouth, inviting him inside. But he waited. Anticipation turned her on, and this was all about Mary.

She shifted against him, a subtle movement of her hips that brought her against the tip of his shaft. He moaned and bit her lower lip in retaliation. He sucked on it to soothe the sting from his teeth and she undulated against him.

The tips of her breasts brushed against his chest, and he wished they were both naked so he could feel her nipples against his flesh.

He slipped his tongue into her mouth for a quick foray, pulling back when she tangled her tongue with his. She shifted her head, trying to move closer to him, but he held her still.

For this one moment he was in control of her. Or so he thought, until he felt her fingers at his neck, her nails scraping down under his shirt collar.

He stopped teasing them both and took her mouth in the kiss he'd been wanting since he'd first seen her again. He thrust his tongue deep inside and let his instincts take over. He stopped thinking and analyzing. Stopped worrying about wooing her and keeping his cool.

No man could be cool around Mary. She was fire and passion. The kind of heat he'd never felt before…

and never would again. She warmed that cold part of him that no one else even realized he had.

His tongue and mouth took hers the way he needed to take her body again. He wanted to reestablish the physical bond between them. To bind her to him as tightly as he could so that she'd never leave him again.

He slowly unbuttoned her blouse. When he had them undone, he pushed the cloth away from her body and put his palm over her breast, loving the full weight of it.

He slipped his hand under the lacy demi-cup of her bra and then paused, savoring the sensation of skin on skin. She twisted her mouth from under his, her breathing hard, her breasts straining.

He leaned back to stare down at her body almost revealed to him. The earth shifted around him and he wondered how he'd ever be content with just a kiss.

Sliding his hands over the smooth skin of her stomach and midriff, he kept his eyes on her. She watched him, watched his big hands move over her small body.

He took her mouth with his once more, even as he knew he couldn't take this any further. Her housekeeper would be coming down the hall any moment, and he didn't want Mary to be embarrassed by anything that passed between the two of them.

Before he could stop himself, he leaned down to kiss the white swell of her breast near the edge of her bra. His tongue swept under the cloth and brushed her nipple quickly. But she tasted so good he couldn't resist tugging the fabric aside with his teeth and sucking her deep into his mouth.

Her hands framed his head, and his world narrowed to this woman and her arousal. He wanted her aroused to the point where she couldn't think of anything but the two of them together.

She moaned and shifted against him, wrapping one thigh around his hips. He lifted his head, glancing down at her. Her exposed nipples were wet and hard from his kisses, the flush of desire making her skin rosy.

He'd never seen Mary more beautiful than she was right now. He twisted his hips between her legs, bringing the tip of his erection in direct contact with her. He used his hands on her butt to rock her, creating a tantalizing friction between them. Her eyes closed and she rubbed herself voluptuously against him.

He kept up the rhythm, kissing her until he felt her jerk against him. She cried out his name as her orgasm rolled through her body. He embraced her against his chest and buried his face in the curve of her neck. He took deep breaths and tried desperately to hold back his own climax.

As the physical sensations ran riot through him, he came to one conclusion. There was no way he was walking away from this woman again. No matter what happened.

Four

Mary jerked out of Kane's arms and headed for the door. What the hell was she thinking? She couldn't give in to the passion between them. She'd known deep inside that Kane was dangerous to her, that the way he made her feel and act would be her downfall…again.

Her body was still on fire for him, and she wanted nothing more than to make love with him. Here, in this room, where she'd endured the most blistering reprimands throughout her life.

The cool air on her breasts made her realize she was still exposed. She pulled the cups of her bra over her aroused flesh and buttoned her blouse.

"Mary." He said her name quietly but with the kind of authority that made her stop.

But she didn't turn around. She couldn't. She needed to leave the room and his presence right now before she gave in to her wild side and did something she would later regret. Letting Kane back into her bed would be one such regret. The secrets she still kept and the truth she wasn't ready to revisit guaranteed it.

"I—I think we've covered enough for today. Any further discussions can be made over the phone or in the presence of other people. Please see yourself out."

She left the room at a clipped pace, heading down the hallway and outside to the beautifully landscaped gardens that once had been her grandfather's refuge and now had become her own. She didn't stop at the pool or the guesthouse cabana but kept walking until she found the old weeping willow tree that had stood on the grounds for years.

The long branches hung to the ground, providing a private sanctuary within. Mary pushed them aside and sat on the small marble bench nestled against the trunk. This was the place she'd always escaped to— a protected spot where no one from the mansion could see her and she could let go.

Tears burned the back of her eyes and she wanted to rail out loud against life. When was it going to get easier? She knew she was on the verge of whining, but she had worked so hard to change her life, to put the sins of her past behind her so that she could make a new start, one that would live up to the Duvall family name. And she'd thought she'd succeeded.

But now she knew the truth.

She hadn't changed at all. She hadn't made the great strides she'd believed she had. No, she was still the same wild child inside.

"Mary."

She glanced up at the sound of Kane's voice to see him standing just inside the willow branches. In her private sanctuary. Where no one else dared to follow her.

She felt a dampness on her cheeks and realized only then that the tears she'd been holding back had fallen. She wiped the wetness away.

"I believe I asked you to leave."

He sat on the bench next to her, casually resting the ankle of his right foot on his left knee. He seemed like a man with no worries and all the time in the world.

"Please, Kane. Just leave."

"Do you really want that?" he asked. "I'm not convinced that you will be happier without me."

She had no idea. She only knew that Kane complicated a situation that was already tricky. "Honestly I'm not sure. But it's not your job to make me happy."

"Of course it is. I'm responsible for hurting you. I have to make up for that."

"When did you hurt me?"

"In Paris."

She closed her eyes, remembering that time. It had

been April and she'd been so ecstatic to see Kane. Ever since she'd learned she was pregnant with their child, she'd been hoping he'd come to find her. To tell her he wasn't marrying his proper English lady. Instead…well, suffice it to say that she'd believed in happily ever after until Paris.

"I don't want to talk about that time."

"I want to make up for what I did."

"You can't. We have to leave those experiences in the past and move on."

"I don't know if I can. I was so jealous when I realized you had a new man in your life and you were pregnant with his child. I know I said some cruel things."

There had been no other lover. She'd never found another man she wanted to touch her the way Kane had. She'd made up that lie when she'd realized that he wasn't leaving Victoria and that the only reason he'd sought her was to ask her to continue being his mistress. She'd been hurt and angry and had lashed out.

"I think we both have regrets of that time."

He smiled then, just briefly, and put his arm around her shoulder, drawing her to his side. He relaxed when she nestled close. Mary hadn't realized how tense Kane was.

When she looked up at him she was surprised to find him staring at her. "Why are you here, Kane? Really?"

He didn't reply for so long that she thought maybe he wouldn't. She wasn't sure why his motives were important, but they were. It seemed to her as though Kane was pursuing her again. Whether she wanted to admit it or not, Kane was the one man that haunted her dreams. The one man who made her forget who she was. The one man who could make her surrender on every level.

"I'm here for you, Mary-Belle. I want you in my life."

"As your mistress?" she asked, overlooking his assertion of support.

He cursed under his breath. "No, not as my mistress."

They were words she would have given anything to hear three years ago, but now she wasn't sure what they meant. And she was too fragile emotionally to ask him right now. But she would later.

"Why now?" she asked.

"I've been searching for you since the day my marriage to Victoria was annulled."

She wasn't sure she believed him. Kane wasn't a man to pine over a woman. "Why was it annulled? I thought you were divorced."

"It's a bit complicated."

Kane held Mary in his arms, fearing for the first time that he might fail in winning her back. There were parts of his life he'd always hidden from the world and his family. And then there were the parts he'd hidden from Mary. Despite his reticence, she was still the person he'd been the most honest with. But now...he didn't know if he could open up the way she wanted him to.

His marriage to Victoria had been wrong from the beginning. But he'd wanted to please his parents, to live up to their expectations just once.

"Tell me about the complicated part of your marriage." Mary's words pulled him from his thoughts.

"Have I ever mentioned my older brother?" he asked even though he knew he hadn't told her. His feelings for Nigel were also complicated. Nigel had been killed in an avalanche while climbing Mount Everest when Kane was twenty-one.

"No. We didn't talk much about family during our time together, did we?"

He suspected that she had liked the idea that they were just two lovers without ties, without commitments, as much as he had. Mary had been bent on escape the same way he had been. She'd left her old life behind when she'd left her country. And he'd run away from his life with her.

"You were an oasis for me, Mary-Belle," he said, rubbing his jaw against the softness of her hair.

"An oasis? That's almost poetic," she said.

It came to him that he needed her to understand she was more important to him than his family or his business interests. It had taken losing her for him to realize how much of himself was tied up in her, how much of himself she'd taken with her.

"Tell me about Nigel," she said. "Are you and he similar?"

"No, he was everything I wasn't. The perfect son, really, and a natural leader—everything my parents could have wished for in a son. He was groomed from childhood to take my father's place as the head of the family business."

"Why were you running it when we met?" she asked.

"Nigel was killed during a climbing expedition. We were all devastated."

She wrapped her arms around him and held him. "You did what you could to step into his role?"

"Yes."

Mary contemplated him with those vivid blue eyes of hers. "I'm not sure what this has to do with your marriage."

Kane took a deep breath, forcing himself to concentrate on the story he was telling instead of on Mary herself. But it was damned hard. "Victoria was engaged to Nigel. When my brother was alive, she was a different person." He didn't like to think about the changes Nigel's death had wrought in her. "Afterward, she was in a deep depression for a long time."

"So you stepped in and offered to marry her?"

"Not at first. I just visited her regularly and we would talk about Nigel. Eventually she started getting out of bed and leaving her room. I took her out a few times, and the next thing I knew, we were engaged."

"Did you take her out while we were together?" she asked.

If he articulated what he'd felt in those days, how pompous and arrogant he'd been, thinking about having both the proper British wife and the wild, sexy mistress, Mary would leave him. But he was done with lying. When his marriage had ended, he'd left behind everything familiar to him—all of his parents' old expectations—and started over as his own man.

And that man was determined to win Mary back, to offer her a place in his life that wasn't hidden in shadows or secrets.

"Yes," he said.

She pulled away from him and he saw the fire in her eyes. He braced himself for her anger. "You arrogant SOB."

She stomped away from him, her entire being radiating her anger. She clenched and unclenched her fists at her sides. He watched her struggle to control her temper.

"Don't stop. I was arrogant and a total ass. I'm so sorry."

She faced him again, her arms crossed under her breasts. "Yes, you were a huge jackass."

She took several deep breaths, and he saw her lips move as she counted to ten. Not once but three times before she finally said, "Finish telling me about your marriage. Why did you get an annulment?"

Kane faced her and tried to find a way to explain

his marriage to someone who hadn't been inside their very cold, very polite house. It was next to impossible, but maybe Mary would understand.

And she deserved to know what he'd left her for. "Before the avalanche, Nigel called me from the base camp and made me promise to take care of his fiancée if anything happened to him. At the time I didn't think anything of it, but afterward..." His words trailed off as he remembered. With effort he pulled himself back. "The truth is, Victoria and I never consummated our marriage."

"You were married for at least a year," Mary stated. "I can't imagine you going without sex for that long."

"How do you know that?"

"I kept track of you after we parted...until I started to despise myself for that weakness."

He hated himself in that moment for what he'd put them both through. "I'm sure your husband must have enjoyed that."

"It was my guilty secret, Kane. Like everything about you, it was hidden from the real world."

"That's why I'm back. I want a chance at a real relationship—an open relationship with you, Mary. A chance to make up for the pain I caused before. And I hope that you'll be able to forgive me in time."

"I can't do this now. Maybe in a few years, when I've established myself here in Eastwick, but not now."

"I can't wait a few years. Our lives are slipping

away and you are the one person I want to share mine with."

He closed the distance between them to take her in his arms. She resisted for a moment before leaning into his chest. He held her tightly to him. "I'm going to do everything in my power to prove to you I'm a new man. An honest man. One worthy not only of your body but also of your love."

For the rest of the afternoon Mary felt like a huge fraud. She had a secret that would hurt Kane as much as the knowledge that he'd dated another woman while she'd been his mistress had affected her. But Mary kept her mouth shut for now.

After their passionate encounter in the study and then the emotional discussion they'd had under the willow tree, she wanted to find some semblance of normalcy.

Carmen set up their drinks and Mary's lunch on a table near the pool. Mary realized that the housekeeper must have figured out she and Kane were fighting. Darn it, she wasn't doing a good job of appearing serene. That was what the therapist that Grandfather had sent her to had told her to strive for—the appearance of serenity.

When she'd told her grandfather why the Duvall inheritance was so important, explaining to him about the baby she'd lost, he'd understood and approved of her plans. But he'd cautioned her that she had to show some signs of carrying on the traditions started by the Duvall women three generations earlier. And that meant being a role model to young women. Since then she'd been slowly figuring out how to comport herself according to those strict rules. And it had never been so difficult as it had since Kane's return.

Mary sighed and took the last bite of her salad. Kane stood as soon as she was finished. "Want to go for a walk on the beach?"

"I'm not exactly dressed for a walk on the beach."

"I'll wait while you change."

"The cabanas are stocked with swimsuits and beachwear if you'd like to change, as well."

"I will. I'll meet you back here in fifteen minutes."

She changed into a long summer skirt and a wrap-around sleeveless top. She started barefoot for the stairs, luxuriating in the cold feel of the tile and then the thick pile of the Berber carpet on the landing beneath her feet. She stopped for a minute, rubbing her toes on the carpet, before she remembered that she was supposed to always wear shoes. The weight of *supposed to, have to* and *should* settled on her, threatening to overwhelm her with guilt and responsibility.

She ran back to her room and found a pair of walking sandals before racing down the stairs as quickly as she could. Sometimes running was the only way she could get rid of the emotions inside her.

She skidded to stop on the bottom step when she

heard Carmen speaking to Channing. Mary hesitated, not wanting to have to speak to her cousin again. She slipped her shoes off and then quickly dashed around the corner and out onto the patio, running full-out.

She ran into Kane, who prevented her fall with his hands on her waist.

"What are you running from?" he asked, his hold on her sliding from her waist to her hips. There was a scant inch of space between their bodies.

"My cousin. I don't want to have to deal with him again today."

Kane dropped his hands and stepped away from her. "I'll take care of him."

She stopped him with a hand on his arm. Though Kane was a very sophisticated man who gave the appearance of being a suave gentleman, she knew him to be a first-rate amateur boxer. And Channing wasn't. As much as she wanted her cousin off her back, she didn't want to see him beaten to accomplish that.

"No, Kane. Let's just go on our walk."

"Are you sure?"

"Yes. Remember what I said about you not fighting my battles?"

"I remember everything you say," he said, taking her shoes from her hands and going down on one knee to help her into them.

He stood, took her hand in his big, warm one, then tugged her toward the path that led down to the beach. She walked beside him somewhat bemused by his attitude.

"What was that about?"

He pulled his sunglasses from his pocket and put them on. Scanning the path ahead of them, he didn't look at her. "I want to take care of you."

There was something in his voice that told her she was missing an important element to what he was saying. And it had more to do with something Kane felt than whatever he was revealing.

"I don't need you to do that," she said. She'd been on her own most of her life. Even when she'd been Kane's mistress she'd lived a solitary existence.

"Part of my mind acknowledges that, but there's this other part that won't listen. You seem so fragile now."

"Fragile? Kane Brentwood, I'm never fragile," she said. She'd always been a solid person both in terms of her physical being and in terms of her personality. She hated that any part of her vulnerability might be obvious to Kane or, worse, the world. "You're probably just seeing my new, more mature behavior."

"I don't think so."

"Why not?"

"I never thought of you as immature before. There's this difference in your eyes now, Mary. A sadness that I want to help lighten."

Her breath caught deep in her body and she had to look away from his penetrating gaze. That sorrow he saw was the grief that lingered from the loss of her child. The grief that not even two and a half years of distance could dull. The grief that she suspected Kane would feel, as well, if he learned the truth of her baby's parentage.

"I don't think anything you do will be able to change that," she said.

"That's not going to stop me trying. I'm going to do everything right this time—romance and wooing, not just sex."

"You're off to a rocky start if that interlude in the study was any indication."

"That's hardly my fault."

"How do you figure?"

"You're a siren, Mary-Belle. A temptress. And I'm defenseless against your pull."

She wanted to warn him that she wasn't the woman he thought she was, but walking hand in hand with him on the beach was too close to the secret dreams she'd once harbored to disturb it. She kept quiet and nurtured a ray of hope deep inside that this time she and Kane would last.

Five

Spending so much time with Mary over the past week was torture on Kane's libido, but it was worthwhile. He savored the emotions she evoked in him, feeling truly alive for the first time in more than three years.

Tonight he'd invited her to dinner at the house he was renting. He'd employed a small house staff and had just finished pouring himself a martini when his butler led Mary into the living room.

She wore a slim-fitting sheath dress that left her arms bare. Around her neck she wore a strand of pearls that he'd given her. Her hair hung in soft waves to her shoulders and she'd tucked the left side behind her ear.

She wore minimal makeup—just something shiny

on her lips that drew his eyes to them. For a moment he couldn't look away, then realized he was staring.

"You look lovely."

"Thank you. I'm sorry I'm a few minutes late. Max called to tell me about a meeting that Channing and Lorette have asked for tomorrow morning at ten and Max was briefing me on what to expect."

"Do you want me to attend?" He had two meetings in the morning—a conference call at nine-thirty that he could probably reschedule and a lunch that he didn't want to move. It was with a real estate agent to visit some business properties; he was planning to move his offices to Eastwick now that Mary would be part of his life again.

"No, I want to do it myself. I have the presentation about the trust that you put together, so I'll take that."

"If you change your mind, I'm close by." He'd once kept their lives carefully separate and he was determined to be accessible this time. It was important to him that Mary see the differences.

"Why did you rent this place?" she asked, making a slow journey around the room before stopping in front of the stone fireplace that dominated one entire wall. She touched the cold stones and he had a glimpse of the sensuous Mary who spent all of her time indulging her senses.

"Commuting was taking too much time. And we could never have drinks and dinner like this."

"Like what?" she asked, tilting her head and

giving him a flirty smile that caused an immediate reaction in him.

God, he wanted this woman. He could scarcely think when they were in the same room. His erection was full, pulsing, pressing against the zipper of his pants. He constantly watched her, waiting for an opening to touch her, any innocent excuse he could find.

"*Alone.* Your house is full of people all the time." Her friends and their new husbands or fiancés were always stopping by. They hadn't been overly welcoming to him until Mary had made it clear she wanted him in her house. Since then he'd been slowly easing his way into the circle of her friends. He'd quickly learned how seriously she took the bond of friendship. Her friends from the Debs Club—a name Mary had explained had come from their younger years as debutantes—were immediately granted Mary's full attention whenever they asked.

"Sorry about that. My friends are an important part of my life."

"I wasn't complaining. I simply wanted a night of you to myself."

"I thought you said this time we weren't all about sex."

"Did I really? I must have been temporarily insane when I said that."

"Is that why we're having martinis? Hoping to get me drunk enough to say yes?"

"Never. Though if it were to happen, I'd try to be noble."

"I have a feeling *noble* wouldn't last very long," she said with a laugh.

It was the first time he'd seen her so open and he was completely charmed.

"I want a chance for us to be reacquainted with each other."

"I approve."

He arched one eyebrow at her. "I'm glad to hear my plan is working. We have about thirty minutes until dinner will be served. Would you like to go out on the deck?"

Kane's house was a split-level with the main entry and living spaces on the second floor.

"I'd love to."

He bent and took the kiss he'd been dying for since she'd entered the room. She set her drink on the nearby table and turned more fully into his embrace. Her hands held his head still while she tipped her own head to the side, angling for deeper penetration. One of his hands rested on her shoulder, his thumb tracing the line of skin exposed by the scoop neckline of her dress.

He struggled to let her control the moment. If he had his way, dinner would be late—much later—and they'd spend the rest of the evening on the soft rug in front of the fireplace.

Finally he gave up his struggle. He set down his

glass, snaked his arm around her waist and lifted her off balance, effectively shifting the power in the embrace to him. He plundered her mouth, taking it the way he longed to take her body.

His free hand slid between their bodies, caressing her breasts through the silk of her dress. He moaned as he encountered only her dress.

"Are you wearing a bra?"

"Can't you tell?"

"Are you trying to make me crazy?"

"Yes," she said, wriggling against him. "I'm wearing a garter belt and stockings, too."

He set her on her feet and took a step away from her. "Do you want to have dinner tonight?"

"Yes."

"Then you need to go outside for a few minutes."

"By myself?"

"Yes."

He pushed her toward the balcony and strode out of the room. Teasing each of them with anticipation was one thing, outright seduction something else. It seemed Mary had her own agenda and Kane needed to make sure everything was perfect if they were to end up in his bed tonight.

Mary sipped her martini, trying to still her nerves. Things weren't as rosy as she'd painted to Kane. Somehow her cousins had found out that she hadn't been married when she'd given birth to her son,

Brent. And now they were determined to find out who the father was.

She took another sip of her drink. The sinking feeling in her stomach made her feel as though she was losing control of the carefully constructed new Mary. She knew it was only a matter of time before they tracked down Jean-Paul Bertrand the gallery owner with whom she'd lived with when she'd fled to Paris.

Jean-Paul would cover for her, she knew that. He'd been too good a friend not to. But she also knew that Albert, Jean-Paul's live-in lover, couldn't tolerate lying and wouldn't lie for her. She felt terrible because she hated his damned honesty.

She finished the martini in one long swallow, glancing out at the water and wishing that, just once, her life would be uncomplicated.

If it were only the inheritance that would be affected, she'd walk away. Kane had been showing her a financial investment plan that would enable her to fund the trust without her grandfather's money. But she knew that Channing and Lorette weren't going to be satisfied with only her leaving—they wanted her to never come back.

When they discovered the truth about Brent's paternity, they'd leak it to a newspaper or some other very public source. She bit her bottom lip and closed her eyes. Not only would the scandal be disastrous for her but also Kane would find out everything—and not from her, as he should.

She had to tell him. All of it. And then…then he'd realize that he wasn't the only one who had something to make up for.

The man had gone to extraordinary lengths to seduce his way back into her life. And not only with sex, which had been the driving factor in their life before, but with a commitment of every little detail of his life.

He'd rented this house to be close to her and, as a result, had done some horrific commuting to his office over the past week. Instead of passing her trust account to a junior partner, Kane had carved the time out of his schedule to handle it personally.

He'd even set about charming her friends and making a place for himself in the circle of her life.

"Ready for a refill?" he asked, coming up behind her and placing his hand on the small of her back. She felt his touch as though the silk of her clothes weren't there.

"Yes," she said. Another Grey Goose martini was exactly what the doctor ordered.

Or maybe not. Getting drunk might not be the best method of gathering her courage to tell Kane the truth.

"Have I thanked you for all your help with setting up my trust?"

"Yes, many times. Aren't you glad I insisted on helping?"

"I'm not sure I should say yes." So much of her current anxiety stemmed directly from the fact that he was in her life and that he would be affected by whatever her cousins uncovered about her past.

He leaned over her, his big body filling her sight, and tenderly brushed his lips against her forehead. "It's okay, darling, we both know that you are."

She wrapped her arm around his waist and laid her head on his chest. The steady beating of his heart under her ear was reassuring. He enfolded her within his arms, and she felt completely surrounded by him. Completely protected by him. She knew it was an illusion, but she wished it were real. She wished that he was her reward for behaving the way her grandmother and mother had always wanted her to.

He tipped her head back with one finger under her chin and kissed her as if he had all the time in the world. When he lifted his mouth, she stared up at him, bemused by this man.

"Do you always have to be right?" she asked, keeping her tone light, but she feared she'd made things worse by accepting his help. She'd never really gotten over Kane. She'd shut down her emotions after losing her son, forced them deep inside her so she'd stop aching. Seeing Kane again made her remember that she'd closed herself off from many good emotions as well as the sad ones.

He shrugged his broad shoulders. "I'm glad you think I'm always right."

"Name one time when you weren't?" she asked, not believing Kane had ever not made the right decision. Or if he'd made a mistake, that he'd eventually come out the winner.

He rubbed her back and then stepped away from her. "When I let you go."

"I'll agree with that, but let's not make this about us tonight. I want to know more about the real Kane Brentwood."

"Ah, you're after my secrets." He took her empty glass into the living room.

She followed him, leaning against the open doorway and watching the way he moved. He'd always fascinated her. She itched for a pad and charcoal pencil to sketch him. It had been so long since she'd felt the urge to do anything artistic.

"Do you have so many?" she asked.

"Don't we all?"

"I asked about you."

"So you did. Well, I'm not sure I'm ready to be that honest with you. I prefer to have you thinking of me as a slayer of dragons."

"Going to slay my dragons?"

"At the very least, I'll slay your cousins."

She smiled at him. He refilled their martini glasses and then rejoined her outside. The setting sun cast long shadows on the balcony, and the breeze from the ocean was warm. Mary turned her face to it and let her cares be swept away. She knew she was postponing her problems, that they'd still be waiting for her in the morning. But she wanted this one night with Kane. One night with the man she was falling for again.

* * *

Mary was a little tipsy from the martinis. Kane was enchanted by seeing a blend of the old Mary he remembered and the new conservative model of perfection. She flirted with him, arousing and exciting him.

At the moment, they were discussing movies, having already covered books. Since they knew each other's likes, there was none of that exploring of tastes that new couples did. Instead they debated each other's favorites and recent discoveries. He'd been surprised that she'd read the latest military history book written by a British scholar. It wasn't her usual type of book, and he wondered if it meant that she'd missed him before his reappearance in her life.

"What do you think of those actresses with pouty lips?" she asked.

He rubbed his jaw, pretending to think about something he'd never noticed before. To him, all women paled in comparison to Mary. He was damned lucky if he could remember any other woman when she was around.

"I've never really considered it."

"Are you sure? What if I had those injections?" She did an exaggerated pout to demonstrate.

As always when he looked at her mouth, he wanted to kiss it. "I think you have the most kissable mouth on the planet."

"Really? Did you know that on Valentine's Day

there was a kissing contest that broke the Guinness world record for most couples kissing at the same time?"

"No, I didn't know that."

"I read about it. Grandfather said all that public affection wasn't a good idea. That passions might be stirred—" She flushed as if recognizing where she was leading this conversation and looked away.

"Your grandfather had a good point."

Kane was beginning to realize that there was more than seduction on Mary's mind tonight. In all the years he'd known her, he'd seen her smashed only twice. Once, on the day she'd heard the news of her parents' and brother's deaths, and the second on the day he'd told her he was getting married to another woman.

Damn. If he'd been thinking with his head instead of his libido, he would have seen something was wrong with her. Reading Mary's moods wasn't as easy as it once had been. Where she used to be as mercurial as the North Sea, now she had the surface tranquility of the Caribbean.

"Where is all this talk of kissing leading?"

"To bed," she said, licking her lips and leaning forward. "That is what you've been wanting, isn't it?"

"Only when you want it, too."

She sighed, pushed her chair away from the table and walked over to him with a gait that was anything but steady.

He shoved his chair back, getting to his feet as she approached, but she pushed him into the chair and sat on his lap.

"I do want you, Kane. I never stopped wanting you. No matter how angry or hurt I was. Your wedding looked really lovely."

"When did you see pictures?"

"They were in the paper. That's when I decided to leave London."

"When did you meet Jean-Paul?"

She flushed again and looked away from him. "I've known Jean-Paul almost as long as I've known you. He owns a gallery in Paris."

It was the guilty expression in her eyes that suggested there was more to her relationship with the gallery owner than she was saying. Kane had always been jealous of the man who'd become her lover after him, always been insane at the fact that she'd carry another man's child so quickly. He'd been keenly aware that Jean-Paul had suited her artist's lifestyle more than a financier had.

"Did you see him at the same time you and I were together?"

"Would that upset you, Kane? It would be a bit hypocritical."

"Hypocritical or not, it pisses me off."

She smiled at him, her hands framing his face and pulling him close for a kiss. Her breath tasted of the sweet wine she'd had with dinner.

"My discomfort makes you happy?"

"Of course not. But I do like the fact that you care enough to be jealous."

If she only knew how possessive his thoughts about her were.

"I didn't date him when you and I were together. In fact, I never looked at another man."

An embarrassing relief flashed through him and he held her closer in his arms. "What has upset you tonight?"

She jerked away and unsettled her balance in the process. He saved her from falling to the floor and stood with her securely in his arms, walking to the living room and the large couch. He sat, still holding her loosely.

"Tell me."

"Why do you think something has upset me?"

"You're not a big drinker, Mary-Belle. And I've seen you like this only twice before."

She turned to press her face against his neck. "I don't want to think about it tonight. I want one perfect night with you."

"And you had to get drunk to enjoy it?"

"No. Getting drunk wasn't part of the plan. Just wanted to forget my troubles for a while. Just…enjoy being with you. Just…forget…everything."

With that she drifted to sleep in his arms. He held her that way for a long time, wondering what part he'd played in her upset. Regardless, he knew that tomorrow he'd have the answers he sought. But tonight he had Mary, even if this wasn't how he'd envisioned spending their first night together again.

Six

Mary groaned as she came awake, remembering drinking a little too much last night. She'd probably also said a bunch of stupid things. She rubbed her hand over her eyes at the thought. Suddenly she realized that she wasn't alone in bed. Kane's warm body was pressed along the back of hers, his arm around her waist anchoring her to him.

This was exactly where she'd wanted to end up, but she'd had a different path to get there in mind. She wished she remembered more of how they'd gotten into bed. She vaguely recalled Kane's questions before she'd fallen asleep on him. Before her mind could reconstruct more of the puzzle of the evening, she felt Kane caress her bare stomach.

She glanced down and saw that the old university T-shirt she wore was bunched up under her breasts. Kane's large hand spanned her entire stomach, his fingers moving in a pattern over her skin. His little finger rested a scant inch from the top of her midnight-blue thong.

She groaned, closing her eyes. She didn't want to see his hands on her. Didn't want to remember the way it felt when he made love to her first thing in the morning with the early light of day spilling through the windows.

The panic that Channing had inspired in her last night had faded away. She wasn't running from her cousins. And she wasn't going to run from Kane.

The past week had proven that Kane was sincere in wanting to be in her life. And she was ready to acknowledge that she wanted him there. More importantly, she wanted him in her bed.

Being his mistress wasn't an option this time— Kane had said as much. But marriage... There was too much history between them for her to even contemplate it.

With her eyes closed, her other senses went on high alert. All her analyzing stopped. Kane's scent and his warmth surrounded her. Damn, he was so hot pressed against her back. She tried to stay still, but when his hand edged up under the cotton shirt and brushed the underside of her breast, she shifted against him thrusting herself against his hand.

He cupped her, his forefinger caressing a circle around her nipple. Her nipple tightened and her breast felt fuller, but no matter how she moved, Kane kept his touch away from where she wanted it the most.

He urged her onto her back, staying on his side so that he was leaning over her, his warm hand still holding her breast. She couldn't think as his fingers moved over her, teasing her areola until she grabbed his wrist and dragged his palm over her nipple, creating the sensation she desired. She rubbed against his hand, closing her eyes and moaning softly.

He drew his hand away and she opened her eyes, fighting not to beg him for what she wanted. But Kane had always been a dominant lover. One who demanded everything she had to give.

"Please," she whispered finally, unable to resist another moment.

"Please what, Mary-Belle?"

"Please touch me."

"I am."

"My nipple."

"I did."

"With your mouth, Kane."

He lowered his head and his mouth settled over her extended nipple through the cotton T-shirt. The wet warmth made her hips arch off the bed.

She buried her hands in his hair. "More."

He lifted his head and stared down at her. "What?"

"I want more, please."

"Over here?" he asked, lowering his head over her other nipple. The air cooled the now exposed wet fabric, garnering an erotic shiver.

Her hips moved again. She wanted more. She *needed* more. "Suckle me."

He sucked stronger at her breast and his hand settled over her other nipple, caressing. She felt the exquisitely delicious pinch of his fingers against one nipple as his teeth bit gently at the other breast. The combined sensation made moisture pool between her legs.

She grabbed for his hips, trying to drag him over her, desperately needing to feel him pressed to her entire body. Now.

"Kane…"

He hummed against her breast, and the sound vibrated against her sensitized skin. She shifted her legs, encountering his hairy leg pressed next to hers on the bed.

She tried again to pull him over her, but he moved his hand from her breast to her stomach and lifted his head. She stared up at him. Her body on fire and that need, she knew, would be clearly in her eyes.

It had been so long since she'd made love. Kane had been her only lover, and fantasies of having him in her bed had sustained her through her long celibacy.

"What do you want, my sweet?"

"I want you over me. Now. I want to feel you

between my legs and against my belly. I need you, Kane."

She swept her hands down his body, pushing her hand through the opening in the front of his boxers and caressing the length of his erection, then lower to cup his sac in her hands. She rolled his balls together, teasing him with her nails on his sensitive skin.

She felt a drop of moisture on the tip of his erection and rubbed her fingers over it, smoothing it down the length of him. He never closed his eyes, never let his control slip.

Finally he grasped her wrist. "Take off your shirt."

As soon as he let go of her hand she did as he'd ordered, pulling the T-shirt up her body and tossing it on the floor.

She glanced down at her breasts and saw her nipples were hard and red. She sighed as Kane rubbed his forefinger over each of them before sliding his hand lower on her stomach.

"Take off your panties."

She pushed them down her legs and then kicked them aside. Now she lay under his gaze completely bare and she remembered the small changes in her body—the ones that time and life had put there. Until this moment, she hadn't considered how vulnerable she would feel.

Before she could cover herself, Kane lowered his head, taking her mouth in a slow kiss that made her insecurities disappear and focused her attention on the fire that he'd started in her.

When he lifted his head, he said, "Remove my boxers."

She nodded and reached for the fabric, but it was hard to do lying on her back, so she shifted to her knees, pushing him onto his back, slowly drawing the fabric over his erection and down his legs. She tossed the last item of clothing on the floor.

She stayed on her knees next to his hips, her fingers caressing his jutting erection. She took her time exploring his length and hardness. His legs shifted apart and she reached between them to cup his sac once again, then slid her touch lower to press against the flesh between his legs, and his hips lifted from the bed.

"No more of that. Are you on the pill?"

"Yes," she said.

"Thank God."

She laughed at the relief in his voice. "You wouldn't wear a condom for me."

"I would, but I enjoy the feel of your heat so much. Part your legs for me."

She did and he slid one finger through the curls at the juncture of her thighs, pushing it into her body, drawing out her moisture and smiling up at her as he used that moisture to lubricate his erection.

"Come here and straddle me," he said.

She did, loving the feel of his big, strong body

under hers. She rubbed her wetness over his erection, not letting him enter her body, just teasing both of them with the anticipation of being so close to one another. She leaned down, rubbing her breasts against his chest and brushing her lips against his neck.

His hands caressed her back, sliding down to her hips, where he spread her legs apart and slipped his shaft against her opening. "Sit up. Take me into your body."

"I want to feel your arms around me," she said.

As soon as the words slipped out she realized she'd said them out loud and that she'd revealed too much. But he only reversed their positions on the bed.

"Watch me take you, Mary. Know that I'm staking my claim on you again."

She swallowed but did as he'd asked, watched him open her body with two fingers and push the broad head of his penis against her. With just the tip nestled inside her body, he grabbed her hips, anchoring her to him as he thrust deep, sliding all the way home. He wrapped his arms around her back and pulled her into his chest as his hips plunged in and out. Driving her to the pinnacle, he held her with one arm, the other hand going between their bodies to stroke her and drive her over the edge before him.

Everything in her body tightened and she felt her orgasm wash over her. But she didn't slide down into dreamy relaxation. Instead Kane's rhythm drove her again to the edge of a climax, his hands holding her head and forcing her gaze to his. He took them both to the edge of their orgasms and held them there.

Finally she couldn't take it anymore. Scoring her nails down his body, she ran her finger along his butt and then lower, pressing against his flesh. She heard him curse her name and jerk against her as he spilled himself inside her. Her climax followed his.

She held him tightly in her arms as he collapsed on her, crushing her to the bed with his weight as they both slowly came back to earth.

He lifted his head. "Good morning."

She pulled his head to hers and their mouths met. Keeping her eyes open, she watched the intensity in his dark gaze sharpen as he kissed her. His mouth moved on hers in a slow, unhurried way, as if he had all day to explore.

He shifted, taking most of his weight on his elbows. His hips still nestled between her legs, his chest brushed her breasts.

He rubbed his mouth over hers, cradling her head in his hands. She smoothed her hands from his neck down to his arms. He was so strong as he held himself over her. She tightened her fingers on his muscles. He had the kind of strength, inside and out, that she'd always wanted.

When she lay in his arms she felt safe, protected and not alone. From the very beginning it had been that way.

He lifted his head expanding the intimacy between

them and their breath mingled. She tried to smile at him, to keep him from guessing how confused she was inside.

Kane closed his arms possessively around Mary, rolling to his back and taking her with him. No other woman had ever affected him the way she did. He wanted her—Mary—and no one else. Now that he had her in his bed, he vowed he'd never let her go again.

He wanted to spend the day here, with her between these sheets. He mentally reviewed his schedule and knew that he was going to piss off a lot of people when he canceled his morning meetings.

Mary snuggled into him, and he shut his eyes as a rush of emotion swamped him. Uncomfortable with the strength of his feelings for her, he crushed her to him, holding on. She embraced him with all the strength in her woman's body.

Kane felt a shift deep inside, something that he'd been afraid to let himself feel before. In fact, he wasn't too damned sure he liked it. But life had proven that Mary was the only woman for him. He wasn't prepared to share the emotion with her, but he planned to keep her by his side forever.

He'd use sex and her dependence on his financial knowledge to bind her to him. He'd use whatever it took to tie her to him in so many ways she wouldn't be able to leave him.

He caressed her entire body, loving the softness

of her skin. He'd missed the freedom to reach out and touch her. Over the past week, when they'd spent long hours working in her office, he'd wanted to touch her so many times. But always he'd been very aware that the privilege hadn't been his. Through his own decisions, he'd given up that right.

But he had it back now and he intended to keep it.

She moved against him and he slid his thigh between hers. She angled her face close, brushing her lips along his, tangling her tongue with his. He nibbled at her jaw, dropping kisses down the side of her neck. She had beard burn on her neck, and he felt a surge of possessiveness that he'd marked her as his own, that there was physical evidence that she'd given her sweet body to him.

He suckled at the skin in the valley between her breasts, leaving another mark. A private one visible to just the two of them.

"You're mine."

She froze and he realized he'd spoken out loud. The possessiveness he felt had spilled over in his words and tone. But he didn't regret them. One of the mistakes he'd made last time had been thinking he could control the force of his feelings for Mary by allocating her to the role of mistress. It hadn't worked and he'd ended up hurting both of them in the process. This time things would be different.

He stared at her. "Aren't you?"

She didn't close her eyes or flinch away from his

gaze, and he could only hope the rawness of what he felt wasn't revealed there. She cupped his jaw in her hands, her long artist's fingers cold against his skin. He waited, even as he wanted to demand she admit she was his.

"Mary?" So much for patience. Where she was concerned, he had none. Too much time had been wasted already.

"Yes. I'm yours. And you're mine. No one else's but mine."

"Damn straight," he said, stroking his hands down her body and sliding between her legs. He drove into her body, felt her flinch as he thrust himself into her while she was still too sensitive and not yet ready for him.

But she didn't push him away. She took him deep, welcomed him into her embrace even though he was hurting her.

Mary was the only person who made him forget the civilized man he was. He cursed, holding himself still.

"I'm sorry."

She soothed him with her caressing hand and held him to her breast. "For what? You didn't hurt me. I was only surprised."

Despite her assurances, he knew that he had. He suckled her pretty breasts and felt her tighten around his erection. He scraped his teeth along her sensitive skin, building the fire again with his kisses and his touch, drawing her along with him. When her hips moved under his, he started thrusting deep into her body. That manic need for her tingled at the back of his spine. He needed more of her. He needed to leave his mark so deep inside her that she'd never forget she belonged to him.

He pushed her thighs farther apart, put his arms under her legs until they were draped over them, granting him more intense access.

She gasped his name. The sound made his balls tighten, then his climax was upon him and he shouted her name, held her under him while he rode out his orgasm. Her muscles contracted around his body, cresting the waves of her own fulfillment.

He settled onto his side, tugging her into his arms. He didn't know if he would ever be sated. Everything about her fueled his passion and made him desire her more. But he didn't want their relationship to be all about sex. He needed to continue to show her that he wanted more than her body.

She shifted in his embrace. "I have a meeting this morning."

He swept his hands down her back and anchored her more fully against him. "Skip it."

She tipped her head back to frown at him. "I'm not your mistress anymore, Kane."

"I didn't think you were."

"I can't skip my meeting because you want to spend the day in bed. I have responsibilities."

"I realize that. It's not as if I'm not planning to re-arrange my day to spend it with you."

"I can't do that."

"Can't or won't?"

"Won't," she said, closing her eyes. "It would be so easy to do this. To stay here with you all day and pretend that the outside world doesn't exist. But it's waiting for me when I go home. And putting it off isn't going to make anything better."

"What are you so afraid of?" he asked. Mary had never been one to really deal with her problems. She abandoned them. She'd run away more than once, and he knew she'd do it again if she had to.

"What makes you think I'm afraid of anything?" she asked in a silky tone that told him he was treading on thin ice.

"You were drinking heavily last night—it's usu-ally a sign."

She pushed against his chest. He knew she wanted out of his arms—not to mention his bed—and for a minute he refused to let he go. He knew once he did that she'd put barriers between them.

"Kane, let me go."

He relaxed his hold and watched her slip from the bed. She bent to pick up his T-shirt from the floor and he couldn't help admiring the curve of her backside. She glanced over her shoulder at him, catching him eyeing her.

She smiled unexpectedly. "Later we can spend time together. I'm free this weekend...all weekend."

Kane rubbed the back of his neck. Part of him hated being in a relationship that included compromise, but he knew that Mary wasn't going to change her mind. "I have to wait four days to make love to you again?"

"No. Only four days to spend all day naked together."

"Okay. I have meetings that I really shouldn't rearrange—one of the men I'm meeting with flew out from L.A. last night." Bill Hutchins was here for an interview. A top-notch finance whiz kid who Kane had spent more than three months trying to convince that working for Brentwood Investments would be his dream job.

"But you would have postponed for me?" she asked.

He would move the world for her if he could. She was his obsession, and it was only now, more than ten years after the first time they'd met, that he acknowledged that fact to himself.

"Yes." Even as he said it, he felt a twinge of anxiety at the feelings that one word evoked. Under the weight of her stare he stalked into the bathroom, knowing that he was attempting to run from emotions that he couldn't escape.

Seven

Kane was withdrawn as they left his house. Mary had walked over last night and he'd insisted on driving her home this morning. She'd already called Max to let him know she'd be late for their meeting.

She knew she was to blame for this awkwardness between her and Kane. When he'd walked away from her in the bedroom she'd understood that she had the power to hurt Kane in ways she'd never contemplated before. And she never wanted to do that to him.

"Thanks for driving me home," she said, enjoying the feel of the wind on her face as they rode in Kane's Jaguar convertible. It was a pretty lame thing to say, but she'd never been good at being tentative.

Breaking the ice had always been something she'd done by being…well, herself. In the old days she would have put her hands between his legs and kissed him hard on the mouth. That action would have shocked him out of his sulk. But having insisted they not focus solely on their sexual relationship, she couldn't use that technique.

"No problem," he said, keeping his eyes on the road and his tone curt.

She watched the scenery pass for a few minutes. She didn't want to start her day with this coldness between them. She wasn't exactly sure how it had happened, but Kane had become her calm oasis in a life that was a chaotic mess and she didn't want to give that up. "I'm sorry I wouldn't—"

"Don't. This isn't about you."

She couldn't have felt worse if he'd slapped her. She withdrew, though her first instinct was to lash out at him, to start the kind of fight she would have in the past. But she wasn't that woman any longer.

She looked at him, at that aristocratic profile, and felt the loud, argumentative words bubbling up inside of her. She tightened her hands into fists, digging her fingernails into her palms.

He pulled into her driveway and entered the code to open the large metal gates that had protected the privacy of the Duvall family for years. As soon as they were beyond the gates, he stopped the car, putting it in Park.

He turned to face her, taking her hands in his own. Opening them gently, he smoothed the crescent marks her nails had made with a brush of his lips.

"What are you hiding?" he asked against her palm.

She shuddered and tried to focus on what he was saying and not what he was doing. That tenderness made her want to bare her soul and tell him the secrets that were her constant companions—the ones that were going to drive a wedge between them the longer she kept silent.

"Mary-Belle?"

"My temper," she admitted. "I'm not doing a very good job of it."

"You don't have to hide it from me," he said, meeting her gaze squarely.

"Yes, I do. I have to remember to keep in control at all times. Ladies don't have outbursts like spoiled children." There were more rules running through the back of her mind like a litany. She heard her mother's voice more frequently now that she was struggling to be the dutiful daughter. The voice was the same stringent one that Mary remembered from childhood.

"Your passionate nature is a part of who you are," Kane said. "Is that why you don't paint anymore?"

She didn't want to talk about her painting. It had been her salvation on the path back to the land of the living. She had revealed more of herself in her latest pieces than she'd wanted to, but the canvas was the only place she had left to be herself. "I'm not really passionate—not anymore."

He shook his head. "Yes, you are. I still catch glimpses of that fervor you always had. No matter how hard you try to hide it, it's there."

"Please don't say things like that. My life is about decorum now. If you think you see passion, ignore it."

"I don't think I can."

"Kane, I'm serious. Don't encourage me to be the way I used to be. I'm weak and—"

"Good, I like you weak. I'm sorry I was an ass before. I'm sulking because I didn't get my way."

"No problem. I don't necessarily like being the conscientious one."

"But you will be."

She *had* to be. Kane would never understand how far she'd fallen after her baby's death. How depressed she'd been and how outrageously she'd acted. *He* may have seen her drink too much only two other times, but he hadn't seen the excesses she'd gone to in Paris after her son died. Kane hadn't seen the way she'd ceased to be the woman he'd known.

The woman she was today was a carefully pieced together version of herself. She sometimes felt like Humpty Dumpty with a fragile eggshell that wasn't going to hold. She feared the cracks left when she'd reassembled her life would gape open and show the vulnerable woman underneath.

"I'm trying to figure out this new you. Each time

I get close I see something else that doesn't fit, a new piece of the puzzle."

"Please don't. You see more clearly than anyone, and right now I'm not ready for that. I don't want to be naked with you when I feel this way."

"We have to move forward, darling. No matter what scars you think you carry, I won't shy away from them."

She wished those words were true. But there was so much of her that Kane didn't know. Too many secrets that were threatening to expose themselves under her cousins' prying eyes.

"Please just drop me off at the house. We can talk about this later."

"If that's what you want."

"It is."

He put the car in gear and didn't say anything again until they'd reached the circular drive in front of her house. He reached over, put his hand on the back of her neck and drew her near to take her mouth in a kiss that left no doubt about the passion he felt for her.

"I told you she couldn't help herself."

Lorette's voice was like a glass of ice water being dumped on Mary. She guiltily pulled away from Kane and turned to face her cousins and their lawyer.

Kane was seriously beginning to dislike Mary's cousins. He watched Mary start to speak and then close her eyes to count quietly, once again battling to maintain her ladylike facade. He also was beginning to really hate that counting thing she did.

"There's nothing scandalous in a man kissing his fiancée," Kane said, pushing open his door and getting out of the car.

"You're engaged?" Lorette asked. The incredulity on her face made Kane's smile deepen.

"Yes. Mary has just now agreed to be my wife."

Mary stared at him with a wildness in her eyes that told him she was going to lose her control in a few seconds. As much as he wanted to see her drop her guard, he knew that she would regret doing so in front of her cousins.

He squeezed her shoulder reassuringly before opening her door and assisting her out of the Jaguar. He leaned down to kiss her again because he knew that this was the right decision. Why hadn't he thought of it before now? His ring on her finger was exactly what he wanted.

Carmen stood in the doorway as Kane glanced up. "Carmen, we're going to need a bottle of champagne on the terrace to celebrate."

"Right away, sir."

Kane put his arm around Mary, tucking her under his shoulder and walking up the front steps past her cousins.

He stopped in front of the third person, a man he didn't know. "I'm afraid we haven't been introduced."

"This is Max Previn. Max, this is Kane Brentwood."

Kane held his hand out to the other man, who shook it firmly. "Are you one of Mary's relatives?"

"No, I'm the Duvall family lawyer. Lorette and Channing were concerned when Mary didn't make our meeting this morning."

"I'm sorry, Max. Didn't your assistant relay my message to you?"

"He just did. But we were already here."

"Carmen told us you've been out all night," Channing said.

Mary flushed, and Kane refused to act as though they'd done anything wrong. This wasn't the Dark Ages. They were adults in an adult relationship.

"That was my fault," he said to Max, ignoring Channing completely because otherwise he'd succumb to the urge to punch the other man. "I knew Mary had an appointment, but I wouldn't let her leave my house until she agreed to marry me."

Max smiled at them and Mary cleared her throat. "Kane, I need to speak to you—privately."

"Certainly, darling," he said, smiling at her. "We'll join all of you on the terrace in a few minutes to toast our engagement."

Kane followed Mary to the study. He leaned against the door after closing it. She turned to him, and he saw the Mary he remembered flashing in those Caribbean-blue eyes of hers.

"What the hell are you thinking? You can't say outrageous things like that in front of them. They are already suspicious of our relationship. Pretending to be engaged isn't going to help matters."

"I'm not pretending. We are engaged."

"Really? I must have missed something, because I don't remember you asking me to marry you."

"Your cousins forced my hand."

"You really want us to get married?" she asked.

"Yes, I really do. I hadn't thought of marriage this soon because I know that I need to rebuild the trust between us. But your cousins are a pain in the ass, and I think an engagement will shut them up."

"I don't want you to marry me to keep my cousins off my back."

He realized that Mary did want to be his wife despite her protests. But he was very close to saying the wrong thing and driving her away from him. He knew he had to handle this carefully and, as always when he was around Mary, his usual eloquence deserted him.

He wanted to order her to marry him. He wanted her to agree and then have her do it. But that wasn't going to happen anytime in this century.

"Mary, tonight I'll ask you properly."

"I can't go out there and lie to them."

"I'm not asking you to lie to them. I want the chance to ask you to be my wife properly."

"Well, I'm not sure I'm going to say yes."

"You said that you were mine," he reminded her, pacing toward her.

She retreated until she collided with the desk and had to stop. He kept walking until only an inch of space was between them. He put his hands on her hips and closed the space.

Lowering his mouth, he kissed her, slowly pouring everything he felt for her into it. He tried to convey his apologies for all the mistakes and missteps he'd taken since the moment they'd met.

"I'm not taking no for an answer. You can either agree to be my wife or I'm going out there and telling your cousins that you were once my mistress."

"Blackmail? Isn't that below you?"

"I'll stop at nothing to make you mine. It's what I should have done the first time I saw you, but I was too overwhelmed by what you made me feel."

"I— Okay, Kane. I'll marry you."

Kane left shortly after Mary agreed to marry him and they'd had their champagne toast. He promised her he'd be back at six for dinner. Lorette and Channing departed with Max a few minutes later. Mary had told them that she'd known Kane when she lived in Europe but that their affair had ended before she'd returned home. Another half-truth that she hoped would appease them.

After that confrontation she felt stretched beyond the limits of her self-control, so she escaped to the small studio her grandfather had had made for her. She locked the door behind her and stripped off the slightly rumpled dress from the previous evening until she was completely naked. She stood still for a minute, breathing in the unaccustomed sensation of freedom. Slowly, the proper-society layers fell away, leaving her feeling more like her true self. She found the brightly colored skirt that she'd hidden in the wardrobe and donned it. Then she pulled out a bright red button-down shirt and knotted the tail ends under her breasts. The transformation was complete.

She stared at the canvas she'd been working on in secret for the last few nights. Though she was best known for her lush landscapes, this piece was a portrait started after Kane had reentered her life. Her guilt and chaotic thoughts faded as she immersed herself in her painting. A sudden knock on the door interrupted her. She grabbed a smock from the hook on the wall to cover her clothing, then unlocked the door, opening it a crack.

"Yes, Carmen?"

"You have guests on the terrace."

"Who?" she asked, not sure she could face Channing and Lorette one more time today.

"Emma Dearborn and Lily Cartwright."

She couldn't send her friends away. As cathartic as her painting was, her friends would boost her spirits. "I'll be down in a few minutes. I have to clean up."

"I'll let them know."

Mary waited until she heard Carmen's footsteps fade, then left the studio, taking care to lock the door behind her. She hurried to her bedroom, where she washed up as quickly as possible and changed into a very proper Ann Taylor sundress. Without time to return to the studio, she tucked her painting clothes in the bottom drawer of her dresser.

She was halfway down the stairs before she remembered she wasn't wearing shoes and ran back up to find some sandals. Finally she made it to the terrace to find her friends relaxing on the Adirondack chairs, soaking up the sun. Each wore sunglasses and held a glass of Carmen's ice-cold lemonade in her hand.

"Hey, there. Sorry to keep you waiting. So to what do I owe the surprise visit?" Mary asked.

"We're on rumor patrol," Lily said, pulling her sunglasses down her nose to stare at Mary.

"Rumor patrol?" Mary asked, feeling a sinking in the pit of her stomach. What had they heard? Had news of her being Kane's mistress leaked out? Or was the fact that she'd had a child in Paris now part of the Eastwick gossip mill? She fumbled for the sunglasses she held in her hand and put them on.

Emma tipped her head to one side. "Yes. Why did we have to hear from Lorette that you are engaged to your gorgeous English guy?"

Oh, the engagement. "Well, they were here when Kane brought me home this morning."

"You spent the night with him? Are we going to get the juicy details?" Lily said, waggling her eyebrows at Mary.

"No, you're not." Mary shook her head and laughed. This kind of silliness was just what she needed. Her friends gave her space to be herself. It was one of the aspects of her new life that she really loved—her renewed friendship with the Debs.

Carmen had left a pitcher of lemonade on the table, so Mary poured herself a glass, then sank into the chair next to Emma.

"Come on, Mary. It's not fair to be so close-mouthed about him. We knew something was up as soon as you fainted into his arms," Lily said.

"I didn't faint into his arms," Mary protested.

"Yes, you did. It was very…un-Marylike. Why did you faint like that?" Emma asked.

Mary was too tired of the all the lies and half-truths she was keeping to make up stories for her friends. "I never thought I'd see him again. I don't know why I passed out, though. I must have looked like an idiot."

Lily reached around Emma to squeeze Mary's hand. "I thought it looked very romantic. He practically ran across the room to catch you."

Mary had known from the moment she'd opened her eyes and felt his arms around her that something had changed between them.

"I bet he was planning to ask you to marry him from that moment," Emma said.

"I don't know."

"So where's the ring?" Lily asked.

"I don't have one."

"Why not?" Emma looked slightly indignant.

Yes, Mary, why not? "Well, um, he's going to ask me properly tonight."

"Properly? How'd he ask you the first time?"

She couldn't tell them that he'd simply announced she'd marry him in front of her cousins. That proposal hardly matched the romantic vision her friends were spinning. Plus it might open a topic of conversation she didn't want to pursue at the moment. "None of your business."

"Ooh, I bet it was a sexy proposal…maybe in his bedroom?" Once again, Lily waggled her eyebrows, clearly hoping for some of those *juicy details* she'd asked about earlier.

"I'm not telling," Mary said, blushing even though she shouldn't be.

Fortunately she distracted her friends with a different discussion. They stayed another thirty minutes, catching up with everything going on in their lives. Mary said goodbye with promises to share the real proposal when it happened. As she watched them drive away, she knew yet another reason to value the Debs—in their presence, she didn't feel like a fraud.

Eight

Kane rarely felt nervous. But he was tonight. He wanted every detail to be perfect, down to the flowers decorating the room.

While he'd convinced Mary to be his fiancée in front of her family and lawyer, he still had his work cut out for him. She wasn't going to marry him unless he could convince her their relationship was the real thing and not a charade.

He'd rescheduled his meetings after leaving Mary earlier because business seemed insignificant compared to the more pressing task at hand—finding the right ring for her. He'd known exactly the ring he wanted; it had been locating it that proved to be the challenge.

He reached into his pocket to ensure the box was still there. He straightened his tie and took one last run through his house. His staff had followed his orders to the letter. Fresh-cut flowers adorned every surface, candles flickered in every room. The hall to the bedroom had been strewn with rose petals and the room itself had been transformed into the ultimate romantic fantasy.

Or at least Mary's romantic fantasy. He knew she liked lush, vibrant material and had a bit of a sheikh fetish. So he'd created a luxurious room worthy of the most arrogant sheikh and his favorite harem girl with candles, pillows and draped fabric.

He stopped in the kitchen to check the last-minute details with his chef before leaving to pick up Mary.

The September evening was cool but comfortable, so he left the top down on his convertible, knowing Mary enjoyed open-air rides. When he arrived at the Duvall mansion, he rang the doorbell and was pleasantly surprised that Mary answered the door.

She wore one of those oh so proper dresses that seemed to fill her current wardrobe. This one was slim-fitting, demurely cut and sleeveless. She looked elegant and poised, although the way she fiddled with the strand of pearls betrayed her nervousness.

"Good evening," he said, taking her hand and dropping a kiss on the back of it.

"Hello, Kane. You look very nice."

He arched one eyebrow at her. "Glad you noticed. You look beautiful as always."

He put his hand at the small of her back to escort her to the car and encountered silky bare skin. He paused as Mary walked in front of him and he admired the daring cut of the dress. The elegant curve of her spine was revealed by the fabric that started right about her buttocks.

"That dress should be illegal," he muttered as he opened the passenger door for her.

"I don't know what you're talking about. It is really demure."

"From the front you look respectable. But the back is pure temptation."

She tipped her head to the side, her eyes twinkling with mischief. "I'm glad."

"Tease."

She just smiled at him as he slipped behind the wheel of the car and roared down her driveway onto the street. That feeling of rightness that Mary always inspired in him swelled to include this place—Eastwick, Connecticut. He knew that he was going to make this town his home—all because of the complicated woman sitting next to him.

"How was your day?" he asked, reaching over to take her hand in his, holding it loosely on his thigh.

"Weird."

"Weird?"

"Yes. This morning some crazy man told me I was going to marry him, my cousins actually left me alone, and I spent time with a couple of my friends."

"That doesn't sound weird to me."

"It wouldn't. You're the crazy man."

"Do you really think it's so crazy to want to marry the woman who sets my body on fire and makes my life fuller?"

"I make your life fuller?" she asked in a soft tentative voice.

"In ways you'll never understand."

"Maybe you're not crazy."

He laughed because he knew she wanted him to, but he couldn't help the niggling worry that sprang to life. Was she feeling pressured to marry him? Working hard to achieve his goals wasn't something he'd ever balked at, but he was realizing that Mary wouldn't always fall into his plans just because he wanted her to. She was going to take all of his concentration.

"What about you—did you have a productive day?"

"No," he said. "You distracted me."

"How did I do that?"

"By agreeing to marry me."

"Really?"

He gave her a measuring look. She knew he didn't make things up.

"Silly question. It's just so hard to imagine you letting something—anything—interfere with business."

He didn't like what that said about the man who Mary had let be her lover in London. She must have felt as though she was a convenience and segregated to only one part of his life. Though he'd certainly acted that way, the opposite had been true.

Then, he'd had to fight the urge to rush to her flat several times a day. He'd forced himself to never visit her more than three times a week. It had been difficult, but she'd been his mistress and he'd thought it necessary to keep the boundaries firmly in place.

"I'm not that man any longer," he said, pulling into his own driveway and braking in front of the house.

"And you're not my mistress, Mary. You are the woman who is going to spend the rest of her life with me."

"Convince me this isn't just one more error in judgment on my part," she said.

"I intend to."

As Kane led her to the terrace off his living room, Mary noticed he'd put a lot of planning into setting the stage for the evening. She was almost afraid to believe his marriage offer had been sincere and not motivated by the wish to protect her.

Why now? The question—or some variation of it—had been going through her mind since the moment Kane had come back into her life. Why was he determined that this time they have a relationship and not an arrangement?

"Would you like a martini?" Kane asked from the door.

"I think I'll pass. I don't want to repeat last night."

Kane smiled as he pulled her into his arms, swaying to the smooth sounds of Sade pouring from the speakers.

"Do you remember the first time we danced together?" he asked, his words a breathy whisper spoken right into her ear.

She did remember. This song, "Diamond Lies," had been playing. She'd been incredibly nervous as it had been her first outing with Kane. Her years growing up in Eastwick had proven that she was horribly inept in any social gathering. But on Kane's arm, all her awkwardness had disappeared. She'd felt beautiful and confident wearing a tasteful but very sexy dress he'd purchased for her.

That night had changed the way she viewed herself. After that, her confidence in herself had started to build.

She rested her head against his shoulder now as his hands roamed along her back to settle low on her hips. Kane was a superb dancer, and she'd always loved going clubbing with him.

"I remember this song," she said. Kane had flown her to a Sade concert for her birthday one year. After the concert he'd given her a stunning diamond-and-sapphire choker, which he'd insisted be the only thing she wore when they went to bed. They'd spent the rest of the weekend making love in their luxurious hotel suite.

The song ended and blended into "Let's Get It On" by Marvin Gaye. She leaned her head back, resting her hands on his lapels. "Not very subtle."

"That one was supposed to come on later," he said, looking chagrined. But his grip on her hips shifted as he canted his hips forward so that his hard-on nudged her lower stomach.

"How much later?" she asked, going up on tiptoe and rubbing her lips over his until his mouth opened and she slipped her tongue inside.

His hand came up to hold the back of her neck, angling her head and taking control of the kiss. He tangled his tongue with hers and kissed her with a thoroughness that left her aching for him.

"After dinner," he said, leaning away and setting her from him.

She didn't want to wait until after dinner. Her breasts felt too full, her skin was flushed and too sensitive, and moisture pooled low in her body. "Will the meal be ruined if we delay it an hour or so?"

"No, but my proposal won't go as planned," he said, cupping her face and kissing her again. She held on to his arms, anchoring herself to this man who had become the center of her world again. Before they lost control, he firmly stepped away to lean against the railing, looking out over the water.

"What do you have planned?" she asked, taking

deep breaths and getting her body back in check. Trying to appear as composed as Kane did, she walked over to stand next to him.

"A surprise," he said, pulling a remote from his pocket and switching CDs. "We'll save Marvin for later. Have you walked through the gardens here?"

"Not since I was a little girl. The Olsteins owned this place then and they had a boy my brother's age. I attended a few birthday parties for him."

"You never talk much about your brother. What was he like?"

She hadn't thought of Alex in years. He had been four years younger than her and cut from the perfect Duvall mold—unlike Mary. "Perfect, at least in my parents' eyes."

"What about in your eyes?"

"He was so cute when he was little. I didn't start to disappoint my mother and the family until I was twelve, so until then, Alex and I got along really well."

"I don't understand much about your relationship with your mother."

"Trust me, Kane, there's nothing to understand. We were complete opposites and she couldn't accept me for who I was. She wanted to have a perfect little model to promote her theories on ladylike child rearing. The memories chilled her. "I don't want to talk about her."

Seeming to accept her pronouncement, Kane escorted her into the garden, which had been draped with strands of clear lights. The entire space looked ethereal, like something from a dream.

"I want to know your family history," he said, proving that he wasn't entirely finished with the topic.

She had always sought to distance herself from her family as well as other people she'd never felt connected to because her very nature made them so dissimilar. But lately she'd recognized that there was more attachment between her and her family than she'd ever realized. Had her parents lived, would she have eventually found her way home to them? Although it was too late to know, the question niggled at her. "There's no one left except me and the cousins. What about you?"

Enough talking about her and relationships that couldn't be changed. She'd have to live forever with the knowledge that her parents had died feeling that she was a failure to them.

"I severed all ties with my family when I made the decision to annul my marriage to Victoria."

"Is there any chance of a reconciliation with them?"

"I doubt it."

Mary heard the finality in his voice. A note of fear entered her being. She sensed that Kane had felt betrayed by his family and their unwillingness to support him in the dissolution of his marriage. Something he could never forgive.

So how would he accept the fact that she'd lied about being pregnant with another man's child?

* * *

Kane wished they'd never started talking about their families and was very glad that they'd arrived at the fountain in the center of the garden. It was the perfect place to propose to Mary.

He'd had a large padded seat cushion put down on the wrought iron bench. The lights gave the night a magical quality and, combined with the music, made him feel as though they had stepped beyond the boundaries of time. And that was how he felt about Mary—she was destined to be his…always.

He was a practical man by vocation and nature, but there was something about this woman that made him believe in things that couldn't be seen or proven. When they were together, something deep inside him felt right. Felt as if he was exactly where he was meant to be.

"You went through a lot of trouble putting this together," she said.

"It wasn't too bad."

"Um…there's something I should tell you before you ask me to marry you. Something about my marriage to Jean-Paul—"

"I don't want to hear it." The very last thing he wanted to discuss with Mary was her first husband. He hated the fact that another man had married her and given her a child and Kane wasn't prepared to be civilized about it.

She bit her lower lip. "I'm sorry."

"I should be a bigger man and more understanding about your ex-husband, but I'm not."

"That's okay, it's just that… Never mind. You're right, this is the wrong time. I should also apologize for what I said earlier—you know, that today was weird and calling you crazy."

She was nervous. He could tell by her inane conversation and the way she was trying to distract him. But he wouldn't let her. "You'll have to make it up to me later."

She arched one eyebrow at him, looking very haughty. "I will?"

"Yes, you will."

"In bed?"

"Yes." He knew exactly how he'd have her when she apologized again. Underneath him, her heels on his shoulders as he brought her to the edge of climax again and again until she was breathless and pleading with him.

"I can't wait," she said.

He skimmed his gaze down her body, noticing that her nipples pebbled simply by his looking at them. "Me either."

He led her to the bench to sit, then turned away to get himself back under control, feeling suddenly anxious. He'd planned what he would say, rehearsed it in his mind. This marriage was about more than their present relationship. It was about bringing closure to and rectifying the way things had ended between them.

He faced her and saw her sitting very properly on the bench—legs crossed at her ankles, hands loosely held together on her lap. She was heartbreakingly beautiful, and he felt a pressure to not only get this right tonight but also to ensure that he kept it right for the rest of their lives.

He cleared his throat. "Antoine de Saint-Exupery once wrote 'Life has taught us that love does not consist of gazing at each other but in looking outward together in the same direction.' Until I met you, Mary, his words seemed like a contrivance."

He took a few steps closer to her. "I've always believed that, as a man, I'd set the course of any relationship I had. I did that with you in London when we first met—made my demands and arranged things so that you could accommodate me. But I realized—" he went down on one knee in front of her, taking both her hands in his "—that I was only fooling myself. No matter how much I wanted to believe I was in control of you and my reactions to you…that wasn't the case."

"Oh, Kane—"

"Shh," he said, putting his fingers over her lips to silence her. "Let me have my say."

She kissed his fingers before he drew them away, then took his hand in hers, staring at him with wide eyes. He felt the import of what he was doing. He understood that he couldn't fail her again the way he had when he'd deserted her to marry Victoria. The deep emotions in Mary's eyes mirrored the ones residing inside his soul—feelings that he hoped he'd never have to name because they'd leave him feeling extremely vulnerable.

"Finding you again, single and alone like I am, made me realize…" He couldn't say that fate wanted them to be together. He'd sound like some kind of pansy even though he did feel that way. Mary was his and she always would be. "Made me realize how much I wanted you in my life."

He reached into his pocket and pulled out the jewelry box. "So I'm asking you to marry me, Mary. Not because your cousins might gossip about us if we don't. Not because my family will approve. But because I want to wake up next to you every day for the rest of my life."

He took out the ring and held it in one hand, hoping he hadn't made a hash of things. He felt unsure what the tears in her eyes meant. Hell, it couldn't be good.

But then she held out her left hand. "I will marry you. I, too, want to wake up next to you every day. I like the thought of spending my life with you, Kane."

He slipped the ring onto her finger and stood, drawing her to her feet with him. He embraced her, kissing her as if she'd just given him the world. Of course, she had.

Nine

Dinner was sumptuous and very romantic, served under the stars in the middle of the garden. The meal was one of her favorites—a seafood dish that was light but filling—which they'd had together every time they'd vacationed in Capri.

As soon as they finished eating, Kane led her to the terrace, where they danced under the stars to all of their favorite songs—both slow and fast tempo. When "Let's Get It On" played again, they were in each other's arms.

Kane held her tightly to him as they danced to the song, letting the lyrics and old memories surround them. His erection brushed against her with each bump of his hips. She smiled up at him.

"Thank you," she said, not sure that the words were enough, but they were all she had right now.

"For?" he asked, dropping kisses along her neck and letting his hands caress her entire body.

She caught his face between her hands and kissed him deeply, not pulling back until she'd done a thorough job of it. "Making this night something out of a dream."

"You're welcome. I intend to make every night we spend together this way."

She knew she should try again to tell him about Jean-Paul, to confess that she'd never married the other man. But this time she stopped for selfish reasons. She wanted this dream night with Kane to never end. She wanted to bask in the tenderness she saw in his eyes. She wanted to be the woman he thought she was, at least for tonight.

"I want to do the same for you," she said at last.

"You already do," he said, lifting her up, and carrying her down the hallway to his bedroom. A path of rose petals directed the way. She was touched again at how much effort he'd put into making this night memorable for her.

No one had ever done anything on this scale for her. The closest thing she could compare it to was her grandfather converting an unused bedroom in the Duvall mansion for her studio. Somehow, that didn't compare. Grandfather David had insisted she keep the door firmly locked and her artwork a secret.

Kane wasn't hiding her or telling her to hide their affection from the world. He was sharing her romantic dreams and fantasies…making them come true.

He set her on her feet outside the bedroom door. "Go inside and get changed. I'll be right back."

"Where are you going?"

"It's a surprise," he said, kissing her quickly on the mouth and walking away.

She opened the door to a room that had been completely done over. She stood on the threshold and felt tears burn the back of her eyes. He'd given her a romantic fantasy straight from her desires.

She entered and felt as if she'd stepped back in time. The room was covered in large pillows—one huge round one the size of a queen bed sat in the middle. It was piled with smaller pillows covered in satins, silks and velvets. Fabric draped from the ceiling to the walls, giving the impression of a tent.

On the edge of the round bed was a garment bag with her name stenciled on it, along with a small velvet pouch. She picked them up and went into the bathroom to change.

She opened the garment bag and saw midnight-blue satin pants and a matching top. Both pieces were adorned with gold coins that jingled when she removed the outfit from the bag.

The pants rode low on her hips, and the top fastened between her bare breasts with a small hook.

The love bite that Kane had left on her this morning was visible just above the fastening.

She opened the velvet bag and found the sapphire-and-diamond choker that she'd returned to him when he'd announced his engagement to another woman. Mary fastened it around her neck, then pulled out a good-size sapphire that she knew to wear in her navel. Using the jewelry adhesive that was also in the bag, she secured the gem in her belly button.

She turned the bag upside down and four other pieces fell out—gold-and-sapphire bracelets and anklets. She put them on, then twirled around in a circle, listening to the music her costume made as she moved.

She smoothed her hands down her body, swaying her hips to the sound of the music in her head. She let everything fall away except the sensual woman deep inside her.

There was a knock on the door as she draped the veil over her head, securing it with the gold circlet and then attaching the transparent fabric that covered her face from the eyes down.

"I'm ready for you, Mary." Kane's deep voice sent shivers coursing through her.

"I'll be right out."

Her overnight bag was sitting on the floor next to the vanity. She grabbed her makeup bag from inside and quickly lined her eyes with the dark eyeliner.

She was more than ready for him. She took one last look at herself in the mirror and felt a settling in her soul that said she was coming close to under-standing who she was meant to be.

Her true self was someone in between the Duvalls' expectations and her rebellious nature. She realized that Kane gave her the freedom to be this woman—the one who liked to be outrageous in private.

And now she wanted to reward him for helping her feel that way. She opened the door and saw him reclining on the round bed, waiting for her.

Kane hit the play button on the CD remote as soon as Mary walked out of the bathroom. The music was slow and sensuous, a CD from the belly-dancing classes she'd taken, which he'd found when he'd cleaned out her London flat.

"Do you want me to dance for you?" she asked. Her demeanor had changed with her clothing—the swaying of her hips was more pronounced, and her arms moved with each step. The bracelets and anklets provided a trilling accent to each movement.

"Hell, yes."

She tossed her head and gave him a look that was meant to seduce—all the more enticing because of the partial covering of her face—and he felt it go straight through his body to his groin.

This moment had occupied his thoughts all day long. Getting through the proposal and the dinner had been a difficult thing, but he'd held onto his restraint and given her the romance that every woman wanted.

She paused in the middle of the room and he held his arms open. "Come to me."

"I thought you wanted me to dance."

"I just plain want you. This night is for you."

She took two steps closer to the bed. He glimpsed the love bite he'd left on her chest earlier and a flare of possessiveness swamped him. Suddenly, he didn't think he had the patience for a slow seduction. He wanted her in his arms, where she belonged. He needed to feel her silky bare limbs entwined with his.

"I want this night for us," she said, reaching behind her back for a moment before lifting her arms over her head and dancing toward him.

The rhythm of her hips made her pants slide lower with each step she took. She must have lowered the zipper in the back to accomplish it. He held his breath, his eyes fixated on the blue gem in her belly button as she undulated her stomach muscles.

Her pants slipped lower as she turned in a half circle. The zipper was open only partway, and he reached out to tug it the rest of the way down.

When she spun again, her pants slid off her body and she delicately stepped out of them. She continued to dance around him, and he watched her with his hand on his erection, stroking it and aching for her.

She toyed with that hook that fastened her top— the only thing keeping him from seeing her bare breasts. She unfastened it and turned rapidly, letting the fabric flare out to expose her in flashes, teasing them both with what she revealed.

She shrugged her shoulders and the top slid down her arms, catching on her bracelets. Another shimmy and she stood in front of him wearing only the veil and her jewelry.

He rose from the bed to go to her. "Dance with me."

"We're both naked."

She wrapped her arms around him and they moved together in a sensuous dance that took Kane to the edge of exploding. He maneuvered them to the bed and gently pushed her onto it.

Kane sank next to her. They were so compatible in bed that he could easily imagine them spending their married lives together in intimacy.

She kissed his thigh, and he shifted, so that he was lying next to her, his erection pressing against her hip.

He took her mouth with his and let his hands wander over her body, still amazed that she was here in his bedroom and in his arms. This time she would be his forever. He knew there were shadows between them that needed to be discussed, and he should have let her tell him whatever it was in her past that she'd wanted to share. Soon, he vowed, but not now.

Her hips undulated, her hands grasping at him, trying to pull him on top of her. "Are you in a hurry?"

She buried her face against his chest. "Yes. No. I don't know. I just want you so much."

He pushed her legs apart, thinking of the ties that

were attached to the bed. He reached between her legs to find her welcoming humid warmth, the evidence of her desire for him.

"I noticed."

"I'm glad. Are you going to do something about it?"

"Yes." He left her side and went to the foot of the bed, finding the velvet ribbon that was attached to the fabric cover of the mattress. He took her left foot in his hand, bending to kiss her ankle before tying the ribbon around it.

"Kane, what are you doing?"

"Something," he said, fastening her other ankle to the opposite side of the mattress so that her legs were spread far apart and her feminine flesh was exposed to him. He crouched between her legs and looked up at her body.

She lifted her hips, a silent invitation for him to do more than look at her. He picked up a handful of the rose petals that littered the floor and dropped them over her body, starting at her feet and working his way up until he covered her to the neck.

She shivered with awareness and her nipples tightened. He arranged the petals on each of her breasts so that her nipples were surrounded by the soft rose petals.

He licked each nipple until it tightened even more. Then he blew gently on the tips. She raked her nails down his back in response.

Her hand covered his. She sat up, displacing the petals on her breasts. She moved the petals on her stomach around until they accented the blue gem in her navel. "How's that?"

"You messed up your breasts," he said.

"That's okay. It gives you a reason to fondle me again."

He did just that, taking his time to fix the petals and draw her nipples out by sucking them. He moved each of the petals on her stomach, nibbling at every inch of bare skin before replacing the petals. Then he knelt between her thighs and looked down at her.

He picked up another handful of petals and dropped them over the dark curls between her legs. She swallowed, her hands shifting on the bed next to her hips.

"Open yourself for me," he said.

Her legs moved, but he took her hands in his, bringing them to her mound. She hesitated before she pulled those lower lips apart. The pink flesh looked so delicate and soft with the red rose petals around it.

"Hold still," he said.

He arranged the petals so that her delicate skin was centered. He blew lightly on her before tonguing that soft flesh. She lifted her hips and he drew her flesh into his mouth, carefully sucking on her. He crushed more petals in both of his fists and rubbed the petals into the skin of her thighs, pushing her legs farther apart until he could reach her core. He pushed his finger into her body and drew out some of her moisture. He lifted his head to look at her.

Her eyes were closed, her head tipped back and her shoulders arched, throwing her breasts, with their berry-hard tips, forward, begging for more attention. Her entire body was a creamy delight accented by the bloodred petals.

He lowered his head again, hungry for more of her. He feasted on her body the way a starving man would, carefully tasting the moist flesh between her legs. He used his teeth, tongue and fingers to bring her to the brink of climax, but held her there, wanting to draw out the moment of completion until she was begging him for it.

Her hands grasped his head as she thrust her hips toward his face. But he pulled away so that she didn't get the contact she craved.

"Kane, please."

At the words he'd been waiting for, he scraped his teeth over her clitoris, and she screamed as her orgasm rocked through her body. He kept his mouth on her until she stopped shuddering and then slid his body along hers.

"Your turn," she said.

He loved the sensuous side of Mary. Loved that she never held anything back in the bedroom.

She took his erection in her hand, touching her finger to the drop of moisture at the tip. She brought her hand to her mouth and licked her finger.

"Untie my legs," she said.

"I like having you open for me."

"I promise you'll like what I'm going to do."

He bent to untie both of her ankles. As soon as she was free, she pushed him back onto the cushions. Kneeling over him, she brought a handful of petals to his erection and stroked them up and down his length. The velvety softness felt incredibly erotic on his skin.

She followed her hand with her tongue, teasing him with alternating quick licks and light touches. She massaged the petals against his sac and lower. With her thumb and forefinger she circled the base of his shaft, while her mouth covered the tip of him and she began to suck.

He arched off the bed, thrusting up into her before he realized what he was doing. The sensations her mouth and hands aroused in him were almost overwhelming. He pulled her from his body, wanting to be inside her when he came.

She straddled his hips, and, using his grip on her own hips, he pulled her down while he pushed his erection into her body.

He thrust harder and harder, trying to get as deep as possible. He pulled her legs forward, forcing them farther apart until she settled even closer to him. She arched her back, thrusting her breasts forward. He captured her nipple in his mouth, sucking on her mercilessly to heighten her response. He thrust harder and felt every nerve in his body tensing. Reaching between their bodies, he touched her in a sensual caress until he felt her body start to tighten around him.

He climaxed in a hot rush, continuing to thrust into her until his body was drained. She collapsed on top of him, laying her head on his chest, and he turned them on their sides, tugging the coverlet over their cooling bodies. He held her lightly in his arms despite his urge to grip her tightly and ensure she was really his. Even though she now wore his engagement ring, he felt something unsettled between them. The feeling in the pit of his stomach said she remained just out of his reach and he hadn't yet found a way to keep her for the rest of their lives.

Ten

Mary was amazed at how quickly Kane meshed their lives together. His job required him to spend at least eight hours a day on the phone and computer, managing investments and talking to his office and clients. She knew that he needed to return to Manhattan, but she had promised to attend the Eastwick ball—an annual charity event at the end of the week—so he'd postponed his trip until the following week.

He always arrived at her house at four in the afternoon and they spent a couple of hours working on the details of her trust. Everything was coming together smoothly under Kane's guidance.

Their relationship was going so well that she was

reluctant to bring up the past and the secrets she kept from him. Even so, she knew it was only a matter of time before she had to tell him.

The phone rang while she waited for Kane one afternoon about a week after their engagement. "Duvall residence."

"Hi, Mary. It's Abby."

Abby Talbot, another member of the Debs Club, had recently lost her mother, Bunny Baldwin. There was a lot of mystery surrounding Bunny's death. Initially, it was presumed she'd died from natural causes, but with investigation it had been ruled suspicious. There was speculation that her gossip column had garnered an enemy or two, possibly one who'd taken extreme measures to prevent Bunny from talking—especially since her secret journals had been stolen, too. Truthfully, though, Bunny's column had never been malicious, and she'd never printed anything that wasn't verifiable.

"Hey, Abby. What's up?"

"I heard something disturbing in town. And you know how I feel about gossip, but I thought you should hear this from a friend." Given her mother's column and the rampant rumors about her death, Abby was sensitive to gossip.

"Maybe you'd better tell me what you heard."

"Did you know that Kane had a mistress?"

Mary blanched. "When?"

"When he was dating his first wife. Apparently

that was the reason for their divorce. I don't know all the details, but Lorette does, and I'm sure she's going to be stopping by your place before long."

Mary felt her throat tighten and her hands get clammy. She should have known that she wouldn't get the chance at real happiness with Kane, that her past and her secrets would haunt her. "Thanks, Abby. It would have been shocking to hear it from Lorette first."

"You're welcome. Friends have to watch each other's backs."

Abby hung up and Mary sat in her grandfather's big chair realizing that everything she'd been working toward since his death was about to come tumbling down around her. How could she have let this happen?

Kane arrived before she'd had time to totally digest what Abby had told her.

"What's the matter?" he asked.

"Uh, our secret is out."

"What secret?"

"That I was your mistress. That I broke up your first marriage. That I'm still not good enough to be a Duvall."

Kane put down his briefcase and crossed the room to her, reaching out to touch her but she flinched away. She didn't want to be comforted. She didn't deserve it.

"Did I really ruin your marriage, Kane?"

He cursed under his breath, leaning against the desk. "No, you didn't."

"Maybe you'd better tell me what really happened. Lorette knows that you had a mistress and thinks that she's the reason your marriage failed."

"You know the details. You know what happened with Victoria. It had nothing to do with you, even though her family did use the knowledge that I'd kept a mistress to try to force me to stay married to her."

She heard the pain in Kane's voice and knew that this wasn't easy for him, either. She put her hand on his thigh, trying to offer him some of the comfort she'd just refused. She didn't want to see him in pain. She didn't want to think of Kane trying to do the right thing by his brother and failing.

"If your cousins are investigating me, then they probably saw the newspaper articles that were written about the dissolution of my marriage. Your name was never mentioned."

"I don't think that's going to matter," she said, wondering if someone knew that *she* had been Kane's mistress. She wondered if Bunny Baldwin had somehow heard that detail and noted it in her private journal, which was said to contain a lot of secret information that never appeared in her column. If that were the case, the thief now knew about Mary's past. The thief could also have found out that Kane was the father of her child, not Jean-Paul. The time for keeping secrets was slipping away. She couldn't delude herself any longer, she needed to tell Kane everything now.

"I say we face this head-on. We'll go speak to Max tomorrow and simply say that I did have a mistress and that you were that woman. Marriage rights all past wrongs."

"Maybe to some people, but my cousins are going to eat up the fact that I was your mistress."

Kane lifted her out of the chair, sat, then pulled her onto his lap. She rested her head on his shoulder, taking solace from the feel of his strong arms around her.

"That was part of the old Mary. Not the new, proper Mary who wouldn't settle for anything but a wedding ring this time around."

"I didn't demand you marry me," she said.

"No, but we'll put that spin on it. I'll put an end to this mistress business."

If only that were her biggest worry. As if sensing her continued anxiety, Kane tipped her head back and said, "Trust me, Mary-Belle. I'll make this right. This was my fault from the beginning by trying to be too many things to too many people."

His words made her ache inside. "It wasn't your fault, Kane."

"Regardless, I'm fixing it."

She knew there was no changing his mind once he made it up. How was she going to tell him the rest of it? That was the real worry that plagued her, tarnishing the happiness she'd found with him.

"Let's get back to work on the Brent Trust," he said. She stood and he went to get his briefcase.

"Why did you pick the name Brent for this charity?" he asked as he settled in a chair, pulling out a sheaf of papers.

"Brent was the name of my son," she said, unable to keep the throaty emotion from her voice. She had so many regrets. For a while, living in Eastwick had been a nice way to escape them, but no longer.

"Do you want to tell me about him?"

"There's little to tell. He was stillborn. I didn't have money for proper prenatal visits, and since I wasn't a French citizen, I wasn't eligible for their medical benefits."

"Didn't your husband provide for you? What kind of man did you marry?"

She took a deep breath. "Jean-Paul and I weren't married."

"He left you while you were pregnant with his child? What kind of a man was he to leave the mother of his child all alone? That's despicable."

Kane stood and paced the room. She could see the anger in each step he took. Her dreams of understanding from Kane about what she'd done died a swift death. He was never going to forgive her for keeping the truth from him.

"No, Kane. I was never married to Jean-Paul. I just said that when you came to Paris to save face. I didn't want you to think that…to realize no one wanted me."

"What the hell are you talking about? *I* wanted you." And he always had. He'd convinced himself that Mary would stay with him once he married Victoria, even though he knew her American sensibility would forbid her from having an affair with a married man. He really had been a jerk back then.

"To be your mistress. You were getting married. Remember that?" she asked.

He didn't want to think about the fact that his choices—no matter how he'd justified them in his own mind—made him directly responsible for what had happened to Mary. *He'd* left her alone. Not Jean-Paul or any other man. Him, Kane Brentwood, the well-respected peer of the realm—a real ass when it came to this woman.

"I'm sorry, Mary. I screwed that up. But I'm planning to make it up to you."

Mary shook her head. "There's enough blame to go around. As I'm sure Channing will point out."

He wasn't going to argue with her. "I'll take care of this. Your cousins might seem big and bad here in Eastwick, but I've done battle with bigger fish."

"Who?" she asked, sounding weary and looking more fragile than he'd seen her since her grandfather's funeral. Sometimes it felt as though a lifetime had passed in the space of a few weeks.

"Victoria's family. They were determined to make me pay for ending our marriage. But there was no way I was staying any longer. I'm getting good at going up against the in-laws."

The blood left her face, and he realized he'd blundered again by saying the wrong thing. Hell, nothing was easy where Mary was concerned, but he knew, no matter how many times he screwed up or said the wrong thing, he wasn't letting her leave this room until she agreed that they were still engaged.

"That's right—you had to deal with all this with the last woman you asked to marry you," she said, looking up at him, her ocean-blue eyes wide with hurt. "What did you do for her, Kane? Did you fill your house with rose petals and seduce her—"

"Nothing. She had the ring from my brother. She announced it to the papers and it was all done."

"Did you want to marry her?" Mary asked. "I've never really been able to forgive that."

He didn't blame her. "I've never wanted any woman the way I want you."

She tipped her head to the side, studying him intently, and he hoped that whatever it was she sought she would find it.

She sighed and paced to the window that overlooked the terrace, putting her hand on the glass and staring out into the garden area. "The easiest thing to do would be to end the engagement. We only said that we were engaged—"

"No, we didn't only say it. I asked you to marry me and you said yes. I'm not letting you change your mind." He crossed the room to stand behind her, placing his hand over hers on the window and twining their fingers together.

He couldn't lose Mary again. These past few weeks had driven home to him how complete she made his life. He liked coming home to her every day, working on the trust with her, having dinner with her and spending the night with her. He liked knowing when he went to bed each night that he'd wake in the morning with Mary in his arms.

"As much as you might like to think so, Kane, you're not the boss of me," she said without looking at him. "I'm a grown woman. No longer the wild child I used to be. And I think it's time I let Channing and Lorette know that."

He wished he was her boss. Life would be much easier if Mary would simply follow his every order. "*The boss of you?* When did I give you the impression that I thought I was?"

"Every time you say something autocratic like 'I'm not letting you change your mind.'"

She pulled her hand out from under his. He knew he was losing this battle. He tried to put his mind to Mary as if she were a financial investment. How would he analyze it and make it work? But Mary wasn't a spreadsheet; she was his obsession, his woman; and it was time she understood that.

"I'm not being autocratic. I'm simply stating the fact that we are getting married." Nothing she could say would change his mind.

"The fact?" she asked.

Her tone let him know she wasn't too pleased

with his handling of this. But he didn't know any other way. "Yes. The first time I handled everything with you the wrong way."

"I don't know about that. We had some good times," she said, and in her voice he heard the memory of the good times they'd shared.

Those memories were of a life that had been half hidden in shadows, and he didn't want that this time. "But we didn't have an open life. We're not hiding anymore. You're my fiancée, and if your cousins don't back off, they'll find out exactly what kind of man they are messing with."

"I don't want you to stay with me because you think I can't fight my own battles."

He wrapped his arm around her waist and pulled her against his body. He lowered his head to rub his jaw against her silky hair. He didn't want to live without her in his life. If that meant taking on her cousins, the town gossips and the ghosts of their past, then he would do it.

"I'm not fighting them for you because I don't think you can win without me. I'm fighting them for you because I want to be your hero."

She turned in his arms, raising her hands to frame his face. "That's the sweetest thing anyone has ever said to me."

He'd take sweet over that anger and fear he'd heard in her voice earlier. In fact, he'd take her any

way she'd have him. He loved this stubborn, complicated, sexy woman. And he wasn't going to let her
escape again.

The day of the Eastwick Fall Ball Mary woke up
alone. Kane had been called to Manhattan for an
emergency meeting. They'd fallen into a tentative
peace the past few days. She'd convinced him to
leave Channing and Lorette to her for now, but only
because she'd agreed to start planning their wedding.

A part of her still wasn't convinced that Kane would
stay with her. The pattern of her life was one of loss.
And she'd never had any relationship that came as
close to normal as the one she was in now with Kane.

She'd suggested going to Felicity to have her help
plan their wedding, but Kane didn't want to wait too
long, saying they could take care of the details themselves. He wanted them to be married in two weeks
on the beach in front of his rented house.

Yesterday she'd received an express-mail package
containing photos of flowers that he thought she'd
like for her bouquet, as well as two original designs
for wedding dresses from Kara Morelli—a designer
friend of theirs who was quickly becoming the "it"
girl for celebrity weddings.

Kara had called Mary yesterday afternoon to
discuss the gown that Mary wanted. In the course of
the conversation Kara had expressed her happiness
that Mary and Kane were finally back together. As

Mary made her way downstairs after her shower, she shook her head, still feeling a little stunned that they *were* together.

"Good morning, Miss Mary. I set your breakfast up on the terrace. Mr. Previn sent over an envelope for you this morning—it's next to your plate."

"Thank you, Carmen."

Mary sat and opened the envelope tentatively. She wasn't sure what he'd be sending her—maybe a formal notice that her behavior still wasn't up to snuff.

She pulled out the papers, reading them as she nibbled on her blueberry muffin. It was a proposal that he thought would keep her cousins off her back for good. This would be a chance to right the wrongs of the past and maybe lay some of the ghosts that haunted her to rest.

He suggested that she write a new edition of the "Duvall Ladies' Etiquette Guide" using what she'd learned from being the ultimate rebel. In fact, that was his recommended title—"The Rebel's Guide to Ladylike Living."

"What's that?"

She glanced up to see Kane striding through the door. "I thought you weren't going to be here until this afternoon."

"I wanted to surprise you," he said. Since their conversation about the engagement and the threat of rumors, Kane had gone out of his way to prove that he wanted to be her hero. "So what's this?"

"A proposal from Max. He's suggesting that I update the 'Duvall Ladies' Etiquette Guide.'"

He leaned down to kiss her thoroughly. "Ah, that's better. I missed you the last few nights. I'd hoped to get here before you got out of bed."

"You just missed me. Thirty minutes earlier and I'd still have been there," she said, realizing she'd missed him more than she wanted to admit.

He pulled out a chair at the table and sat, reaching for the coffee carafe and the empty mug that Carmen had left on the table. She must have known Kane was coming home and set out the extra dishes.

"I don't suppose I can convince you that you need a nap?" he asked, arching one eyebrow. "The ball tonight will go late."

"A nap at nine in the morning?" Though she wouldn't mind going back to bed with Kane.

"I guess not."

He sounded so disappointed she couldn't help but smile at him. "I might be sleepy this afternoon."

"I'm sure I will be. I stayed up all night finalizing the paperwork for your trust. By the end of the month you should be able to start looking for office space and hiring your staff."

She was touched at how he'd made the trust a priority. Without his help she knew she'd still be trying to figure out which steps to take first.

"I'm not sure where to start the hiring process. I'm

on the board of trustees for the Eastwick Art Council, but that's mostly a local group."

"I've got a few contacts who are experts in developing and running successful charitable trusts," Kane said, handing her a folder that was a quarter of an inch thick. "According to everyone I spoke to, you'll need at least eight people on staff. You'll also need a first-rate Web designer to create the site for the foundation and give people a place to register for the services."

Kane's investment strategy had made it possible for Mary to make the Brent Trust a twofold operation—one that would endow hospitals with neonatal wings and a second separate operation for low-income mothers to apply for money to help pay for prenatal care.

"Thank you so much for all the work you put into this."

"It was nothing," he said.

But she knew it had been something. And more important to her than he probably realized. Or maybe he did realize the importance of this trust and that was why he'd worked so hard to make it come together.

"It is everything, Kane. You took my dreams to help others and made it a reality. I can't thank you enough."

"I didn't do it for thanks, Mary-Belle," he said, taking her hand in his and meshing their fingers together.

No, he'd done it for her. Because he cared about her. She knew that he was still trying to make amends for the past, but there were no further reparations to be made. In the face of his sincerity, her secret felt cold and dark—dirty as it lay in her mind. She needed to tell him he'd been Brent's father. Needed to get that out in the open. But this morning, with the sun shining down on them, she didn't want to say anything.

She stared at Kane for a long time, watching him as he read over Max's proposal and made notes in the margin. Her heartbeat sped up as she acknowledged how much she loved Kane. She'd never really stopped loving him. No matter what happened in the future—if her cousins succeeded in driving a wedge between them, and they had to live their lives apart— she'd always love him.

Eleven

Kane's cell phone rang while they were walking on the beach later that afternoon. "I've got to take this."

"No problem. You don't have to entertain me every second of the day."

"I want to," he said.

"Take your call and then we can talk."

He answered the phone, and Mary moved a few feet away to give him privacy. He wrapped up the conversation quickly, then came up behind her, resting his hands on her shoulders as they stared toward the ocean.

"I'm going to have to participate in a conference call in about ten minutes. Can I use the phone in your study?"

"Yes. I guess it's a good thing we didn't take a nap," she teased.

"As much as I hate to admit it, you're right."

At the house, Mary left Kane to his conference call and went to her studio. She wasn't sure how to tell Kane the truth about Brent. Every time she started to, she stopped.

Her motives were selfish. For the first time in her life she actually felt accepted for who she really was. She wasn't playing a role—the rebel for her family or the sexy mistress for Kane or even the bohemian artist for herself—to get that acceptance. Regardless of how she acted, Kane stood by her.

She was actually making peace with the strictures her grandfather's will had put on her. It was as if, dammit, she was finally growing up. The process wasn't as painful as she'd always thought it would be.

Still, she did have to confess the one lie that lingered between her and Kane—the one thing that was keeping her from fully embracing their relationship.

She locked the door behind her and quickly changed into her painting clothes. She moved her easel into the center of the room, where she had good light from the sun and the overhead track lighting.

Kane's portrait had started out featuring only him. Working on it had given her a chance to explore the new lines on his face that age and life had put there, to reacquaint herself with his familiar looks.

But then almost without conscious thought she'd added herself to the picture, placing herself securely in his arms.

Now, as she dwelled on how to tell Kane about his son, she toyed with the idea of adding Brent to the picture, transferring the mental image of his sweet, peaceful face onto canvas.

It would be the easiest way for her to tell Kane. Words were always a struggle for her when her emotions were involved.

She started painting Brent into the portrait.

As the image emerged, she recognized the elements of the family she'd always craved—loving husband and wife, cherished child. With Kane she finally had an opportunity to see her dream realized. Hope surged through her at the prospect.

For almost two hours she worked, until a knock on the door brought her back to this world.

"Who is it?"

"Kane."

She hurriedly moved her easel so that the canvas wasn't visible from the doorway before opening the door.

"You're painting," he said, rubbing his finger over her cheek. When he lifted his hand she saw a smudge of cerulean on his finger.

"I'm...well, I'm working on a private piece right now. But I have a commission to do a new series similar to my Paris pieces that I need to start soon."

"Can I have a preview?" he asked, tucking her under his shoulder as he walked into the room.

She halted, taking both of his hands in hers, wondering if this would be the moment when the truth just spilled out. It was unexpected, but many of the moments that defined her life were.

"This painting isn't like my normal work, and I'm not sure about it."

"I'm sure it's fabulous like all of your other pieces. Has anyone seen it yet?"

"No. No one here in Eastwick knows that I'm Maribel D."

"How can you keep something like that a secret? Especially now that you are gaining recognition."

"It's a very personal part of me, Kane. I don't want the artist and the Duvall heiress to be linked in public."

"I'm glad to be one of the few you trust with your secrets," he said, his words a double-edged sword. He cupped her face, kissing her lingeringly. "So can I see what you've worked on?"

She shook her head, letting the opportunity to confess pass again. "Not yet. But soon I'll show it to you."

"I can hardly wait."

Now that she'd decided to use her art to share her secret she wanted every detail of the painting to be perfect. She needed to make sure that Kane saw their son as he'd been in her eyes—beautiful, sweet and far too fragile. She shuddered as she remembered holding his tiny body.

Kane pulled her into his arms, stroking her back. "You okay?"

She rested her head against his chest, letting him surround her. She didn't want to respond. She only wanted to close her eyes and pretend that Kane would always want to hold her, that once she made her confession he wouldn't loathe her. Unfortunately reality would not recede. She knew from the way he'd reacted to the news that Jean-Paul had left her alone to give birth to her baby that Kane wasn't going to forgive easily.

She wished now that she hadn't acted in anger on that long-ago day when she'd first lied to Kane. Ironic that she wished now that she'd behaved the way Grandfather had urged her to. Because if she'd counted to ten a few thousand times and kept her temper, she and Kane might have a different history. There might not be so many wasted years between them.

Kane had hired a limo and driver for the evening. Sitting in the back of the car, Mary watched him fiddle with his tie, which was, of course, perfectly knotted.

"What are you doing?" she asked.

"Are you sure a dinner jacket is going to be fine?"

"Yes. You look dashing…like 007."

"Double-oh seven?"

Mary waggled her eyebrows at him. "Don't I look like a Bond girl?"

He caught her by the back of the neck, drawing her closer to him and taking her mouth with his. He didn't pull back until she was leaning against him and holding onto his shoulders for support.

Mary had spent a little more time on her painting before they'd left for the evening and knew that it was ready. Tonight was the night. When they returned home, she'd take him up to her studio to show him the truth of the past. Afterward, they could work out how to have a future together. Having made the decision to tell him, she felt lighter, as if the weight of guilt had left her.

"Come on, Bond girl, we don't want to be any later than we already are."

The chauffeur opened the door and they both exited the car. Kane put his hand on the small of her back—half of his palm rested on the fabric of her evening dress, the other half on the bare skin of her back. He stroked his forefinger gently over her flesh, and she felt a shiver of sensual awareness start deep inside her.

"Do you have to socialize and work the room or do you want to dance?" Kane asked when they entered the ballroom.

"I definitely want to dance with you, but I think I see Abby over there and I want to talk to her. Would you mind getting me a drink?" After their talk the other day, Mary needed to check with Abby to see if she'd heard anything else.

"Not at all. Do you want a martini?"

"Yes, please. Too bad I can't go with you and have you do that Bond thing—*shaken, not stirred.*"

"You are teasing me, Mary-Belle."

"Yes, I am. I intend to drive you out of your mind tonight."

"You already do," he said, kissing her and then firmly pointing her in the direction of her friend. "Fifteen minutes?"

She nodded. It took a few minutes to get across the crowded room to Abby. She appeared to be without her husband, Luke.

"I thought Luke was going to be here tonight," Mary said, hugging her friend.

"He is. I don't know when he'll show up." Abby sipped her glass of champagne. Abby's husband was gone a lot on business.

"You can hang out with Kane and I until he does."

"Thanks, Mary. Where is Kane?" Abby asked, finishing her drink and signaling one of the waitstaff to collect her empty glass.

"Getting some drinks at the bar. I'm not much of a champagne drinker."

"I am," Abby said, taking another glass from a passing tray.

"I can see that. Listen, I wanted to talk to you alone for a minute."

"About?" Abby asked.

Mary looked around the ballroom. This might not be the best place for the conversation, but she couldn't let this opportunity pass. She took Abby's arm and drew her away from the other people to a quiet corner.

"That rumor about Kane's past that you heard the other day…"

"What about it?"

"I wondered if you knew any more details, possibly from another source."

"I told you everything I heard. Why?"

"With Kane and I being the targets of speculation, I'm worried that maybe your mother found out something about my past that I don't want made public."

"I haven't read anything about you in her diaries, if that helps."

Mary was only partially relieved. Just because there was nothing in Bunny's diary didn't mean that there hadn't been notes on Mary's past in the stolen journal.

"My cousins have found out part of it, which is what you heard. The truth is that *I* was Kane's mistress when we lived in London. He paid for my flat and living expenses plus provided me with an investment portfolio in exchange for—"

Abby put her hand on Mary's arm in a show of support. "You don't have to justify yourself to me. I'm not judging you."

Until that moment Mary hadn't realized how much her friend's respect meant to her. She hadn't acknowledged the depth of her fear that Abby might have read something damning about her and withdrawn her friendship as a result.

"I'm finally figuring out some things about my life that I should have a long time ago," Mary said.

"Because of Kane?"

"I think so." She paused. "You know, there's a part of me that can't believe we're really going to get married."

"I like him," Abby said. "He's made you seem…I don't know, not so sad."

"I didn't realize anyone noticed."

"You just haven't been yourself lately."

"I'm not sure that's a bad thing."

"Your mother never understood you, Mary. You were proper in your own way."

Mary smiled at her friend. As she watched Abby drain her glass, she felt compelled to address her friend's consumption. "You seem to be drinking a lot tonight. Is anything wrong, Abby?"

Her friend snagged a third glass of champagne from a passing waiter. It wasn't like Abby to drink this much, but before Mary could pursue it further, they were interrupted.

"Hello, Mary and Abby. Mind if we join you? You look like a couple of wallflowers hiding out," Delia Forrester said. She was wearing a tight dress that left no doubt to her assets, which, rumor had it, had been enhanced by several plastic surgeries.

Yes, Mary thought. This was a part of Eastwick she could do without. She really wanted to find out if Abby was okay and instead she would be forced to chat it up with Delia and Frank Forrester. She actually liked the seventysomething Frank. He'd been a friend of her grandfather's, and the two men had played golf together once a week.

Delia was almost thirty years Frank's junior. Mary didn't really understand their relationship, but Frank seemed happy with his wife.

Mary wanted to say something catty back to Delia, but Kane arrived then and she decided Delia wasn't worth her time. As he handed Mary a martini glass, he lowered his head to give her a very proprietary kiss. "Miss me, darling?"

"Yes."

"I'm afraid we haven't met your fiancé, Mary," Frank said.

"Frank and Delia Forrester, this is Kane Brentwood. Kane, Frank and Delia."

Kane shook Frank's hand. "Nice to meet you."

"What a sexy accent you have," Delia said. "It's no wonder Mary scooped you up so quickly."

"I'm the one who claimed her," Kane said.

Mary shook her head at him. He was in a good mood tonight. But then, he shone in social settings. Apparently she wasn't the only one who saw his appeal, since Delia had settled her hand on Kane's arm. Mary stepped closer to her fiancé in a distinctly possessive move. Kane arched one eyebrow at her, then wrapped his arm around her waist to accommodate her. Their actions effectively squeezed Delia out.

Mary lifted her martini to clink her glass against Kane's. "To our life together."

They both took a sip of their drinks. She loved the icy perfection of a Grey Goose martini.

"That is so touching. You two are picture-perfect. How did you meet?" Delia asked in that saccharinely sweet way of hers.

"We met in a shop in London," Kane said.

"When was that? Tell us all the juicy details," Delia said.

Mary stared at her for a moment, not sure what to say. "There's nothing juicy to tell."

"I'm sure there is," Delia said, taking a sip of her white wine.

"Frank, I heard you had a medical scare a while back," Abby said, forcing the subject away from Mary and Kane's relationship.

"He did, right about the time your mother died, Abby," Delia said.

Mary mouthed a *thank-you* to her friend when Delia turned away. Abby just lifted her champagne flute and took another sip.

"It's kind of strange actually," Frank said. "I'd mixed up my morning and evening medication. Ended up double dosing on my heart medicine. I was lucky to get to the hospital in time."

"Such a close call must have frightened you both," Mary said.

Delia pressed a kiss to her husband's cheek. "It certainly did. We've hired a nurse to make sure that doesn't happen again."

The band returned from their break, playing a cover of "We Are Family." Abby and Mary looked at each other and smiled. "Come on, Kane. This is our song."

"I thought our song was 'Let's Get It On.'"

"I meant this is the Debs' song. We always meet in the middle of the dance floor when it comes on."

"Excuse us, Frank and Delia, my lady wants to dance. It was nice meeting you both."

Mary followed Abby onto the dance floor, keeping hold of Kane's arm. Felicity Farnsworth, Emma Dearborn, Lily Cartwright and Vanessa Thorpe joined them, some with their men in tow some without. They laughed and danced together, enjoying their ritual. Kane disappeared for a few moments but returned before the song ended.

The tempo changed to a slower beat, and Kane drew her into his arms as the first notes of "Let's Stay Together," the classic Al Green song that Tina Turner had made popular, started.

"Did you request this song?" she asked.

"Yes, they didn't know 'Let's Get It On.'"

She wrapped her arms around his shoulders as he led her around the dance floor. His entire body caressed hers as the lead singer's voice played over them. The words of the song took on special resonance as she recognized how aptly they applied to her and Kane.

She reached up to frame his face in her hands and kissed him with all the love and passion that she felt. He held her with the kind of possessiveness that made her feel that there was nothing they couldn't overcome together.

Twelve

Dancing with Mary turned Kane on. And he knew it affected Mary, as well. When the band took another break, he led her off the dance floor. "Ready to go home?"

"Yes, but I want to check on Abby before we leave."

Kane searched for Abby over the crowd and was surprised to find her in the embrace of a man. "I think her husband arrived."

"Really? Where? I can't see over the crowd the way you can."

Kane maneuvered them around until Mary could see her friend from a distance. "Okay. Then I'm ready to go."

"Excellent."

"You sound…"

"Excited?"

"Tired. I think we'll have to go straight to bed."

He laughed at her. "We are definitely going straight to bed. You've kept me waiting all day, and time's up."

He put a protective arm around her waist as they moved through the throng to the exit. While they were waiting for the limo, Emma and her husband, Garrett Keating joined them.

"Did you notice that Luke showed up?" Mary asked.

"Yes. Just in time, if you ask me," Emma replied.

"Just in time for what?"

"Someone poisoned Abby's champagne."

"What? How did she know there was poison in her drink?" Mary was stunned.

"I'm not sure. I think Luke could tell by the scent that it was tainted and stopped her from drinking it."

"Was it deliberate?"

"How could it be?" Kane asked. "All the waiters had trays of champagne."

"I don't think anyone really knows who the target was," Garrett added.

"Well, the rumor mill will be busy tomorrow with speculation," Mary said. She wondered if the attempted poisoning was linked to Bunny's death and the missing journal.

Before she could voice her theory, their limo

arrived. Mary and Emma made plans to visit Abby in the morning to check on her.

"Alone at last," Kane said as the car pulled away from the country club. He drew Mary onto his lap, found her mouth with his and kissed her the way he'd wanted to all night—long, deep and thoroughly. He found the zipper at the side of her dress and lowered it.

"Not quite alone," Mary said, grabbing his wrist to prevent him from cupping her breast. "There's a driver up front there."

"So?" he asked, tugging at her dress until her arms were trapped and the tops of her breasts revealed.

He lowered his head and dropped tiny nibbling kisses along the border of the fabric. Her nipples tightened and she undulated in his arms. He pulled the fabric lower, revealing the edges of her areolae, brushing his tongue across them.

Her hands came up to his head, holding him to her breasts. She shifted her shoulders and one nipple burst free. He suck her deep into his mouth, holding her still with his hands on her waist.

Only when he had her in his arms did he feel as though she was completely his. The rest of the time she seemed to keep a wall between them.

But as he made love to Mary in the car he knew there were no obstacles between them. They were perfectly compatible. He loved her scent, the womanly smell that was unique to Mary. He loved her taste, the sweet-salty flavor of her skin. He loved her breathy little sighs as her passion built.

Suddenly their car screeched to a halt, throwing them off balance. Kane wrapped his arms around Mary as they both rolled to the floor. He took the impact of the fall, holding her close to him, keeping her safe in his arms.

She pulled the bodice of her dress into place as Kane lifted her back onto the seat. He lowered the partition between them and the driver.

"What happened? Are you okay?" Kane asked the driver. There were lights from another car off the other side of the road.

"A deer jumped out and the car in front of me slammed on the brakes. I'm fine. Are you both okay?"

"Yes," Kane said. "Does the other driver need our assistance?"

"I'll go check. The car spun around when he tried to stop."

"I'll call 911 and get some help," Mary said.

Kane got out with the driver and checked on the other vehicle. Although the other driver appeared unhurt, the ambulance arrived a few minutes later and the paramedics checked him over. A police officer arrived on scene, as well, to take everyone's statements.

Once they were back in the limo, Kane raised the partition. He held Mary close. "Are you okay?"

"I'm fine. How about you? You took the weight of our fall."

"Are you sure?" He ignored her query as he ran his hands over her arms and back. He didn't like the thought that she could be hurt.

"Yes, Kane, I'm fine. What about you?"

"That doesn't matter."

"Did you get hurt?"

"No."

She cuddled close to his side. "Thank you for being my hero."

Carmen was waiting for them when they got home. "You had a call, Mr. Brentwood. The caller said it was urgent."

"Thank you, Carmen," he said, accepting the paper with a phone number on it from her. He'd been expecting to hear from Bill Hutchins regarding the job offer Kane had made him the last time they'd spoken. Even though it was eleven o'clock here, it would only be about eight on the west coast, so Kane could still return the call.

"Why don't you use the study, Kane?" Mary suggested. "I'll put together a nightcap for us on the terrace."

"I'd rather you put together something for us—"

"Kane." She interrupted him by putting her fingers over his lips. A faint blush covered her cheeks, and he knew she was conscious of Carmen's awareness of their intimate lives.

He squeezed Mary's hand. "That sounds wonderful. I'll meet you on the terrace."

He heard Carmen asking about the ball as he closed the door to the study. Since he'd started using Mary's office for business calls, he'd installed one of his company phones that had a digital-recording feature that they used to record all investment calls. It was a safeguard that Kane used against investors' selective memories when stocks didn't perform the way they'd expected.

He'd use that feature tonight so that he'd have an accounting of everything that he and Bill negotiated in terms of employment and benefits.

He dialed the phone, frowning when he didn't recognize the number at Bill's. Maybe it was a cell phone. When the call connected he said. "This is Kane Brentwood."

"Are you alone?" a voice asked. It sounded like a woman, but he couldn't place the voice.

That this call wasn't from Bill was a disappointment. He wanted to wrap this up quickly so he could get back to Mary and his plans for the rest of this night.

"Yes. Who is this?" Kane asked, ready to hang up.

"A concerned friend," the woman replied.

"Why concerned?" Kane asked, trying to identify the speaker. Was it Victoria? The last time they'd talked she'd been livid about Mary.

"Because Mary is a dangerous woman."

"Victoria?"

"No, I'm not your ex-wife."

This was ridiculous. "I'm not interested in hearing this kind of garbage."

"Did you know that she has a secret? One that affects you?"

"What are you talking about?" As much as he wanted to, Kane couldn't bring himself to end the call just yet.

"I think you'd be interested to know that Mary has never been married before."

"That's hardly cause for concern." Kane couldn't believe this person had dug into Mary's past and clearly thought that Mary hadn't confided in him. He was surprised this person hadn't discovered that he'd kept Mary as his mistress for years before her relationship with Jean-Paul.

"She was pregnant in Paris. An unwed mother."

"This is a complete waste of my time."

"Ask Mary who the father of her baby is."

Kane hesitated. "Why?"

"Just do it," the woman said before hanging up.

He returned the phone to the cradle, then sat back in the leather chair. Had Mary been involved with a third man? He didn't think it was possible.

He checked that the digital recording was saved and then went to find Mary. He paused in the doorway leading to the terrace. A bucket of ice with a bottle of champagne chilling in it sat in the middle of the table. There were two champagne flutes next to the bucket.

Mary was standing beside her easel a short distance away. The torches around the edge of the patio had been lit, and the pool and landscape lighting was on. The moonlight contributed ambience to the area.

The scene was at odds with the conversation he'd just had. Whoever had called him had done so in an attempt to hurt this woman. The woman whom he had vowed to protect from being harmed again—by him or by anyone else.

She lifted the canvas from the chair where she'd rested it and set it on the easel.

"Is this a private showing?"

She turned around quickly, a tentative smile on her face. "Yes. Just for you. Did Bill accept your employment offer?"

"The call wasn't from Bill."

"Who was it from?" she asked, nervously adjusting the fabric that covered the canvas.

"I don't know. Some woman who warned me about you," he said, leaning against the wall and watching her.

"What? What did she say?" she asked.

"She wanted me to believe you'd had secrets you'd do anything to keep quiet."

Mary didn't respond. With each passing moment he felt an inexplicable anxiety rise in him, which was crazy given that she was the victim.

"You said it was a woman who told you this," Mary said finally, not addressing his comment about her secrets.

"Yes," Kane said, crossing the terrace to stand next to her.

"I wonder who it could be. Did you recognize the voice?"

"No, but I did record the call. We can both listen to it later."

"Why later?"

"She told me to ask you something, Mary."

"What?"

"Who is the father of your child?"

All of the color washed out of Mary's face and she reached behind her to grab the chair for support. At her response, Kane's anxiety launched into full-scale dread. This couldn't be good.

Mary felt her knees collapse, but Kane was there before she could fall. She wanted to rest against him, to let his strong arms wrap around her and keep the world at bay. But she'd waited too long in silence and the time for accepting his comfort had passed.

Who was Kane's mystery caller and where had she gotten her information? Was she the thief—and perhaps Bunny's murderer—who had stolen Bunny's private journal? Or had the thief spread the information and the caller was trying to create mayhem? It was possible that none of this was related to Bunny, that the caller had discovered Mary's secret some other way.

"I think I need to sit down," she said, pulling away

from Kane to sit on one of the Adirondack chairs. Kane took a seat in the one next to her.

"Are you going to answer me?"

"Yes. I'd been planning to talk to you about that very subject tonight."

"Really? Why?"

"Because I never slept with Jean-Paul. I tried to tell you the night you asked me to marry you. I wanted to get this out in the open before we started a new life together."

"There was another man, though. Someone else you were involved with."

She took a deep breath. He was angry at the thought of her being with another man, but she knew that he wouldn't be relieved when she told him there hadn't been anyone else. She was a little afraid of how he'd react. Afraid that he would walk out of her life. But there was no more hiding.

"No, Kane. There's never been any other man for me except you."

"But then that means…"

"You were the father of my child."

He said nothing but sank back in the chair, closing his eyes.

"I received two pieces of news the day I left London. The first from my doctor telling me I was pregnant. The second…well, that came from the newspaper telling me that the father of my child was engaged to another woman."

Kane opened his eyes, looking at her with emotions that she really couldn't read. She swallowed hard and forced herself to go on. "I didn't know what to do. I knew I couldn't stay only to see you marry someone else, so I fled to Paris and Jean-Paul. He offered me a place to stay."

"Why didn't you tell me this when I tracked you down?" Kane demanded, his tone harsh and irate.

"I almost did. But then you asked me to be your mistress. Do you remember that, Kane? You asked me to live in that same luxurious flat, where I'd had you all to myself, and be your second—your hidden life. I couldn't do that to a child. I couldn't accept that for us. And I think I knew even then that you wouldn't abandon your own child."

"So you made up a lie. You took my child from me, Mary," Kane said. "All this time you've kept this knowledge from me. You let me try to make amends for Victoria when this big lie lay between us."

Mary shook her head. "I paid for that. I'm still paying for it."

"Tell me all of it. How did our child die?"

"I didn't have any money in Paris. You'd put a hold on all my accounts and I was cut off from my family. Jean-Paul was kind enough to give me a place to stay, but I couldn't take money from him, as well. So I didn't have regular doctor's visits."

Mary stood, unable to stay seated while she talked about that period of her life. It was at once the best time of her life because she'd wanted to be a mother and the worst because she'd felt so alone and so afraid that her decisions weren't the right ones. "I started working in Jean-Paul's gallery and saved my money to hire a midwife to attend the birth."

"The labor was long and intense, and when the baby was born the umbilical cord was wrapped around his neck. He died during the labor. Even with proper prenatal care, there was little that could have saved him."

She wrapped her arms around her waist, holding herself tightly to contain the emotions that were straining to get free. She wanted to rant at Kane, but she knew that the blame for Brent's death lay on her shoulders. She'd lied to Kane to try to hurt him, and the backlash had hurt her.

"I was devastated. I can't begin to tell you what it was like to be so close to having a family of my own only to have it taken away so quickly—"

"Actually I can understand that. It's the same thing you've done to me by lying about your pregnancy. You stole my chance at those dreams, Mary."

"Be honest, Kane. You wouldn't have left Victoria for me and our child."

Kane stalked over to her. "Neither of us knows what I would have done."

She knew then that revenge ran both ways. In trying to cause him pain, she'd pained herself. There was nothing she could say to make it up to him. She saw the sadness in his eyes and knew he was mourning their child.

"I'm so sorry. If I'd been less stubborn, maybe we'd have our child today. But I couldn't ask you for help, not after you'd left."

"I can't accept your apology. This goes beyond a simple *I'm sorry.*"

"I know, Kane. I think I've known it from the very beginning. That's why I put off telling you for so long," she said through the tears streaming down her face. "I know there's nothing left to say between us."

Mary left the terrace and went into the cold, empty house. Secure in the knowledge that she'd spend the rest of her life here…alone.

Thirteen

Kane watched Mary leave but didn't follow her. He needed time alone away from her. He walked through the garden down to the beach. With the wind blowing in from the water, he sank to the sand.

He'd had a son. When Mary had told him of her little boy, he'd felt sadness because the boy's death had obviously hurt her. But now the pain was sharper because it was *his* son. Tears burned the backs of his eyes and he pushed the heels of his hands against his eyes until the burning stopped.

He pushed to his feet and started walking, his mind focused on the past—a past he couldn't change. He hated the feeling of impotence that came with that knowledge. When he came to the beach entrance of his house he went inside.

It was cold, quiet, empty. He should return to Manhattan, where he'd at least have the noise of the city to fill the background and provide the illusion that he wasn't alone.

He went to the liquor cabinet and found the bottle of single malt scotch that he kept in the back. He poured himself a glass and tossed it back quickly. It stung as it went down, and Kane refilled his glass, then took the bottle and glass with him to sit.

He remembered the night Mary had come here and drunk too much. Remembered the shadows in her eyes and understood for the first time what she'd been battling. Hell, she'd been living with the fact that their son had died for three long years. She'd also been living with the fact that her lover didn't care enough to pay attention to details he should have.

He put the bottle on the floor beside him and thought about all he knew of Mary. She'd been battered by their relationship the same way he had and she hadn't trusted him. She hadn't trusted him enough to tell him they'd had a son together. He could only blame himself because he hadn't given her much to trust in.

Kane rubbed the back of his neck. He didn't want to go back to the life he'd had without Mary. The past few weeks had been the best of his life. And he needed Mary…he'd always known that even if he didn't always admit it. He wasn't about to let her slip away again.

They belonged together in a way Kane couldn't explain. He stood up, glancing at the clock and realizing several hours had passed. It was nearing sunrise. He wanted to go to Mary right now and hash things out with her. He wanted her to understand that they weren't going to spend the rest of their lives apart.

He went to his bedroom to shower and change and then retraced his steps along the beach to her house. Someone had moved the canvas and easel into the living room, Kane noticed as he entered the house from the terrace door.

He removed the fabric to look at the painting Mary had been working on so hard. His breath caught in his chest. He now knew what his son looked like.

Tears burned his eyes again and this time he didn't wipe them away. He let them fall for the family that might have been. He vowed that he and Mary would have more children, that their dream of a family would come true.

The doorbell rang, the chimes echoing through the quiet house. Kane went to answer and encountered Mary at the bottom of the stairs. She looked tired, as if she hadn't gotten any more sleep last night than he had. He wanted to take her in his arms and hold her, tell her that he was sorry for the way he'd acted.

"I didn't realize you were still here," she said.

"I just came back. We have to talk."

The doorbell rang again.

"Where's Carmen?" he asked.

"She doesn't get here until eight."

Kane crossed the foyer and opened the door, wanting to deal quickly with whoever was there so he could then get everything settled with Mary.

Channing and Lorette stood on the doorstep. "A little early for a social call, isn't it?" Kane asked.

"We're here about a legal matter," Channing said, trying to push past Kane into the house.

Kane didn't budge.

"Don't mess with me, Brentwood. You have no idea the trouble I can cause you. I know all your dirty little secrets."

"I doubt that, Moorehead."

"Mary, let us in. You're going to want to hear what we've found out about this man," Lorette said.

Mary came up behind him. Putting her hand on his where he held the door, she slowly peeled his fingers away. "Let them in, please."

Kane did as she asked, stepping out of the way to let them pass. He barely resisted the urge to trip Channing as he entered the foyer.

Kane closed the door. "We can do this here. No use in both of you getting comfortable."

"Why not? Once we go see Max, this house and the entire Duvall fortune will be ours."

"Just get to the good part," Kane said.

"Yes, the good part. Well, it seems that Kane's

lover had his child. Did you know that, Mary?" Channing's smug voice grated on Kane.

Mary went completely white. "Yes, I knew that."

Lorette stepped closer to Mary, her eyes narrowing on her cousin. Kane placed himself between the two women to prevent contact between them. "That's it. That's the big news you've uncovered? You should know Mary isn't responsible for my actions."

"Yes, she is. *She* was your mistress. We know all about it. And that kind of behavior doesn't fit with the stipulations of Uncle David's will," Lorette declared.

"No wonder Mary told me she had no family when we met in London. You people don't know the first thing of what it means to care about someone."

"That doesn't change the fact that once word gets out about you and Mary, the inheritance will come to us," Channing boasted.

"You're not going to say a word about Mary or me to anyone."

"Why not?"

"If you do, I'll ruin you financially. I'm not bluffing. If you've spent as much time digging into my background as it appears you have, you know I can do it."

"Why would you do that? You didn't care enough for Mary to stay with her when she was pregnant with your child."

"You know nothing about my feelings for Mary. You can leave. I'll contact Max this morning for full disclosure. We're not hiding the facts of our past from anyone. There's no scandal where there is truth." Kane opened the front door. "Now get out."

Channing and Lorette left without another word. Kane turned to face Mary, only to find himself alone in the foyer. Before he went to find her, he needed to call her attorney and make sure that her cousins couldn't do any damage to Mary or the funds she wanted to use to set up her charitable trust.

Mary went outside to the gardens beyond the pool and sat on a bench. She'd left when Lorette had said that Kane didn't care about her or their child. She couldn't bring herself to listen to Kane's blunt response. He wasn't a man to lie—even to spare her feelings—and she knew the truth of his commitment to her.

It had been plain last night that love was the last emotion he felt for her. Loving him was a dull ache because she knew that he wasn't about to forgive her, wasn't going to suddenly realize he couldn't live without her. She'd spent the night tossing and turning, trying to think of some way for the two of them to have a relationship.

She'd tried to imagine what she could say to change his mind. To convince him that once she'd made up her stubborn mind about keeping her pregnancy secret, it had been too late to change it. Her pride and her humiliation at being the other woman had kept her silent.

She'd made a real mess of her life, a mess that

she'd finally figured out how to straighten up. But it was too late for her and Kane.

"Mary?" Kane called her name from somewhere near the pool.

She almost didn't answer. If she didn't talk to him this morning, maybe she could find a way around the obstacles between them. But she was through running, she reminded herself.

"Over here."

He came up the path a few moments later. He looked tired as he approached her. She wrapped her arms around her waist, holding herself so that she wouldn't reach out to touch his face and smooth the lines around his eyes and mouth.

He walked right up to the bench and went down on one knee in front of her.

"What are you doing?"

"Asking you to forgive me. Until I heard your cousin's words I didn't realize how you must have felt when I left you for Victoria. I didn't understand how the world would see you and I until that moment. I can't bear the thought that I hurt you that way when all I've ever wanted to do is protect you."

"You can't protect me from the past, Kane. We both made choices that led to—"

He sat on the bench beside her and took her hands in his. "We can't undo the past. But we can make our future a better one."

"What future?" she asked. "I can't live with you

if you don't love me. I was willing to give it a try, but last night I realized that I was still settling for less than what I need from you."

"I don't want you to settle. We need each other, Mary-Belle. We always have. From the moment we met I told myself you were an obsession. That time would dull the sharp ache I had for you."

"Did it?"

"No. Never. From the moment I first made love to you I felt wrapped up in your affection. I know your family wasn't the loving kind, yet you always showered affection on everyone who came into your life. I lived for the hours I spent in your arms in that flat. And yet I almost regret that time together."

She tugged her hands free of his, not sure she could believe him. But Kane had never lied to her. Not once. Even when it would have been in his best interest to do so, he'd stuck to the truth.

"What are you trying to say?"

"That I wish I could go back to when we met in Harrods and do things differently...properly."

"Why?"

"Because I knew from that moment that—"

He pulled her into his arms, holding her so tightly she could barely breathe. His lips brushed her ear, and she felt his mouth move, but she couldn't hear what he said.

She leaned away and looked into his dark eyes. "What did you say?"

He shook his head. "I—I love you, Mary Duvall. I can't imagine living without you. I shouldn't have wasted a moment of our lives together by making you my mistress. I should have asked you to be my wife."

Her breath stopped for a second, then she framed his face with her hands and kissed him softly. "I love you, too."

Kane lifted her into his arms and started walking to the house.

"Where are you taking me?"

"To bed. I want to make love to you and then spend the day talking about our future together."

* * * * *

THE PART-TIME WIFE

BY
MAUREEN CHILD

Dear Reader,

What if you found out the man you married wasn't who he said he was at all? Would you be able to forgive him for lying to you—if he had a really good reason?

In *The Part-Time Wife*, Abby Baldwin is finding out all sorts of interesting things about her husband, Luke Talbot. And Luke is caught between the lies he's told and the woman he loves more than anything.

I had so much fun being a part of the SECRET LIVES OF SOCIETY WIVES. I hope you enjoy your time in Eastwick as much as all the authors did! And I hope you'll continue to buy and read our novels—we love writing them for you.

Love,

Maureen

PS Be sure to check out my website, www.maureen child.com, for information about my newest releases.

Maureen Child is a California native who loves to travel. Every chance they get, she and her husband are taking off on another research trip. The author of more than sixty books, Maureen loves a happy ending and still swears that she has the best job in the world. She lives in Southern California with her husband, two children and a golden retriever with delusions of grandeur.

For my niece, Maegan Carberry, because she always
wanted a dedication all to herself! Love you, Mae!

One

"Let's hear it for the Debs!" Abby Baldwin Talbot said, lifting her champagne glass in a toast to the five women who were her best friends.

"Way to go, us!" Felicity chimed in and the others lifted their glasses, as well.

Abby looked from one to the other of them and smiled at each in turn. There were the original members of the Debs Club...girls who'd gone through Eastwick Academy together and survived their "coming-out" society debut arm in arm. Emma, Mary, Felicity and Abby had known each other forever and their bond was unbreakable. But if it couldn't break, it did bend, at least far enough to welcome two new members into their circle. Lily and Vanessa had slipped into the group seamlessly and now Abby couldn't imagine her life without all of these women in it.

Especially now, she thought, but didn't say. With everything else in her world crumbling around her, she needed the familiarity, the love she found with her friends more than ever.

"Okay, hate to break up the moment," Mary said with a quick grin. "But as much as I love you guys, I want to claim a dance with Kane." Then her grin faded a little as she asked, "You all right, Abby?"

"I'm terrific," she lied, smile wide. She took another sip of champagne to ease the dryness in her throat. "Go. Boogie the night away."

"Sounds like a plan," Felicity agreed.

"Right behind you," Vanessa said, then glanced at the three remaining women standing at the back of the country club ballroom. "You guys coming?"

"I am," Lily said, smoothing the front of her gown unnecessarily.

"I'll be along in a few minutes," Abby told her friends. "I just want to stand back here and watch the party for a while."

"Okay," Vanessa told her, pointing her index finger at her. "But if you're not out on the dance floor in fifteen minutes, I'm coming to find you."

Abby nodded. "Consider me warned."

Vanessa and Lily dissolved into the crowd and Abby took a long, deep breath. It was agonizing trying to keep up a cheerful front for the people she loved best. But damned if she would ruin this party they'd all worked so hard on. With that thought firmly in mind, she glanced up at her much taller friend.

"You did an amazing job on this place, Emma."

"You mean *we* did an amazing job," Emma countered, as her gaze drifted around the crowded, noisy ballroom.

It seemed as though everyone in Eastwick had turned out for this year's Autumn Ball. Diamonds winked at throats and ears, and hands glittered with enough jewelry to give a security company a collective heart attack. Women wore bright colored gowns as if trying to enliven the fall and stave off the coming winter. They greeted each other with hugs and air kisses, then whispered with their friends about everyone else in the room. Men in tuxedos gathered in tight knots to talk about whatever it was men found so fascinating. Football? The stock market?

Didn't matter, Abby told herself. All that mattered was, that the Debs Club had managed to make the old country club shine for the night. Soft lights, a live band playing old standards with a few classic rock-and-roll songs tossed in for flavor. A champagne fountain—tacky, but fun—stood proudly in the middle of the room and sharply dressed waiters moved through the crowds, balancing trays of artfully arranged canapés.

The Debs Club.

Abby smiled and thought about that. She and her friends had nicknamed themselves the Debs in

honor of the night they'd been society debutantes.
It had all seemed so silly, so old-fashioned back
then. But the friendships forged in high school and
at that cotillion had stood the test of time. Now
here they were, years later, still a force to be reck-
oned with.

So much had changed, though, Abby thought,
glancing around the room and picking out the faces of
her friends. So many things had happened over the past
several months, that she could sense a strained atmosphere in the room, as if everyone present were holding
their breath, waiting for the next bombshell to hit.

And who could blame them? Murder and extortion were just not the norm in Eastwick. Or at least,
they never used to be.

Abby's eyes filled with tears and she wasn't sure
if her blurry vision was from the attempt not to cry
or the champagne she'd been drinking steadily since
she arrived. She probably should have had something to eat, but she simply hadn't been able to even
consider choking down food. Not with her stomach
in knots and her nerves jangling.

This was all Luke's fault, she told herself grimly,
as her husband's face rose up in her mind. He should
have been here. Had *promised* to be here. But, like
most of Luke Talbot's promises, they weren't worth
the breath he used to make them.

"Ab?" Emma asked, staring into her eyes, "Are
you okay?"

Oh, she hadn't been okay for a long time. And she

was getting less okay with every passing day. *Less okay?* That sounded stupid. She met Emma's violet gaze and did what she'd been doing for months now. She lied to one of her best friends.

"I'm *fine,* Emma." She plastered her practiced smile on her face and inhaled sharply. "Really. I'm good. Better than good," she said and stepped closer, stumbling just a bit on the hem of her cranberry-colored, floor-length gown.

"Hey, careful," Emma urged.

"Oh, I'm always careful," Abby said. "That's me. Careful Abby. Always looking before she leaps. Always doing the right thing. Always— What were we talking about?"

Emma frowned at her, then shifted a look around the room, as if searching for backup. Giving up, she said, "I think you should come and sit down for a while. I'll get you something to eat."

"Not hungry. I'm just enjoying myself, Em. No worries." Abby took another sip of her champagne, slipped her arm through the crook of Emma's and whispered, "We all worked really hard to pull this ball off— you more than anyone. So let's just party tonight."

"I think you've had enough party."

"Emma." Waving with her champagne glass, Abby said "Oops," as some of the bubbling wine sloshed over the crystal rim to drip down the back of her hand. "I'm fine, fine," she insisted as Emma stopped a passing waiter to snag a couple of cocktail napkins. "Everything's good."

"Abby, how much of that champagne have you had?"

"Not nearly enough," Abby answered, the fake smile she'd been wearing all night slipping just a little.

Her world was crashing down around her and nobody knew it but she and the man she'd once thought she knew so well. What would the Debs have to say if they knew she'd seen a lawyer? If they knew that she was having Luke served with divorce papers? If they knew what Abby had only discovered the week before—that she'd married a liar, a cheat, a *bastard.*

She took another gulp of air, straightened and blinked the blurries out of her vision. Facing Emma, she lifted her chin and said, "I'm really fine, Em. Go find that new husband of yours and have some fun, okay? I'm just going to go sit down on the patio."

"It's freezing out there," Emma countered.

"I have a wrap. I'll be fine." To prove it, Abby tossed her black cashmere stole across her left shoulder, then set her nearly empty glass of champagne down on a passing waiter's tray. "See? I'm good. Go. Play. Dance."

"Okay…" Emma bent down to plant a kiss on Abby's cheek. "But I'll catch up with you again later."

"I'll be here," Abby quipped, making her smile brighter, her voice lighter. *Alone,* she added silently.

She watched as Emma moved through the crowd, stopping to say hello, smiling at friends, then finally, being swooped into her new husband Garrett's welcoming embrace. As the two deliriously happy people began to dance, an awful sense of envy crawled through Abby.

God, she was a terrible human being. How could she begrudge Emma her hard-won happiness? Answer? Abby didn't. Not really. But oh, how she wanted to feel that way again. She could remember so clearly how she'd felt when she and Luke had first gotten together. She remembered that quickening of her pulse, the jumping in the pit of her stomach.

But it had been so long since she'd felt anything but *alone,* she wanted to weep for the loss of what she and her husband had once had.

Now, she was standing in a crowded ballroom, surrounded by people and she felt lonelier than she could ever remember feeling. The music washed over her. A soft, cool breeze drifted in through the open French doors leading onto the patio. Laughter, snatches of conversation rose in the air and settled over her like an uncomfortable blanket.

"Shouldn't have come," she whispered, low enough that no one around her could overhear.

Of course, she'd had to show up. The Debs were responsible for the success of the ball and she had owed it to her friends to be here. But God, she wished she were anywhere else. She could hardly stand being at the club anymore. Nothing was the same. Nothing felt…safe anymore.

A chill that had nothing to do with the late-October air swept along her spine. Staring at the faces in the crowd, she didn't see familiarity. She saw suspicion. She saw guilt. Fear. Ever since discovering that the death of her mother, Bunny Baldwin, hadn't been an accident, but murder, Abby had been forced to admit that perhaps everyone she knew and trusted weren't what they seemed.

Starting with her husband.

And God help her, in spite of everything, she wished that he were there with her right now. Not as he was now, though. But as he had been when they'd first met. First fell in love. Wistfully, she blanked out the ball she cared nothing about and let memories swarm through her mind.

The day after her graduation from college, Abby struck out on her first adventure. Two weeks in Paris. Alone. She had plans to explore the city, sit at sidewalk cafés and look properly bored. She wanted to drink wine in a park, see the Eiffel Tower and wander through Notre Dame.

She had planned every minute of the trip she'd been looking forward to for years. There wasn't a single impulsive bone in her body. She believed in organization. Clarity. Plans. She even had an itinerary, which went right out the window the minute Luke Talbot took the seat beside her on the flight to France.

She watched him enter the plane and look around and she held her breath until he came to her row of seats and smiled down at her.

"Well, this long flight suddenly looks a lot more

interesting," he said, and stowed his carry-on above the first-class seats. Then he dropped into the aisle seat beside hers and held out his right hand. "Luke Talbot."

As soon as she touched him, Abby knew this moment was...special. Different. Something hot and exciting and totally unexpected zinged from her palm up the length of her arm and then rattled around in her chest like a BB in the bottom of an empty can.

She looked into his eyes and couldn't look away. "Abby Baldwin."

He released her hand reluctantly and Abby folded her fingers into her palm as if trying to hold on to that jolt of electrical energy.

"First trip to Paris?" he asked.

"How can you tell?" Abby wondered.

"There's excitement in your eyes."

"Really?" she asked, just a little disappointed. "And here I was trying to look like an experienced world traveler."

"Oh, this is better. Trust me."

Abby's stomach dipped and rolled as his dark brown eyes collided with hers. His hair, also dark brown, was shaggy, a little rumpled and he wore a gray sweater with blue jeans. He looked a little collegiate and very sexy. What better way to start her adventure than with a little flirting?

"What about you?" she asked. "First time to Paris?"

His eyes darkened a bit, then the shadows lifted again and he shook his head. "Nope. I make this trip pretty regularly for business."

"What do you do?"

"I'm a rep for a software company." He gave her a slow smile. "What about you?"

"I just graduated from college."

"Congratulations—a degree in what?"

"Thanks—and my degree's in communications. Minor in foreign languages."

"Well, that's disappointing," he said, his gaze moving over her features. "I was sort of hoping you'd need an interpreter."

She smiled, enjoying the twist and pull of nerves in the pit of her stomach. "I don't need an interpreter," she admitted then took a breath and a risk at the same time. She couldn't believe she was going to do this. She didn't even know this guy. But something inside her demanded that she *get* to know him. "But if you're interested, I could use a guide who knows his way around Paris."

His mouth curved in a smile that sent a lightning-like bolt of sheer lust slicing through her.

"I'd like that, Abby Baldwin."

She jolted a little and grabbed hold of the armrest as the plane lurched into the taxi down the runway.

"Nervous about flying?" he asked, covering her hand with his own.

"A little," she admitted, through gritted teeth. "Well, not the actual flying part. That's okay. It's the takeoff that gets me. I never really believe they're going to be able to get up into the air."

He picked her hand up off the armrest, cradled it between both of his and said, "Believe, Abby. The plane will go up and we'll discover Paris together."

And they had, she thought on a sigh. For two weeks, they'd spent nearly every moment with each other. Sure, Luke had had to work, but mostly, it had been just the two of them.

Sweet little bistros, dancing in the dark to the music from a street musician just beneath the Eiffel Tower, its light glittering in the darkness. Shared wine and fresh baguettes, picnics along the banks of the Seine and long, slow afternoons, locked away in a tiny hotel room three stories above a loud, bustling alley.

They'd made love for hours, discovering each other over and over again. Their bodies were joined, their hearts engaged and before the two weeks were over, they each knew that their lives would never be the same again.

Tugging her cashmere wrap tighter around her shoulders, Abby sighed and headed for the French doors leading to the balcony. Luke had proposed on that last, wonderful night in Paris. He'd kissed her in front of the Louvre, and promised to love her forever.

She'd been so blinded by happiness, so lost in

love, she had never questioned what they felt for each other. When he'd reminded her that he would have to travel for business, she hadn't cared. Knowing that he would be coming home to her was more than enough.

Love caught them both unawares.

And now, so many years later, it wasn't love keeping them together. Now it was just habit. A habit, Abby told herself, that it was more than time to break.

"Champagne, ma'am?" A waiter asked, pausing beside her and giving her a half bow.

She looked past him to the man hurrying across the crowded room to her side. Luke. He had finally arrived after all.

And she wished desperately that her heart hadn't leaped into her throat with just one look at him. How could she still love him, even knowing that he'd been lying to her for who knew how many years?

"Ma'am?" the waiter prodded gently. "Champagne?"

"Yes," she said, reaching for the glass. "I think I will."

TWO

Luke Talbot slipped through the crowd, hardly causing a ripple of awareness from the people around him. But even if he had, he wouldn't have cared—or noticed. His gaze was locked on his wife.

He was late, but there'd been no way to avoid it. Hell, it was a miracle he'd been able to make it to the ball at all. But he knew how hard Abby and her friends had worked to make this event a success and he'd wanted to be here. For her.

Not entirely true, he thought as he got closer to the wife who didn't look particularly happy to see him. He'd wanted to be here because being away from Abby was miserable.

He was the first to admit that his trips for work

were necessary. He knew that his job was an important one and he consoled himself with the fact that
he had warned Abby going into this marriage that he
would have to be gone. A lot. But it was getting
harder and harder to leave her.

When he was close enough to look directly into
her pale blue eyes, he clearly saw the gleam of
emotion stirring there. She was furious. Maybe no
one else would see it. But Luke did.

"Babe," he said, forcing a smile to combat the
light of battle in her eyes, "I made it."

"So I see."

He leaned in to kiss her and she stepped back
hastily, stumbling slightly before she could catch her
balance. His eyes narrowed on the still-full glass of
champagne she clutched in a white-knuckle grip.
"How much of that stuff have you had?"

"That really isn't any of your business, is it?" she
asked through gritted teeth.

God, even furious, Abby was enough to take his
breath away. That soft blond hair of hers was pulled
up at the back of her head and the blond ends sprayed
out into a fall of gold. She wore the ruby necklace
he'd given her on their first Christmas together and
the thumb-sized stone lay nestled in her cleavage,
displayed proudly by the dark red gown she was
wearing. The matching earrings, an anniversary
present, shone darkly at her ears like drops of blood
against her pale, white skin and he cringed inwardly
at the metaphor.

She wasn't tall, but every inch of her was packed nicely. She was the kind of woman who haunted a man's dreams. His, anyway. And she had from the first moment he'd met her.

"Why are you here, Luke?" she asked, her voice a touch louder now.

"What's that supposed to mean?" he countered, glancing around him to make sure no one was listening.

"It means," she said tightly, "I can't quite figure out why you would even bother to show up at the ball."

"I told you I'd be here."

"Oh." She nodded and her mouth twisted into a parody of a smile. "And you never lie to me, do you, Luke?"

Slippery ground here, he thought and stuffed his hands into his pockets to keep from grabbing her. The safest answer was the one he usually took. Answer a question with a question. Distract and disarm. "Why would I lie to you, babe?"

"Just what I was wondering," she said, her voice lifting a notch or two. Enough to have a couple of the people closest to them turning to glance their way.

"Abby…" He glared at the older man beside him and the guy turned away, but Luke wasn't stupid enough to believe he'd stopped listening. "This isn't the place to—"

"To what?" she asked, swinging her champagne glass wide and sloshing some of its contents onto the floor. "To talk about why my *husband* lies to me?"

Luke gritted his teeth, pulled his hands from his pockets and made a grab for her. She stepped back quickly, though, and the way she was avoiding his touch cut at him.

"I didn't lie to you." *Until right this minute,* he thought with an inward groan.

He had been so damn careful over the years. Always couching his excuses in half-truths. Disguising everything he said in shades of gray, so that he could reassure himself in the middle of lonely nights that he wasn't actually *lying* to the woman he loved.

Should have known that couldn't last forever.

"Liar," she whispered and her voice carried the sting of hurt. Louder, she said, "I called you at your hotel in Sacramento a couple of days ago."

Confused, he said, "Yeah. I know. We talked for like a half an hour."

"Hah!" She lifted her chin and looked down at him. Not easy considering she was nearly six inches shorter than Luke. "But I called the hotel before that, too," she said and started swaying unsteadily.

Luke's gaze narrowed on the champagne. Clearly she'd already had too much. "Abby…"

"I didn't have the number you gave me in my purse, so I called information and got the hotel's phone number myself."

Oh, God.

"Wanna know what they said?" she taunted, and her voice lifted again. Loud enough now that several people were turning to listen.

"I think you've had all the champagne you need," he said and snatched her glass from her hand.

"Hey! I wasn't finished with that."

"Oh yeah, you were," he said, clutching the glass with one hand and catching her elbow with the other. Determinedly, he turned her around, steered her through the French doors and out onto the semideserted stone patio.

Out here, the music was softer. Conversations were no more than a rippling undercurrent of sound. The couples besides Luke and Abby who had braved the chilly October night air, were sprinkled around the large patio, giving them a semblance of privacy.

He had a feeling they were going to need it. Setting the flute down on the patio railing, he let go of Abby when she yanked herself free.

Below them, the manicured golf course stretched out in shadowy acres lit by the moon and a few discreetly placed lawn lamps. Pools of light formed on the grass and splintered against the trees that lined the fairway. In the adjacent parking lot, a car's engine growled into life and water danced eagerly in a fountain at the far edge of the patio.

Abby looked at him and Luke wanted nothing more than to pull her into his arms—but he knew she wouldn't welcome it. Her eyes were filled with hurt and it tore at him to see her features twisted with pain *he* had caused. He hadn't meant to hurt her. Ever. But he'd known all along that it would happen eventually.

"The hotel in Sacramento never *heard* of you,

Luke," she said, swinging her cashmere wrap around her shoulders and holding on to it tightly. A single strand of blond hair fell across her eyes and she whipped her head back to toss it aside. "You weren't registered there. Had *never* been registered there."

Damn it.

A shaky laugh escaped her throat. "I explained how you always stayed there when you were in town. That I'd spoken to you in your room only two days before." Her blue eyes narrowed on him. "They thought I was crazy."

"I can explain…" Not really. But he'd try. God help him, he'd try.

She held up one hand for silence. "When I got home, I used the number *you* left with me and voilà! The hotel operator—a woman with a very deep, very sexy voice, by the way—put me right through to your 'room.' Interesting, isn't it?"

"Abby, there's a perfectly reasonable explanation." She'd never believe the truth, so he'd have to find an alternate story to tell. Fast.

"Of course there is!" She kept one hand on her wrap and reached up with the other to push that loose strand of hair irritating her back into place. "It's all very clear to me now," she said, her words beginning to slur just a little.

He reached out to steady her when she stumbled again and she leaped back.

"Don't touch me again," she muttered thickly. "I don't want you to touch me."

He winced as though her words had actually delivered a physical blow.

"You lied to me, Luke," she said and for the first time, he saw tears pool in her eyes. "Maybe you've been lying to me all along. Is that it? Right from the beginning?"

"No, Abby," he said hotly, half expecting his tongue to fall off with yet another lie. "No."

She shook her head, unconvinced. "A couple of months ago, Delia Forrester hinted that when you left me, you weren't really off on business trips. That you were with other women."

Delia Forrester. A woman with a sharp mind and a calculator for a heart. At forty, her husband, Frank, was thirty years older than she and, though she seemed to dote on the man, she didn't have too much trouble coming on to younger guys. Including Luke. He'd brushed her off as politely as possible, but now, it looked as though she'd found a way to get back at him for refusing her.

"Delia Forrester's a bitch and you know it."

"Doesn't mean she was wrong," Abby countered quickly. "I stood up for you, you know. Defended my *husband*. Now I have to wonder. Are you really my husband? Are we even legally married?"

"Of course we are. Hell, we got married right here," he reminded her in a tight, hot voice. "In this club."

"Doesn't make it legal," she said, slowly shaking her head. "Doesn't mean you don't have twenty other wives all over the damn country. Heck." She hiccuped, covered her mouth and whispered, "Maybe even a few in Europe."

"What?" he demanded. "Now I'm a bigamist?"

"Why not?" she argued. "You lie to me so well, that tells me you get plenty of practice." She stepped in close, put both hands on his chest and gave him a hard shove that didn't budge him. Her wrap fell down to her elbows and she snatched it back up. "Our whole life is a *lie,* Luke. I can't believe anything you've ever said to me. For all I know, you met me on that plane on purpose. To set me up. To marry me and pretend to love me and then to—"

Luke's heart twisted as she ranted, but he knew he'd never slow her down now, so he let her go on. Get it all out. Once she was finished or exhausted or both, he'd try to talk to her. To find a way to explain without explaining. To give her what he could while he held on to what was most important to him.

God, this was killing him. Just watching her as she paced in tight circles in front of him, so clearly in pain, so deeply hurt. He'd had no right, he told himself, to bring her into his messed-up life. Had no right to try to find some normalcy for himself.

He'd known from the instant he sat down beside her on that plane so long ago, that she was the one woman in the world for him. Those two weeks in Paris had given him a glimpse of what he might have if he were anybody else. And when it came time to say goodbye, he had known he couldn't do it.

The thought of living without her was so repellent,

he'd done the one thing he had always promised himself he would never do. He'd dragged an innocent person into his world. All because he hadn't been able to stand the thought of losing her.

Now, it seemed he was going to lose her anyway.

His eyes narrowed into slits as he watched the woman he loved cry. Abby never cried. She was always in control. Always smiling. Even after her mother's death, she'd held it together.

It killed him to know that *he* was the one who'd pushed her over the emotional edge. Throat dry, heart hammering in his chest, he reached for the champagne glass he'd taken from her only a few minutes ago and lifted it for a sip.

He stopped just short of his mouth when he detected a familiar scent. Frowning down at the glass, he inhaled again, just to be sure. But it was unmistakable.

Bitter almonds.

Cyanide.

Ice collected in his veins. He slanted a glance at the club, where the party was in full swing. From his vantage point, he saw at least three waiters, all of them carrying trays of drinks and appetizers. Any one of them could have given Abby the doctored drink.

Hell, maybe it had been a random attack. Not meant for any one person in particular.

Autumn moonlight shone from the sky and enveloped Abby in a silvery glow that made her seem luminescent. Despite the pain in her tear-filled eyes and the unhappy curl of her lips, she was still the most beautiful woman he had ever seen.

And if he hadn't arrived at the ball when he did, she would be dead.

Cyanide wasn't a pleasant way to die, but it was quick. Everything in him went cold and hard. Someone in that room had nearly killed his wife. The one person in the whole damn world that meant everything to him.

"Let's go," he said abruptly.

"What?" She stopped ranting, surprised at his abrupt command. "Go where?"

"Home."

"I'm not going back there with you."

"Oh, yes you are," he muttered and holding the champagne flute carefully, he grabbed her arm with his free hand and started half walking, half dragging her off the patio and down the steps to the parking area.

"Luke, let me go," she ordered, putting every ounce of her New England blue blood ancestry into her voice.

If he hadn't already been chilled to the bone, that tone would have frozen him solid. As it was, he had to get her away from here, whether she liked it or not. Whether she fought him or not. He wasn't about to stick around and give someone else a shot at killing Abby.

He stopped dead, met her furious gaze with a quelling glare and said tightly, "Abby, we're finishing this at home. You can either walk or I can throw you over my shoulder and give the parking attendants a free show. Your choice."

Stunned shock glittered in her eyes. "You're a cold bastard, Luke Talbot."

"Not the first time I've heard that."

"First chance I get," she said, her voice withering, "I'm going to make you pay for this."

"Get in line."

Then they were through talking. He tightened his grip on her elbow and took the steps at a pace that had her stumbling along in his wake. Still, he held the crystal flute carefully by its base. Didn't want to spill a drop. Didn't want to further damage any fingerprints that might be on the glass.

Damn it.

He had to find a way through this.

Had to find a way not only to convince his wife he loved her, but to keep her alive long enough to win back her trust.

Their house sat far back on a tidy, landscaped lawn. Even in the moonlight, the blooming chrysanthemums made quite a splash of color against the gray brick home. Leaded glass windows in diamond shapes lined the front rooms and a soft lamp burned behind them, sending out golden spears of light onto the lawn.

Abby swallowed hard as Luke pulled the car into the driveway. He'd driven all the way home in silence, steering one-handed and carefully holding the champagne flute in his free hand. She was grateful for the quiet between them. After all, what had been left to say? Her mind was a little blurry, her throat a little scratchy from all the ranting she'd done on the club patio and her heart was aching for all she'd lost.

Once, she'd loved this house.

When they had first bought the place, she and Luke had christened every room with their lovemaking. Sex in the living room, dining room, kitchen. Heck, she couldn't even go up the stairs without remembering herself splayed across them and Luke kneeling between her legs.

Now when she walked through the house, she felt empty. There were no sounds of children, because Luke had wanted to wait to have babies. She had gone along, wanting him to herself as long as possible, and knowing that one day, they'd begin the family they had talked about so long ago in Paris.

He turned off the engine, turned to look at her and said, "We have to talk."

"I wonder how many marriages have come to an end with those immortal words," she said, her voice a whisper.

"Abby, I don't want our marriage to end."

She turned her head to look at him and in the shadows, she told herself that there was apology in his eyes. But she knew that it was too little too late. She had loved him for so long, and so fiercely. It was hard to believe that it could all come to a shattering end.

"It's too late for that, Luke," she said and climbed out of the car, without waiting for him to open her door.

As she walked around the front of the car,

though, he was there. Waiting. And still holding her glass of champagne.

"Why'd you bring that with you?"

"I'll tell you inside."

His face was shuttered, his eyes distant and she knew it would be pointless to argue with him about it. Besides, if the truth be told, she simply didn't have the heart for another argument. She felt exhausted. Drained. All she wanted now was her bed and eight hours of oblivion.

She followed him along the walk and her heels clicked noisily against the bricks as if they were marking off the last remaining seconds of a marriage that had seemed so perfect in the beginning.

He opened the front door and stepped into the foyer. For some ridiculous reason, that solitary lamp left on in welcome made her want to cry. Welcoming them home. Probably for the last time together.

"Come into the living room," he said, as he walked across the hall, hit a light switch and entered the huge main room.

The gray brick walls looked cold and impersonal, but paintings of vivid landscapes and bright splotches of color gave life to the room. Overstuffed furniture in tones of cream and beige were artfully arranged and boasted throw pillows in jewel tones. The massive fireplace was dark and empty and a vase of freshly picked chrysanthemums spiced the air.

While she watched, Luke set the crystal flute on the mantel, then walked quickly across the gleaming hardwood floor to the front windows. There, he yanked at a cord and closed the drapes, sealing them in, shielding them from prying eyes. Better that way, Abby thought. No point in putting on a show for the neighbors.

At that thought, she almost laughed. The homes in Eastwick were so big, so far apart, she could probably scream bloody murder and no one would hear her. She could dance naked in front of the windows and no one would see her. She knew this for a fact because, once upon a time, she and Luke had tested the theory.

But that was then and this was now.

Luke turned to look at her and in his eyes, she saw something she had never seen before.

Fear.

Three

"What is it?" Abby asked, taking a half step in his direction before she realized that she shouldn't *care* what was bothering Luke.

He blew out a breath and came toward her. Abby held her ground. There were still shadows in his eyes and a firm set to his mouth that she couldn't remember ever seeing before. "There's something you have to know," he said finally.

"If this is another lie, don't bother," Abby said, guarding her heart carefully. Of course it was like locking up the house after the burglar had left with all your diamonds, but it was the intention that mattered, right?

"I haven't lied to you…exactly," he said, reaching

out and grabbing her shoulders, holding her in place in case she tried to bolt for the stairs.

"Really? So the hotel where you were supposed to be staying made a mistake when they told me they never heard of you?"

"I can explain."

"With another lie. No thank you."

"Abby something's going on here—"

"No kidding?"

"I mean," he muttered, grip tightening on her shoulders, "something more than what's happening between us."

Her heart deflated. Like a balloon in the hands of a nasty child with a pin, all of the air went out of her. "So it's not *us* you're worried about," she said flatly, surprised that the pain could keep on coming. "It's something else. Something, no doubt, way more important than our pesky little marriage."

"Damn it, will you listen to me?"

"You're not saying anything, Luke. Why should I listen?" Her gaze locked on his and she tried to see into his mind. To read the thoughts he kept hidden from her. But he was far too practiced at keeping her out. That shouldn't still have the ability to surprise her, but it did. "I don't want any more lies, Luke. I don't want you to pretend that our marriage—that *I* matter to you. I can't keep acting as if everything is wonderful between us. I can't go on living this deception."

"I *love* you, Abby," he said, "that's no deception."

His voice was no more than a breath. A hushed prayer of sound that once would have swayed her to believe everything he told her.

Now, she wouldn't allow herself that belief.

"How can I believe you?"

His shoulders slumped and his grip on her loosened just enough that she stepped out from under his touch. The fact that her skin felt cold without his hands on her meant nothing. Only that she would have to work even harder to distance herself from him.

"I'm sorry you feel that way, babe," he said at last and his voice had a thread of steel in it. "And I swear, I'll try to find a way to change your mind. But right now, there's something else you have to know."

Brush her aside and move on, was that it? *Oh, don't believe I love you? Well okay, we'll fix that later, but first…*

Suddenly exhausted, Abby felt as though she just couldn't handle one more thing thrown at her tonight. "Can't it wait until morning?"

"No."

"Fine." Resigned, she stiffened her spine. "Then tell me so I can go to bed."

"Your champagne was poisoned."

A second or two ticked past. She knew because she felt her heartbeat thudding in her chest. Luke's gaze fixed on her, Abby opened her mouth to speak, but couldn't make a sound. *Poisoned?*

"I almost drank it myself, that's when I noticed,"

Luke said, with a quick glance at the champagne flute, resting on the mantel.

In the lamplight, the wine inside the crystal looked like liquid gold. Clear. Beautiful. And, apparently, deadly.

"What?" she finally managed to say on a squeak. "You noticed what? How did you notice? Did you drink it? You didn't drink any of it, did you?" She flew at him, hands patting his shoulders, his chest, as if looking for a wound or something and even in her blind panic, she knew she was being ridiculous. If he *had* tasted the wine and it *was* poisoned, he'd be dead.

"I caught the scent of almonds just before I took a sip," Luke told her, grabbing both of her hands and holding on to them tightly. "That's cyanide, Abby. If you had drunk that champagne…if I hadn't come to the ball and taken it away from you…"

His gaze moved over her features lovingly and she felt the heat of it as surely as she would have his caress. His words filled her mind, her heart, her soul and a wild sense of dread rushed through her. "God, Luke. If you hadn't smelled the wine— How did you smell it on the wine?"

"Just lucky, I guess."

"Lucky." Yes, so very lucky, she thought. If he hadn't been so quick to notice. If he had tasted that wine. He would have died there on the patio, with the sound of her rant ringing in his ears.

And though she knew she couldn't live with him

anymore, Abby also realized she couldn't live knowing he was dead.

"How?" she asked, followed quickly by, "Why? And who?"

"I don't know," he answered. "But I swear I'll find out."

Cyanide?

"Someone killed my mother, Luke." Her mom, Bunny, had diligently taken her digitalis medicine—unaware that someone had switched those tablets for placebos that were no help at all when she desperately needed them. Abby's gaze latched onto Luke's. "Do you think it's the same person trying to kill me? Or maybe not. Maybe it was an accident."

He started to talk, but she cut him off.

"No," she said quickly. "You don't *accidentally* drop cyanide into champagne. But maybe I wasn't the intended victim." Abby's mind filled with the images of the crowded ballroom. Of people laughing, talking, dancing. All of them having a good time. Well, all but one of them. A murderer wandering through the room with impunity.

How could she ever imagine one of the people she'd known most of her life as a cold-blooded killer? But then, she already knew someone had murdered her mother. Was it such a stretch to admit that that someone was on a roll now and looking to edge up his scorecard?

"There's no way to know if you were the intended victim," Luke said softly.

"So it could be. Could be a mistake that I got that flute."

"Possibly," he said, but his tone said he didn't believe that.

"We should tell someone."

"We will."

"Luke…"

His hand cupped her cheek, then he speared his fingers through her hair, tugging the thick, blond mass from the diamond-studded clip. She heard it clatter onto the floor behind her and couldn't have cared less. His fingertips stroked her scalp and goose bumps raced along her spine.

"You're so beautiful, Abby," he murmured, his gaze moving over her face before locking on her eyes. He pulled in a deep breath, released it slowly and whispered, "My God, it kills me to even think about what might have happened tonight."

"Oh, me, too, Luke. Me, too." She shook her head and blinked back tears as she looked up at him.

This was a mistake.

She knew it.

But she didn't care.

If she and Luke were going to divorce, if she was never going to see him again, then she wanted tonight. She wanted to be in his arms again. Feel his body fill hers. Especially now. Now when she knew just how closely they'd both come to dying.

To losing each other forever in a way that could never be changed.

"You're everything, Abby," he whispered and bent his head to hers. A brief kiss. Featherlight. A touch of lips to lips.

And fire erupted inside her.

It had always been this way between them. A single touch was all it took to ignite the embers that were always just beneath the surface.

Then he deepened the kiss and Abby clutched at his shoulders, hanging on as her world tipped wildly. His mouth covered hers, his tongue invaded and tangled with hers while they both fought for breath.

Here was the magic, she thought, her mind clouding as sensation roared through and shut down rationality. Here was what had brought the two of them together. This was the fire that had forged them.

And no matter what else was happening in their lives, this was always good.

"I need you," he said, tearing his mouth from hers, dipping his head to kiss her throat down to the curve of her shoulder.

Abby's head fell back and she closed her eyes, concentrating on the touch of his lips against her skin. His hands moved over her, undoing the single button that held her wrap closed around her shoulders and letting the cashmere slide to the floor in an elegant heap.

Then he touched her, smoothing his palms over her arms, her back, her chest and across the tops of her breasts, displayed by the low-cut gown. Idly, he picked up the ruby pendant and held it between his fingers. Looking into her eyes, he smiled. "You wore this for me tonight."

She wanted to deny it. Hell, she hadn't even expected him to show up at the ball. But the simple truth was that he was right. She *had* worn the rubies tonight for him. As she had dressed, she had imagined his eyes on her, watching the fat ruby as it lay nestled between her breasts.

"Do you remember when I gave it to you?"

"Yes," she said on a sigh, looking into his eyes and seeing that memory reflected back on her.

"It was our first Christmas together. Christmas Eve, we sat in here, the only light in the room coming from the tree."

She swayed into him, mesmerized by his voice, by the feelings he stirred within her.

"I gave you this then because I couldn't wait for morning." His thumb stroked the cabochon stone and Abby could have sworn she felt that strong, sure touch on her skin. "You cried," he said. "You told me it was so beautiful it deserved tears."

"Luke…"

"I put it around your neck and then we made love, right here in front of the Christmas tree." He let go of the ruby and trailed his fingertips across the tops of her breasts, making her shiver. "I can still see you that night, Abby. Naked, but for the pendant, with the shine of a hundred colored lights flashing on your skin."

Her throat squeezed shut.

"And you were so beautiful," he whispered, "*you deserved tears.*"

"Luke…" She fell into him, throwing her arms around his neck, clinging to him as though he were a life preserver tossed into a stormy, churning sea. She turned her face into the curve of his neck and inhaled his familiar scent. Spice and male.

His hands swept to the back of her dress and skillfully worked the zipper and the hook and eye closure at the top. When she was freed, he set her back from him and let the dress drop to the floor. His eyes popped.

"Naked?" he asked, staring at her with frenzied wonder. "You were naked under that dress? At the ball?"

She stepped out of her heels. "Couldn't have panty lines, now could I?" And she went to him as she had that first Christmas Eve, wearing only the blood-red stone he'd given her.

"I could have lost you tonight," he murmured, dipping his head to kiss her forehead, her eyes, her nose, her mouth. "I could have lost you forever."

She squeezed her eyes shut and refused to think about the sad truth. That though she had survived an attempt to kill her outright, he'd already lost her.

Still, for this one night, she would pretend. She would let go of the hurt, the pain, the betrayal and give herself over to the wonder that was Luke.

"Touch me," she said softly.

"Abby." Her name came on a groan as she pushed his tuxedo jacket off his shoulders, then quickly moved to unbutton his shirt. He tore at his belt at the same time and was pushing his slacks down and off as she divested him of the shirt and ran her palms over his broad, muscled chest.

Never ceased to amaze her, Abby thought now, hungrily exploring her husband's flesh. He looked so lean and wiry in his clothes, yet naked, the man was solid muscle. Dark brown hair matted his chest and arrowed down across a taut, flat abdomen. Her gaze dropped and her blood pressure skyrocketed. He was already hard and ready for her.

He reached out, flicking his thumbs across her hardened nipples and Abby gasped as the jolt of sensation shot through her and settled in the hot, damp core of her.

"Don't think I'm gonna be able to wait to get upstairs to the bed," he said.

"Beds are highly overrated." Abby went up on her toes, slanted her mouth across his and met his tongue with hers.

He groaned into her mouth, swept one hand down her body to the juncture of her thighs. She gasped again as he cupped her heat, working her body with his fingers until tingles of hot, demanding expectation roared into life inside her. She parted her thighs for him even as she continued to kiss him, her tongue tangling with his in a pitched battle of hunger.

One finger, then two, slipped inside her and Abby moaned, rocking her hips against his hand, needing that touch more than she needed anything else in the world.

Her body tightened, poised on the edge of completion and for that one heart-stopping moment, she wanted to freeze time. Then the moment passed in a vision-splintering explosion of sensation. Her body jolted, rocked against him and he held her tightly as his fingers brought her to a climax that nearly shattered her.

And even before the last of the tremors had eased away, he was laying her down on the closest couch, then covering her body with his.

"Gotta have you now, Abby. Now."

"Yes, Luke. *Now.*"

She hooked her legs around his middle and lifted her hips to meet him as his body plunged into hers. He filled her completely, invading not only her body, but her soul. It was always this way with Luke. He touched her more deeply than any man ever had.

His hips rocked against hers. She opened for him, sliding her arms around his neck, dragging her fingernails along his spine as he set a rhythm that she raced to follow.

Again and again, they separated only to come together again. Her body quickened again, ready for another shattering release. She held her breath and shifted beneath him, increasing the tension, the friction of flesh against flesh. And when neither of them could stand another moment of waiting, he pushed her over the edge one more time and in the next moment, let himself follow.

Only minutes later, Luke eased away from her,

picked her up and holding her close to his chest, carried her out of the room, across the foyer and up the stairs to the master bedroom.

Moonlit darkness greeted them, silver slices of light spearing through the open drapes to lie across the wide, duvet-covered bed. Luke paused only long enough to grab one end of the down quilt and toss it to the foot of the bed.

He hadn't had enough of his wife yet tonight. Doubted that he ever could. With the knowledge of the tainted champagne foremost in his mind, he felt as though he had to keep touching her, loving her, to reassure himself that she was well and with him.

The problems they had, he would find a way to iron out. He wouldn't lose her. *Couldn't* lose her.

He laid her out on the sweet-smelling sheets and took a long moment to simply look his fill. Her eyes were hazy with spent passion, her lips full from his kiss and her body limp with release. The ruby pendant lay against her skin and her blond hair spread out beneath her head on the blue sheets.

She looked like an ancient pagan goddess.

And he wanted her desperately.

Just as he had from the first moment he saw her. "Luke…"

His name came on a sigh and the sound shuddered through him.

She lifted her arms to him and he went into her embrace like a man finding home after a long, exhausting search. Skin to skin, heat to heat, rough to smooth, their bodies lay against each other and the fire between them rekindled.

He slid down her length, taking his time, stopping along the way to nibble at her body. He took first one hardened, peaked nipple into his mouth, and then the other. He suckled her, drawing at her flesh, feeding off the soft moans of passion that slipped from her lips.

His hands moved over her body, defining every line and curve. She drew one knee up and he smiled against her breast, knowing what she wanted…needed. He slid his right hand down across her abdomen past the nest of blond curls to the heat that awaited him.

She shivered in his arms at his first touch and lifted her hips into his hand, rocking, silently demanding more. But now that the first wave of passion had been slaked, he planned to take his time. To treasure her, to stoke the fires burning within so high that neither of them would survive the inferno.

Shifting position, Luke slid off the edge of the bed, knelt on the floor and taking hold of her legs, pulled her closer. She went up on her elbows and looked at him, her hair wild, her eyes flashing with a pale blue light that never failed to leave him breathless.

He lifted her legs, draped them over his shoulders and slowly, as she watched him, lowered his mouth to her center. His gaze met hers as he tasted her. Tasted her heat, her sex. His tongue swept over the core of her, that one, tiny, sensitized nub of flesh that contained the power to send her into a frenzy of need.

She reached for him, her fingers stroking through his hair as he continued his gentle invasion. His tongue swept over her inner folds, and he felt her body jerk in response. She whimpered quietly and arched her back, tightening her grip on his hair as he worked her flesh over and over again.

"Luke, it's so good," she whispered brokenly, her heels digging into his back. "So good."

He scooped his hands beneath her, lifting her hips from the mattress, holding her tightly as she writhed beneath him. She held his head to her as if half-afraid he would stop what he was doing to her.

But he only took her higher, higher, until finally the tension in her body exploded. She screamed his name and he held her safe while the world around them shattered.

Four

Abby curled into Luke's side, her head pillowed on his chest. His arm came around her, holding her close and the sound of his heartbeat beneath her ear was both comforting and painful.

This was the last time they would be like this. The last night they would be together and her heart broke at the thought of living the rest of her life without him. Yet even as she thought it, she wondered if Luke really was the man she'd thought she knew. After all, if he had lied to her about some things, perhaps he'd lied about everything. Even down to the most basic things she'd always taken for granted. Who he was. What he was.

She closed her eyes and a single tear escaped to roll down her cheek and onto his chest.

"Abby…"

"Don't—" She stopped him, going up on one elbow to look down into his eyes. The moonlight pooled in the room, soft, incandescent. "Luke, don't say anything now. Let's just…have this night and leave the rest for morning."

He looked as though he wanted to argue. She recognized the firm set of his mouth and the slight narrowing of his dark brown eyes. But then he thought better of it, cupped her cheek in the palm of his hand. "Abby, I can guess what you're thinking about me… but you're wrong."

She let out a pent-up breath and rubbed her cheek against his palm. What felt like a cold fist tightened around her heart. "I wish that were true."

"If you'll just listen," he whispered, voice strained, eyes pleading.

She couldn't. Not now. The sting of betrayal was still too fresh. She recalled all too clearly how she had felt a few days ago, when she'd discovered that the husband she had trusted for years had lied to her about where he was. No matter what he said now, the point was, the hotel he had told her he was staying at had never heard of him.

And she couldn't forget that a woman had answered the number Luke had given her.

"I can't, Luke," she said. "I can't."

His eyes closed but not before she saw and recognized a flash of pain in their depths. She was sorry for it, but her own pain went so deep the knowledge of his brought her only a slight twinge.

Reaching out blindly for her, he wrapped his arms around her and drew her down on top of him. Holding her tightly to him, he buried his face in her hair and sighed heavily. "This is all screwed-up, Ab," he said quietly.

"I know," she answered, laying her head in the crook of his neck.

"It isn't what I wanted."

Another fresh ache rattled through her. Hardly a consolation to know that he hadn't wanted her to discover his lies.

"Please, Luke," she said, her mouth against his skin. "Don't say anything more."

His hands swept down her spine, cupped her behind and squeezed. She lifted her head, looked into his eyes and saw the fire burning there.

"If you won't let me *tell* you what I feel," he said, meeting her gaze with a steely determination that shook her to her bones. "Then all I can do is *show* you."

He flipped her over onto her back and a surprised squeak shot from her throat. He caught her chin in his hand, tipped her head back on the pillow and stared into her eyes. "I've told you before, Abby." His fingers tightened on her face. "You're *everything*."

Pushing his body into hers, he claimed her again in an ancient way. She groaned and moved with him, dancing to his rhythm again. Moving with him, opening for him, welcoming him. In this, always in this, they were in tune. They filled each other and closed off the empty places inside.

In this, they were honest.

In this, there were no lies.

"Take me," he whispered, sitting up and back onto his haunches and dragging her with him. Abby sat on his lap, impaled on his body, feeling him touch her so deeply, she thought she would never be completely alone again. "Take me, Abby. And let me take you."

She moved on him. Swiveling her hips, rocking, easing up and down on him, slowly at first, quickening the pace as their breath mingled and sighed out around them. As she moved on him, he bent his head to her breast and took her nipple into his mouth. Licking, tasting, suckling, he drove her fast and hard as she took him to the brink of oblivion.

Luke inhaled her scent, wrapped his arms tightly around her middle, holding her as closely as he could and when his release finally slammed into him, he looked into her eyes and lost himself in the blue depths that would always be *home* to him.

The next morning, Abby woke up alone.

Luke's scent was still on his pillow and her body felt limber and well used. But her husband was gone.

She sat up, looked around the room, then dropped back, disgusted, onto the bed. This shouldn't surprise her. She knew that all too well. But somehow, during those long hours of lovemaking, she'd half convinced herself that maybe their marriage wasn't over. Maybe, if they could still reach each other so completely on such an elemental level, that there was still a chance for them.

"Apparently not," she muttered into the stillness. She scooted back, and stuffed a pillow behind her, braced on the headboard. "For Pete's sake, Luke. Somebody tried to *kill* me last night. You couldn't stick around an extra hour?"

Her gaze swept the room and the only sign that Luke was back in town were his discarded clothes from last night, tossed onto a chair in the corner. Okay, maybe the cyanide hadn't been aimed at her. But the point was that she had almost drunk it! She could be dead right now. And Luke would probably *still* go into work. "Well," she whispered to the empty room, "at least I know where I stand."

Sadly, she reached out for the phone on the bedside table. Yes, it was Sunday morning, but for the amount of money she was paying her attorney, he could darn well take her call anyway.

"Louis?" she asked when a man answered.

"Mrs. Talbot?"

"Yes," Abby said, gripping the phone receiver tightly. "I know that it's Sunday, but I'd like you to have the papers delivered to my husband today."

"Today? But—"

"Please. Just do this. I already gave you his company's address. No doubt you'll find him there." One thing she could say about Luke. He was a fiend for work. He put in more hours at his job than anyone she had ever known. If he had devoted half as much energy to their marriage, this day wouldn't have come.

Her lawyer hemmed and hawed for a few seconds, then said, "A private messenger on a Sunday will be prohibitively expensive."

She didn't care.

She just wanted this over.

Her heart ached again and she rubbed her chest with her free hand as if to try to massage away the pain. It didn't help.

"It doesn't matter," Abby said. "Please, just have the papers delivered to him within the hour."

"Of course, I'll get right on it—"

"Thanks." She hung up and let her fingers rest atop the phone for a long minute, as if she could undo what she had just done. But the bottom line was, this decision had been made weeks ago. She was only following through on it now. And it would be best to have it done quickly. Then she and Luke could both move on with their lives.

Alone.

At work, Luke was haunting the lab rats—the technical geeks who can decipher any mystery once it's put on a glass slide.

"There's got to be something," he snapped, standing right behind Bernie Burkower as he huddled over the gazillion-dollar, super-duper, electron-something-or-other microscope.

"Yeah," Bernie said, sitting up and pushing his

black horn-rims up higher on his sharp, beaklike nose. "There's cyanide."

"Well, I *knew* that," Luke practically snarled. He stomped around the perimeter of the lab, hardly glancing at the beakers and glass-fronted drawers and the steel tables where evidence lay spread out for examination. "What I want to know is who put it in the champagne."

Bernie's myopic gaze followed him around the room. He shrugged. "Can't tell you that, Agent Talbot. Unless it was you or your wife who did it. Yours are the only fingerprints on the crystal."

"Perfect," he muttered and stopped dead directly opposite Bernie. "I want you to go over it again. Check the rim of the base. Or the stem of the glass. You might get a partial."

Bernie gave him one of the superior looks that all of the tech guys saved for the field agents. The one that said, *If you were as smart as me, you'd be doing this job, so back off.* "I've already tested every square inch of that glass," he said tightly. "Except for yours and your wife's prints, there's nothing on it. I can run some more tests on the cyanide, maybe find unique characteristics that could lead us to possible sources."

Frustration simmered in Luke and he felt as if he were going to explode. Last night with Abby, he'd held her, loved her and today, he was finding out there was no way to be sure she was safe. If there had been fingerprints on the champagne flute, he might have been able to figure out who the intended victim was by discovering the identity of the would-be murderer. At the very least, he'd have had someone to lock up!

Turning his head to the glass wall separating the lab from the rest of the office, he looked out at his fellow agents at their desks, on the phone, surfing the Net. Everyone out there was diligently working on cases assigned to them.

Everyone but Luke.

But how the hell could he take on a new assignment when there was every chance someone was out to kill his wife?

A phone rang and Bernie stretched out one hand to grab it. "Burkower." A pause. "Right. I'll tell him."

Luke glanced at him.

Bernie hung up and shrugged. "The director wants to see you. Like now."

Scraping one hand across his face, Luke nodded, then jabbed one finger at the crystal glass still on Bernie's desk. "Check it again."

He stomped out of the lab without waiting for an answer or a smart-ass retort from Bernie. Outside the lab, the office wasn't so quiet. Keyboards clattered, telephones rang, dozens of conversations were taking place at once and from down the hall came the furious shouts of a handcuffed suspect.

To the outside world, this company was just another software developer. A leader in computer programming. Only a select few people beyond the walls of the building knew its real purpose.

Luke stalked down the long hallway, moving past cubicles, glassed-in offices and undercover agents who looked like gangbangers. He knew this world. He'd been a part of it since his senior year of college.

Recruited by a top government agency, Luke had adapted to the covert life of an operative like a chameleon. He could go from a tuxedoed guest at an embassy ball to the alleys of Hong Kong seamlessly. He became whoever he needed to become on a moment's notice.

And he loved every minute of it all.

It wasn't just the adrenaline rush of the danger and the chance to play real-life spy. It was the notion that he was doing a service for his country. Making the world a little safer for the children he hoped to have one day with Abby.

Abby.

Just short of the director's office, he stopped to pull himself together.

From the moment he'd met Abby on a plane to his Paris assignment, he had known that she was different. That she was the woman he had been born to love. And even knowing that a marriage to a civilian would be difficult, he hadn't been able to keep himself from reaching for the brass ring.

Maybe it had been selfish of him. Maybe it would have been better for her if he had walked away from what he was feeling. But he simply hadn't been able to. Life without Abby in it was no life at all.

Yet now, his marriage was crumbling, dissolving

under the mountain of half-truths he'd been forced to tell her over the years. He didn't want to be cagey with her. Wanted to be able to share everything with her.

But if he did, he would be putting her life in danger.

Still, he reminded himself, her life was already at risk. Hadn't she had a narrow escape just the night before? And who had been behind it? The same someone who had killed Abby's mom? Or was it one of Luke's enemies, trying to even a score?

God.

If he was responsible for the attack on Abby, how would he ever live with himself?

The door beside him was flung open and a tall, burly sixty-year-old man with a bald head and a bristling gray mustache glared at him. "When I send for an agent," Tom Kennedy snarled, "I mean for him to come *into* my office. Not just stand outside it staring into space."

The man turned and headed to his desk and Luke followed, closing the door behind him. A big room, as befitted the director of an agency who reported only to the President, the office was neat to the point of painful—except for the desk. Tom's desk was a vast expanse of glass and steel and the top of it was covered by files, photographs, memos, a half-eaten sandwich and a scattering of jelly beans spilling out of a tipped-over jar.

And if he had to, Tom could put his finger on absolutely anything in that pile within a heartbeat. A sort of jumbled organization.

"Sorry," Luke said to the man he'd been reporting to for eight years. "I've got some things to think about."

"You've got *plenty* to think about," Tom admonished him. "For example, your trip to Prague." He tossed a manila file to the edge of his desk, knocking a few pieces of candy to the floor. "The paperwork's all in there. Itinerary, tickets, name of your contact once you arrive. You leave in two days."

Luke picked up the folder, flipped it open, glanced at the contents, then closed it again. He ignored the quickening of his heartbeat. Hell, he always liked to start a new job. The rush. The risk. The satisfaction of getting away with something under the very noses of the guys supposed to prevent it from happening.

But today was different. Tossing the file back onto the desk, he shoved both hands into his pockets and said, "Can't do it."

"You'll be meeting with Schuman when you leave Prague for Berlin." Tom picked up a black pen, made a note on a file, then spun around in his chair and stacked it neatly on the shelf behind him.

"You're not listening," Luke said through gritted teeth. "I'm not going."

Turning back to the front, Tom kept talking. "You'll give the chip to Schuman and he'll have it coded and electronically transferred back here."

Luke had worked with the German agent many times. That wasn't a problem.

"You'll have to send someone else on this trip. Send Jackman."

Tom snorted. "Jackman doesn't speak German."

"Then send someone else."

"Check your tickets now," Tom said, leaning back in his chair and studying Luke through slitted eyes. "Make sure they're in order *before* you leave this time."

Damn it, one time. One lousy time, he'd arrived at the airport to discover that the travel arrangements made for him were with the wrong airline. He'd found a way around the situation. Just as he always had.

"I don't care if the tickets are in order, because I'm not going."

"Your flight will put you into Prague with three hours to spare before the meet."

"Damn it, Tom," Luke said, slamming both hands down onto the desk. "I told you I can't do this one."

"I heard you," the older man said, bracing his elbows on the arms of his leather chair and steepling his fingertips. "I'm just not listening."

"Well, you'd better start. I can't leave right now. Things at home are—"

"Abby?"

Luke shoved one hand through his hair and bit back a growl. "She tried to call the hotel in Sacramento direct. Naturally, they didn't have me registered there."

Tom shook his head grimly. "An oversight that won't happen again."

"It's not the point," Luke told his old friend and mentor. "The point is, Abby doesn't trust me."

"Why should she?"

"Excuse me?"

"Think about it, Luke." Tom stood, came around the desk, then perched on the corner of it. "You've been lying to her since you met. And to keep doing your job you're going to have to keep on lying to her."

"Maybe I shouldn't be doing this job anymore."

"You're too good to quit."

Luke swiveled his head to stare at his boss, his friend. "I won't lose Abby over this."

"And I'm not going to lose my best agent," Tom countered. "Look, we all make sacrifices. Marrying a civilian is tough."

"If I could tell her what I do. Why I had to lie."

Tom straightened up and shook his head. "Not an option."

Regret settled in the pit of Luke's stomach. "I know."

"You could endanger her."

"I think I already have."

Tom frowned. "The lab nerds tell me there's no way to be sure *who* was behind that cyanide drop at the party."

"I'll find out," Luke promised, his eyes narrowing, his lips thinning into a fierce, grim line. "That's why I won't be on the plane to Prague on Tuesday. I'm not leaving while Abby's in danger."

"Damn it, Jackman sucks."

Luke laughed and turned when someone knocked on the office door then opened it.

"Sorry to interrupt, sir," a young woman said, holding out a large brown envelope to Luke. "But this just came by special messenger for Agent Talbot."

Luke took it, watched the woman leave again, then ripped the envelope open. Yanking out the sheaf of papers inside, he stared at them, then lifted his gaze to Tom's.

"They're *divorce* papers. Abby's divorcing me."

Tom whistled, low and long. "Apparently, your wife doesn't want you around when she's in danger. Prague looking a little better to you now?"

Five

"I really owe you guys," Abby said and reached for her glass of chilled white wine.

"No problemo," Felicity said, after a sip of her margarita. "The Debs are ready for any emergency meeting. Right guys?"

The other women gathered around the glass-topped table nodded in solidarity. And Abby wanted to kiss each one of them.

After talking to her lawyer and arranging for Luke to get the divorce papers, she'd put in a call to Emma, looking for a little sympathy. What she had received was over and above the call of sisterhood. Emma had called everyone else and now they were all together at the Emerald Room at the country club.

They had a patio table, with a view of the pool and the lushly landscaped grounds. Pansies lined the flower beds, their bright, jewel-colored faces turned toward a watery fall sun. From the nearby tennis courts, the rhythmic slap of a ball against a racket sounded like a heartbeat. In the nearby bar, music played over the speakers and a few older men sat together arguing about their golf scores.

There was only one other patio table occupied—by two elderly women in their Sunday best, sharing tea and scones. The weather was a little cool and the wind was petulantly kicking up, but being outside assured the Debs of not being overheard.

"So," Mary said, sipping her iced tea. "What's going on, Ab?"

"Yeah," Lily asked, "what's the emergency?"

"It's Luke." Abby gripped her white wine a little tighter. She'd already sniffed at the liquid, unobtrusively checking for the scent of bitter almonds. Seemed ridiculous in the bright light of day to even consider the fact that she might have been killed the night before. But the honest truth was, it had happened—and now she was cautious. But this wine was fine. Crisp and clean and the color of sun-washed straw.

"What's wrong with him?" Mary asked, concern etched onto her features. "Is he sick?"

"No," Abby said, setting her glass down again, "but he's probably pretty furious right about now."

"Uh-oh," Felicity put in. "That doesn't sound good."

"I had him served with divorce papers today."

There. She'd said it all in one breath, rushing the words out. But hearing them said out loud gave her a cold shiver. God. She was really doing it. Really ending her marriage to a man she'd thought she would spend the rest of her life with.

Worse, a man she still loved desperately.

"Oh, girl," Emma said with sympathy, reaching across the table to pat her hand.

"It's terrible," Mary chimed in.

"Well, I can't say I'm surprised," Vanessa said softly. "You've been so sad for so long, Abby."

Tears filled her eyes but she blinked them back. They wouldn't do her any good and she certainly didn't want to give anyone at the club something new to gossip about.

Which was ironic when she stopped to think about it. Her mother had been the maven of gossip. Her column *The Eastwick Social Diary,* had detailed the goings-on in Eastwick society for eager readers all over the city.

She had lived for gossip. Not that Bunny was malicious or anything. She had just loved the scandalous idea of keeping her friends and acquaintances on their toes. Her journals were legendary—she'd written down every nugget of information, every rumor, every innuendo—which was probably why they'd been stolen by whoever killed her.

Which brought Abby right back to the danger of gossip. She didn't want other people commenting on her life, her marriage. It was bad enough that Delia

Forrester was already spinning tales about how *poor Abby* didn't have the sense to see that her own husband was cheating on her.

She winced at the thought and hunched her shoulders against unseen eyes staring at her…pitying her.

"Abby," Mary said, "are you really sure this is what you want? It's so obvious that you still love him."

"I know," she agreed sadly, tracing the tip of one finger around the rim of her glass. "And that will never change, damn it. I do love him. Always have. And, I still believe that divorcing him is the right answer, but last night…"

"Ah," Felicity whispered, "a little last-minute loving?"

"Not a little." Abby slumped back against her white wicker chair. "A *lot*."

"Mmm…" Emma sighed heavily. "So I'm thinking that a divorce is the last thing on Luke's mind today."

"Are you really sure?" Mary asked again. "I mean, if the fire's still there, maybe it's not really over."

"It's not like I *want* to divorce him," Abby told her sincerely. "I thought when I married Luke that it was forever. We talked about having kids, building a family. But he's been stalling about the baby thing for two years now and then, to top it all off…I just discovered he's been lying to me for who knows how long and—"

"What kind of lies?"

She almost told them, but Abby couldn't quite

bring herself to confess that perhaps Delia had been right. That there was a chance that Luke was having an affair. Maybe only the latest in a long line of women he'd cheated on her with.

"Doesn't matter," she said grimly, swallowing hard past the knot of regret nearly choking her.

"It does, too," Felicity said sharply. "I always liked Luke. But if the bastard isn't treating you right, then you absolutely divorce him."

Abby smiled at her friend's quick defense.

"What about counseling?" Lily asked.

"No," Abby said softly, imagining her husband lying to whatever counselor they might see. What would be the point? "He'd never go and I don't think it would solve anything, either."

"I just hate to see it," Emma added. "You two always looked so good together."

They *had* been good. Once upon a time, they had been the best. But that felt so long ago now, Abby could hardly remember that sharp blade of happiness. There had once been a time when they could look into each other's eyes and know what the other was feeling.

But there had also been a time when Luke could tell Abby where he would be on a business trip and Abby could believe him. That ship had clearly sailed. Anger twisted together with pain inside her and she sighed again at how badly her life was turning out. Here it was, a lovely Sunday afternoon, when she and Luke could have been cozied up at home together, but instead, Abby was here with her friends and Luke...

"Oh, God," Abby said on a groan, "I had them deliver the divorce papers to his office."

"Ouch," Lily said.

"Hey," Mary retorted, looking from one woman to the next, "we're on Abby's side, remember."

"Oh, no doubt." Felicity lifted her glass. "We're here for you, Ab," she said, waiting for the others to join in her toast. "No matter what. You need us, we're here."

The tightness in her chest hadn't eased a bit, but somehow, the knot in her throat was dissolving. Yes, she was losing her husband. Something she might never recover from, emotionally. But she still had her friends. That said, maybe she wasn't as completely alone as she'd thought she was.

Luke was waiting for her when she walked in.

Divorce papers rolled up and gripped tight in one fisted hand, he slapped them against his thigh as if to remind himself why he was damn mad.

He heard the door open, heard her drop her keys onto the hall table. The wall clock behind him ticked loudly in the silence. Sunlight poured in through the diamond-shaped leaded windows and shone on the tables that gleamed with the lemon polish that scented the air. He listened to the click of her heels as she walked across the foyer headed for the living room and his gaze locked on the open doorway.

Her eyes widened and she sucked in a gulp of air.

"Surprised to see me?" he asked, silently congratulating himself on the calm, even tone of his voice.

"I thought you were at work."

"It's Sunday. We used to spend Sundays together."

"We used to do a lot of things," she said and started to back out of the room, clearly trying to avoid any kind of confrontation.

He wasn't going to let her.

"Like talk?" he asked.

"Yes."

He nodded, and tossed the furled divorce papers onto the coffee table, but kept his gaze locked on her. "So you mean, in the old days, you would have actually *told* me before serving me with divorce papers?"

Abby winced and it gave him no pleasure. But instead of stepping back into the hall, she came forward into the living room. "In the old days, there wouldn't have *been* divorce papers."

"I can't believe you're doing this, Abby."

He hadn't wanted to let her know just how deep the hurt went. But damn it, how was a man supposed to cover that up? Luke looked at her and felt the swell of love rushing to compete with the ache centered around his heart. He'd known that she wasn't happy.

But he hadn't known she was unhappy enough to walk out on him. And whether it was right or not, a sense of betrayal settled over him. Last night, when they were together, he'd felt all the jagged pieces of his soul fall back into place. As if the fight with Abby had never happened. As if they were still as they'd once been.

They had rediscovered the passion that had drawn

them together in the first place. They'd reconnected in a basic, elemental way. And Luke had convinced himself that they would find a way past their present problems—only to find out that Abby had secretly been planning to divorce him.

Cut a man's legs out from under him.

Add that to the fear still chewing at him—he hadn't forgotten that Abby's life had been threatened the night before—and he was in no mood to be reasonable.

"I *have* to do this, Luke," Abby said, laying one hand on her chest as if trying to hold her heart in place. "I have no choice."

"There's always a choice."

"No. Not for me." She shook her head fiercely and her blond hair flew wildly about her head. "I can't keep living this half life."

"Half life? What the hell does that mean?" He jammed both hands into his pockets and fisted them helplessly.

"It's what we have, Luke," she cried and this time her voice broke, chipping away at his heart at the same time. "I live here—you live...God. I don't even know where. What I do know is you don't live here. With me."

"This is crazy."

"No it's not," she insisted and a solitary tear escaped her eye and rolled down her cheek. "This house is no more than a place to store your stuff. You check in from time to time, but you're never really *here*."

Pain slapped at him again and Luke wanted to

argue with her. Hard to do, though, considering she was too close to the truth. "Abby..."

"Even when we're in the same room together, your mind is somewhere else, Luke." She moved to stand behind one of the twin sofas, keeping its bulk between them. Her hands gripped the chenille fabric until her knuckles whitened. "I can't keep being a part-time wife, Luke. I want the marriage we should have had. I want the babies we used to talk about. I want—"

His throat tight, he managed to say, "Go ahead. You want what?"

Her gaze locked on his and he felt the pain shining there as deeply as he felt his own.

"Mostly, I want to be able to trust my husband. And I don't."

He opened his mouth to combat that charge, but she rushed on quickly.

"No," she said, lifting one hand to keep him quiet. "You wanted to hear this, so I'm going to say it. I don't trust you anymore, Luke. You lied to me. And if you lied this time, you've probably been lying to me for years. You weren't at the hotel where you said you were going to be. And that *woman* answered when I dialed the phone number you gave me."

"I can ex—"

"I won't stay with a man who thinks so little of me that he's off having affairs with God knows how many women. I won't do it."

"Affairs?" Insult stung sharply. Over the years, he'd been away on more assignments for the government than he could count. He'd had to pretend to be married a couple of times for covert ops and he'd even had to pick up women in bars or kiss someone to keep his cover intact. But never once had he *ever* considered cheating on the only woman he'd ever loved. "I've never cheated on you, Abby."

"Oh." She drew her head back, gave him a wide-eyed look of feigned happiness and added, "You didn't? Well, why didn't you say so? Then sure. Everything's okay now. I believe you."

"Damn it."

"No," she countered quickly, hotly. "You're not going to talk your way out of this, Luke. I know something's going on. I know you're lying to me and the only thing that makes any sense of this at all is that you're a cheating husband."

"That's great," he snapped and before she could back up, stalked around the edge of the couch and grabbed hold of her shoulders. "That's just perfect. You're supposed to be the one person in the world who knows me better than anyone else. And you seriously believe I would cheat on you?"

Her head fell back and she looked up at him. Luke saw the sheen of tears in her eyes and wanted to do whatever he had to, to wipe them away. But damn it, he didn't know what he *could* do. He was sworn to secrecy about his job and even though his marriage—the only truly sacred thing to him in his life—was on the line, he didn't have the right to disregard the vow he'd made to his country.

"I don't want to believe it," Abby said, her gaze locked with his. "But what choice do I have, Luke?"

His fingers dug into her shoulders and only loosened slightly when she winced and he realized he was hurting her. "Abby, when we met in Paris, I told you that I had to travel. A lot. For my job. I didn't lie to you about that. You knew going in what it would be like."

"And in Paris," she countered, "we talked about having a family. Remember that, Luke? We wanted three kids. We even named them."

He did remember. Lying beside Abby on a narrow bed in a splash of moonlight, they'd laid out their plans for their life together. And Luke, even knowing that his job with the agency was going to make a normal life tough to manage, had wanted it all as badly as she had.

Now it was his turn to wince.

"But," she said softly, sadly, "every time I bring up the subject of us having a baby, you shut me down. You say, 'in a few months, babe'…or, 'next year, babe, when things slow down at work.'"

Luke sighed, knowing she was right and wishing she weren't. "It's not that I don't want kids. Of course I want kids with you, Abby…"

She shook her head. "It's not just that, Luke, at least not that alone. It's everything. Yes, you travel, but now I know you don't always tell me where you really are."

"I want to tell you, Abby," he admitted. "I just— *can't*."

She laughed shortly, humorlessly. "That's great. You've made my point for me, Luke. You don't trust me. And I won't live with a man I can't trust."

The phone rang and though Luke would have ignored it, Abby made a beeline for it, as if grateful for the interruption.

"Hello?" She frowned, disgusted, before saying, "I don't know why you keep calling here. I've told you over and over again, there is no Lucy living here."

She hung up and shook her head. "At least once a month, some man calls for *Lucy*. Doesn't matter how often I tell them they've got the wrong number, someone's always looking for that woman. She must be really popular."

Luke was hardly listening. *Lucy* was the code name the agency used to call him into the office. But, he told himself, since Abby was clearly more suspicious than she ever had been before, looked like they were going to have to change the protocol.

The phone rang again a split second later and this time, Luke grabbed it before Abby could. "Hello?"

"You know," Bernie Burkower grumbled, "you could answer the phone yourself sometimes so I wouldn't have to listen to your wife yell at me."

"Yes, I understand," Luke hedged, smiling and nodding at Abby while she watched him.

"She's standing right there, isn't she?" Bernie asked.

"That's right."

"Well, this could be fun," Bernie continued. "What's she wearing?"

Perfect. Luke was straddling a bottomless canyon filled with danger and Bernie wanted to make jokes. When he got back to the office, first thing he was going to do was punch him dead in the nose. Luke's hand tightened on the receiver. "I'll get right on it."

"Not gonna tell me?" Bernie whined.

"Who is it?" Abby asked.

"The office," Luke told her, then to Bernie, said tightly, "You have something for me?"

"Fine. If you're not going to cooperate, back to business then," the other man complained. "Yeah, I'm finished running the champagne and the glass."

"And…?"

"I might have found something with the cyanide."

A cold chill crawled along his spine. He glanced at Abby and she looked so beautiful and vital and so damn *alive* in the sunlight that outlined her body like a halo—it was impossible to believe that she'd come so close to dying only the night before.

"What do they want?" Abby asked, stepping closer. Sunlight scattered over her hair like liquid gold and glittered in her still-tear-filled eyes.

He couldn't tell her what was going on, yet for the first time in his marriage, he was sorely tempted to confess everything.

His wife?

Or his country?

And why the hell did it have to be one or the other?

"I'm going to have to go in again," Luke told her

and watched her determinedly blink back the tears until her eyes were cold and dry.

"If you're coming in, why am I still on the phone?" Bernie demanded.

"No reason," Luke said sharply and hung up, with Bernie still babbling.

"You're going into work," Abby said. "In the middle of—"

"You know what you said earlier about having no choice?" Luke asked. "Well, this time, neither do I."

"You said there was always a choice."

"I was wrong."

He had to find out everything Bernie knew. Had to figure out who had tried to kill Abby before they tried again. God, he'd always imagined that he'd been able to strike a real balance between his secret agent life and his home life. But apparently, he'd been fooling himself. Not only was his marriage dissolving around him, but while he had been out saving the world, someone was trying to kill his wife.

"It's okay, Luke. I was wrong, too," Abby said softly and reached out as if to touch his cheek. Then, before she made contact, she let her hand drop to her side. "About a lot of things."

Six

Abby could actually *see* Luke withdraw.

He was standing a mere foot from her but he might as well have been on the moon. It didn't matter that they were in the middle of dissecting their marriage. His focus had clearly shifted to whatever was happening at the office.

Obviously the computer software business was far more fascinating than she would have guessed.

When Luke hung up the phone Abby waited to hear what had been so darn fascinating that he was willing to walk away from their most important conversation to go back to work.

"Abby," he finally said, "this morning, while you

were still sleeping, I took that champagne glass to a lab."

"What lab?" she asked.

"Doesn't matter," he answered quickly. "I've uh, got an old friend who works at a top-of-the-line facility. He ran some tests for me."

He.

Was he telling the truth? Or was this yet another lie?

"And…?"

"And I was right. The champagne was doctored."

She swallowed hard. "Cyanide."

"Yeah."

It felt as if all the air had been sucked from her lungs. Okay sure, she'd been living with the information since the night before, when Luke had told her his suspicions. But this was confirmation. She'd blithely accepted a flute of champagne from a passing waiter and if Luke hadn't shown up, she would have died right there at the country club ball.

Sinking onto the couch behind her, Abby lifted one hand and covered her mouth.

Luke took a seat on the coffee table in front of her. He tossed the phone onto a sofa cushion, then took both of her hands in his. "My friend says the only prints on the glass were yours and mine. I want you to think back. When you got that champagne, did the waiter hand it to you?"

That moment popped into her mind and she was there again, surrounded by people and feeling so alone. She heard the music, felt the wind off the terrace and heard the waiter saying, "Ma'am? More champagne?"

"He offered it to me a couple of times," she murmured, remembering it all so clearly. "At first, I wasn't paying attention and then…" Her gaze met Luke's. "No, he didn't hand it to me. I took it off the tray."

"Was there more than one glass on the tray?"

His eyes were steely, his voice a slash of low-pitched sound filled with determination.

"Why is that important?"

"If there was more than one, if this waiter, whoever he was, was offering you a choice, then the poisoning was random. Could have been meant for anyone."

God.

The poisoning.

"No," she said, shaking her head, but keeping her gaze locked with his. "There was only one glass. I remember thinking that everyone must be having a great time, because the champagne was really moving."

Abby laughed shortly, a painful scrape in her throat and Luke's hands tightened on hers.

"Someone tried to kill me," she whispered.

He nodded. "Looking that way."

"But why?" It was a question that had no answer, but it was one she couldn't shake.

"That's what we have to find out," he told her, lifting his hands to cup her face. "And we *will* find out, Abby. I swear it."

It felt so good to have his hands on her. To feel

the warmth of his skin on hers. To savor the connection that always flared into life between them. But a part of her knew that it was foolish to take comfort here. Because Luke wasn't going to be a part of her life anymore. Allowing herself to lean on him, depend on him, would only stretch out the pain of their eventual split.

Because nothing had really changed.

Despite everything else going on around them, the painful truth was that she couldn't trust Luke anymore. And though her heart was breaking, she knew she had to defend against further pain.

She pulled back, away from his touch, and fought her instinct to move in close again. "Luke, I appreciate your help—and believe me when I say I'll accept all the help I can get to figure out what's going on."

"I hear a *but* in there."

"But," she said nodding, "I haven't changed my mind about the divorce."

"Damn it, Abby, if you think I'm going to leave you while—"

"I'm perfectly safe in my own home," she said, interrupting him quickly. At least, she *hoped* she was safe here. She'd hate to think that she was in danger in the home she loved so much. "And I don't think it's a good idea for you to continue living here."

"Tough."

"Excuse me?"

"I said tough." Luke leaned back on the table, but his hard, unforgiving gaze met hers and she knew he wasn't going to budge an inch on this. "I'm not going anywhere."

"Luke, our marriage is—"

"The marriage and divorce talk can wait, Abby." He stood, looked down at her and said, "I'm not leaving you. Not when there's somebody after you. Not until I know you'll be safe."

But who, she wondered, would keep her safe from *him?* If he stayed, if they spent more time together, it would only make their eventual parting more painful. And as it was, the pain was staggering.

"Luke," she said, standing, too, to meet him on a more or less equal basis. Even though she had to look up to stare into his eyes. "What happened between us last night—that won't be happening again."

"Fine." His jaw tight, his mouth a grim slash, he looked at her. "You don't want me in your bed, that's your choice and I'll respect it. You want me to leave you to face danger on your own and I'll fight you on it."

Her heartbeat quickened as she heard the tension in his voice and sensed it pouring off him in thick waves. She wished she could believe his feelings were based on the love she'd once counted on so completely.

"I have to get into the office," he said abruptly and checked his wristwatch. "Shouldn't be more than an hour. So get ready for some conversation when I get back. We're going to find a way to get to the bottom of this, Abby. Whether you want me in this with you or not…you're stuck with me."

* * *

Luke went directly to his supervisor.

"Tom, I need a leave of absence. A few days—" He caught himself, shook his head and admitted, "Maybe more. I can't leave Abby alone until I find out what's going on. She was almost poisoned last night."

The big man sighed and leaned back in his chair. Grimly, he studied Luke for a long minute before saying, "This is going to put us in a bind. We already went over this. We need you in Prague."

"Anyone can make that connection. Only *I* can keep Abby safe."

"You know, I could arrange for someone to keep an eye on your wife while you go on this mission."

Luke shook his head. "No. I'm not leaving her. But," he added, "I'll take you up on the extra eyes. I'd like to get one of the guys to follow her during the day. Keep her safe when I'm not with her."

"I'd want the same thing for my wife if I was in your shoes. You pick the agent you want as your wife's tail. I'll take care of the rest." Sitting up straight, Tom reached for his desk phone, punched in a set of numbers and muttered grimly, "Find Jackman. Tell him he's going to Prague."

Relief shot through Luke. He'd still have duties around this office, but he wouldn't be out of the country. Plus he'd be able to get one of his friends to watch over Abby when he couldn't. And he'd be at her side every night. Whether she wanted him there or not.

When Tom hung up, he grimaced. "Good thing

Schuman speaks English. Jackman's German wouldn't get him a cup of coffee."

"I owe you, Tom."

"Damn straight you owe me," the other man said, waving one beefy hand in dismissal. "Get this thing with your wife straightened out so you can get back to work."

"Oh," Luke promised him, "I'll get this situation sorted out. Fast. *Nobody* threatens my wife."

The next night over dinner, conversation was strained. In the old days, Abby used to love having this hour with her husband. They had a chance to talk. To share the events of their day. To laugh together.

Now, however, there were too many shadows in the room for them to pretend that they were easy with each other anymore. They were eating in the huge, farm-house style kitchen. A round pedestal table sat before a bay window where potted herbs thrived on glass shelves. The sunshine-yellow walls shone in the lamp-light, but outside the windows, the darkness crouched.

"It's good," Luke said, breaking the silence that had seemed thick enough to slice. "Always did like your lasagna."

Abby forced a smile that felt stiff and she wondered if he noticed. "Thanks. I needed something complicated today. Something to keep my mind off—" *You,* she added mentally.

"You didn't go to work?" he asked.

"No." She'd called in sick, something she never

would have done even a year ago. But these days, she didn't feel like going into work and was seriously considering just giving notice and walking away. And that was part of the problem lately, too, she admitted. Her job contributed to the dissatisfied feeling that was so much a part of her lately.

Not so very long ago, she had loved going into work. Loved being an executive at a perfume company. It was exciting to be in on the marketing decisions. To be listened to and respected when she made suggestions. She used to enjoy sitting behind her desk, talking to clients on the phone, going to lunch with the company president and discussing strategic plans for the future.

But in the last year, her job—like her marriage—had lost its shine. She felt as though there were other things she could be doing. Other, more fulfilling things. Maybe she could try painting. Or writing.

Or, being a mother?

In her heart of hearts, she admitted that what she wanted most was children. She and Luke had always talked about them. Although now, the chances of that happening were slim to none.

Pain, old and familiar, rippled through her and she shut down that train of thought because she simply couldn't bear to think about it anymore.

"Have you found out anything else about the champagne?" she asked, the silence in the room, her own thoughts forcing her to speak or deal with emotions she didn't want to face.

"Nothing that I haven't already told you."

Both of her eyebrows lifted in question.

"I *mean* it," he said gruffly. "I told you what I know about the damn champagne and the glass it was in. There's just nothing."

"That doesn't make me feel any better."

"It shouldn't. Something's going on here in Eastwick. And nobody's going to be safe until we figure it out."

Abby picked up her glass and drank a healthy gulp of wine. It didn't help to settle her suddenly tumbling stomach, but it did ease the dryness in her throat. "Do you think this all has something to do with my mother's murder?"

"Possibly." He watched her and Abby felt her own tension ease a little at the steadiness in his gaze. Funny that just having him close was comforting. Especially when she'd claimed not to want him around.

"Did you tell me everything you know about Bunny's death?"

"Yes," she said, still holding on to her wineglass as if it were a life preserver. She stared down into the deep red liquid as if looking for answers she would never find and said, "The pills she thought were her digitalis were really placebos." She tried very hard not to think about her mother suffering, in pain, futilely waiting for her pills to ease the strain on her heart. "*Someone* switched those pills. But the police don't have any ideas. No leads. No suspects."

"None?" he asked, and for the first time a wry smile curved one corner of his mouth.

She gave him a half smile in return. "Okay, touché. The problem is, not that there are *no* suspects, but that there are too *many* suspects in Mom's death. The killer could have been any number of people she wrote about in her column."

"Have to give Bunny credit," Luke mused wryly. "She knew more about dishing dirt than a landscape designer."

"Yeah, she did." Her mother hadn't always been popular with the people who appeared in her columns, but Abby had loved her deeply. And most of her friends had been very sweet since Bunny's death. Only one or two people had even hinted at being more relieved than grieved at Bunny's passing. As that thought settled in, she spoke up. "You know, there was something else."

His gaze sharpened. "What?"

"It's probably nothing, but not long after Mom died, Frank Forrester said something that I didn't think anything of at the time."

"But now…"

"Now, I don't know."

"Tell me."

His eyes were so dark they were nearly black and he was so focused on her that Abby had to fight the urge to fidget. "It's probably nothing," she hedged, feeling a little foolish now for even mentioning it, but the more she thought about it, the more she wondered.

"Just tell me."

"Right. Okay. I forget where we were," she said, going back in her mind now to try to pull up the correct memory, "probably at the club, though. Yeah." She brightened up, gave him a smile and said, "It was a Debs lunch at the club. I got up to get another drink from Harry, the bartender, and Frank was there, getting a refill for some of his golfing cronies."

"Frank?"

"Yes. He told me how sorry he was about Mom, and then he said that not too long ago, he'd had a close call of his own with his digitalis." She frowned. "He said something vague about a screwup with his dosage or something. Then he mentioned he's now put Delia in charge of his medication."

"Scary thought," Luke said.

"Totally." Abby smiled, recalling how many times she and Luke had admitted that they found Delia Forrester cold and a little intimidating. And just for a second or two, it was good between she and Luke again. Easy. As it used to be. The two of them enjoying sharing the same thoughts and sense of humor. But that moment passed all too quickly.

"I'll check into it," Luke said. "See what I can find out about Frank's close call and—"

"How're you going to do that?" Abby asked, frowning. "You're not with the police, Luke. People aren't going to tell you anything."

He swallowed hard and mumbled something about a *friend* he could call on for help.

"Who is this friend?"

"No one you know."

"Perfect," Abby said and took another sip of wine as the sigh of disappointment washed over her. "Even more secrets."

"Abby…"

"No, never mind." God, she didn't want to talk about it again. Didn't want to rehash everything they'd already said. Especially didn't want to hear more of Luke's lies. "Let's just drop it, okay?"

"Okay." Luke took a relieved breath and changed the subject entirely. "What's new in the perfume business?"

Abby looked at him for a long moment. "You don't really care, do you?"

"Of course I care. What's important to you is important to me."

"I wish I could believe that." It tore at her that she couldn't. Couldn't believe anything he said, really. He'd lied to her so well, so completely, how would she ever know truth from lie?

He blew out a breath and picked up his wineglass. Taking a sip of the dark, rich burgundy, he set the glass back down and said quietly, "Okay, so we won't talk about work."

"We can talk about *your* work," she said, eyeing him. "For example, when's the next 'business' trip?"

His gaze snapped to hers. "I was supposed to leave tomorrow."

"Supposed to?"

"I'm not going." He took another bite of lasagna and talked around it. "Told the boss to send someone else."

"You shouldn't have done that."

"Why the hell not?"

"Because I don't want you here," Abby said flatly and wondered if he knew that for the lie it really was. Could telling lies make you an expert at *identifying* them? Another interesting question she supposed she'd never get an answer to. "I think you should move out. I filed for divorce, in case you've forgotten."

His fork dropped onto the plate with a clatter that made her wince.

"Not likely to forget that," he assured her. "It isn't every day that a man gets served with divorce papers at the office."

"I—" she held up both hands "—I just wanted it over with. Done and over."

"What's between us will never be over, Abby."

"Don't, Luke. Don't do this. Don't make this harder on both of us than it has to be." She stood, carrying her plate to the sink.

He was right behind her, so quickly she hardly heard him move. Grabbing hold of her, he spun her around and pulled her so close to him she had to tip her head back to meet dark eyes filled with fury.

"It *should* be hard, Ab," he said through gritted teeth. "Ending our marriage should be damn near impossible. Why would I want to make it easy for you?"

"Why are you so determined to hold on?"

"Because I *love* you."

Abby's heart twisted in her chest and air was suddenly hard to come by. The ring of truth sounded in his voice, but what did that mean? She'd been fooled before.

Besides, now that she knew their bond was so fragile, love simply wasn't enough. She needed to know he trusted her. Needed to know…oh God, she needed to know *she* could trust *him*.

His grip on her loosened as the expression on his features softened. Sliding his hands up and down her arms, stroking her skin as if trying somehow to soothe her, he whispered, "Abby, I never cheated on you. Never."

Tears stung her eyes and his image wavered and blurred. She wanted to believe him—more than she'd ever wanted anything. But how could she? Hadn't she herself caught him in a lie? Hadn't a woman answered the phone when she called him on his last business trip?

"Please, Abby," he said, his voice a caress. "Believe me."

"I want to," she admitted, which was more than she had intended to say. "But to do that, you have to tell me the truth. What's going on with you? Where were you *really* on that last trip? Who was the woman who answered the phone pretending to be a hotel operator?"

"If I could tell you, don't you think I would?"

"I think you've been lying to me for so long now, it's become second nature."

Several long seconds ticked past and she held her breath, hoping, waiting. Unreadable emotions flashed across his eyes and his jaw worked as though he was literally biting back the words that were fighting to get out. Finally, though, he dropped his forehead to hers.

"Babe, I wish I could tell you what you want to know. You have no idea how badly I wish it," he said, voice hard-edged, steely. "But I can't. I'm sorry."

Abby's eyes closed tightly, briefly. His hands on her arms were warm and familiar, but that warmth didn't negate the cold creeping through her bones. Regret choked her and she had to fight for breath. She hadn't known she could still feel fresh pain. But it seemed that there was always more.

When she opened her eyes, she stepped away from the man she'd once thought she knew better than anyone. She needed that distance between them. Needed a physical reminder that what they'd once had was long over. That there was no going back.

As long as he insisted on keeping her in the dark.

"I'm sorry, too, Luke," she said and turned away from him. She flipped up the stainless steel lever over the faucet and watched as a rush of hot water splashed into the sink. "Now, if you won't leave the house, then you can at least move into the guest room."

"Abby, whatever you're thinking, we're still married."

"Not for long," she said firmly, despite the sheen of tears blurring her vision. "I can't be married to a man I don't trust, Luke. More, I *won't* be married to a man who doesn't trust me or respect me enough to tell me the truth."

Seven

Over the next few days, Luke and Abby reached a sort of armed truce.

At least, that's how she thought of it. He stayed in the house, but he slept in the guest room, just next door to the master bedroom. Abby had thought that if he were in another room, it would make this whole situation easier.

It didn't.

She lay awake every night, listening to him prowl the confines of his own room. She wondered what he was thinking, why he was so restless. And she wondered if he was spending as much time thinking about her as she was thinking about him.

The nights seemed to last forever, but the days

flew past. She tried to keep as busy as possible. She even went into work and did her best to focus on the tasks at hand. But it was nearly impossible.

She'd blown a meeting with a prospective client and then had forgotten to call another one back. So much for being the dedicated executive. If she didn't quit soon, Abby had the distinct impression she might be fired.

This is what her world had come to.

But how was she supposed to be concerned with next year's perfumes when there were so many other things—more important things—to obsess about?

The attempt on her life.

Her mother's murder.

Luke.

"And that's the bottom line, ladies and gentlemen," she murmured, throwing back the blanket and jumping out of bed. She couldn't think because Luke was occupying all of her thoughts.

Clearly, even divorce wasn't going to be enough to get him out of her mind. Her heart.

She walked across the big room, the plush, pale blue carpet soft beneath her bare feet. At the French doors leading to the stone terrace, she stopped, pulled back the sheer drapes and stared out into the night.

"Bottom line," she whispered into the silence, "I still love him. Always have. Always will."

Her grip on the curtains tightened until she deliberately relaxed her grip and smoothed the creases in the fabric.

Fine. She loved her husband.

A man she *knew* was lying to her.

A man she *suspected* was cheating on her.

How had it all come to this? They'd started out so well. So happy. So perfectly matched. It was as if they'd been made for each other.

Now, Abby wasn't sure of anything anymore.

As she stood there in the shadows, she heard a voice. Muffled, but distinct. Frowning, she moved to the wall separating her room from Luke's. Leaning in, she put her ear to the wallpaper, closed her eyes and listened intently.

"No," he said clearly, then there were a few words she missed, followed by, "take out."

Take out? She pulled her head back, stared at the wall as if she had X-ray vision or something and then instantly put her ear back against the wall. She held her breath and strained to hear more.

"Follow *mumble mumble mumble* tail and don't *mumble mumble mumble* her."

"Oh for heaven's sake," she muttered, frustrated and more intrigued than ever.

"Counting *mumble* you to *mumble* cover her *mumble mumble* until *mumble mumble*."

Gritting her teeth, Abby realized she'd never hear well enough through the stupid wall. Following her instincts, she moved quietly across the room, eased the door open and stepped out into the hall. A draft skittered past her and sent goose bumps racing up and down her spine.

This was just perfect. She'd been reduced to sneaking around her own house in the middle of the night to listen in on her husband's phone conversations. She had actually become the betrayed wife in every old movie she had ever seen. All she needed to do to complete the picture was hire some hard-boiled private detective to follow Luke around and snap blurry pictures.

Hmm. She tilted her head to one side and seriously considered it. For a half second or so. Then she dismissed it and tiptoed to the guest-room door. Bracing both hands on the doorjamb, Abby *very* carefully swung her hair out of the way and then gently placed her ear against the wood panel.

His voice was a little clearer here, she thought with an inward smile of victory. Now maybe she'd get some answers. Maybe she'd actually hear him talking to whatever woman he was cheating with.

Abby winced and closed her eyes. Did she really want to hear Luke talking to another woman? No. Was she determined to? Yes.

Swallowing back her distaste for the whole situation, Abby held her breath and listened.

"I don't care," Luke said. "I told you this is important to me. You have to understand that I'm not going to leave until I get what I'm after."

Her breath left her in a rush. *What he's after?*

"You do this my way, Katherine."

Abby muffled a groan. The bitch had a name. And

a nice name at that. Why couldn't she have been a Bambi or a Musty or something?

"All you have to do is stay out of sight, damn it. How hard is that?"

She leaned in closer to the door, tears brimming in her eyes even as she strained to hear more.

Luke's voice dropped and Abby frowned tightly. Darn it. She hadn't heard enough. He couldn't hang up. Not yet.

The door flew open and, unbalanced, Abby fell into the room, bounced off Luke's bare chest and stumbled backward into a table, knocking the Tiffany lamp to the floor with a shattering crash.

"Damn it, Abby, watch out," he shouted as she backed away from him.

"Me?" She slapped one hand to her chest. "I should look out? You better watch your own step, buddy boy."

"Buddy boy?"

Abby held out one hand, palm up, to keep him at bay. She couldn't let him touch her. Wouldn't let him near her. "*Katherine* probably wouldn't want you getting too chummy with me, now would she?"

"Kath—" Clearly disgusted, he tossed the cordless phone onto the bed. "You were listening."

"Damn straight I was and, hey, I got an earful." Her anger propelled her into the room.

"Abby, you don't understand—" He broke off and shouted, "Stop!"

"No— OW!" She stepped on a shard of glass and

before she could even slump with the pain, Luke was there, scooping her up into his arms.

Physical pain radiated up her leg, but emotional pain far outweighed everything else. She pushed at his chest, her hands skidding across his chest and not budging him one bit. The man might look lean, but every inch of him was solid muscle.

"Put me down."

"Right. Put you down so you can walk barefoot through broken glass some more. Great idea." He tightened his grip on her, stalked into the attached bathroom.

"I'm serious, Luke," she said as he plopped her butt down onto the green granite counter. "I don't want you to even touch me."

"Tough." He grabbed her bleeding foot, swung her around so that it was in the sink, then turned on the water.

"That hurts!" She struggled in his grip, but she might as well have tried to push at a mountain. The man had no intention of letting her go. "Turn it off."

He shot her a furious glare and snapped, "Shut up, Abby."

"Shut up? You're telling me to— OW!" She slapped his shoulder, hard, but couldn't make him stop his ministrations. And to give him his due, his big hands were gentle on her foot as he carefully pulled out the small piece of glass and threw it into the trash can. Then, holding her steady, he kept her foot under the stream of warm water until the bleeding eased a bit.

Finally, he shut off the water, grabbed a hand towel from the nearby stainless steel ring and pressed it to the bottom of her foot.

"Not that towel, it's—" She blew out a breath. "Never mind."

"Hold this in place till I get back."

"Back? Where are you going?"

"To clean up the rest of the broken lamp before you slice off your leg."

She gave him a dismissive smirk. "Very amusing."

"Nothing about this is amusing, Abby. Now hold that towel against your foot with steady pressure."

Abby's nightgown was hiked up her thighs and her bottom was icy cold, sitting on the darn granite. The harsh overhead light shone down on Luke, creating shadows on his rugged face that made him look a little more dangerous than she could ever remember seeing him. Funny how a trick of the light could make her calm, sweet-natured husband look like the Terminator.

"You have no right to give me orders," she said, but held on to the towel anyway.

"Seems like I just gave you one. So do it."

"Or what?"

Muffling a tight growl of fury, he leaned in close, braced both hands on either side of her and glared directly into her eyes. "Don't push me, Ab."

"Fine," she said with a shrug. "I don't want to bleed to death or anything, so I'll do it."

"Good."

"But *not* because you told me to."

"Whatever." He pushed away from the counter, turned his back on her and stalked into the bedroom.

He didn't see her stick her tongue out at him. But she enjoyed doing it anyway.

Wincing, Abby awkwardly shifted on the granite counter and dragged her injured foot out of the sink and onto her lap.

"Are you moving?" he called from the other room.

"Yes, master, I'm doing the tango," she snapped angrily.

"Well, sit the hell down."

She heard him throwing broken glass into a trashcan and flinched at every crash and tinkle of what had been a really lovely lamp. Her own fault. She'd obviously made enough noise that he'd heard her at the door. Some spy she'd make.

Pulling the towel away from her foot, she looked at the slice in her skin and flinched.

"Put it back," he ordered from the other room and she stared at the open doorway.

"How did you know it was off?"

"I know *you*."

"I used to be able to say the same about you, you know," she called back, as she once again tucked her now-ruined, bloody designer hand towel to her injured foot.

"Abby…"

"Who is she?"

Another crash of glass hitting the trash can, then silence.

"Luke?"

He appeared in the open doorway. Bare-chested, he wore a pair of old jeans that were worn and faded and fit him like a second skin. The denim hung low on his hips and the top two buttons were undone. The hem of his jeans stacked up atop his bare feet and Abby had to swallow hard against a sharp jolt of lust and hunger that she really didn't want to be feeling at the moment.

She had to force herself to remember what she'd overheard. He'd told Katherine that he was going to stay here, with Abby, until he had what he was after. And though she didn't know exactly what that meant, it didn't fill her with giddy joy.

"Katherine," she repeated. "Who is she? Do I know her?"

"No," he said on a sigh, "you don't know her."

Inside her, something broke. Shattered, just as completely as that antique lamp.

She'd suspected another woman.

But, oh God, how she'd been hoping she was wrong.

"It's not what you think."

Abby laughed and it sounded brittle, even to her. "I wonder how many husbands have said that to how many trusting wives."

He came into the room and lifted her foot off her lap.

"Don't. I don't want you to help me. I don't want—"

"I don't give a good damn what you want, Abby."

"Oh, I think that's perfectly obvious, but thanks

for saying it out loud." She sniffed and hated herself for it. While he inspected her injury, she wiped away a few stray tears with the backs of her hands.

"You don't understand."

"Then explain it to me."

"I can't."

"You won't. There's a difference."

"You should have stitches."

"No. No doctors. No hospitals."

He glanced at her, and probably saw both the fear and pain in her eyes. Because he slowly nodded and said, "Okay. We'll take care of it here."

Abby blew out a shuddering breath. "Okay."

"Good thing you always keep a first-aid kit in all the bathrooms."

"Yeah, that's me. Born under a lucky star."

His jaw worked, but he didn't say anything as he reached into a cupboard, pulled out the white box marked with a big red cross and opened it.

"Why were you listening at the door?" he asked as he situated a couple of butterfly bandages over the cut on her foot.

"Why do you think?" She answered his question with a question and knew this conversation wouldn't go anywhere.

"Because you don't trust me."

"Bingo. And it seems I have good reason."

"Things aren't always what they seem, Abby." When he was satisfied with the butterflies, he took a roll of gauze and carefully wrapped several layers around her foot, then cut some adhesive tape to hold it in place.

But he didn't let her go. Instead, he cradled her foot in the palm of his hand and slowly, gently, stroked her skin.

"Luke, I don't want you—"

"Now who's the liar?" he asked, his voice a low rumble of sound that seemed to reverberate inside her.

Her heart ached, making it nearly impossible to draw a breath. She looked into his eyes and saw the man she'd fallen in love with so long ago. She felt his touch and still fired to it. But it wasn't that easy anymore. No matter how much she wanted him…he simply wasn't the man she had thought she knew.

"I just heard you on the phone with another woman," she reminded him. "Is it really so easy for you to move from me to her and back again?"

A muscle in his jaw twitched and his eyes narrowed. "I've already given you my word that I've never cheated on you, Abby."

"Yes, but what's your word worth these days, Luke?"

He took a breath and released it slowly, keeping his gaze fixed on hers. Gently setting her injured foot back in her lap, he picked up her hands and smoothed his thumbs across her skin. "I know I'm asking a lot here. I know you think you have reason to doubt me—"

"I *think?*"

"But," he interrupted sharply, "I'm asking you to try to trust me. To reach back, to look at all of our years together and try to find that trust again." He dropped her hands, lifted his and cupped her face in his palms. "Please, Abby. Just try to trust me for a little while. Can you do that?"

She covered his hands with hers and though she felt the warmth of him, it didn't dispel the chill inside her. "I don't know."

He closed his eyes as if against a wound so deep he couldn't bear it. And when he looked at her again, there was grim resolve in his dark eyes. "Try Abby," he said softly. "Just promise me you'll try."

The following morning, Abby's foot throbbed and her head felt as though it was stuffed with cotton. She hadn't gotten any sleep and a quick look in her mirror told her that those sleepless hours had been etched onto her face.

Her eyes felt gritty and her stomach seemed to be in a perpetual spin and lurch. She couldn't forget Luke's gentleness with her and yet, the memory of him talking to another woman was just as clear. She felt as if she was a Ping-Pong ball, slamming back and forth between players bent on smashing her.

"Ms. Talbot?"

Abby jerked at the intrusion and looked up to find her assistant standing in the open doorway of her office. God, she was so unfocused she hadn't even heard the door open.

"What is it, Donna?"

"Phone call for you on line two. Our French

office. I tried buzzing you," Donna said, barely concealing her impatience, "You didn't respond."

"Sorry," Abby shook her head, tried to get her mind back on business. "Who's on the line?"

Donna rolled her eyes. "I just told you that. The French office. You were supposed to call them first thing this morning."

Abby sighed, rubbed at a spot between her eyes and murmured, "I guess I forgot."

"Mr. Wainwright isn't happy about this," Donna said, and the fiftyish woman looked as snippy as an old maid librarian shushing constant whisperers.

"*Thank you,*" Abby said, and bit her lip to keep from firing the woman. After all, it was Abby's own fault the work wasn't getting done.

Donna checked a memo pad she held in one hand. "When you've dealt with Michel, you have a twelve-thirty lunch with marketing and then a two o'clock with the buyer from London."

"Fine," Abby muttered, already reaching for the phone.

"And, you should know," Donna added before she could pick up the receiver, "Mr. Wainwright wants to see you in his office before you leave today."

Perfect.

Abby's head pounded and her throat tightened. Stress, she thought. Too much stress. Her mother's murder. The attempt on her own life. Luke's lying. A divorce. Her foot hurt, her stomach was churning and her eyes felt like two marbles in a bucket of damp sand.

There was just too much.

Too much to think about.

Too much to worry about.

And now she had to soothe Michel Andre's feelings because she'd forgotten to call him. Then the lunch meeting. Then Mr. Wainwright.

Her fingers tapped idly on the receiver, but she didn't pick it up. She glanced at the blinking white hold light on the phone and knew she should pick up the darn phone.

But she just couldn't make herself do it.

"Ms. Talbot?" Donna prompted. "Line two?"

Abby hardly heard her over the roaring in her own ears. She couldn't do this anymore. Couldn't pretend that this job, the perfume industry, mattered to her in the slightest. It wasn't as if she needed the income. It wasn't as if she *had* to be doing a job she no longer cared about.

So why was she here?

She couldn't come up with a single reason.

"That's it," she said, grabbing her purse from the bottom right desk drawer and then standing up. She looked at Donna's surprised expression and nearly laughed. Shrugging into her suit jacket, she said, "Tell Mr. Wainwright I won't be able to come to his office today."

"He won't be happy."

"Curiously enough," Abby said as she walked to the door, forcing Donna to step aside to make room, "that's not my problem anymore. I quit."

Eight

That afternoon, Katherine Shaker checked her ear mic and then pulled her short brown hair over her ears to cover it. "I'm set," she said, picking up her purse and flipping it open to make sure her nine millimeter was tucked inside. It was.

"Fine," Luke said, slipping his own gun behind his back, under the waistband of his jeans. Pulling his sweatshirt down to cover the bulge, he grabbed his keys from his pocket and jingled them in the palm of his hand. "Keep the tail on Abby. Don't let her out of your sight."

"I've been on her ass for the past two days, remember?" Katherine smirked at him. "I've been doing this a long time, Talbot. I really don't need you to tell me how to do my job."

"Yeah?" Luke asked, glancing around the crowded central office to make sure no other agents were close enough to overhear. "If you're so damn good at your job, you'd know enough not to call me at home."

She had the grace to flush a little, but immediately stiffened her spine and lifted her chin. "An error I regret."

"No more than I do," he countered, remembering finding Abby at his bedroom door, eavesdropping on his conversation with Katherine.

He could recall with utmost clarity the look of wounded betrayal in her eyes and he wanted to kick his own ass. But what could he have done differently? It wasn't as though he could tell her that he had been talking to a fellow agent about Abby's safety.

Tom had assigned Katherine Shaker to help Luke out, knowing that the woman's elegant look and manner would fit in well around the country club and Eastwick society. She had a good cover story—the estranged wife of a wealthy older man, shopping for a new home. That way, she could move among the locals, frequent the country club and be able to keep tabs on Abby without her getting suspicious.

Or, more suspicious than she already was.

"Look, Abby's walking a fine line right now," Luke said, inwardly cringing at the understatement. He hated admitting, even to himself, that *he* himself had added to Abby's worries. "She knows her mother was murdered—probably by one of the people she considers a friend. She damn near died herself, and she can't trust her husband anymore."

For the first time since he'd known her, Luke saw sympathy flash in Katherine's eyes for a split second. "It's hard, I know," she said, swinging her purse strap over her shoulder. "Hell, Luke. Marriage is tough enough under normal circumstances. And God knows nothing about our job is *normal.*"

"True," he acknowledged and wondered again if he shouldn't just tell Abby the truth and damn the consequences.

"Telling her wouldn't be a good idea," Katherine said, as if she were reading his mind.

He laughed shortly, ruefully. "What're you, psychic?"

"No," Katherine said wryly, "it's just that you're not the first agent to consider telling their spouse the truth about what they do."

The normal, everyday office noise faded into the background. It was as if all the keyboards had been silenced and all the other agents had left the room. Katherine's pretty features were blank, revealing nothing and yet, Luke had known her for a few years. He knew she had once been engaged to a medical doctor, but that the relationship had ended. Badly.

"Did you?" he asked quietly.

She shifted a look first right, then left, then back to him. "Yeah. If you ever repeat this, I'll deny it, call you a liar and maybe even put out a contract on you," she warned with only a slight smile on her face. "But yes. I told my fiancé the truth. I know it was against regs, but I felt like he deserved to know who he was marrying. What I did for a living."

"And…?"

"And," she repeated, "you know who my husband is. You know he works for this agency. And you know he's not a doctor."

"He didn't take it well." Luke eased down to perch on the edge of his desk.

"You could say that," Katherine admitted with a half shrug. "You could also say I saw sparks from the soles of his feet as he ran away from me at top speed."

"I'm sorry."

She shrugged again. "So was I. At the time. You know, David wasn't a bad guy. He just wasn't pre-pared to hear that the woman he thought he loved was a spy, not a computer software analyst." Inhaling sharply, she straightened up and said, "So, enough of memory lanc. I'vc got to get moving if you want me to start the tail on your wife this afternoon."

"Right. And thanks, Kat."

"Later."

The tall, self possessed woman walked across the busy room, head held high, but Luke wasn't fooled. He had heard the old sadness in his friend's voice and knew the betrayal by her fiancé still hurt her. He ap-preciated the fact that she'd told him any of this at all—she'd taken a chance. If their supervisors ever found out she'd talked about the agency to a civilian, her career would be over. But at the same time, he wondered if Abby would react the same way? Would she be appalled? Or relieved?

He would probably never know.

"Thanks for coming," Mary said when she opened her front door to Abby an hour later. "Kane really wants you to hear the tape."

"I can't believe he's still got it," Abby said, tossing her purse down onto the hall table in her friend's elegant foyer. Favoring her injured foot, Abby fought the urge to kick off her designer mules. She'd worn them that morning to avoid having to wear closed shoes over the bandages. But after several hours, the throbbing was starting to reverberate throughout her body and all she really wanted to do was go home and prop up her foot.

"Oh, Kane's too thorough to ever throw something like that away. The police have a copy, but he kept the original. I don't think they know that, but…" Mary shrugged and tucked her hair behind her ear.

Abby glanced around the house as she followed her friend down the hall and then up the stairs to Kane's office. Paintings, done by Mary herself, dotted the walls, bright splashes of vivid color. The house itself was quiet and cool, and Abby appreciated the peace.

Ever since she'd walked out on her job, her brain had been clamoring with silent shrieks, all demanding that she explain herself. But she couldn't. All she knew for sure was that leaving that office, she'd taken her first easy breath in weeks. It was as if she'd escaped prison. Where she would go from here, she had no idea. But that first step had officially been taken and, despite the rational voice in her mind trying to guilt her into going back, she was confident with her decision.

Trying to refocus her mind, Abby asked, "This is the call Kane received from some woman accusing you of killing my mother?"

"Yes." Mary paused on the stairs, turned back and looked at Abby. "I can't tell you how much it means to me, knowing that you believe I would never have hurt Bunny. Even as furious as she could make me," Mary acknowledged, "I would never have hurt her."

Instinctively, Abby reached out, took one of Mary's hands in hers and gave it a squeeze. "Honey, I know that." Then, forcing a smile and a chuckle she didn't really feel, she added, "Besides, Mom could make *anybody* nuts. Including me."

Mary's eyes filled, but she blinked the tears back and smiled in return. "Thanks. Really. Thanks."

"You bet." Abby let her go and continued up the stairs when Mary started walking again. She and Mary had known each other forever. When they were kids, Mary had had a wild, bohemian streak that had made her lively and fun to be around. And though she was quieter now, more centered, there was simply no way that a woman as inherently sweet and gentle as

Mary could murder *anyone*. Least of all, the mother of one of her best friends.

At the landing, Mary turned right and led the way into a room that had been outfitted as a top-of-the-line office space. Filing cabinets, a sleek computer and a fax machine-copier lined the walls and a sofa and comfortable armchair completed the furnishings. There were paintings on the walls and two or three framed photographs of a smiling Kane and Mary together standing on the wide, mahogany desktop.

Kane stood, smiled and held out one hand to Abby. His blue eyes were sharp and he looked casually elegant in black slacks and a white dress shirt, open at the collar. When he spoke, his British accent flavored every word. "Abby. Thank you for coming."

"Of course. Anything I can do." She smiled at Mary, then shifted her gaze back to Kane. "I want to find out who murdered my mother. I *have* to find out. But I want to make it clear, I know that person wasn't Mary."

Kane smiled and draped one arm around Mary's shoulders. When she leaned into him and laid one hand on his chest in a comfortingly familiar gesture, Abby's heart twisted in envy. There was a time she and Luke had been that close. That comfortable together. How she missed it.

"Well then, shall we play the tape so you can try to identify the caller?"

"Yes," Abby said and moved to the desk, Mary standing beside her, gripping her hand for support.

The minute Kane hit the play button, a strange,

distorted voice filled the room. Her words were clear, as the woman implicated Mary in Bunny's death. But her voice was muddy. Indistinct. In fact, if Kane hadn't identified her as a woman, Abby would have been hard-pressed to guess whether it was a male or female voice.

Still, the venom in the caller's tone came through loud and clear. Mary's fingers tightened on Abby's cold hand and stayed like that until the tape was finished and Kane turned the machine off.

"Any ideas?" he asked, watching Abby intently.

"None," she admitted sadly. "Though I feel like I want to burn that tape and cleanse the house with burning sage and cinnamon candles."

"Yeah, that voice gives me the heebies, too," Mary said softly, staring at the machine as if half expecting the caller to step right out of the recorder and threaten them all in person.

"Who would do that?" Abby whispered.

"Someone trying to keep suspicion off herself."

"You're sure it's a woman talking? Kind of hard to tell, isn't it?"

"The expert I took the tape to insists that the cadence of speech and some of the colloquialisms definitely point the way to female."

"I'll take your word for it," Abby said with a shudder. "I'm just glad this tape didn't incriminate Mary."

"Not a chance," Kane said and reached for the woman he loved, pulling her into a close embrace and kissing the top of her head for good measure.

Envy pricked at her again and Abby told herself she should be ashamed of the feeling. Mary deserved her happiness with Kane. Just because Abby herself was miserable, didn't mean she wanted to see all of her friends in the same boat.

"I'm sorry you didn't recognize the caller," Kane said, disappointment clear in his tone. "But thank you for trying."

Abby nodded. "The police say they still have no leads in my mother's death."

"Was the killer really that clever, you think?"

"Clever enough to escape detection so far," Abby said.

"No crime is perfect," Kane told them both. "After all, if criminals were smart, the prisons wouldn't be so crowded, now would they?"

Abby smiled in spite of her day from hell. "Good point." She checked her wristwatch and sighed. "I'm sorry, but I should run."

"Oh," Mary said, "stay and have some coffee." She paused and added in a coaxing voice, "I have cake…."

"Chocolate?" Abby asked.

"Is there another kind?" Mary teased.

"Sold," Abby said. "Coffee and chocolate. Sounds like just what I need after the day I've had."

"Bad?"

"Doesn't begin to describe it," Abby assured her.

"I'm all ears." Then she turned to Kane. "Would you like to join us?"

Kane, a wise man, shook his head and sat down

at his desk. "No, thank you, love. I'll leave you to it and get some of my own work done."

Mary bent down for a quick kiss, then straightened, and smiled at Abby. "Okay, let's go gorge on chocolate while you tell me what's wrong."

"Deal," Abby said, heading out of the room.

"Hey," Mary asked, following behind her, "why are you limping?"

Frustrated, and stuffed with chocolate and coffee, Abby headed home an hour later.

"So," she said, with a quick glance at her own reflection in the rearview mirror. "A bumper day for you. Hell, a record week. Murder attempt. Philandering husband. And now, unemployed."

Her hands tightened on the steering wheel of her sleek, two-seater sports car. When the signal turned from green to yellow, she slowed down, preparing to stop. Classic rock poured from the sound system and the dashboard clock read four forty-five.

The sky was dark and heavy with rain clouds. The wind rushed past her car, picked up dry leaves and twirled them off down the street. A kid on a bicycle popped a wheelie, tumbled off the back end of the bike and cracked his helmeted head on the sidewalk.

"Ouch," Abby muttered, then relieved, watched the kid bound up, jump onto his bike and wheel off down the sidewalk. As she turned her head to the front, she caught a glimpse of a blue car behind her.

For a second or two, she didn't think anything of

it. Then a niggling thought gnawed at the edges of her mind. Over the past couple of days, she'd seen that blue car behind her half a dozen times or more. It was never very close, usually keeping at least one car between them, but it was *there*.

Just like now.

Without turning her head, she glanced again into the mirror and tried to notice everything without actually staring. A woman sat at the wheel. Vaguely familiar and yet, a stranger. Brown hair, dark glasses, despite the lowering gloom of the day and a nondescript, late-model blue compact.

Idly tapping her fingers to the beat of the music, Abby kept tossing glances at the woman behind her, trying to place her. Trying to remember where she'd seen her and when. But it just wasn't coming.

Still, it creeped her out enough that her insides were jumping and her heart rate accelerated. *Someone* had tried to kill her. *Someone* had poisoned her champagne. Maybe this was the person. Maybe she'd tired of being sneaky and had decided to just run Abby off the road somehow. Make her death look like a tragic traffic accident.

Mouth suddenly dry, Abby reached out and punched the radio off button. Silence dropped onto her like a suffocating blanket. Rummaging one-handed into her purse, Abby blindly found her cell phone, flipped it open and hit speed dial for Luke.

"Overreacting much?" she asked herself, trying to find humor in the situation and missing completely. This wasn't funny. And it wasn't her imagination. She'd seen that car before. Seconds ticked past as she listened to Luke's phone ring. And ring. And ring. No answer.

One hand fisted on the steering wheel, Abby glanced from the woman behind her to the traffic light in front of her, anxiously awaiting her turn to get moving. Meanwhile, Luke's voice mail kicked in. Abby hung up, then dialed again, never taking her free hand off the steering wheel.

When the light turned green, Abby punched the gas pedal to the floor and held on while her car's powerful engine jumped to life. Instantly, the tiny sports car leaped off the line like a cheetah going from zero to sixty in a blink.

She tore down the road and noted that the blue car behind her kept pace. Always leaving room between them, the car nonetheless stayed right with her. Abby could hardly draw breath. Her lungs felt as though they were in a vise and her heartbeat thundered in her chest, pounding against her rib cage as if it was trying to escape its prison and fly free.

"Abby?" Luke's voice came, warm and familiar in her ear.

God, he sounded good.

"Luke, somebody's behind me. I mean following me. In a blue car." She took a right turn, barely braking and felt her tires skid slightly, then find purchase again. Trees were whizzing past as she headed for the interstate on-ramp. She wasn't going to keep driving at high speeds on city streets where she could run down a kid chasing a ball into the street.

"What?" he asked. "Following you?"

"Yes," she screamed in a sudden burst of fury at men who don't listen. "Aren't you listening to me? A blue car. A woman driving. I've seen her a lot the past few days. Just didn't notice till now."

"Ah, God. Abby…" His voice dropped a notch.

Abby steered around a slow-moving minivan and blew into the fast lane, wishing she were closer to the damn interstate. Eastwick had never seemed so big before. The blue car was closer now. She flew through a red light and the honking horns that blasted in her wake made her cringe and say a silent prayer.

"It's not stopping," she said through gritted teeth. "What do I do? Where do I go?"

"Abby, listen. You don't have to be scared," Luke was saying, his voice urgent now.

She laughed hysterically, heard the sound and took a gulp of breath to steady herself. "How can I help being *scared?*" she shouted frantically. "Somebody's trying to kill me again!"

"No, babe," he said, "it's okay. The driver of the blue car is a friend of mine."

"What?" She threw another glance in the rear-view mirror, her foot easing off the gas pedal incrementally. Did the blue car slow down, too?

"A friend, Abby. The driver is just keeping an eye on you. To keep you safe."

"Safe?" She eased up further on the gas. Fury was quickly replacing the stark terror she'd known only a moment or two ago. How could he do this to her? How could he terrify her like this? He knew she was already on an emotional cliff ready to topple. "I'm driving like a maniac, running red lights and speeding through town trying to get away from your *friend?*"

"I can explain."

"No, you son of a bitch," Abby shrieked, gripping the phone so tight, she was surprised Luke wasn't choking in response, "you *can't*. You scared me. You set up a stranger to follow me. You should have *told* me!"

She took her foot off the gas completely and kept her gaze on the rearview mirror as the blue car came closer…fast. Narrowing her eyes, she tried to see the driver, but the sun's glare on the windshield made that impossible.

Fear came back in a rush.

"Luke…"

"What's wrong?" he said, picking up on the worry in her voice.

"The car…" she said in short bursts, filled with exploding terror. "Oh…my…God…it's…not…slowing…down…"

He shouted into her ear. "What do you mean?"

"Oh God!" Abby dropped the phone, grabbed hold of the steering wheel and screamed as the blue car rammed her squarely. Her little car screeched sideways across the pavement. Eyes wild, heart pounding, she watched, helpless as she careened toward a light pole with no way to stop,

The last thing she heard was Luke's voice screaming her name.

Nine

Luke couldn't breathe.

With the sound of Abby's scream still ringing in his ears, he drove like a crazy man, following the GPS signal he was picking up from her car. From a distance, he saw an ambulance, a couple of fire trucks and three police cruisers parked in a semicircle around the scene of an accident.

As he slammed on the brakes, he noted a spiral of smoke dancing and twisting in the air as it lifted from the crushed hood of a car.

Abby's car.

"Ah, God, no…"

He threw his car into Park, turned off the engine then bolted into the gathering crowd. Only half listening to the whispered shock in the voices of the people straining to see, he pushed through them all, straight-arming his way to the front of the crowd.

He couldn't remember ever knowing this kind of bone-deep terror. It was as if his whole body was wrapped in ice that was slowly squeezing the life out of him. Abby's face floated in the forefront of his mind and was the only thing that kept him moving when he thought he couldn't take another step. Luke fought the fear jangling inside, as he'd been taught to do. But he knew, deep in his core, that if Abby were hurt bad— or worse—nothing in his life would be worth a damn.

"Stop it! I'm telling you, I'm fine, so quit trying to poke and prod at me!"

Abby's voice lifted over the muttering crowd and sounded so angry, so full of life and temper, relief plowed into Luke with the force of a freight train. His step faltered as he closed his eyes, grinned and took his first easy breath in way too long. His heartbeat kicked into life again as he heard her, clearly furious, tear a strip off somebody. He'd never heard anything more beautiful in his life.

"Somebody get me a phone," she demanded in her best Queen to Peasant tone. "Or find *my* phone. It's in my car—or what's left of my car."

"We'll get you a phone later," a deep voice said.

"Now," Abby responded and Luke wished the guy arguing with his wife luck. Because when Abby used that tone in her voice, heads were about to roll. God, he loved that woman.

"Lady, if you don't let me check your eyes for signs of concussion…" the EMT spoke quietly, with a sort of forced patience.

"I'll show you a concussion," Abby shouted and Luke pushed to the front of the crowd in time to see her give the poor man trying to help her a vicious shove.

"Ma'am?" A young patrol cop approached her hesitantly and Luke couldn't blame him for his caution. "If you'll just tell us exactly what happened…"

Luke watched as his delicate, beautiful wife ripped the blood pressure cuff off her upper arm and threw it at the EMT before turning on the cop, who looked as though he would rather be *anywhere* else.

"I've *told* you already," Abby snarled. "Pole. Car." Her palms smacked together. "Car hit pole." She threw her hands wide. "How hard is that to understand? Now, listen carefully. I. Need. A. Phone."

"Geez, lady…" The young cop backed up a step.

"Abby!" Luke called her name and she spun around fast. She had a small cut above her eye, but other than that, didn't seem to have a mark on her and for that, Luke thought, he would be forever in debt to whoever had kept her safe.

Her gaze caught his and relief, followed quickly by fury, flashed across her eyes.

"Luke!" She took a step toward him, then stopped and looked at the cop. "I don't need the phone now, after all. This is my husband."

The cop gave him a sympathetic glance, then backed off.

"Abby," Luke said again, stalking across the few feet separating them. Damn it, call him crazy, but he *loved* seeing that furious glint in her eyes. Even if it was directed at him. He'd been so scared. So terrified that he'd lost her. Never again get to hold her, kiss her, tell her that he loved her.

Then he got close, Abby muttered, "You son of a bitch!" and slapped him hard.

He felt as though his eyeballs were jittering with the force of the blow but before he could respond, she leaped at him, wrapping her arms around his neck and holding on as if it meant her life.

"I'm sorry," she muttered thickly, "I didn't mean to hit you. I'm just—"

"It's okay, baby," he assured her, his tone soothing, his hands moving up and down her back in a caress meant to comfort.

She burrowed even closer, shaking her head, tightening her grip on him. "God, Luke, I was so scared."

"Me, too, baby," he whispered, burying his face in the curve of her neck. He inhaled her scent, kissed the pulse point at the base of her throat and held her until she stopped trembling. "Me, too."

The emergency workers stayed back, giving them as much privacy as being in the center of a crowd could afford. After a long couple of minutes, though, when Luke was pretty sure he could stand letting go of her briefly, he pulled her off him and held her at arm's length. "Are you okay?"

"I'm fine," she said, but her voice had a hitch in it. "I just can't seem to stop shaking."

"Shock," he whispered, smoothing her hair back from her face with a gentle touch. Right now, she was holding it together. He knew that soon, the shock would really settle in and she'd be lucky to stand up under her own power.

"If you want my opinion," the EMT said, as he gathered up his blood pressure cuff and rolled it tightly, "we don't know if she's fine or not, since she wouldn't let us examine her."

She turned and fixed a glare on the guy. "My blood pressure is a little high because somebody ran me off the road!"

"What're you talking about?" Luke demanded, grabbing her arm and turning her back around to face him. "This wasn't an accident?"

"The only accident," Abby told him quietly, "is that I'm still alive." She shoved her hair back and Luke noticed that her eyes looked a little wild. Too much adrenaline in her system.

"I'm talking about your *friend*," Abby snapped, "the one who was following me."

"Impossible," he said thickly, instinctively scanning the area around them for the signs of the blue car Katherine Shaker had been driving. But there was nothing. Not a sign of her.

And wasn't that unusual?

If Katherine had seen Abby's accident, she would have stayed with her until help came. So

why wasn't she there? And if she wasn't there...
where the hell was she?

Abby swayed unsteadily against him and Luke
shut down every thought but his wife's safety.

"Come on. You need to sit down." He walked her
to the curb, one arm around her waist, and eased her
down carefully, as if she were made of the most
fragile porcelain. "You're not okay, Ab..."

"She might have a concussion." The EMT
shrugged and shook his head. "Can't tell because
she won't let me check her out."

"I told you I don't need to be checked," Abby
said, temper sparking again as she lifted her gaze to
Luke's. Those beautiful eyes of hers filled with tears
and the beginnings of pain he knew would soon start
screaming at her. "I just want to go home."

Luke watched her and noted how pale she was,
how glassy her eyes suddenly looked and he worried
about that cut on her forehead. She was walking and
talking now, but adrenaline would keep her moving
for a couple hours. When that wore off and shock set
in, she was going to start feeling aches and pains in
muscles she didn't even know she had.

"Abby," he said, dropping to one knee in front of her,
taking both of her hands in his. "You're going to ride
to the hospital with these guys and get checked out."

"No, I'm not." Scowling first at Luke, then the
EMT and then back again, "I don't need a hospital
and you can't make me go."

One eyebrow lifted. "Wanna bet?"

The police were dispersing the crowd and the fire-fighters were putting their gear away. Nearly sundown, the shadows were long and the temperature was cool and dropping fast. Abby shivered and Luke shrugged out of his old, brown leather bomber jacket and draped it around her shoulders.

"Abby," he said, meeting her gaze and holding it, "you're going to the hospital. Now, you can go under your own steam or I'll tie you to a gurney."

She frowned at him. "You'd do that to me?"

"In a heartbeat."

She studied him for a long minute or two, trying to decide whether or not he meant what he was saying. Finally, she lowered her gaze and muttered, "Fine."

"Good choice," Luke said and helped her to stand again. Walking her to the open doors of the ambulance, he handed her off to the paramedic and said, "I'll follow you."

She stopped. "You're not riding with me?"

He wanted to. Wanted to be right by her side, insuring that nothing else bad would ever happen to her. But there were a couple of things he had to check out. For her sake as well as his own.

"I'll be right behind you."

She nodded stiffly, then glanced past him to where her cute little sports car sat smoking, crumpled around the base of the lamp pole.

Luke followed her gaze and stiffened. The passenger side was crunched completely, shoved so far into the interior of the car that Abby, sitting on the driver's side, had probably felt the cold steel brush her body. Thank God, no one had been with her. Thank God the driver's side was relatively unscathed.

"Thank God for air bags," she muttered, as if reading his mind.

"Amen to that." Luke dropped a kiss on her forehead, then waved at one of the paramedics. "Go on and don't give these guys a hard time. I'll see you at the hospital."

Once she was inside the truck and the doors were closed, he stood back and watched as the ambulance roared off. Then he turned his gaze onto what was left of the curious crowd, searching for a familiar face. When he didn't find it, Luke walked over to the closest cop, flashed his ID badge and asked, "Any witnesses?"

The young cop's eyes bulged with surprise as he looked from the government ID to Luke's hard, cold eyes. "No, sir. There's some evidence that another car was involved like your wife said. Some blue paint on the rear right panel of your wife's car. Otherwise, nothing."

"Fine." Luke left the younger man to fill out his report and walked over to what was left of Abby's car. He checked out the rear panel himself and squatting beside the wreck, he saw the streak of blue imbedded in the scarred metal.

Careful not to touch it, for fear of disturbing evidence, Luke studied that paint as his mind raced. If Katherine had run Abby off the road, then someone had gotten to her. Which he just didn't believe.

Katherine Shaker was not only one of their best agents, she was a friend. Luke had trusted her with his life on more than one occasion.

So, if his fellow agent hadn't been behind this accident, that meant someone else had. And if they were driving Katherine's car, then where was Katherine? And who in Eastwick had been good enough to take out a trained, experienced agent?

He stood up, forced his anger into a tight, hard ball in the pit of his stomach and grabbed for his cell phone. Punching the speed dial, he called Tom Kennedy.

When the other man answered, Luke asked abruptly, "Have you heard from Katherine?"

"No. Nothing in three hours. She missed her last check-in."

"This doesn't look good."

"You think?" Tom's voice was tight and gruff. "How's your wife?"

"Probably fine, considering. She's on her way to the hospital."

"Go join her. We'll find Katherine."

"Keep me posted," Luke said and hung up, shoving his phone into his shirt pocket. Then he forgot about everything else, climbed into his car and followed his heart to Abby.

Every square inch of her body ached.

Abby winced as she pushed herself higher on the pillows at her back, then sighed in relief to be safe in her own house, in her own bed.

With her husband right beside her.

Luke had been great. Okay, he'd bullied her into going to the hospital, but he'd sat with her in the emergency room and held her hand while she was being examined. Then he'd carried her from the car to their bedroom and tenderly undressed her and tucked her into bed.

She closed her eyes and felt his hands on her again.

"Going to sleep?" Luke asked as he came into the room, carrying a tray.

Abby's eyes flew open and she watched him cross the room to stand by her side. "No," she said. "I'm too wired to sleep and too sore to be awake."

"I'm just grateful that you're *only* sore," he said, setting the tray holding a cup of tea and some soup down on the table beside the bed. "You were lucky."

"I know," she said and reached for his hand. Tugging him down onto the edge of the mattress, she looked up into his eyes so she could watch him as she asked him, "Did the police find your 'friend'?"

Those eyes she knew so well shuttered, locking her out and confirming her fears that Luke was still lying to her, keeping her at arm's length, no matter how differently his actions spoke.

"No," he said, then added, "but it wasn't Katherine who hit you."

"Katherine?" she repeated. "The woman I heard you talking to the other night?"

"Yes." He watched her and she knew he must have seen what she was thinking on her face because he said quickly, "I'm not having an affair with Kath erine. She's a friend. From work."

Abby let go of his hand and turned her face away from him. A short, harsh laugh shot from her throat. "From work? You had a computer analyst following me to keep me safe? Please, Luke. At least lie convincingly."

The phone rang and Luke reached for it. Abby didn't want to look at him, but couldn't help herself. She turned her head on the pillow and watched as her husband's features tightened and his eyes darkened until they were almost black.

"I understand," he said. "When?"

Tension spiraled in the room and Abby scooted up on the pillows again until she was almost sitting straight up. She hardly felt the aches and pains simmering in her body. Instead, every sense was locked on Luke.

She noted the ramrod stiffness of his spine, the white-knuckled grip he had on the phone and the grim slash of his mouth as he nodded to whoever was speaking to him.

"Tomorrow then," Luke said. "Fine." He hung up with a forced carefulness that told Abby what he really wanted to do was throw the phone across the room.

"What is it?" she asked, hoping that this time he wouldn't lie. That this time, she'd be able to see in his eyes that he was being honest with her.

He turned his head and speared her with a look. "That was the office."

"The office?" she repeated in disbelief. "A *computer* problem upset you this much?"

He gave a strangled laugh, then reached up and shoved both hands through his hair before scraping his palms across his face. Finally, he looked at her again, with a thoughtful, considering air.

"What?" she demanded, feeling nerves begin to flutter to life in her belly. "What is it? Luke, please just *tell* me. I can take anything but more lies."

"I think you can," he said finally, nodding to himself as if he'd made a decision. Then, speaking slowly, he picked up one of her hands and held it tightly. "I should have told you this a long time ago. But I wasn't allowed. It's against the rules."

"What rules?" Abby didn't understand any of this, but just thinking that someone else had been behind her husband lying to her made her furious. "You mean you've been lying to me because you were forced to?"

"Yeah," he acknowledged, his eyes still dark, his features still tight. "That's about it. In my business, you never tell the truth. Lies keep you alive."

Fear blossomed in her chest and she clung to his hand. "Alive? Luke, I don't—"

He cut her off. "Abby, I'm going to tell you something that I'm not supposed to reveal to anyone."

Her nerves had nerves now. The spinning, churning sensation in her stomach quadrupled and she was suddenly grateful she hadn't eaten recently. Luke's expression was so still, so serious, she was half-terrified to hear what he wanted to tell her.

But she'd had enough of subterfuge.

She wanted answers.

No matter what they were.

"First, it wasn't Katherine who rammed your car," he said.

"How do you know?" she managed to ask and studied his face in the soft glow of lamplight. Because she was watching him so closely, she saw fury glitter in his eyes before it was shut down in the next instant.

"Because she was just found, unconscious in an alley."

Abby sucked in a gulp of air then released it slowly, half-afraid she wouldn't be able to draw another when she needed it. "Is she all right?"

"She will be," Luke said, and tightened his grip on her hand. "Whoever bashed her over the head used her car to run you off the road. The car hasn't been found yet, but when it is, we're hoping there'll be some evidence to point to whoever did this."

Abby shook her head as she stared at him. "None of this makes sense, Luke."

"It does if you have the missing piece of the puzzle," he said tightly.

"Which is…?"

He blew out a breath. "Katherine's not a computer analyst, Abby. Neither am I."

This, she hadn't expected. Cheating on her, yes. Lying to her definitely. But why would a man lie about his *job?* She swallowed hard and braced herself. "What exactly are you saying?"

He locked his gaze with hers and said simply, "I'm a spy."

Ten

Luke watched her, waiting for her reaction.

When it came, it wasn't what he'd been expecting.

Her laughter spilled from her in long, breathless explosions of sound. Pushing free of his grasp, she flopped back against the pillows, closed her eyes, gasped for breath and laughed even harder.

"Oh, that's wonderful," she finally said, tears streaming down her cheeks. She lifted one hand and shook her head. "Oh God, a *spy?*"

Luke stood up and glared down at her. "What the hell is so damn funny?"

"Please…" A few more giggles escaped before she was able to control herself again. When she did, she wiped away her tears, blew out a breath and looked up at him. "Of all the silly, stupid stories to come up with. Honestly, Luke, if you're going to continue lying to me, at least make them *believable* lies."

"I'm not lying."

"Right," Abby said, still half smiling, "and as soon as Prince Charles arranges for a divorce, I'll be leaving you and setting up house in Windsor Castle."

"Funny."

"No funnier than your story."

Here was irony for you, he thought grimly. He finally spilled his guts, broke his oath to the agency and she thought it was just one more lie.

"Do you mean now that I'm actually telling you the truth, you don't believe me?"

"Truth?" Blue eyes narrowed, her laughter fading, smile slipping away, she pushed herself up and stared at him as though she'd never seen him before. "You're telling me that you, my husband the computer software analyst, are really James Bond?"

Luke shoved both hands into his jeans pockets and fisted those hands in helpless frustration. "Just so you know? We *hate* those movies."

"Oh do *we?*" She snorted. "Can't imagine why. All those wonderful toys."

She threw the blankets off and stood facing him. Luke noted the high color on her cheeks, the flash of temper sparking in her eyes and knew that this wasn't going to be easy, truth or not. Her blond hair hung loose around her shoulders and her breasts beneath her dark green, silk nightgown heaved with every breath.

"James Bond is fiction. What I do is *real*. Abby, I took an oath to never tell anyone what I do for a living. And until tonight, I never had."

"An oath."

"That's right."

"And you're a spy."

"I prefer the term undercover operative."

"Oh, sure," she nodded, those sparks in her eyes glittering hotly, "wouldn't want to use the wrong term."

He took her upper arm in a firm grip, but she yanked herself free and backed up a step or two. "Don't. Just don't even touch me right now," she warned. Her steps hesitant at first, then fed by the temper churning within, she stomped around the perimeter of the master bedroom.

Her bare feet were soundless on the thick carpet, but her breath huffed in and out of her body in impatient bursts. "Why would you tell me something like this?" she demanded, never stopping long enough for him to get a hold of her again.

"Because I'm tired of lying to you," Luke said, standing still, letting only his gaze follow her erratic movements.

She glared at him.

"I'm not going to lose you because you think I'm having a damned affair."

"So you're not having an affair, you're just a spy."

"Right."

She stopped, folded her arms across her chest and tapped one foot against the carpet. "Who's Katherine?"

Hell, he'd already told her this much. Might as well go for the whole story. "Another operative. I've known her for years."

One blond eyebrow lifted.

Luke sighed. "She's married to an upper-level agent. They have three kids."

Abby's features relaxed a little as she tipped her head to one side. "So Katherine the spy is also a mother?"

"Yes."

"And you're not having an affair with her?"

"No."

"Who are you having an affair with?"

He smiled at her. "No one. My wife is an amazing woman—and she's the jealous type."

"No I'm not," she argued, but there was no heat in it.

"You don't have reason to be," Luke assured her, walking carefully across the room. He advanced on her warily, like a man forced to approach a hungry lion.

"I'd like to believe you," she said softly and Luke felt an infinitesimally small flicker of hope spark to life inside him.

"I'm not lying, Abby," he said and reached for the bomber jacket he'd tossed across the foot of the bed. Reaching into the inside pocket, he pulled out a worn leather wallet and handed it to her.

She took it, opened it and stared silently for several long seconds. When she finally lifted her eyes to his, she said, "It's true? You work for the government?"

"It's true."

"Not a software analyst."

"Wouldn't know how to analyze it."

Shaking her head, she looked down at his official ID again and smoothed her fingertips across the photograph of him. "This is surreal."

"I know how it sounds, but it's all true." He took another step toward her. "When we met on the plane to France?"

She looked up at him.

"I was going to Paris to interrogate a suspected terrorist."

"Oh, my…"

"Those phone calls for Lucy you've intercepted? They're from the office. A signal to get me to call in or report in."

"Passwords?"

"In a way." God, how was she taking this? So hard to tell. Hard to know if he'd done the right thing. Hard to know if he'd only made things worse.

Tom Kennedy wouldn't be happy when he heard about this, but damn it, Luke wasn't willing to lose the most important person in his life because of a promise made before he'd even known her. He *wouldn't* lose Abby. Not without a fight.

"Oh, boy," she whispered and, clutching the ID wallet, she walked to the end of the bed and sat. After a moment or two, she asked, "Your last business trip. Why weren't you at the hotel when I called? Were you even in Sacramento?"

"Yes," he said, taking a seat beside her. "I was. I wasn't in the hotel, though. I stayed at a safe house there while investigating the sale of top secret government files to a foreign power."

"Safe house."

"It was an oversight—the hotel not putting you through to a room where the call would have been transferred to me."

"Top secret."

"Abby?"

She blew out a breath and looked down at his ID, still in her hand. "Government files. Foreign powers. Spies. Terrorists."

"You okay?"

"I don't know," she admitted, lifting her head to stare at the man she'd thought she knew so well. Now, everything she had accepted for years was tumbling down around her like a house of cards in a hard wind. "Luke, I just don't know what to think."

"I know it's a lot to take in."

"It really is," she said, handing him his ID and looking deeply into his dark eyes.

"I never wanted to hide this from you, Abby," he said, lifting one hand to cup her cheek. His thumb smoothed over her skin gently. "But I didn't want to risk endangering you by telling you what I do."

"I understand," she said and she really did. It still hurt that he'd kept so much of his life separate from her, but she could at least appreciate why he'd done it.

The room was quiet. Drapes drawn, only the lamplight kept the darkness at bay. She felt her heartbeat tick off the passing seconds and knew she should say something. But darned if she could think of anything.

"By keeping you out of that part of my life, I was supposed to be keeping you safe," Luke said, and reached out to smooth one hand through her hair. "Now, though, I'm wondering if just being married to me isn't enough to put you in danger."

Her gaze snapped to his as she instantly understood what he was talking about. "You mean the cyanide? You think that someone who knows who you really are tried to poison me?"

He scowled thoughtfully. "It's a possibility I have to consider." His hand stilled at the back of her neck. "But it doesn't seem likely."

"No," Abby agreed, her mind now beginning to click along at top speed. "It doesn't. No one in Eastwick suspects who you are and it wouldn't make sense for an enemy agent to expose himself or herself," she allowed, "by trying to poison a civilian at a charity dinner." She stopped, blew out a breath. "Wow. I can't believe I actually used a sentence with the words *enemy agent* in it."

He smiled and gave her neck a little squeeze. "Takes a little getting used to, huh?"

Abby turned to look right at him. His features were so familiar. His eyes the same, dark chocolate color she'd always known. His smile still curved one side of his mouth slightly higher than the other. He was the same man she'd always known. And yet…

now that she knew his secret, she imagined she was noticing new things, too.

The sharpness in his eyes. The hard planes of his jaw and the strength that helped him work behind the scenes, undercover, in danger, to serve his country.

And just like that, a swirl of something hot and delicious and overwhelming swept through her. Every bone in her body ached from the accident earlier, but the fresh desire bubbling in her veins was more compelling.

Leaning in toward him, Abby scooted close and clambered into his lap.

"Hey…" His arms came around her middle and held her in place while at the same time, he was looking at her in question. "You're supposed to be resting."

"Don't want to rest," she whispered and brushed her mouth over his, pausing only long enough to tug at his bottom lip with her teeth.

He groaned. "Abby…"

She wiggled her bottom against him and he went hard and ready in an instant.

"Mmm…" Clearly enjoying herself, she squirmed against him again, her bare heat sliding across the fly of his jeans.

His hands slid up and down her back, then dipped beneath the hem of her nightgown and smoothed along her spine, his fingertips dancing gently over her skin. "This is probably not a good idea," he managed to grumble. "You've got to be in some pain and—"

"No," she said, with a soft shake of her head that

sent her hair dancing around her shoulders. "I'm not. Not now."

She kissed him again, this time putting everything she had into it. His lips parted for her and her tongue tangled with his. She felt his heartbeat accelerate, pounding against hers as he held her so tight, she thought her ribs might crack. But she didn't care.

Yes, she had some aches and pains. But her hunger for her husband outstripped every other sensation. She wanted him so badly, she could hardly breathe. This man. The man she'd loved for so long.

When he finally pulled his head back, breaking the kiss that had left them both breathless, he stared into her eyes and whispered, "From the moment I saw you on that plane—" he shook his head and gave her a half smile "—you were all I wanted. All I'll ever want."

She didn't say anything to that, only reached down and quickly undid the buttons on his jeans. He kept a tight grip at her waist and held his breath while she worked. When she freed him, she ran her fingers up and down his thick, rigid length and watched his eyes roll back in his head.

Then she rubbed her thumb over the sensitive tip of him and when his eyes fixed on her again, she confessed, "When that car hit me, when I was sliding into that pole and knew that I could die in an instant, all I could think was...*I'll never touch him again. Never kiss him again.*"

He laid his forehead against hers and whispered her name in a broken sigh.

Her hand tightened on his length and she slowly went up on her knees. Looking down at him, she said softly, "Luke, I thought I was going to die. And I couldn't bear the thought of never being with you again. I need you. I need to feel you inside me."

"I need that, too, baby," he said and held his breath as she lowered herself onto his length. Inch by inch, she took him within her heat, surrounded him in a tight, damp sheath that filled them both with a glory they'd never found anywhere else.

In the lamplit darkness, they moved together, gazes locked, bodies joined, and together, they chased the elusive explosion that would consume them. Time stood still and all that existed was that room and the heat blossoming between them.

And finally, when she threw her head back, screamed his name and clung to his shoulders, Luke groaned, and emptied himself inside her. Then tightening his grip on her, he fell back on the bed and held his world close.

An hour or two later, Abby listened to the steady beat of Luke's heart beneath her ear as she cuddled in close to him. He was sleeping, one arm draped around her shoulder, holding her to his side.

But Abby hadn't been able to close her eyes. She kept seeing that lamppost headed toward her. Kept imagining Luke in dark alleys with guns pointed at him. Every old espionage movie she had ever seen came rushing back in the darkness to taunt her. Haunt her. Terrorize her with thoughts of the kinds of things that Luke faced every time he left their home to go to work.

And she'd never once guessed.

In all the time she'd known him, she had never suspected that he had had such a secret. Which told her exactly how good he was at his job. He was a man who had learned how to compartmentalize. A man who knew how to juggle a life of intrigue with a home life of normality.

She slid her left arm across his broad, bare chest and for just a moment, enjoyed the solid, warm comfort of him. And silently, she realized that as hard as his lies had been on her, how much worse it had been for him. What must it have been like for Luke, to come into their home and keep up a pretense. To never allow himself to fully relax. To always be on his guard.

Her eyes closed on a sigh as she thought about what she'd been putting him through for the last several months. Hurt, she'd attacked, wanting to be let in, wanting to know why she felt such a distance between them. And Luke must have been so torn. Wanting to take her into his confidence and not being able to.

How had he been able to do his job? How had he been able to concentrate on staying alive while worries about her were niggling at the back of his mind? Had she endangered him, however unknowingly?

"Abby?"

She turned her head and looked into his eyes. "I thought you were sleeping."

One corner of his mouth lifted. "I could hear you thinking."

Raising herself up, she braced her forearm on his chest and ran her free hand through his thick, dark hair. "I was thinking about a lot of things," she admitted.

"I'm guessing by the look in your eyes, they weren't exactly happy thoughts."

"No," she said sadly, knowing suddenly exactly what she had to say. What she had to do. "Luke, I do love you."

"I love you, too, baby." His hands swept up and down her naked back and she sighed, memorizing the feel of his fingers on her flesh.

"I know," she said, "that's what makes this so hard."

"What?" His hands stilled and his eyes narrowed.

"Luke, I'm so glad you finally told me everything. It means so much to me that you trusted me enough to be honest with me."

"Abby…" Wariness colored his voice.

She gulped in air and silently prayed for the courage she'd need to say what she had to say. "I'm still going to get a divorce."

He shot straight up, grabbing hold of her and dragging her across his lap. "What the hell are you saying?"

Lamplight threw harsh shadows over his features and his eyes glittered dangerously.

"It's the only way, Luke. The only way I can be sure you're safe. If you don't have me to worry about, you'll be able to concentrate on your job." She lifted one hand, cupped his cheek and dropped a quick kiss on his mouth. "I don't want to make you choose between your duty to your country and your marriage to me. Not anymore."

He tightened his grip on her. "Abby, I don't want a damn divorce."

"Neither do I, Luke," she said softly. "But for your sake, I'm still going to get one."

Eleven

Luke could have sworn he felt the earth literally shake beneath him. Staring into his wife's lake-blue eyes, he could hardly believe what he was hearing.

He'd thought it was settled. Thought they'd broken through the mistrust, the anger, the hurt of the past several months and found their balance. Now, when he'd finally told her everything, she wanted to leave him to protect him?

"Not a chance in hell I'm letting you go, Ab," he ground out through clenched teeth.

She wrenched herself free of his grasp, climbed off his lap and scooted off the edge of the bed. She grabbed up the nightgown she'd tossed to the floor a couple of hours ago and shimmied into it. Once she was dressed, she stabbed one finger at him and said, "We're going to get a divorce, Luke. Whether we want one or not."

He shook his head fiercely. "Do you even *hear* how stupid that sounds?"

"Stupid?" she countered. "What's stupid is sending my husband out to fight for his country and knowing that his mind isn't on his work. Worrying that he'll be thinking about me instead of protecting himself. *That* would be stupid."

"Now you're telling me how to do my job?"

"Somebody has to," she snapped.

Feeling at a decided disadvantage while naked, he jumped off the bed, grabbed his jeans and yanked them on. He didn't bother buttoning them up before stomping around the edge of the bed to stalk to her side. "Believe it or not, I'm damn good at my job. And I don't need my *wife* protecting me."

She shoved at his chest and didn't budge him an inch. "Do you think I'll be able to relax and go about with my life—lunching with the Debs, finding a new job, doing…idiotic, mundane things, all the time knowing that you're slinking through some dark alley with guns pointed at you?"

"You've got to stop watching those movies."

"So you're never in danger?"

He plowed his hands through his hair and briefly thought about snatching himself bald. And would have, if he thought it would help. "Of course there's some danger. There's danger anywhere.

Hell, Abby, you were nearly *poisoned* at a country club dance!"

"That's different."

"No, it's not," he said tightly, grabbing her upper arms and pulling her to him. "You think I would choose my job over *you?* You're wrong. I'll quit in a heartbeat if that's what it takes to keep you with me."

"I won't make you choose between me and our country, Luke."

"There are other things I can do. I don't have to be an operative."

"It's what you love," she argued.

"*You're* what I love," he said.

She dropped her forehead onto his chest and sighed heavily. "This is so hard."

His arms came around her. "Baby, it'll get better. We're going to figure all this out. We'll find out who slipped you the poison. Find Bunny's murderer. Then we'll figure out where we stand."

"We already know where we stand, Luke."

"Yeah, we do," he said, and tipped her chin up with his fingertips until his gaze met hers. "We stand *together,* Abby. Always."

At the company, Luke was like a man possessed. For two weeks, he snarled at coworkers, snapped at lab techs and growled at interns. His work was suffering because he couldn't get his mind off Abby. In that, she'd been only too right. Images of her face, her tears were with him always and he heard her voice whispering the word *divorce* over and over again in his imagination.

Every night, when he held her, when he made love to her, he promised himself he would never lose her. Then in the light of day, he was faced with her immovable decision to give him up for his own sake.

The damn woman was more stubborn than he'd given her credit for. Now that she knew who he was and what he did, she was determined to leave him—because she loved him. Now what the hell sense did *that* make?

Outside his miniscule office, the company floor was a cacophony of sound. Keyboards rattled, faxes hummed, phones rang and conversations rose and fell like waves on the ocean. But Luke wasn't a part of any of it. He'd locked himself away, not only to work, but to avoid interaction with his fellow agents. For their own good.

Everyone was walking a wide berth around him. Conversations halted when he came near and people lowered their gazes whenever he looked up from a desk that was littered with files, notes and investigative reports.

"Tom wants to see you in five."

Luke muttered a curse at the intrusion and glared up at…Katherine. His perpetual frown was replaced with a relieved grin. Good to see her up and around again. "Hey, you're looking better than the last time I saw you."

Wryly, she quipped, "Yeah, well, unconscious and bleeding's not my best look."

"You okay?"

"Yeah." She waved away his concern and strolled around the edge of his desk. "God knows we've both been through worse. Belgium springs to mind."

"True." That op had gone wrong from the start. He and Katherine had just barely managed to make the extraction point and get out to safety in time.

"You really should get yourself a better office," Katherine mused. "With your seniority, you shouldn't be working in this rat hole."

He shrugged and glanced around. "Suits me. Since I'm usually in the field, why have a big damn office sitting here empty most of the time?"

"I guess. But it's a damn mess, too." Pushing a pile of crap off the only other chair in the office, she sat down, crossed her legs and stared at him. "So, you want to tell me why Bernie's complaining about being an indentured servant?"

Luke leaned back in his chair and scrubbed both hands across his face. He'd had Bernie going over and over the tests already run on the champagne flute and its contents looking for something. Anything they might have missed. And the little lab geek was really being a pain in the ass about it.

Luke couldn't blame him. He was the best lab tech in the agency. If there had been something to find, Bernie would have found it. It was only Luke's desperation making him push the man to find the impossible.

So far, nothing. But he was determined. He had

every agent available looking for clues, trying to uncover the mystery of his mother-in-law's death.

"I need a break and Bernie's the best one to find it for me."

"Not necessarily," Katherine said and tossed the manila file folder she was holding onto his desk.

"What's this?"

"Take a look." She leaned back in her chair and smiled as she watched him. "You know how you wanted me to look into Delia Forrester? That bit with her husband's accident with the digitalis?"

"Yeah?" He flipped the folder open and quickly scanned the contents. As he read, his blood pumped and his pulse rate jumped into high gear.

"Seems dear Delia's got something of a track record when it comes to husbands. Thought you might make something of it."

Luke read the first page, then turned to the second. By the time he was finished, his eyes were flashing with determination. "This is good, Kat."

"Thought you'd like it."

"There's no evidence, though, right?"

"Not yet," Katherine said. "But there's plenty there to think about."

"Got that right," Luke agreed, tapping one finger against the file. "And I'm thinking that there's a way for us to get the proof we need."

"Just tell me what you want me to do."

Luke grinned. "I was hoping you'd say that."

* * *

"We've got something."

Abby looked up as Luke stalked across their brick patio to where she knelt in front of a flower bed, weeding. Since quitting her job and finding out the truth about her husband, she'd been too unsettled to sit still for long. And weeding gave her the satisfaction of having instant results to her work. The gardener might not appreciate her help, but being outside gave her time to think.

And heaven knew, there was plenty to think about.

She watched Luke coming toward her. Her heartbeat quickened just to see him move. She'd always felt a burst of lust whenever her husband walked into a room. But now, everything about him seemed just a little different.

Oh, he was still the man she'd always loved. But since telling her the truth about himself, it was as if Luke had decided to let her see the *real* him. His every movement radiated confidence and strength and she wondered how she had ever convinced herself that he was a man who would be satisfied sitting behind a desk.

"Abby?" He snapped his fingers in front of her face.

"What?" She blinked herself out of her daydream and grinned up at him. "Sorry. Mind wandering."

He squatted beside her and leaned in to plant a quick kiss on her mouth. Abby licked her lips as if savoring the taste of him, then took a deep breath and let it slide from her lungs on a sigh of regret. Soon, too soon, she would lose him. She would be alone, wondering what he was doing. If he was safe.

If he was missing her.

"You're doing it again," Luke said quietly, smoothing her hair back and tucking it behind her ear.

The fall sunshine was weak, but warm enough to keep the October chill at bay. A soft breeze rattled the gold and red leaves of the trees in the yard.

Abby smiled, leaned back, pulled off her gardening gloves and laid both hands on her thighs. "Okay. I'm here. Listening. Tell me."

He handed her a file folder and before she could open it, he started talking. "You already know that I've had every spare body at the company working on finding an answer to your mother's murder and the attempt on your life."

"Yes…"

"We've been looking into the backgrounds of everyone in Eastwick. Been a lot of paperwork generated on this case."

"I bet that's gone over well," she said, stroking the file folder with the tips of her fingers.

"They've been happy to help me out with this, Abby. When one of us—or our families—is attacked, everyone takes it seriously."

"What've you found?" she whispered, still a little reluctant to open that file.

"Well, the standard background checks didn't give up much. But we dug a little deeper and found something interesting." He eased down to sit on the grass opposite her. Wrapping his arms around his up drawn knees, he gave her another quick grin and added, "In fact, found a lot of interesting stuff."

Curiosity piqued inside her, but Abby stifled it. "I don't think I want to know everyone's secrets," she said. "Mom did. She loved every little morsel of gossip and savored each tiny tidbit of information—" She paused and sighed. "Which is probably why she was killed, eventually. But I've recently discovered that some people have a reason for keeping secrets."

He reached out, took one of her hands and gave it a squeeze. "And some secrets," he said, "are much easier to keep when they're shared."

Linking her fingers with his, she nodded and said, "You're right. Go on. Tell me what you found."

"Most everyone here has something in their pasts that they're either not proud of, or trying to hide. But one person in particular jumped out at us."

"God," she whispered, afraid of what Luke had found out, hoping that whatever it was, it wouldn't affect someone she loved. One of her friends. "Who?"

"Delia Forrester."

Surprise jolted her a bit. Oh, Abby had never liked the woman, but she had never seemed anything other than what she appeared to be. A fortyish trophy wife of a wealthy, much-older man. Delia and Frank had only been married about a year and, though she seemed to dote on her husband, Delia hadn't really bothered to mix with the people in Eastwick. She never volunteered at the charity functions, avoided joining the club committees, and in general focused her attentions on her husband.

Sure, she was annoying and occasionally hurtful with the constant jabs and withering remarks she made a point of issuing. But what on earth could she have in her past that would so interest an investigative search of her life?

"Really?" Abby asked and kept her gaze locked on his face. "She always seems so…ordinary. Well," she corrected, "sort of *flamboyantly* ordinary, I guess."

Confused, he said, "One day, you'll have to explain to me how you can be flamboyantly ordinary."

She grinned. "Sure. But for now…"

"Right." He reached for her bottle of water, unscrewed the cap and took a long drink before speaking again. "We've looked into everyone, right down to the bartender in the Emerald Room."

"Harry?" She pulled her head back in shock and stared at him. "Please don't tell me Harry's a bad guy."

"Nope." Luke laughed. "He's just who he says he is. A cranky bartender."

"Thank God."

"Back to Delia. Remember when you told me that Frank Forrester said something once about an *accident* with his medication?"

"Yes." She recalled clearly. "He was commiserating with me after Mom's death. He even made a point of saying that Delia was going to be in charge of his medication from now on, to make sure there were no more accidents."

"Yeah, well, I'm figuring he's going to be rethinking that decision."

"Luke, tell me. What's going on?"

"First you tell me. What do you know about Delia?"

"Not much," she admitted. "She hasn't made many friends here. Seems determined *not* to. She dresses a little too flashy, her hair's a little too platinum blond and her jewelry's gaudy." Shrugging, she added, "If you didn't guess, I don't like her much."

"Glad to hear it," he said and handed her the water bottle. He waited while she took a sip, then said, "Because flashy, gaudy Delia has a background that gave a couple of very experienced agents cold chills."

"You're kidding."

"Oh, no," he said and opened the folder still lying closed on her lap. "Take a look at that."

Abby's gaze dropped to the first page of the file and her mouth dropped open when she saw Delia Forrester's mug shot. "Oh, my God."

"Yeah," Luke said wryly. "We had to go down a couple of levels to find this information. Somewhere along the line, Delia paid out some serious cash to have her file buried."

"I can't believe this."

"Well, the police photographer didn't exactly capture her best side."

"I'll say." The woman in the photograph stared out at Abby through flat, cold brown eyes. Her makeup was harsh, her hair atumble, but it was those eyes that caught and held Abby's attention. "When was this picture taken?" she asked, even as she lifted her gaze to read the information typed onto the sheet.

"About ten years ago," Luke said, and idly pulled a weed encroaching on Abby's bright gold chrysanthemums. "She was arrested for passing bad checks in New York."

"A forger?"

He nodded. "Small-time. She used to steal checks out of bill envelopes people left out on their mailboxes." He shook his head almost in admiration. "Then she'd wash the ink off, let the check dry and fill them out again for whatever she wanted."

"You can *do* that?" Astonished, Abby just stared at him.

"It's not easy, and these days, more check companies are making it even harder, with new security measures taken with the paper they use," he paused. "But yeah. Someone who knows what they're doing can make a real killing fairly easily."

"How'd she get caught?"

Luke smiled. "A cashier at an upscale department store demanded to see her ID when she wrote the check and wasn't convinced by the phony driver's license. She alerted store security, they called the local cops."

"So we know she's a thief," Abby said. "But that doesn't make her a murderer."

"I haven't gotten to the good part yet."

"There's more?"

"Plenty." Luke caught her gaze with his and held it. "Seems little Delia wasn't satisfied with petty theft. She's moved on up. Now, she's a genuine Black Widow."

A cold chill raced along Abby's spine and she shivered. "What does that mean, exactly?"

"It means that she's made a career out of marrying older, wealthy men. As far as we can tell so far, she's had five husbands—including Forrester."

"Five?"

"The kicker is, every last one of them died. Within fifteen months of marrying sweet Delia."

Twelve

"This is highly irregular," Tom Kennedy said the following day as he stood behind his desk and glared first at Luke, then at Abby, who stood by his side. "No offense, Ms. Talbot, but you don't belong here."

"Please call me Abby and, believe me, I know," she said, and would have said more, but Luke cut her off.

"This was the easiest way, Tom. She knows everything already anyway."

The huge, bald man didn't look at all happy about that little piece of news and Abby worried that Luke had compromised not only his job, but maybe his life by taking her into his confidence. What happened to spies who couldn't be spies anymore?

She glanced around the big office, idly taking in

everything at once. It was almost cavernous and as tidy as a church. Somehow it wasn't what she'd expected. But then nothing about this place was anything like her imagination had painted it. The main floor looked as though it could be any ordinary run-of-the-mill office building.

The fact that it was so nondescript, was almost a letdown.

"Yeah," Tom practically growled at him. "And we're going to be having a talk about your breach of security, real soon."

"Mr. Kennedy." Abby threaded her fingers through Luke's and held on tightly while she continued. "I'll never repeat anything my husband has told me—you have my word. And I'm happy to sign whatever paper you think is necessary."

The big man huffed out a breath, his jaw worked for a minute or two, making his substantial gray mustache twitch and then finally, he nodded abruptly. "I appreciate that, Abby. And for now, we'll just take your word at face value and leave it at that."

Luke smiled down at her and Abby felt a thread of relief unspool inside her. Even if she and Luke couldn't be together, she wanted to know that he was happy. Doing the job he loved.

She would always worry about him, but at least now, she'd have the image of his workplace in her mind and she would be able to picture him here.

"Now that that's out of the way," Luke said, keeping a tight grip on Abby's hand, "I want to talk about our plan."

"It's crazy," Katherine muttered from her chair beside the desk.

Abby looked at her briefly. Now that she knew Luke wasn't having an affair with the woman, Abby was feeling a bit more magnanimous toward her. After all, the woman had been injured in an attempt to keep Abby safe.

"It'll work," she said, meeting the woman's direct gaze.

"With you as bait," Katherine pointed out.

"I'll be right there with her," Luke said, glancing at her himself. "And so will you. Along with Baker and Hernandez. Hell, you can even bring your husband along."

"A night without the kids?" Katherine said, brightening up. "Maybe it's not so crazy after all."

Abby laughed. "You consider setting a trap for a possible killer as a good night out?"

Katherine smiled easily. "You don't know my kids."

"I do," Luke said. "She's right."

"All right now," Tom said, lifting both hands in an attempt to silence them all. "If I understand this correctly," he said, looking from one to the other of them, "you want to throw a party at your house."

"That's about the size of it," Luke agreed. "We'll invite everyone, including Delia."

"And this accomplishes…?"

"At the party," Abby put in, "we're going to trap her into a confession."

Luke nodded and took over. "There's plenty of suspicion about her former husbands' deaths, but there's no proof. If we play this right, we should be able to take her down."

"Unlikely," Tom murmured.

"I don't think so," Luke argued. "Delia's a woman on the edge. She's worried about being found out. Worried that at any moment, her past will come to light and that would be enough to get her latest husband to divorce her and run for the hills before she can get her meat hooks on his money."

"True…"

"*And,*" Abby added, "I believe she killed my mother because she had discovered something Delia wanted kept quiet. I've already put out the word that I found copies of my mother's journals and that I was going to read them before locking them up in a safety-deposit box."

"Seems risky."

Abby saw the disgusted look Tom shot at Luke and she spoke up. "Don't blame him. This was my idea. I didn't even want to tell *you,* but Luke insisted."

"Lady—" Tom started to say.

"This has nothing to do with you or your agency," Abby said, cutting him off neatly. "This is about me. And my family."

The very thought that Delia Forrester was a free woman when she might very well have killed Abby's mother was too much to stand. And from what Luke said, Bunny wasn't the woman's only victim. It was long past time that someone stopped her before other innocents died.

"She's a civilian," Tom said. "She doesn't know the dangers of—"

"I don't need your approval," Abby told him, lifting her chin and locking her gaze with the older man's. "I know what I'm doing and I insist on doing it. On my own if I have to. Doing it with your help will be a lot safer."

Luke dropped one arm around her shoulders, linking them and she was grateful for it.

"I don't like it." Tom said, then frowned when his office door flew open after a perfunctory knock. "I said no interruptions!"

"Sorry, Director," the harried-looking, middle-aged woman blurted, then shot everyone a look of apology. "But we've got trouble. Our contact in Russia is on line two and our translator is held up in traffic."

Tom stomped out from behind his desk. "Well, get someone else on it."

"There is no one else."

"Damn it, you mean to tell me there isn't one other person in this place who can speak Russian?"

"There's me," Abby offered quietly and every eye in the room turned to look at her.

"What?"

Abby shrugged. "I'd be happy to help. I do speak several languages. Always had a knack for them and—"

"Get Ms. Talbot a phone," Tom shouted, impatiently waving at Abby to hurry along with him. "Can you type, too?"

"Eighty words a minute," she said.

"That'll do," Tom said, taking her arm and practically dragging her out of the office and plunking her down into an empty cubicle.

Luke and Katherine were right behind her, watching the whole thing. Katherine looked shocked, but Luke was clearly enjoying the situation.

"Translate the information," Tom said, "and type it up exactly as you hear it. Inflections, pauses, everything. Got it?"

"Got it," Abby said, slipping the headphones on and settling behind the desk.

"Good. Get busy." Tom punched a blinking white light on the phone console.

And then Abby was too busy to think. Her fingers flew over the keyboard as the far-off Russian operative passed along information he'd gathered.

As she did the work, she smiled to herself, realizing that somehow or other, she'd just become a junior agent. She was doing something *important*. She was helping. In a very small way, she knew exactly what Luke felt when he reported to work every morning.

And she envied him.

* * *

At midnight, Abby finally gave up on trying to sleep.

She sat up, braced the pillows behind her back and stared out the French doors at the night beyond. Cold outside, the trees at the edge of the yard swayed in a wind that tore off fall leaves and tossed them like confetti.

Abby glanced at the empty bed beside her and wished Luke were there. But he was still sleeping in the guest room. With the divorce action hovering over their heads like a black cloud trying to decide whether to rain or not, Abby had told him it was best if they kept their distance.

Especially now.

Sex would only make things harder between them. How could she ever leave Luke if he was still making love to her? She closed her eyes as a wave of nausea so thick her head spun, rolled through her. Just the thought of being without Luke made her sick. How would she ever live without him in her life? How would she be able to get through the long lonely nights stretching out ahead of her through the coming years? On the other hand, how could she stay married to him, knowing his love for her might endanger him—cause him to hesitate when it might cost him his life?

Her stomach dipped again and Abby tossed the blankets back and slid off the bed. Sleep wasn't going to happen. What she needed was some hot tea. She moved quietly across the room, stopping only long enough to grab her robe from the foot of the bed. Slipping it on, she tied the green silk sash at her waist and eased her bedroom door open. No sense making enough noise to wake Luke up.

She headed downstairs, her bare feet making no sound at all on the carpeted wood steps. Shadows reached for her, but they were friendly shadows. She loved this house. Had from the moment she and Luke had first seen it. Abby had always felt safe here and the thought of leaving it broke her heart.

But she couldn't imagine living in it without Luke.

Moonlight spilled through the open windows in the dining room, and she walked through the silvery patches, with only a glance at the night sky. She walked into the kitchen and didn't bother with the light switch. She knew where everything was. Grabbing the teakettle off the stove, she took it to the sink, filled it, then set it down again on the back burner. With the gas flame shining blue in the darkness, she got down a cup and a tea bag, then sat at the kitchen table to wait.

"Isn't this handy?"

Abby jolted and spun around on her chair, staring into the dark. Her heart was still jittering in a rapid beat when Delia Forrester stepped out of the shadows. Moonlight reflected in her eyes and glinted off the edge of the knife she held in her right hand.

"Delia—"

"Please," the other woman said with a smirk. "Don't pretend to be surprised. I know you know."

"Know?" Abby stalled, looking around the kitchen, past Delia to the door into the dining room, hoping to see Luke appear like an avenging angel.

But there was nothing.

"Don't play games, I don't have the time," Delia snapped and stepped up close, grabbing Abby with one hand and holding the knife in front of her face with the other. "I want the copies of your mother's journals."

Damn. Abby had expected Delia to make a move for the diaries at the party they'd planned. For some reason, she had never thought the woman would break into the house and try for them early. Stupid.

"*Now*, Abby," Delia warned.

"Fine. Fine. They're in the, uh…" She remembered finally where she and Luke had told everyone they'd stashed the nonexistent copies of the journals. "Living room."

"Great. Let's go." Delia yanked her out of the chair and Abby had a moment to wonder if the woman was really that strong, or did crazy people just get a burst of muscle when they needed it most?

Prodding her across the floor, Delia kept the knife close to Abby's side as they left the kitchen. Halfway across the dining room, an earsplitting whistle sounded—the teakettle on the stove had reached the boiling point.

Delia hesitated, then gave Abby a push. "Never mind. Hurry up. Get the journals and I'm out of here."

Fear shaking inside her, Abby stepped into the living room and walked toward the farthest bookcase. Her gaze swept the room, calculating escape plans. Looking for something to use as a weapon. Bottles of liquor? Too far away. Lamp? Too heavy to grab and throw in time. Damn it. *Luke! Wake up!*

She had to do something, Abby thought wildly, as the very real fear of dying grabbed at her and wouldn't let go.

"Drop the knife, Delia." Luke turned on the lights at the same time as he spoke and there was a brief moment of sheer blindness, going from dark to light so quickly.

But Delia recovered far faster than Abby did. She grabbed hold of Abby, spun her around to face Luke and held the knife close to her captive's rib cage. "Back off now, or I'll kill her."

"No you won't."

God, he looked good. And fierce. Like an avenging angel. His dark eyes were narrowed and full of fury. She'd wished for him and here he was. Like her own personal cavalry.

Delia laughed and the sound was like nails on a chalkboard. Abby winced, but Luke never flinched. Barefoot, in jeans, his features grim, he braced himself and held his pistol in both hands, its barrel pointed at Delia.

"I can drop you right here," he promised.

"Not before I cut her, you can't."

"I've got a shot," someone else said and Delia darted a look at the far corner, as Katherine Shaker stepped out from behind a leather couch where she'd been hidden.

"Me, too." Another man's voice, this time coming from behind the bar.

"Damn it!" Delia's voice hitched as she muttered the curse and her grip on Abby tightened even further. "I swear to God I'll kill her. I've done it before. One more dead bitch won't bother me."

"Touch her and you're dead."

"So predictable," Delia hissed. "Men are so damn easy. You want to be her white knight? Then back off before you get her killed."

Abby's gaze remained locked on Luke and she didn't look away when he idly waved off the agent behind the wet bar.

"It was all so easy," Delia muttered, more talking to herself than anything else. "All those men, so easy to make them fall in love with me. Even easier to kill them. Disgusting, slobbering old farts. Did they really think I *wanted* them? Men. As a gender, you're all pretty useless," she pointed out to Luke. "It took a *woman* to figure it all out."

"My mother?" Abby whispered and for her trouble, felt the edge of the knife press through the sheer fabric of her robe and into her side. She yelped as a trickle of blood rolled down her skin.

"Keep still," Delia said with a sneer. "Don't want me to get nervous, do you?"

"I'm okay," Abby shouted to Luke and winced as the knife bit into her again.

"Your mother just kept sticking her nose into my business," Delia muttered as if she still couldn't believe it had all gone so wrong so fast. "You're just like her. Questions. Always questions. The bitch should have understood! She should have been on *my* side. Woman to woman. But no. She didn't see it that way. So she had to go."

"You killed my mother."

"Not like I wanted to," Delia argued. "She didn't give me a choice. It was her own damn fault. Nosy bitch was asking for it."

Abby saw red. Actual red. The edges of her vision clouded and swam with the fury nearly choking her. Before she could think about it, before she could worry about the repercussions, she spun out of Delia's hold, turned and slammed her closed fist into the other woman's jaw.

Delia staggered back as if she'd been hit by a truck and before she could recover, Luke was there, knocking the knife out of her hand and pushing the older woman to the floor. In a couple of seconds, he had her facedown on the carpet, wearing a shiny pair of handcuffs and screaming about revenge and the stupidity of men in general.

While the other agent dragged Delia to the car waiting outside, Katherine sprinted to the kitchen to turn off the still-shrieking teakettle.

Luke gathered Abby in his arms and held on tight.

"Ow," Abby complained as his grip came down on the slice in her side. Instantly, he released her.

"God, you idiot, she could have killed you," he

murmured, pushing her robe aside and lifting her nightgown to get a look at the cut. "Going to need stitches."

"Great," Abby said shakily, "I hate needles."

Then she swayed a little unsteadily and Luke grabbed her again, face tucked into the curve of her neck.

"She killed Mom," Abby said, squirming in as close as she could get to her husband's broad, bare chest. "And she wasn't sorry. She just made me so mad, I—"

"It's all over now, baby. It's over." He ran one hand over her hair and the other up and down her spine, as if reassuring himself of her safety.

"How'd you know she was here?" Abby asked, her voice muffled against him.

"I followed you when you went downstairs. Katherine and Hank were positioned in here just in case Delia made a preemptive strike for the journals."

"Good call," she managed to say.

"Thanks."

In the background, the teakettle's whistle abruptly ended and Abby knew that it was all over. God, she couldn't believe it. She was safe. Luke was safe. And her mother's killer was going to be behind bars for a long, long time.

"Luke?" Katherine called from the doorway and he looked up. "We're taking the nutball into the company for interrogation. You want to be there?"

"In an hour or two. First I'm taking Abby to the hospital. The bitch cut her."

Katherine scowled and glanced at Abby. "You gonna be okay?"

"Yes. Thanks."

The other woman smiled, lifted one hand and walked out the front door, closing it behind her.

"It's over."

"Not yet," Luke said and stepped back from her only far enough that he could cup her face in his hands. Looking into her eyes, he said tightly, "I know you've got some big ideas about leaving me for my own good, but I'm not letting you go, Abby."

"Luke…"

"I'm through being a spy," he said, staring into her eyes, willing her to believe him. "There are lots of jobs I can do for the company without being a field agent. From now on, I'm only playing secret agent with you. In our bedroom."

Abby looked up at him through teary eyes and oh God, she really wanted to let him make that sacrifice. She didn't want to go through life without him. But… "You'll regret that decision. You know you will. Luke, I don't want you to resent me someday for forcing you to give up the job you love."

"You're not forcing me to do anything. I made my choice Abby. It's you."

"I wish it was that easy."

"It *is*," he said softly, a gentle smile curving his amazing mouth. "It's only hard if you fight me on it. And I warn you, you'll lose."

His eyes were so warm and dark and full of love,

it stole her breath. And Abby so wanted to let him do this. Yet still, she hesitated.

He bent down, pressed his lips to hers for a long second or two, then straightened up and said, "The only thing I would ever regret is losing *you*. Nothing means anything to me without you in my life, Abby. Don't you get that?"

Everything she needed to know was in his eyes. His voice. His touch.

"I do," she said, smiling now, even as the tears rolled down her face. "I love you so much, Luke. And I don't want to lose you, either."

He exhaled and gave her a grin that made her toes tingle. "Never gonna happen, babe."

She reached up to hug him and yelped as the pain in her side screamed at her.

"Right," Luke said, scooping her up into his arms. "First things first. Stitches. Then interrogating the bitch from hell."

"Can I watch?" she asked, cuddling in close to her own personal Secret Agent Man.

"Wouldn't have it any other way," Luke told her, and headed for the front door.

They had the planned party anyway a few nights later.

With smooth jazz sliding from the stereo, and all of her friends gathered in her home, Abby smiled and enjoyed the sensation of having every-thing right with her world. Her gaze slanted over the couples laughing and talking and she smiled at all of them.

Jack and Lily had brought baby Grace with them—they couldn't bear to be apart from her just yet. Emma and Garret were standing close to them and the look in Emma's eyes told Abby that babies were definitely on her good friend's mind. Felicity and Reid were dancing, oblivious to everyone else and Mary and Kane were standing in a corner arguing about something—and clearly enjoying the spirited debate. Vanessa and Tristan were talking to Katherine Shaker and her husband and Abby grinned. Katherine had demanded her invitation to the party be upheld. She had really wanted a night out.

And then there was Luke, smiling at her from across the room. Her heart jumped in her chest and she dropped one hand to her abdomen. God, just a month ago, she never would have believed she could be this happy. She took a sip of her tonic water and lime and held out one hand to Luke when he came toward her.

"Thanks for coming, everybody," Luke said just loudly enough to get everyone's attention.

Emma grinned. "How could we resist? Not only a party, but the answers to what's been going on in Eastwick."

Luke dropped one arm around Abby's shoulders and gave her a squeeze. "Right. Well, you all know Delia Forrester's been arrested."

"Still can't believe she actually killed Bunny," Mary murmured.

"Believe it. There's no clear evidence to prove that she also killed all of her previous husbands, but there's enough suspicion that I don't believe she's going to be getting out of jail any time soon."

"But why?" Felicity asked. "Why Bunny?"

Abby spoke up. "Apparently, Mom was there when Frank had some chest pains and she noticed that until Delia spotted Mom watching, she was moving really slow in getting help. But Mom didn't realize that she'd actually thwarted a murder attempt."

"Until much later," Luke added.

"Right," Abby said. "You know that Mom wrote down *everything* in her journals. Well, I guess she started keeping an eye on Delia after that. Making notes, tracking little things. Enough to make Delia worry about her. Eventually, Delia decided to kill Mom the way she had planned to kill Frank. By replacing Mom's digitalis with placebos." She looked over at Mary. "The day Mom died, Delia saw Mary leave Mom's house after an argument."

Mary dipped her head, but Kane gave her a supportive hug that had her smiling a moment later.

"When Mary left Bunny," Luke said, taking up the story, "Delia slipped inside and forced Bunny at gunpoint to hand over her journals. The stress and fear sent Bunny into cardiac arrest. She tried to take one of her pills, but dropped it as she died. Delia says she took the pills with her when she left, but apparently, she missed the one Bunny dropped when the housekeeper's approach sent her running."

"Good God," Garrett muttered.

"Poor Bunny," Felicity said.

"A while later," Luke started talking again, "Delia phoned Kane, disguised her voice and implicated Mary in Bunny's death."

"What about all of the other blackmail attempts after Bunny died?" Vanessa asked.

"It seems that killing Bunny was about self-preservation," Luke said, hugging Abby again. "But the other blackmail attempts were just about greed. And spite. We found all of Bunny's journals hidden away in Delia's house."

"They're still around?" Mary whispered.

"Don't worry," Abby said, smiling. "I burned them myself last night."

"Good," Jack said. "I think Eastwick's had enough of the scandalous."

"Amen to that," Reid said.

"Well, I don't know," Abby told them all, snaking one arm around her husband's waist. "I have had an anonymous offer to continue Mom's column. It seems someone out there thinks there are still plenty of scandals to write about."

"Oh, no," Emma said, laughing. "You're kidding."

Everyone laughed and talked at once and in the hubbub, Luke leaned down to whisper into his wife's ear. "So, are you going to tell them all about your new job?"

"I think that can wait. After all, to all of them, it'll only look like I'm going to work at your company with you. No one will ever know that I'm a translator for spies." She could hardly believe it herself. But her shiny new ID badge was real enough.

He wiggled his eyebrows and winked at her. "Now we can ride to work together."

"Except for next week," she reminded him. "When you'll be in Hong Kong."

Luke's smile faded and he looked a little worried. "Just this one more mission, baby. I swear."

Abby ignored her friends and concentrated solely on the man she loved. "Don't worry. I know just how good you are at your job. And now that I'm an assistant spy, I'll be able to keep closer tabs on you."

"I call that a win," Luke said, dropping a kiss on her forehead. "So. You feeling okay? You need to sit down or something?"

Abby laughed in delight. She felt as though she'd been grinning like an idiot ever since Luke had taken her to the hospital to be stitched up and the doctors had discovered she was *pregnant*. "Luke, I came through a car accident and a near stabbing by a psycho. I'm fine. *We're* fine."

"Damn right you are." His mouth curved again. "Do you want to make the announcement, or do you want me to do it?"

"Let's do it together," she said, threading her fingers in his.

"Always, baby," he said. "Always."

Then, he raised his voice, lifted his glass and called out, "Everybody, we'd like to make a toast."

"To what?" Someone asked.

Abby lifted her glass, too, looked at Luke with love shining in her eyes, then with him, she faced their friends and they both said, "To our baby."

Cheers roared and soon they were surrounded by all of the people who were most important to them. And when the last congratulations had been said, Abby lifted her glass again, looked at every one of her friends in turn and knew she'd never been happier. Each of them had been through so much in the last year. And they'd all come out the other side, stronger. Happier.

The circle of her friends gathered around her and she said softly, "To the Debs. Friends forever."

* * * * *

A sneaky peek at next month...

By Request

RELIVE THE ROMANCE WITH THE BEST OF THE BEST

My wish list for next month's titles...

3 stories in each book - only £5.99!

In stores from 21st October 2011:

❏ Blackmailed Into His Arms
  – Heidi Betts, Margaret Mayo
  & Elizabeth Power

❏ Christmas Marriages & Miracles
  – Lucy Gordon, Caroline Anderson & Alison Roberts

In stores from 4th November 2011:

❏ The Bravos: Family Ties – Christine Rimmer

Available at WHSmith, Tesco, Asda, Eason, Amazon and Apple

Just can't wait?

Special Offers

Every month we put together collections and longer reads written by your favourite authors.

Here are some of next month's highlights— and don't miss our fabulous discount online!

On sale 21st October   On sale 21st October   On sale 4th November

Have Your Say

You've just finished your book. So what did you think?

We'd love to hear your thoughts on our 'Have your say' online panel
www.millsandboon.co.uk/haveyoursa

- 🌹 Easy to use
- 🌹 Short questionnaire
- 🌹 Chance to win Mills & Boon® goodies

Visit us Online

Tell us what you thought of this book now at
www.millsandboon.co.uk/haveyoursay

YOUR_SAY